The Death Shot
A Story Retold

By

Captain Mayne Reid

The Death Shot
A Story Retold
by Captain Mayne Reid

ISBN: 978-93-61154-13-3

Published by

DOUBLE 9 BOOKS

2/13-B, Ansari Road
Daryaganj, New Delhi – 110002
info@double9books.com
www.double9books.com
Tel. 011-40042856

ABOUT THE AUTHOR

Thomas Mayne Reid, an Irish-American novelist, participated in the Mexican–American War. His numerous books on American life discuss colonial policy in the American colonies, the horrors of slave labor, and the lifestyles of American Indians. "Captain" Reid created adventure stories similar to those of Frederick Marryat and Robert Louis Stevenson. They were primarily situated in the American West, Mexico, South Africa, the Himalayas, and Jamaica. He admired Lord Byron. Dion Boucicault turned his anti-slavery novel Quadroon (1856) into a drama called The Octoroon (1859), which was staged in New York. Reid was born in Ballyroney, a hamlet near Katesbridge in County Down, Northern Ireland, as the son of Rev. Thomas Mayne Reid Sr., a senior clerk of the General Assembly of the Presbyterian Church in Ireland, and his wife. Reid's father intended him to become a Presbyterian pastor, so he enrolled at the Royal Belfast Academical Institution in September 1834. He stayed for four years, but lacked the ambition to finish his studies and graduate. He returned to Ballyroney to teach at a school.

CONTENTS

Preface

Long time since this hand hath penned a preface. Now only to say, that this romance, as originally published, was written when the author was suffering severe affliction, both physically and mentally—the result of a gun-wound that brought him as near to death as Darke's bullet did Clancy.

It may be asked, Why under such strain was the tale written at all? A good reason could be given; but this, private and personal, need not, and should not be intruded on the public. Suffice it to say, that, dissatisfied with the execution of the work, the author has remodelled—almost rewritten it.

It is the same story; but, as he hopes and believes, better told.

Great Malvern, September, 1874.

Chapter One
Two sorts of Slave-Owners

In the old slave-owning times of the United States—happily now no more—there was much grievance to humanity; proud oppression upon the one side, with sad suffering on the other. It may be true, that the majority of the slave proprietors were humane men; that some of them were even philanthropic in their way, and inclined towards giving to the unholy institution a colour of *patriarchism*. This idea—delusive, as intended to delude—is old as slavery itself; at the same time, modern as Mormonism, where it has had its latest, and coarsest illustration.

Though it cannot be denied, that slavery in the States was, comparatively, of a mild type, neither can it be questioned, that among American masters occurred cases of lamentable harshness—even to inhumanity. There were slave-owners who were kind, and slave-owners who were cruel.

Not far from the town of Natchez, in the State of Mississippi, lived two planters, whose lives illustrated the extremes of these distinct moral types. Though their estates lay contiguous, their characters were as opposite, as could well be conceived in the scale of manhood and morality. Colonel Archibald Armstrong—a true Southerner of the old Virginian aristocracy, who had entered the Mississippi Valley before the Choctaw Indians evacuated it—was a model of the kind slave-master; while Ephraim Darke—a Massachusetts man, who had moved thither at a much later period—was as fair a specimen of the cruel. Coming from New England, of the purest stock of the Puritans—a people whose descendants have made much sacrifice in the cause of negro emancipation—this about Darke may seem strange. It is, notwithstanding, a common tale; one which no traveller through the Southern States can help hearing. For the Southerner will not fail to tell him, that the hardest task-master to the slave is either one, who has been himself a slave, or descended from the Pilgrim Fathers, whose feet first touched American soil by the side of Plymouth Rock!

Having a respect for many traits in the character of these same Pilgrim Fathers, I would fain think the accusation exaggerated—if not altogether untrue—and that Ephraim Darke was an exceptional individual.

To accuse *him* of inhumanity was no exaggeration whatever. Throughout the Mississippi valley there could be nothing more heartless than his treatment of the sable helots, whose luckless lot it was to have him for a master. Around his courts, and in his cotton-fields, the crack of the whip was heard habitually—its thong sharply felt by the victims of his caprice, or malice. The "cowhide" was constantly carried by himself, and his overseer. He had a son, too, who could wield it wickedly as either. None of the three ever went abroad without that pliant, painted, switch—a very emblem of devilish cruelty—in their hands; never returned home, without having used it in the castigation of some unfortunate "darkey," whose evil star had caused him to stray across their track, while riding the rounds of the plantation.

A far different discipline was that of Colonel Armstrong; whose slaves seldom went to bed without a prayer poured forth, concluding with: "God bress de good massr;" while the poor whipped bondsmen of his neighbour, their backs oft smarting from the lash, nightly lay down, not always to sleep, but nearly always with curses on their lips—the name of the Devil coupled with that of Ephraim Darke.

The old story, of like cause followed by like result, must, alas! be chronicled in this case. The man of the Devil prospered, while he of God came to grief. Armstrong, open-hearted, free-handed, indulging in a too profuse hospitality, lived widely outside the income accruing from the culture of his cotton-fields, and in time became the debtor of Darke, who lived as widely within his.

Notwithstanding the proximity of their estates, there was but little intimacy, and less friendship, between the two. The Virginian—scion of an old Scotch family, who had been gentry in the colonial times—felt something akin to contempt for his New England neighbour, whose ancestors had been steerage passengers in the famed "Mayflower." False pride, perhaps, but natural to a citizen of the Old Dominion—of late years brought low enough.

Still, not much of this influenced the conduct of Armstrong. For his dislike to Darke he had a better, and more honourable, reason—the bad behaviour of the latter. This, notorious throughout the community, made for the Massachusetts man many enemies; while in the noble mind of the Mississippian it produced positive aversion.

Under these circumstances, it may seem strange there should be any intercourse, or relationship, between the two men. But there was— that of debtor and creditor—a lien not always conferring friendship. Notwithstanding his dislike, the proud Southerner had not been above accepting a loan from the despised Northern, which the latter was but too eager to extend. The Massachusetts man had long coveted the Mississippian's fine estate; not alone from its tempting contiguity, but also because it looked like a ripe pear that must soon fall from the tree. With secret satisfaction he had observed the wasteful extravagance of its owner; a satisfaction increased on discovering the latter's impecuniosity. It became joy, almost openly exhibited, on the day when Colonel Armstrong came to him requesting a loan of twenty thousand dollars; which he consented to give, with an alacrity that would have appeared suspicious to any but a borrower.

If he gave the money in great *glee*, still greater was that with which he contemplated the mortgage deed taken in exchange. For he knew it to be the first entering of a wedge, that in due time would ensure him possession of the *fee-simple*. All the surer, from a condition in that particular deed: *Foreclosure, without time*. Pressure from other quarters had forced planter Armstrong to accept these terrible terms.

As, Darke, before locking it up in his drawer, glanced the document over, his eyes scintillating with the glare of greed triumphant, he said to himself, "This day's work has doubled the area of my acres, and the number of my niggers. Armstrong's land, his slaves, his houses,—everything he has, will soon be mine!"

Chapter Two
A flat refusal

Two years have elapsed since Ephraim Darke became the creditor of Archibald Armstrong. Apparently, no great change has taken place in the relationship between the two men, though in reality much.

The twenty thousand dollars' loan has been long ago dissipated, and the borrower is once more in need.

It would be useless, idle, for him to seek a second mortgage in the same quarter; or in any other, since he can show no collateral. His property has been nearly all hypothecated in the deed to Darke; who perceives his long-cherished dream on the eve of becoming a reality. At any hour he may cause foreclosure, turn Colonel Armstrong out of his estate, and enter upon possession.

Why does he not take advantage of the power, with which the legal code of the United States, as that existing all over the world, provides him?

There is a reason for his not doing so, wide apart from any motive of mercy, or humanity. Or of friendship either, though something erroneously considered akin to it. Love hinders him from pouncing on the plantation of Archibald Armstrong, and appropriating it!

Not love in his own breast, long ago steeled against such a trifling affection. There only avarice has a home; cupidity keeping house, and looking carefully after the expenses.

But there is a spendthrift who has also a shelter in Ephraim Darke's heart—one who does much to thwart his designs, oft-times defeating them. As already said, he has a son, by name Richard; better known throughout the settlement as "Dick"—abbreviations of nomenclature being almost universal in the South-Western States. An only son—only child as well—motherless too—she who bore him having been buried long before the Massachusetts man planted his roof-tree in the soil of Mississippi. A hopeful scion he, showing no improvement on the paternal stock. Rather the reverse; for the grasping avarice, supposed to be characteristic of the Yankee, is not improved by admixture with the reckless looseness alleged to be habitual in the Southerner.

Both these bad qualities have been developed in Dick Darke, each to its extreme. Never was New Englander more secretive and crafty; never Mississippian more loose, or licentious.

Mean in the matter of personal expenditure, he is at the same time of dissipated and disorderly habits; the associate of the poker-playing, and cock-fighting, fraternity of the neighbourhood; one of its wildest spirits, without any of those generous traits oft coupled with such a character.

As only son, he is heir-presumptive to all the father's property—slaves and plantation lands; and, being thoroughly in his father's confidence, he is aware of the probability of a proximate reversion to the slaves and plantation lands belonging to Colonel Armstrong.

But much as Dick Darke may like money, there is that he likes more, even to covetousness—Colonel Armstrong's daughter. There are two of them—Helen and Jessie—both grown girls,—motherless too—for the colonel is himself a widower.

Jessie, the younger, is bright-haired, of blooming complexion, merry to madness; in spirit, the personification of a romping elf; in physique, a sort of Hebe. Helen, on the other hand, is dark as gipsy, or Jewess; stately as a queen, with the proud grandeur of Juno. Her features of regular classic type, form tall and magnificently moulded, amidst others she appears as a palm rising above the commoner trees of the forest. Ever since her coming out in society, she has been universally esteemed the beauty of the neighbourhood—as belle in the balls of Natchez. It is to her Richard Darke has extended his homage, and surrendered his heart.

He is in love with her, as much as his selfish nature will allow—perhaps the only unselfish passion ever felt by him.

His father sanctions, or at all events does not oppose it. For the wicked son holds a wonderful ascendancy over a parent, who has trained him to wickedness equalling his own.

With the power of creditor over debtor—a debt of which payment can be demanded at any moment, and not the slightest hope of the latter being able to pay it—the Darkes seem to have the vantage ground, and may dictate their own terms.

Helen Armstrong knows nought of the mortgage; no more, of herself being the cause which keeps it from foreclosure. Little does she dream, that her beauty is the sole shield imposed between her father and impending ruin. Possibly if she did, Richard Darke's attentions to her would be received with less slighting indifference. For months he has been paying them, whenever, and wherever, an opportunity has offered—at balls, *barbecues*, and the like.

Of late also at her father's house; where the power spoken of gives him not only admission, but polite reception, and hospitable entertainment, at the hands of its owner; while the consciousness of possessing it hinders him from observing, how coldly his assiduities are met by her to whom they are so warmly addressed.

He wonders why, too. He knows that Helen Armstrong has many admirers. It could not be otherwise with one so splendidly beautiful, so gracefully gifted. But among them there is none for whom she has shown partiality.

He has, himself, conceived a suspicion, that a young man, by name Charles Clancy — son of a decayed Irish gentleman, living near — has found favour in her eyes. Still, it is only a suspicion; and Clancy has gone to Texas the year before — sent, so said, by his father, to look out for a new home. The latter has since died, leaving his widow sole occupant of an humble tenement, with a small holding of land — a roadside tract, on the edge of the Armstrong estate.

Rumour runs, that young Clancy is about coming back — indeed, every day expected.

That can't matter. The proud planter, Armstrong, is not the man to permit of his daughter marrying a "poor white" — as Richard Darke scornfully styles his supposed rival — much less consent to the so bestowing of her hand. Therefore no danger need be dreaded from that quarter.

Whether there need, or not, the suitor of Helen Armstrong at length resolves on bringing the affair to an issue. His love for her has become a strong passion, the stronger for being checked — restrained by her cold, almost scornful behaviour. This may be but coquetry. He hopes, and has a fancy it is. Not without reason. For he is far from being ill-favoured; only in a sense moral, not physical. But this has not prevented him from making many conquests among backwood's belles; even some city celebrities living in Natchez. All know he is rich; or will be, when his father fulfils the last conditions of his will — by dying.

So fortified, so flattered, Dick Darke cannot comprehend why Miss Armstrong has not at once surrendered to him. Is it because her haughty disposition hinders her from being too demonstrative? Does she really love him, without giving sign?

For months he has been cogitating in this uncertain way; and now determines upon knowing the truth.

One morning he mounts his horse; rides across the boundary line between the two plantations, and on to Colonel Armstrong's house.

Entering, he requests an interview with the colonel's eldest daughter; obtains it; makes declaration of his love; asks her if she will have him for a husband; and in response receives a chilling negative.

As he rides back through the woods, the birds are trilling among the trees. It is their merry morning lay, but it gives him no gladness. There is still ringing in his ears that harsh monosyllable, "*no*." The wild-wood songsters appear to echo it, as if mockingly; the blue jay, and red cardinal, seem scolding him for intrusion on their domain!

Having recrossed the boundary between the two plantations, he reins up and looks back. His brow is black with chagrin; his lips white with rancorous rage. It is suppressed no longer. Curses come hissing through his teeth, along with them the words, —

"In less than six weeks these woods will be mine, and hang me, if I don't shoot every bird that has roost in them! Then, Miss Helen Armstrong, you'll not feel in such conceit with yourself. It will be different when you haven't a roof over your head". So good-bye, sweetheart! Good-bye to you.

"Now, dad!" he continues, in fancy apostrophising his father, "you can take your own way, as you've been long wanting. Yes, my respected parent; you shall be free to foreclose your mortgage; put in execution; sheriff's officers—anything you like."

Angrily grinding his teeth, he plunges the spur into his horse's ribs, and rides on—the short, but bitter, speech still echoing in his ears.

Chapter Three
A Forest Post-Office

From the harsh treatment of slaves sprang a result, little thought of by the inhuman master; though greatly detrimental to his interests. It caused them occasionally to abscond; so making it necessary to insert an advertisement in the county newspaper, offering a reward for the runaway. Thus cruelty proved expensive.

In planter Darke's case, however, the cost was partially recouped by the cleverness of his son; who was a noted "nigger-catcher," and kept dogs for the especial purpose. He had a natural *penchant* for this kind of chase; and, having little else to do, passed a good deal of his time scouring the country in pursuit of his father's advertised runaways. Having caught them, he would claim the "bounty," just as if they belonged to a stranger. Darke, *père*, paid it without grudge or grumbling—perhaps the only disbursement he ever made in such mood. It was like taking out of one pocket to put into the other. Besides, he was rather proud of his son's acquitting himself so shrewdly.

Skirting the two plantations, with others in the same line of settlements, was a cypress swamp. It extended along the edge of the great river, covering an area of many square miles. Besides being a swamp, it was a network of creeksy bayous, and lagoons—often inundated, and only passable by means of skiff or canoe. In most places it was a slough of soft mud, where man might not tread, nor any kind of water-craft make way. Over it, at all times, hung the obscurity of twilight. The solar rays, however bright above, could not penetrate its close canopy of cypress tops, loaded with that strangest of parasitical plants—the *tillandsia usneoides*.

This tract of forest offered a safe place of concealment for runaway slaves; and, as such, was it noted throughout the neighbourhood. A "darkey" absconding from any of the contiguous plantations, was as sure to make for the marshy expanse, as would a chased rabbit to its warren.

Sombre and gloomy though it was, around its edge lay the favourite scouting-ground of Richard Darke. To him the cypress swamp was a precious preserve—as a coppice to the pheasant shooter, or a scrub-wood to the hunter of foxes. With the difference, that his game was human, and therefore the pursuit more exciting.

There were places in its interior to which he had never penetrated—large tracts unexplored, and where exploration could not be made without great difficulty. But for him to reach them was not necessary. The runaways who sought asylum in the swamp, could not always remain within its gloomy recesses. Food must be obtained beyond its border, or starvation be their fate. For this reason the fugitive required some mode of communicating with the outside world. And usually obtained it, by means of a confederate—some old friend, and fellow-slave, on one of the adjacent plantations—privy to the secret of his hiding-place. On this necessity the negro-catcher most depended; often finding the stalk—or "still-hunt," in backwoods phraseology—more profitable than a pursuit with trained hounds.

About a month after his rejection by Miss Armstrong, Richard Darke is out upon a chase; as usual along the edge of the cypress swamp, rather should it be called a search: since he has found no traces of the human game that has tempted him forth. This is a fugitive negro—one of the best field-hands belonging to his father's plantation—who has absented himself, and cannot be recalled.

For several weeks "Jupiter"—as the runaway is named—has been missing; and his description, with the reward attached, has appeared in the county newspaper. The planter's son, having a suspicion that he is secreted somewhere in the swamp, has made several excursions thither, in the hope of lighting upon his tracks. But "Jupe" is an astute fellow, and has hitherto contrived to leave no sign, which can in any way contribute to his capture.

Dick Darke is returning home, after an unsuccessful day's search, in anything but a cheerful mood. Though not so much from having failed in finding traces of the missing slave. That is only a matter of money; and, as he has plenty, the disappointment can be borne. The thought embittering his spirit relates to another matter. He thinks of his scorned suit, and blighted love prospects.

The chagrin caused him by Helen Armstrong's refusal has terribly distressed, and driven him to more reckless courses. He drinks deeper than ever; while in his cups he has been silly enough to let his boon companions become acquainted with his reason for thus running riot, making not much secret, either, of the mean revenge he designs for her who has rejected him. She is to be punished through her father.

Colonel Armstrong's indebtedness to Ephraim Darke has become known throughout the settlement—all about the mortgage. Taking into consideration the respective characters of the mortgagor and mortgagee, men shake their heads, and say that Darke will soon own the Armstrong plantation. All the sooner, since the chief obstacle to the fulfilment of his long-cherished design has been his son, and this is now removed.

Notwithstanding the near prospect of having his spite gratified, Richard Darke keenly feels his humiliation. He has done so ever since the day of his receiving it; and as determinedly has he been nursing his wrath. He has been still further exasperated by a circumstance which has lately occurred — the return of Charles Clancy from Texas. Someone has told him of Clancy having been seen in company with Helen Armstrong — the two walking the woods *alone!*

Such an interview could not have been with her father's consent, but *clandestine*. So much the more aggravating to him — Darke. The thought of it is tearing his heart, as he returns from his fruitless search after the fugitive.

He has left the swamp behind, and is continuing on through a tract of woodland, which separates his father's plantation from that of Colonel Armstrong, when he sees something that promises relief to his perturbed spirit. It is a woman, making her way through the woods, coming towards him, from the direction of Armstrong's house.

She is not the colonel's daughter — neither one. Nor does Dick Darke suppose it either. Though seen indistinctly under the shadow of the trees, he identifies the approaching form as that of Julia — a mulatto maiden, whose special duty it is to attend upon the young ladies of the Armstrong family, "Thank God for the devil's luck!" he mutters, on making her out. "It's Jupiter's sweetheart; his Juno or Leda, yellow-hided as himself. *No* doubt she's on her way to keep an appointment with him? No more, that I shall be present at the interview. Two hundred dollars reward for old Jupe, and the fun of giving the damned nigger a good 'lamming,' once I lay hand on him. Keep on, Jule, girl! You'll track him up for me, better than the sharpest scented hound in my kennel."

While making this soliloquy, the speaker withdraws himself behind a bush; and, concealed by its dense foliage, keeps his eye on the mulatto wench, still wending her way through the thick standing tree trunks.

As there is no path, and the girl is evidently going by stealth, he has reason to believe she is on the errand conjectured.

Indeed he can have no doubt about her being on the way to an interview with Jupiter; and he is now good as certain of soon discovering, and securing, the runaway who has so long contrived to elude him.

After the girl has passed the place of his concealment—which she very soon does—he slips out from behind the bush, and follows her with stealthy tread, still taking care to keep cover between them.

Not long before she comes to a stop; under a grand magnolia, whose spreading branches, with their large laurel like leaves, shadow a vast circumference of ground.

Darke, who has again taken stand behind a fallen tree, where he has a full view of her movements, watches them with eager eyes. Two hundred dollars at stake—two hundred on his own account—fifteen hundred for his father—Jupe's market value—no wonder at his being all eyes, all ears, on the alert!

What is his astonishment, at seeing the girl take a letter from her pocket, and, standing on tiptoe, drop it into a knot-hole in the magnolia!

This done, she turns shoulder towards the tree; and, without staying longer under its shadow, glides back along the path by which she has come—evidently going home again!

The negro-catcher is not only surprised, but greatly chagrined. He has experienced a double disappointment—the anticipation of earning two hundred dollars, and giving his old slave the lash: both pleasant if realised, but painful the thought in both to be foiled.

Still keeping in concealment, he permits Julia to depart, not only unmolested, but unchallenged. There may be some secret in the letter to concern, though it may not console him. In any case, it will soon be his.

And it soon is, without imparting consolation. Rather the reverse. Whatever the contents of that epistle, so curiously deposited, Richard Darke, on becoming acquainted with them, reels like a drunken man; and to save himself from falling, seeks support against the trunk of the tree!

After a time, recovering, he re-reads the letter, and gazes at a picture—a photograph—also found within the envelope.

Then from his lips come words, low-muttered—words of menace, made emphatic by an oath.

A man's name is heard among his mutterings, more than once repeated.

As Dick Darke, after thrusting letter and picture into his pocket, strides away from the spot, his clenched teeth, with the lurid light scintillating in his eyes, to this man foretell danger—maybe death.

Chapter Four
Two good girls

The dark cloud, long lowering over Colonel Armstrong and his fortunes, is about to fall. A dialogue with his eldest daughter occurring on the same day—indeed in the same hour—when she refused Richard Darke, shows him to have been but too well aware of the prospect of impending ruin.

The disappointed suitor had not long left the presence of the lady, who so laconically denied him, when another appears by her side. A man, too; but no rival of Richard Darke—no lover of Helen Armstrong. The venerable white-haired gentleman, who has taken Darke's place, is her father, the old colonel himself. His air, on entering the room, betrays uneasiness about the errand of the planter's son—a suspicion there is something amiss. He is soon made certain of it, by his daughter unreservedly communicating the object of the interview. He says in rejoinder:—

"I supposed that to be his purpose; though, from his coming at this early hour, I feared something worse."

These words bring a shadow over the countenance of her to whom they are addressed, simultaneous with a glance of inquiry from her grand, glistening eyes.

First exclaiming, then interrogating, she says:—

"Worse! Feared! Father, what should you be afraid of?"

"Never mind, my child; nothing that concerns you. Tell me: in what way did you give him answer?"

"In one little word. I simply said *no*."

"That little word will, no doubt, be enough. O Heaven! what is to become of us?"

"Dear father!" demands the beautiful girl, laying her hand upon his shoulder, with a searching look into his eyes; "why do you speak thus? Are you angry with me for refusing him? Surely you would not wish to see me the wife of Richard Darke?"

"You do not love him, Helen?"

"Love him! Can you ask? Love that man!"

"You would not marry him?"

"Would not—could not. I'd prefer death."

"Enough; I must submit to my fate."

"Fate, father! What may be the meaning of this? There is some secret—a danger? Trust to me. Let me know all."

"I may well do that, since it cannot remain much longer a secret. There *is* danger, Helen—*the danger of debt*! My estate is mortgaged to the father of this fellow—so much as to put me completely in his power. Everything I possess, land, houses, slaves, may become his at any hour; this day, if he so will it. He is sure to will it now. Your little word 'no,' will bring about a big change—the crisis I've been long apprehending. Never mind! Let it come! I must meet it like a man. It is for you, daughter—you and your sister—I grieve. My poor dear girls; what a change there will be in your lives, as your prospects! Poverty, coarse fare, coarse garments to wear, and a log-cabin to live in! Henceforth, this must be your lot. I can hold out hope of no other."

"What of all that, father? I, for one, care not; and I'm sure sister will feel the same. But is there no way to—"

"Save me from bankruptcy, you'd say? You need not ask that. I have spent many a sleepless night thinking it there was. But no; there is only one—that one. It I have never contemplated, even for an instant, knowing it would not do. I was sure you did not love Richard Darke, and would not consent to marry him. You could not, my child?"

Helen Armstrong does not make immediate answer, though there is one ready to leap to her lips.

She hesitates giving it, from a thought, that it may add to the weight of unhappiness pressing upon her father's spirit.

Mistaking her silence, and perhaps with the spectre of poverty staring him in the face—oft inciting to meanness, even the noblest natures—he repeats the test interrogatory:—

"Tell me, daughter! Could you marry him?"

"Speak candidly," he continues, "and take time to reflect before answering. If you think you could not be contented—happy—with Richard Darke for your husband, better it should never be. Consult your own heart, and do not be swayed by me, or my necessities. Say, is the thing impossible?"

"I have said. *It is impossible!*"

For a moment both remain silent; the father drooping, spiritless, as if struck by a galvanic shock; the daughter looking sorrowful, as though she had given it.

She soonest recovering, makes an effort to restore him.

"Dear father!" she exclaims, laying her hand upon his shoulder, and gazing tenderly into his eyes; "you speak of a change in our circumstances—of bankruptcy and other ills. Let them come! For myself I care not. Even if the alternative were death, I've told you—I tell you again—I would rather that, than be the wife of Richard Darke."

"Then his wife you'll never be! Now, let the subject drop, and the ruin fall! We must prepare for poverty, and Texas!"

"Texas, if you will, but not poverty. Nothing of the kind. The wealth of affection will make you feel rich; and in a lowly log-hut, as in this grand house, you'll still have mine."

So speaking, the fair girl flings herself upon her father's breast, her hand laid across his forehead, the white fingers soothingly caressing it.

The door opens. Another enters the room—another girl, almost fair as she, but brighter, and younger. 'Tis Jessie.

"Not only my affection," Helen adds, at sight of the newcomer, "but hers as well. Won't he, sister?"

Sister, wondering what it is all about, nevertheless sees something is wanted of her. She has caught the word "affection," at the same time observing an afflicted cast upon her father's countenance. This decides her; and, gliding forward, in another instant she is by his side, clinging to the opposite shoulder, with an arm around his neck.

Thus grouped, the three figures compose a family picture expressive of purest love.

A pleasing tableau to one who knew nothing of what has thus drawn them together; or knowing it, could truly appreciate. For in the faces of all beams affection, which bespeaks a happy, if not prosperous, future—without any doubting fear of either poverty, or Texas.

Chapter Five
A photograph in the forest

On the third day, after that on which Richard Darke abstracted the letter from the magnolia, a man is seen strolling along the edge of the cypress swamp. The hour is nearly the same, but the individual altogether different. Only in age does he bear any similarity to the planter's son; for he is also a youth of some three or four and twenty. In all else he is unlike Dick Darke, as one man could well be to another.

He is of medium size and height, with a figure pleasingly proportioned. His shoulders squarely set, and chest rounded out, tell of great strength; while limbs tersely knit, and a firm elastic tread betoken toughness and activity. Features of smooth, regular outline—the jaws broad, and well balanced; the chin prominent; the nose nearly Grecian—while eminently handsome, proclaim a noble nature, with courage equal to any demand that may be made upon it. Not less the glance of a blue-grey eye, unquailing as an eagle's.

A grand shock of hair, slightly curled, and dark brown in colour, gives the finishing touch to his fine countenance, as the feather to a Tyrolese hat.

Dressed in a sort of shooting costume, with jack-boots, and gaiters buttoned above them, he carries a gun; which, as can be seen, is a single-barrelled rifle; while at his heels trots a dog of large size, apparently a cross between stag-hound and mastiff, with a spice of terrier in its composition. Such mongrels are not necessarily curs, but often the best breed for backwoods' sport; where the keenness of scent required to track a deer, needs supplementing by strength and staunchness, when the game chances, as it often does, to be a bear, a wolf, or a panther.

The master of this trebly crossed canine is the man whose name rose upon the lips of Richard Darke, after reading the purloined epistle— Charles Clancy. To him was it addressed, and for him intended, as also the photograph found inside.

Several days have elapsed since his return from Texas, having come back, as already known, to find himself fatherless. During the interval he has remained much at home—a dutiful son, doing all he can to console a sorrowing mother. Only now and then has he sought relaxation in the chase, of which he is devotedly fond. On this occasion he has come down to the cypress swamp; but, having encountered no game, is going back with an empty bag.

He is not in low spirits at his ill success; for he has something to console him—that which gives gladness to his heart—joy almost reaching delirium. She, who has won it, loves him.

This she is Helen Armstrong. She has not signified as much, in words; but by ways equally expressive, and quite as convincing. They have met clandestinely, and so corresponded; the knot-hole in the magnolia serving them as a post-box. At first, only phrases of friendship in their conversation; the same in the letters thus surreptitiously exchanged. For despite Clancy's courage among men, he is a coward in the presence of women—in hers more than any.

For all this, at their latest interview, he had thrown aside his shyness, and spoken words of love—fervent love, in its last appeal. He had avowed himself wholly hers, and asked her to be wholly his. She declined giving him an answer *viva voce*, but promised it in writing. He will receive it in a letter, to be deposited in the place convened.

He feels no offence at her having thus put him off. He believes it to have been but a whim of his sweetheart—the caprice of a woman, who has been so much nattered and admired. He knows, that, like the Anne Hathaway of Shakespeare, Helen Armstrong "hath a way" of her own. For she is a girl of no ordinary character, but one of spirit, free and independent, consonant with the scenes and people that surrounded her youth. So far from being offended at her not giving him an immediate answer, he but admires her the more. Like the proud eagle's mate, she does not condescend to be wooed as the soft cooing dove, nor yield a too easy acquiescence.

Still daily, hourly, does he expect the promised response. And twice, sometimes thrice, a day pays visit to the forest post-office.

Several days have elapsed since their last interview; and yet he has found no letter lying. Little dreams he, that one has been sent, with a *carte de visite* enclosed; and less of both being in the possession of his greatest enemy on earth.

He is beginning to grow uneasy at the delay, and shape conjectures as to the cause. All the more from knowing, that a great change is soon to take place in the affairs of the Armstrong family. A knowledge which emboldened him to make the proposal he has made.

And now, his day's hunting done, he is on his way for the tract of woodland in which stands the sweet trysting tree.

He has no thought of stopping, or turning aside; nor would he do so for any small game. But at this moment a deer—a grand antlered stag—comes "loping" along.

Before he can bring his gun to bear upon it, the animal is out of sight; having passed behind the thick standing trunks of the cypresses. He restrains his hound, about to spring off on the slot. The stag has not seen him; and, apparently, going unscared, he hopes to stalk, and again get sight of it.

He has not proceeded over twenty paces, when a sound fills his ears, as well as the woods around. It is the report of a gun, fired by one who cannot be far off. And not at the retreating stag, but himself!

He feels that the bullet has hit him. This, from a stinging sensation in his arm, like the touch of red-hot iron, or a drop of scalding water. He might not know it to be a bullet, but for the crack heard simultaneously—this coming from behind.

The wound, fortunately but a slight one, does not disable him; and, like a tiger stung by javelins, he is round in an instant, ready to return the fire.

There is no one in sight!

As there has been no warning—not a word—he can have no doubt of the intent: some one meaning to murder him!

He is sure about its being an attempt to assassinate him, as of the man who has made it. Richard Darke—certain, as if the crack of the gun had been a voice pronouncing the name.

Clancy's eyes, flashing angrily, interrogate the forest. The trees stand close, the spaces between shadowy and sombre. For, as said, they are cypresses, and the hour twilight.

He can see nothing save the huge trunks, and their lower limbs, garlanded with ghostly *tillandsia* here and there draping down to the earth. This baffles him, both by its colour and form. The grey gauze-like festoonery, having a resemblance to ascending smoke, hinders him from perceiving that of the discharged gun.

He can see none. It must have whiffed up suddenly, and become commingled with the moss?

It does not matter much. Neither the twilight obscurity, nor that caused by the overshadowing trees, can prevent his canine companion from discovering the whereabouts of the would-be assassin. On hearing the shot the hound has harked back; and, at some twenty paces off, brought up beside a huge trunk, where it stands fiercely baying, as if at a bear. The tree is buttressed, with "knees" several feet in height rising around. In the dim light, these might easily be mistaken for men.

Clancy is soon among them; and sees crouching between two pilasters, the man who meant to murder him—Richard Darke as conjectured.

Darke makes no attempt at explanation. Clancy calls for none. His rifle is already cocked; and, soon as seeing his adversary, he raises it to his shoulder, exclaiming:—

"Scoundrel! you've had the first shot. It's my turn now."

Darke does not remain inactive, but leaps—forth from his lurking-place, to obtain more freedom for his arms. The buttresses hinder him from having elbow room. He also elevates his gun; but, perceiving it will be too late, instead of taking aim, he lowers the piece again, and dodges behind the tree.

The movement, quick and subtle, as a squirrel's bound, saves him. Clancy fires without effect. His ball but pierces through the skirt of Darke's coat, without touching his body.

With a wild shout of triumph, the latter advances upon his adversary, whose gun is now empty. His own, a double-barrel, has a bullet still undischarged. Deliberately bringing the piece to his shoulder, and covering the victim he is now sure of, he says derisively,—

"What a devilish poor shot you've made, Mister Charlie Clancy! A sorry marksman—to miss a man scarce six feet from the muzzle of your gun! I shan't miss you. Turn about's fair play. I've had the first, and I'll have the last. Dog! take your *death shot*!"

While delivering the dread speech, his finger presses the trigger; the crack comes, with the flash and fiery jet.

For some seconds Clancy is invisible, the sulphurous smoke forming a nimbus around him. When it ascends, he is seen prostrate upon the earth; the blood gushing from a wound in his breast, and spurting over his waistcoat.

He appears writhing in his death agony.

And evidently thinks so himself, from his words spoken in slow, choking utterance,—

"Richard Darke—you have killed—murdered me!"

"I meant to do it," is the unpitying response.

"O Heavens! You horrid wretch! Why—why—"

"Bah! what are you blubbering about? You know why. If not, I shall tell you—*Helen Armstrong*, After all, it isn't jealousy that's made me kill you; only your impudence, to suppose you had a chance with her. You hadn't; she never cared a straw for you. Perhaps, before dying, it may be some consolation for you to know she didn't. I've got the proof. Since it isn't likely you'll ever see herself again, it may give you a pleasure to look at her portrait. Here it is! The sweet girl sent it me this very morning, with her autograph attached, as you see. A capital likeness, isn't it?"

The inhuman wretch stooping down, holds the photograph before the eyes of the dying man, gradually growing dim.

But only death could hinder them from turning towards that sun-painted picture—the portrait of her who has his heart.

He gazes on it lovingly, but not long. For the script underneath claims his attention. In this he recognises her handwriting, well-known to him. Terrible the despair that sweeps through his soul, as he deciphers it:—

"Helen Armstrong.—For him she loves."

The picture is in the possession of Richard Darke. To him have the sweet words been vouchsafed!

"A charming creature!" Darke tauntingly continues, kissing the carte, and pouring the venomous speech into his victim's ear. "It's the very counterpart of her sweet self. As I said, she sent it me this morning. Come, Clancy! Before giving up the ghost, tell me what you think of it. Isn't it an excellent likeness?"

To the inhuman interrogatory Clancy makes no response—either by word, look, or gesture. His lips are mute, his eyes without light of life, his limbs and body motionless as the mud on which they lie.

A short, but profane, speech terminates the terrible episode; four words of most heartless signification:—

"Damn him; he's dead!"

Chapter Six
A coon-chase interrupted

Notwithstanding the solitude of the place where the strife, apparently fatal, has occurred, and the slight chances of its being seen, its sounds have been heard. The shots, the excited speeches, and angry exclamations, have reached the ears of one who can well interpret them. This is a coon-hunter.

There is no district in the Southern States without its coon-hunter. In most, many of them; but in each, one who is noted. And, notedly, he is a negro. The pastime is too tame, or too humble, to tempt the white man. Sometimes the sons of "poor white trash" take part in it; but it is usually delivered over to the "darkey."

In the old times of slavery every plantation could boast of one, or more, of these sable Nimrods; and they are not yet extinct. To them coon-catching is a profit, as well as sport; the skins keeping them in tobacco—and whisky, when addicted to drinking it. The flesh, too, though little esteemed by white palates, is a *bonne-bouche* to the negro, with whom animal food is a scarce commodity. It often furnishes him with the substance for a savoury roast.

The plantation of Ephraim Darke is no exception to the general rule. It, too, has its coon-hunter—a negro named, or nicknamed, "Blue Bill;" the qualifying term bestowed, from a cerulean tinge, that in certain lights appears upon the surface of his sable epidermis. Otherwise he is black as ebony.

Blue Bill is a mighty hunter of his kind, passionately fond of the coon-chase—too much, indeed, for his own personal safety. It carries him abroad, when the discipline of the plantation requires him to be at home; and more than once, for so absenting himself, have his shoulders been scored by the "cowskin."

Still the punishment has not cured him of his proclivity. Unluckily for Richard Darke, it has not. For on the evening of Clancy's being shot down, as described, Blue Bill chances to be abroad; and, with a small cur, which he has trained to his favourite chase, is scouring the timber near the edge of the cypress swamp.

He has "treed" an old he-coon, and is just preparing to ascend to the creature's nest—a cavity in a sycamore high up—when a deer comes dashing by. Soon after a shot startles him. He is more disturbed at the peculiar crack, than by the mere fact of its being the report of a gun. His ear, accustomed to such sounds, tells him the report has proceeded from a fowling-piece, belonging to his young master—just then the last man he would wish to meet. He is away from the "quarter" without "pass," or permission of any kind.

His first impulse is, to continue the ascent of the sycamore, and conceal himself among its branches.

But his dog, remaining below—that will betray him?

While hurriedly reflecting on what he had best do, he hears a second shot. Then a third, coming quickly after; while preceding, and mingling with the reports are men's voices, apparently in mad expostulation. He hears, too, the angry growling of a hound, at intervals barking and baying.

"Gorramity!" mutters Blue Bill; "dar's a skrimmage goin' on dar—a *fight*, I reck'n, an' seemin' to be def! Clar enuf who dat fight's between. De fuss shot wa' Mass' Dick's double-barrel; de oder am Charl Clancy rifle. By golly! 'taint safe dis child be seen hya, no how. Whar kin a hide maseff?"

Again he glances upward, scanning the sycamore: then down at his dog; and once more to the trunk of the tree. This is embraced by a creeper—a gigantic grape-vine—up which an ascent may easily be made; so easily, there need be no difficulty in carrying the cur along. It was the ladder he intended using to get at the treed coon.

With the fear of his young master coming past—and if so, surely "cow-hiding" him—he feels there is no time to be wasted in vacillation.

Nor does he waste any. Without further stay, he flings his arm around the coon-dog: raises the unresisting animal from the earth; and "swarms" up the creeper, like a she-bear carrying her cub.

In ten seconds after, he is snugly ensconced in a crotch of the sycamore; screened from observation of any one who may pass underneath, by the profuse foliage of the parasite.

Feeling fairly secure, he once more sets himself to listen. And, listening attentively, he hears the same voices as before. But not any longer in angry ejaculation. The tones are tranquil, as though the two men were now quietly conversing. One says but a word or two; the other all. Then the last alone appears to speak, as if in soliloquy, or from the first failing to make response.

The sudden transition of tone has in it something strange—a contrast inexplicable.

The coon-hunter can tell, that he continuing to talk is his young master, Richard Darke; though he cannot catch, the words, much less make out their meaning. The distance is too great, and the current of sound interrupted by the thick standing trunks of the cypresses.

At length, also, the monologue ends; soon after, succeeded by a short exclamatory phrase, in voice louder and more earnest.

Then there is silence; so profound, that Blue Bill hears but his own heart, beating in loud sonorous thumps—louder from his ribs being contiguous to the hollow trunk of the tree.

Chapter Seven
Murder without remorse

The breathless silence, succeeding Darke's profane speech, is awe-inspiring; death-like, as though every living creature in the forest had been suddenly struck dumb, or dead, too.

Unspeakably, incredibly atrocious is the behaviour of the man who has remained master of the ground. During the contest, Dick Darke has shown the cunning of the fox, combined with the fiercer treachery of the tiger; victorious, his conduct seems a combination of the jackal and vulture.

Stooping over his fallen foe, to assure himself that the latter no longer lives, he says,—

"Dead, I take it."

These are his cool words; after which, as though still in doubt, he bends lower, and listens. At the same time he clutches the handle of his hunting knife, as with the intent to plunge its blade into the body.

He sees there is no need. It is breathless, almost bloodless—clearly a corpse!

Believing it so, he resumes his erect attitude, exclaiming in louder tone, and with like profanity as before,—

"Yes, dead, damn him!"

As the assassin bends over the body of his fallen foe, he shows no sign of contrition, for the cruel deed he has done. No feeling save that of satisfied vengeance; no emotion that resembles remorse. On the contrary, his cold animal eyes continue to sparkle with jealous hate; while his hand has moved mechanically to the hilt of his knife, as though he meant to mutilate the form he has laid lifeless. Its beauty, even in death, seems to embitter his spirit!

But soon, a sense of danger comes creeping over him, and fear takes shape in his soul. For, beyond doubt, he has done murder.

"No!" he says, in an effort at self-justification. "Nothing of the sort. I've killed him; that's true; but he's had the chance to kill me. They'll see that his gun's discharged; and here's his bullet gone through the skirt of my coat. By thunder, 'twas a close shave!"

For a time he stands reflecting—his glance now turned towards the body, now sent searchingly through the trees, as though in dread of some one coming that way.

Not much likelihood of this. The spot is one of perfect solitude, as is always a cypress forest. There is no path near, accustomed to be trodden by the traveller. The planter has no business among those great buttressed trunks. The woodman will never assail them with his axe. Only a stalking hunter, or perhaps some runaway slave, is at all likely to stray thither.

Again soliloquising, he says,—

"Shall I put a bold face upon it, and confess to having killed him? I can say we met while out hunting; quarrelled, and fought—a fair fight; shot for shot; my luck to have the last. Will that story stand?"

A pause in the soliloquy; a glance at the prostrate form; another, which interrogates the scene around, taking in the huge unshapely trunks, their long outstretched limbs, with the pall-like festoonery of Spanish moss; a thought about the loneliness of the place, and its fitness for concealing a dead body.

Like the lightning's flashes, all this flits through the mind of the murderer. The result, to divert him from his half-formed resolution—perceiving its futility.

"It won't do," he mutters, his speech indicating the change. "No, that it won't! Better say nothing about what's happened. They're not likely to look for him here..."

Again he glances inquiringly around, with a view to secreting the corpse. He has made up his mind to this.

A sluggish creak meanders among the trees, some two hundred yards from the spot. At about a like distance below, it discharges itself into the stagnant reservoir of the swamp.

Its waters are dark, from the overshadowing of the cypresses, and deep enough for the purpose he is planning.

But to carry the body thither will require an effort of strength; and to drag it would be sure to leave traces.

In view of this difficulty, he says to himself,—

"I'll let it lie where it is. No one ever comes along hero—not likely. At the same time, I take it, there can be no harm in hiding him a little. So, Charley Clancy, if I have sent you to kingdom come, I shan't leave your bones unburied. Your ghost might haunt me, if I did. To hinder that you shall have interment."

In the midst of this horrid mockery, he rests his gun against a tree, and commences dragging the Spanish moss from the branches above. The beard-like parasite comes off in flakes—in armfuls. Half a dozen he flings over the still palpitating corpse; then pitches on top some pieces of dead wood, to prevent any stray breeze from sweeping off the hoary shroud.

After strewing other tufts around, to conceal the blood and boot tracks, he rests from his labour, and for a time stands surveying what he has done.

At length seeming satisfied, he again grasps hold of his gun; and is about taking departure from the place, when a sound, striking his ear, causes him to start. No wonder, since it seems the voice of one wailing for the dead!

At first he is affrighted, fearfully so; but recovers himself on learning the cause.

"Only the dog!" he mutters, perceiving Clancy's hound at a distance, among the trees.

On its master being shot down, the animal had scampered off—perhaps fearing a similar fate. It had not gone far, and is now returning—by little and little, drawing nearer to the dangerous spot.

The creature seems struggling between two instincts—affection for its fallen master, and fear for itself.

As Darke's gun is empty, he endeavours to entice the dog within reach of his knife. Despite his coaxing, it will not come!

Hastily ramming a cartridge into the right-hand barrel, he aims, and fires.

The shot takes effect; the ball passing through the fleshy part of the dog's neck. Only to crease the skin, and draw forth a spurt of blood.

The hound hit, and further frightened, gives out a wild howl, and goes off, without sign of return.

Equally wild are the words that leap from the lips of Richard Darke, as he stands gazing after.

"Great God!" he cries; "I've done an infernal foolish thing. The cur will go home to Clancy's house. That'll tell a tale, sure to set people searching. Ay, and it may run back here, guiding them to the spot. Holy hell!"

While speaking, the murderer turns pale. It is the first time for him to experience real fear. In such an out-of-the-way place he has felt confident of concealing the body, and along with it the bloody deed. Then, he had not taken the dog into account, and the odds were in his favour. Now, with the latter adrift, they are heavily against him.

It needs no calculation of chances to make this clear. Nor is it any doubt which causes him to stand hesitating. His irresolution springs from uncertainty as to what course he shall pursue.

One thing certain—he must not remain there. The hound has gone off howling. It is two miles to the widow Clancy's house; but there is an odd squatter's cabin and clearing between. A dog going in that guise, blood-bedraggled, in full cry of distress, will be sure of being seen—equally sure to raise an alarm.

On the probable, or possible, contingencies Dick Darke does not stand long reflecting. Despite its solitude, the cypress forest is not the place for tranquil thought—at least, not now for him. Far off through the trees he can hear the wail of the wounded Molossian.

Is it fancy, or does he also hear human voices?

He stays not to be sure. Beside that gory corpse, shrouded though it be, he dares not remain a moment longer.

Hastily shouldering his gun, he strikes off through the trees; at first in quick step; then in double; this increasing to a rapid run.

He retreats in a direction contrary to that taken by the dog. It is also different from the way leading to his father's house. It forces him still further into the swamp—across sloughs, and through soft mud, where he makes footmarks. Though he has carefully concealed Clancy's corpse, and obliterated all other traces of the strife, in his "scare," he does not think of those he is now making.

The murderer is only—cunning before the crime. After it, if he have conscience, or be deficient in coolness, he loses self-possession, and is pretty sure to leave behind something which will furnish a clue for the detective.

So is it with Richard Darke. As he retreats from the scene of his diabolical deed, his only thought is to put space between himself and the spot where he has shed innocent blood; to get beyond earshot of those canine cries, that seem commingled with the shouts of men—the voices of avengers!

Chapter Eight
The coon-hunter cautious

During the time that Darke is engaged in covering up Clancy's body, and afterwards occupied in the attempt to kill his dog, the coon-hunter, squatted in the sycamore fork, sticks to his seat like "death to a dead nigger." And all the time trembling. Not without reason. For the silence succeeding the short exclamatory speech has not re-assured him. He believes it to be but a lull, denoting some pause in the action, and that one, or both, of the actors is still upon the ground. If only one, it will be his master, whose monologue was last heard. During the stillness, somewhat prolonged, he continues to shape conjectures and put questions to himself, as to what can have been the *fracas,* and its cause. Undoubtedly a "shooting scrape" between Dick Darke and Charles Clancy. But how has it terminated, or is the end yet come? Has one of the combatants been killed, or gone away? Or have both forsaken the spot where they have been trying to spill each other's blood?

While thus interrogating himself, a new sound disturbs the tranquillity of the forest—the same, which the assassin at first fancied was the voice of one wailing for his victim. The coon-hunter has no such delusion. Soon as hearing, he recognises the tongue of a stag-hound, knowing it to be Clancy's. He is only astray about its peculiar tone, now quite changed. The animal is neither barking nor baying; nor yet does it yelp as if suffering chastisement. The soft tremulous whine, that comes pealing in prolonged reverberation through the trunks of the cypresses, proclaims distress of a different kind— as of a dog asleep and dreaming!

And now, once more a man's voice, his master's. It too changed in tone. No longer in angry exclaim, or quiet conversation, but as if earnestly entreating; the speech evidently not addressed to Clancy, but the hound.

Strange all this; and so thinks the coon-hunter. He has but little time to dwell on it, before another sound waking the echoes of the forest, interrupts the current of his reflections. Another shot! This time, as twice before, the broad round boom of a smooth-bore, so different from the short sharp "spang" of a rifle.

Thoroughly versed in the distinction—indeed an adept—Blue Bill knows from whose gun the shot has been discharged. It is the double-barrel belonging to Richard Darke. All the more reason for him to hug close to his concealment.

And not the less to be careful about the behaviour of his own dog, which he is holding in hard embrace. For hearing the bound, the cur is disposed to give response; would do so but for the muscular fingers of its master closed chokingly around its throat, at intervals detached to give it a cautionary cuff.

After the shot the stag-hound continues its lugubrious cries; but again with altered intonation, and less distinctly heard; as though the animal had gone farther off, and were still making away.

But now a new noise strikes upon the coon-hunter's ears; one at first slight, but rapidly growing louder. It is the tread of footsteps, accompanied by a swishing among the palmettoes, that form an underwood along the edge of the swamp. Some one is passing through them, advancing towards the tree where he is concealed.

More than ever does he tremble on his perch; tighter than ever clutching the throat of his canine companion. For he is sure, that the man whose footsteps speak approach, is his master, or rather his master's son. The sounds seem to indicate great haste—a retreat rapid, headlong, confused. On which the peccant slave bases a hope of escaping observation, and too probable chastisement. Correct in his conjecture, as in the prognostication, in a few seconds after he sees Richard Darke coming between the trees; running as for very life—the more like it that he goes crouchingly; at intervals stopping to look back and listen, with chin almost touching his shoulder!

When opposite the sycamore—indeed under it—he makes pause longer than usual. The perspiration stands in beads upon his forehead, pours down his cheeks, over his eyebrows, almost blinding him. He whips a kerchief out of his coat pocket, and wipes it off. While so occupied, he does not perceive that he has let something drop—something white that came out along with the kerchief. Replacing the piece of cambric he hurries on again, leaving it behind; on, on, till the dull thud of his footfall, and the crisp rustling of the stiff fan-like leaves, become both blended with the ordinary noises of the forest.

Then, but not before, does Blue Bill think of forsaking the fork. Descending from his irksome seat, he approaches the white thing left lying on the ground—a letter enveloped in the ordinary way. He takes it up, and sees it has been already opened. He thinks not of drawing out the sheet folded inside. It would be no use; since the coon-hunter cannot read. Still, an instinct tells him, the little bit of treasure-trove may some time, and in some way, prove useful. So forecasting, he slips it into his pocket.

This done he stands reflecting. No noise to disturb him now. Darke's footsteps have died away in the distance, leaving swamp and cypress forest restored to their habitual stillness. The only sound, Blue Bill hears, is the beating of his own heart, yet loud enough.

No longer thinks he of the coon he has succeeded in treeing. The animal, late devoted to certain death, will owe its escape to an accident, and may now repose securely within its cave. Its pursuer has other thoughts—emotions, strong enough to drive coon-hunting clean out of his head. Among these are apprehensions about his own safety. Though unseen by Richard Darke—his presence there unsuspected—he knows that an unlucky chance has placed him in a position of danger. That a sinister deed has been done he is sure.

Under the circumstances, how is he to act? Proceed to the place whence the shots came, and ascertain what has actually occurred?

At first he thinks of doing this; but surrenders the intention. Affrighted by what is already known to him, he dares not know more. His young master may be a murderer? The way in which he was retreating almost said as much. Is he, Blue Bill, to make himself acquainted with the crime, and bear witness against him who has committed it? As a slave, he knows his testimony will count for little in a court of justice. And as the slave of Ephraim Darke, as little would his life be worth after giving it.

The last reflection decides him; and, still carrying the coon-dog under his arm, he parts from the spot, in timid skulking gait, never stopping, not feeling safe, till he finds himself inside the limits of the "negro quarter."

Chapter Nine
An assassin in retreat

Athwart the thick timber, going as one pursued—in a track straight as the underwood will allow—breaking through it like a chased bear—now stumbling over a fallen log, now caught in a trailing grape-vine—Richard Darke flees from the place where he has laid his rival low.

He makes neither stop, nor stay. If so, only for a few instants, just long enough to listen, and if possible learn whether he is being followed.

Whether or not, he fancies it; again starting off, with terror in his looks, and trembling in his limbs. The *sangfroid* he exhibited while bending over the dead body of his victim, and afterwards concealing it, has quite forsaken him now. Then he was confident, there could be no witness of the deed—nothing to connect him with it as the doer. Since, there is a change— the unthought-of presence of the dog having produced it. Or, rather, the thought of the animal having escaped. This, and his own imagination.

For more than a mile he keeps on, in headlong reckless rushing. Until fatigue overtaking him, his terror becomes less impulsive, his fancies freer from exaggeration; and, believing himself far enough from the scene of danger, he at length desists from flight, and comes to a dead stop.

Sitting down upon a log, he draws forth his pocket-handkerchief, and wipes the sweat from his face. For he is perspiring at every pore, panting, palpitating. He now finds time to reflect; his first reflection being the absurdity of his making such precipitate retreat; his next, its imprudence.

"I've been a fool for it," he mutters. "Suppose that some one has seen me? 'Twill only have made things worse. And what have I been running away from? A dead body, and a living dog! Why should I care for either? Even though the adage be true—about a live dog better than a dead lion. Let me hope the hound won't tell a tale upon me. For certain the shot hit him. That's nothing. Who could say what sort of ball, or the kind of gun it came from? No danger in that. I'd be stupid to think there could be. Well, it's all over now, and the question is: what next?"

For some minutes he remains upon the log, with the gun resting across his knees, and his head bent over the barrels. He appears engaged in some abstruse calculation. A new thought has sprang up in his mind—a scheme requiring all his intellectual power to elaborate.

"I shall keep that tryst," he says, in soliloquy, seeming at length to have settled it. "Yes; I'll meet her under the magnolia. Who can tell what changes may occur in the heart of a woman? In history I had a royal namesake—an English king, with an ugly hump on his shoulders—as he's said himself, 'deformed, unfinished, sent into the world scarce half made up,' so that the 'dogs barked at *him*,' just as this brute of Clancy's has been doing at me. And this royal Richard, shaped 'so lamely and unfashionable,' made court to a woman, whose husband he had just assassinated—more than a woman, a proud queen—and more than wooed, he subdued her. This ought to encourage me; the better that I, Richard Darke, am neither halt, nor hunchbacked. No, nor yet unfashionable, as many a Mississippian girl says, and more than one is ready to swear.

"Proud Helen Armstrong may be, and is; proud as England's queen herself. For all that, I've got something to subdue her—a scheme, cunning as that of my royal namesake. May God, or the Devil, grant me like success!"

At the moment of giving utterance to the profane prayer, he rises to his feet. Then, taking out his watch, consults it.

It is too dark for him to see the dial; but springing open the glass, he gropes against it, feeling for the hands.

"Half-past nine," he mutters, after making out the time. "Ten is the hour of her assignation. No chance for me to get home before, and then over to Armstrong's wood-ground. It's more than two miles from here. What matters my going home? Nor any need changing this dress. She won't notice the hole in the skirt. If she do, she wouldn't think of what caused it—above all it's being a bullet. Well, I must be off! It will never do to keep the young lady waiting. If she don't feel disappointed at seeing me, bless her! If she do, I shall curse her! What's passed prepares me for either event. In any case, I shall have satisfaction for the slight she's put upon me. By God I'll get that!"

He is moving away, when a thought occurs staying him. He is not quite certain about the exact hour of Helen Armstrong's tryst, conveyed in her letter to Clancy. In the madness of his mind ever since perusing that epistle, no wonder he should confuse circumstances, and forget dates.

To make sure, he plunges his hand into the pocket, where he deposited both letter and photograph—after holding the latter before the eyes of his dying foeman, and witnessing the fatal effect. With all his diabolical hardihood, he had been awed by this—so as to thrust the papers into his pocket, hastily, carelessly.

They are no longer there!

He searches in his other pockets—in all of them, with like result. He examines his bullet-pouch and gamebag. But finds no letter, no photograph, not a scrap of paper, in any! The stolen epistle, its envelope, the enclosed *carte de visite*—all are absent.

After ransacking his pockets, turning them inside out, he comes to the conclusion that the precious papers are lost.

It startles, and for a moment dismays him. Where are they? He must have let them fall in his hasty retreat through the trees; or left them by the dead body.

Shall he go back in search of them?

No—no—no! He does not dare to return upon that track. The forest path is too sombre, too solitary, now. By the margin of the dank lagoon, under the ghostly shadow of the cypresses, he might meet the ghost of the man murdered!

And why should he go back? After all, there is no need; nothing in the letter which can in any way compromise him. Why should he care to recover it?

"It may go to the devil, her picture along! Let both rot where I suppose I must have dropped them—in the mud, or among the palmettoes. No matter where. But it does matter, my being under the magnolia at the right time, to meet her. Then shall I learn my fate—know it, for better, for worse. If the former, I'll continue to believe in the story of Richard Plantagenet; if the latter, Richard Darke won't much care what becomes of him."

So ending his strange soliloquy, with a corresponding cast upon his countenance, the assassin rebuttons his coat—thrown open in search for the missing papers. Then, flinging the double-barrelled fowling-piece— the murder-gun—over his sinister shoulder, he strides off to keep an appointment not made for him, but for the man he has murdered!

Chapter Ten
The eve of departure

The evil day has arrived; the ruin, foreseen, has fallen.

The mortgage deed, so long held in menace over the head of Archibald Armstrong—suspended, as it were, by a thread, like the sword of Damocles—is to be put into execution. Darke has demanded immediate payment of the debt, coupled with threat of foreclosure.

The demand is a month old, the threat has been carried out, and the foreclosure effected. The thread having been cut, the keen blade of adversity has come down, severing the tie which attached Colonel Armstrong to his property, as it to him. Yesterday, he was owner, reputedly, of one of the finest plantations along the line of the Mississippi river, an hundred able-bodied negroes hoeing cotton in his fields, with fifty more picking it from the pod, and "ginning" the staple clear of seed; to-day, he is but their owner in seeming, Ephraim Darke being this in reality. And in another day the apparent ownership will end: for Darke has given his debtor notice to yield up houses, lands, slaves, plantation-stock—in short, everything he possesses.

In vain has Armstrong striven against this adverse fate; in vain made endeavours to avert it. When men are falling, false friends grow falser; even true ones becoming cold. Sinister chance also against him; a time of panic—a crisis in the money-market—as it always is on such occasions, when interest runs high, and *second* mortgages are sneered at by those who grant loans.

As no one—neither friend nor financial speculator—comes to Armstrong's rescue, he has no alternative but submit.

Too proud, to make appeal to his inexorable creditor—indeed deeming it idle—he vouchsafes no answer to the notice of foreclosure, beyond saying: "Let it be done."

At a later period he gives ear to a proposal, coming from the mortgagee: to put a valuation upon the property, and save the expenses of a public sale, by disposing of it privately to Darke himself.

To this he consents; less with a view to the convenience of the last, than because his sensitive nature recoils from the vulgarism of the first.

Tell me a more trying test to the delicate sensibilities of a gentleman, or his equanimity, than to see his gate piers pasted over with the black and white show bills of the auctioneer; a strip of stair carpet dangling down from one of his bedroom windows, and a crowd of hungry harpies clustered around his door-stoop; some entering with eyes that express keen concupiscence; others coming out with countenances more beatified, bearing away his Penates—jeering and swearing over them—insulting the Household Gods he has so long held in adoration. Ugh! A hideous, horrid sight—a spectacle of Pandemonium!

With a vision of such domestic iconoclasm flitting before his mind—not a dream, but a reality, that will surely arise by letting his estate go to the hammer—Colonel Armstrong accepts Darke's offer to deliver everything over in a lump, and for a lamp sum. The conditions have been some time settled; and Armstrong now knows the worst. Some half-score slaves he reserves; the better terms secured to his creditor by private bargain enabling him to obtain this concession.

Several days have elapsed since the settlement came to a conclusion—the interval spent in preparation for the change. A grand one, too; which contemplates, not alone leaving the old home, but the State in which it stands. The fallen man shrinks from further association with those who have witnessed his fall. Not but that he will leave behind many friends, faithful and true. Still to begin life again in their midst—to be seen humbly struggling at the bottom of the ladder on whose top he once proudly reposed—that would indeed be unendurable.

He prefers to carry out the design, he once thought only a dreamy prediction—migrating to Texas. There, he may recommence life with more hopeful energy, and lesser sense of humiliation.

The moving day has arrived, or rather the eve preceding it. On the morrow, Colonel Archibald Armstrong is called upon by the exigency of human laws,—oft more cruel, if not more inexorable, than those of Nature—to vacate the home long his.

'Tis night. Darkness has spread its sable pall over forest and field, and broods upon the brighter surface of the stream gliding between—the mighty Mississippi. All are equally obscured—from a thick veil of lead-coloured cloud, at the sun's setting, drawn over the canopy of the sky. Any light seen is that of the fire-flies, engaged in their nocturnal cotillon; while the sounds heard are nightly noises in a Southern States forest, semi-tropical, as the wild creatures who have their home in it. The green *cicada* chirps continuously, "Katy did—Katy did;" the *hyladae*, though reptiles, send forth an insect note; while the sonorous "gluck-gluck" of the huge *rana pipiens* mingles with the melancholy "whoo-whooa" of the great horned owl; which, unseen, sweeps on silent wing through the shadowy aisles of the forest, leading the lone traveller to fancy them peopled by departed spirits in torment from the pains of Purgatory.

Not more cheerful are the sounds aloft: for there are such, far above the tops of the tallest trees. There, the nightjar plies its calling, not so blind but that it can see in deepest darkness the smallest moth or midge, that, tired of perching on the heated leaves essays to soar higher. Two sorts of these goatsuckers, utter cries quite distinct; though both expressing aversion to "William." One speaks of him as still alive, mingling pity with its hostile demand: "Whippoor-Will!" The other appears to regard him as dead, and goes against his marital relict, at intervals calling out: "Chuck Will's widow!"

Other noises interrupt the stillness of a Mississippian night. High up in heaven the "honk" of a wild gander leading his flock in the shape of an inverted V; at times the more melodious note of a trumpeter swan; or from the top of a tall cottonwood, or cypress, the sharp saw-filing shriek of the white-headed eagle, angered by some stray creature coming too close, and startling it from its slumbers. Below, out of the swamp sedge, rises the mournful cry of the quabird—the American bittern—and from the same, the deep sonorous bellow of that ugliest animal on earth—the alligator.

Where fields adjoin the forest—plantation clearings—oft few and far between—there are sounds more cheerful. The song of the slave, his day's work done, sure to be preceded, or followed, by peals of loud jocund laughter; the barking of the house-dog, indicative of a well-watched home; with the lowing of cattle, and other domestic calls that proclaim it worth watching. A galaxy of little lights, in rows like street lamps, indicate the "negro quarter;" while in the foreground a half-dozen windows of larger size, and brighter sheen, show where stands the "big house"—the planter's own dwelling.

To that of Colonel Armstrong has come a night of exceptional character, when its lights are seen burning later than usual. The plantation clock has tolled nine, nearly an hour ago. Still light shines through the little windows of the negro cabins, while the larger ones of the "big house" are all aflame. And there are candles being carried to and fro, lighting up a scene of bustling activity: while the clack of voices—none of them in laughter—is heard commingled with the rattling of chains, and the occasional stroke of a hammer. The forms of men and women, are seen to flit athwart the shining windows, all busy about something.

There is no mystery in the matter. It is simply the planter, with his people, occupied in preparation for the morrow's moving. Openly, and without restraint: for, although so near the mid hour of night, it is no midnight flitting.

The only individual, who appears to act surreptitiously, is a young girl; who, coming out by the back door of the dwelling, makes away from its walls in gliding gait—at intervals glancing back over her shoulder, as if in fear of being followed, or observed.

Her style of dress also indicates a desire to shun observation; for she is cloaked and close hooded. Not enough to ensure disguise, though she may think so. The most stolid slave on all Colonel Armstrong's plantation, could tell at a glance whose figure is enfolded in the shapeless garment, giving it shape. He would at once identify it as that of his master's daughter. For no wrap however loosely flung over it, could hide the queenly form of Helen Armstrong, or conceal the splendid symmetry of her person. Arrayed in the garb of a laundress, she would still look the lady.

Perhaps, for the first time in her life she is walking with stealthy step, crouched form, and countenance showing fear. Daughter of a large slave-owner—mistress over many slaves—she is accustomed to an upright attitude, and aristocratic bearing. But she is now on an errand that calls for more than ordinary caution, and would dread being recognised by the humblest slave on her father's estate.

Fortunately for her, none see; therefore no one takes note of her movements, or the mode of her apparel. If one did, the last might cause remark. A woman cloaked, with head hooded in a warm summer night, the thermometer at ninety!

Notwithstanding the numerous lights, she is not observed as she glides through their crossing coruscations. And beyond, there is but little danger—while passing through the peach orchard, that stretches rearward from the dwelling. Still less, after getting out through a wicket-gate, which communicates with a tract of woodland. For then she is among trees whose trunks stand close, the spaces between buried in deep obscurity—deeper from the night being a dark one. It is not likely so to continue: for, before entering into the timber, she glances up to the sky, and sees that the cloud canopy has broken; here and there stars scintillating in the blue spaces between. While, on the farther edge of the plantation clearing, a brighter belt along the horizon foretells the uprising of the moon.

She does not wait for this; but plunges into the shadowy forest, daring its darkness, regardless of its dangers.

Chapter Eleven
Under the Trysting Tree

Still stooping in her gait, casting furtive glances to right, to left, before and behind—at intervals stopping to listen—Helen Armstrong continues her nocturnal excursion. Notwithstanding the obscurity, she keeps in a direct course, as if to reach some particular point, and for a particular reason.

What this is needs not be told. Only love could lure a young lady out at that late hour, and carry her along a forest path, dark, and not without dangers. And love unsanctioned, unallowed—perhaps forbidden, by some one who has ascendancy over her.

Just the first it is which has tempted her forth; while the last, not the cold, has caused her to cloak herself, and go close hooded. If her father but knew of the errand she is on, it could not be executed. And well is she aware of this. For the proud planter is still proud, despite his reverses, still clings to the phantom of social superiority; and if he saw her now, wandering through the woods at an hour near midnight, alone; if he could divine her purpose: to meet a man, who in time past has been rather coldly received at his house—because scarce ranking with his own select circle—had Colonel Armstrong but the gift of clairvoyance, in all probability he would at once suspend the preparations for departure, rush to his rifle, then off through the woods on the track of his erring daughter, with the intent to do a deed sanguinary as that recorded, if not so repulsive.

The girl has not far to go—only half a mile or so, from the house, and less than a quarter beyond the zigzag rail fence, which forms a boundary line between the maize fields and primeval forest. Her journey, when completed, will bring her under a tree—a grand magnolia, monarch of the forest surrounding. Well does she know it, as the way thither.

Arriving at the tree, she pauses beneath its far-stretching boughs. At the same time tossing back her hood, she shows her face unveiled.

She has no fear now. The place is beyond the range of night-strolling negroes. Only one in pursuit of 'possum, or 'coon, would be likely to come that way; a contingency too rare to give her uneasiness.

With features set in expectation, she stands. The fire-flies illuminate her countenance—deserving a better light. But seen, even under their pale fitful coruscation, its beauty is beyond question. Her features of gipsy cast—to which the cloak's hood adds characteristic expression—produce a picture appropriate to its framing—the forest.

Only for a few short moments does she remain motionless. Just long enough to get back her breath, spent by some exertion in making her way through the wood—more difficult in the darkness. Strong emotions, too, contribute to the pulsations of her heart.

She does not wait for them to be stilled. Facing towards the tree, and standing on tiptoe, she raises her hand aloft, and commences groping against the trunk. The fire-flies flicker over her snow-white fingers, as these stray along the bark, at length resting upon the edge of a dark disc—the knot-hole in the tree.

Into this her hand is plunged; then drawn out—empty!

At first there is no appearance of disappointment. On the contrary, the phosphoric gleam dimly disclosing her features, rather shows satisfaction— still further evinced by the phrase falling from her lips, with the tone of its utterance. She says, contentedly:—"*He has got it!*"

But by the same fitful light, soon after is perceived a change—the slightest expression of chagrin, as she adds, in murmured interrogatory, "Why hasn't he left an answer?"

Is she sure he has not? No. But she soon will be.

With this determination, she again faces towards the tree; once more inserts her slender fingers; plunges in her white hand up to the wrist—to the elbow; gropes the cavity all round; then draws out again, this time with an exclamation which tells of something more than disappointment. It is discontent—almost anger. So too a speech succeeding, thus:—

"He might at least have let me know, whether he was coming or not—a word to say, I might expect him. He should have been here before me. It's the hour—past it!"

She is not certain—only guessing. She may be mistaken about the time—perhaps wronging the man. She draws the watch from her waistbelt, and holds the dial up. By the moon, just risen, she can read it. Reflecting the rays, the watch crystal, the gold rings on her fingers, and the jewels gleam joyfully. But there is no joy on her countenance. On the contrary, a mixed expression of sadness and chagrin. For the hands indicate ten minutes after the hour of appointment.

There can be no mistake about the time—she herself fixed it. And none in the timepiece. Her watch is not a cheap one. No fabric of Germany, or Geneva; no pedlar's thing from Yankeeland, which as a Southron she would despise; but an article of solid English manufacture, *sun-sure*, like the machine-made watches of "Streeter."

In confidence she consults it; saying vexatiously:

"Ten minutes after, and he not here! No answer to my note! He must have received it: Surely Jule put it into the tree? Who but he could have taken it out? Oh, this is cruel! He comes not—I shall go home."

The cloak is once more closed, the hood drawn over her head. Still she lingers—lingers, and listens.

No footstep—no sound to break the solemn stillness—only the chirrup of tree-crickets, and the shrieking of owls.

She takes a last look at the dial, sadly, despairingly. The hands indicate full fifteen minutes after the hour she had named—going on to twenty.

She restores the watch to its place, beneath her belt, her demeanour assuming a sudden change. Some chagrin still, but no sign of sadness. This is replaced by an air of determination, fixed and stern. The moon's light, with that of the fire-flies, have both a response in flashes brighter than either—sparks from the eyes of an angry woman. For Helen Armstrong is this, now.

Drawing her cloak closer around, she commences moving off from the tree.

She is not got beyond the canopy of its branches, ere her steps are stayed. A rustling among the dead leaves—a swishing against those that live—a footstep with tread solid and heavy—the footfall of a man!

A figure is seen approaching; as yet only indistinctly, but surely that of a man. As surely the man expected?

"He's been detained—no doubt by some good cause," she reflects, her spite and sadness departing as he draws near.

They are gone, before he can get to her side. But woman-like, she resolves to make a grace of forgiveness, and begins by upbraiding him.

"So you're here at last. A wonder you condescended coming at all! There's an old adage 'Better late than never.' Perhaps, you think it befits present time and company? And, perhaps, you may be mistaken. Indeed you are, so far as I'm concerned. I've been here long enough, and won't be any longer. Good-night, sir! Good-night!"

Her speech is taunting in tone, and bitter in sense. She intends it to be both—only in seeming. But to still further impress a lesson on the lover who has slighted her, she draws closer the mantle, and makes as if moving away.

Mistaking her pretence for earnest, the man flings himself across her path—intercepting her. Despite the darkness she can see that his arms are in the air, and stretched towards her, as if appealingly. The attitude speaks apology, regret, contrition—everything to make her relent.

She relents; is ready to fling herself upon his breast, and there lie lovingly, forgivingly.

But again woman-like, not without a last word of reproach, to make more esteemed her concession, she says:—

"'Tis cruel thus to have tried me. Charles! Charles! why have you done it?"

As she utters the interrogatory a cloud comes over her countenance, quicker than ever shadow over sun. Its cause—the countenance of him standing *vis-à-vis*. A change in their relative positions has brought his face full under the moonlight. He is *not* the man she intended meeting!

Who he really is can be gathered from his rejoinder:—

"You are mistaken, Miss Armstrong. My name is not Charles, but Richard. I am *Richard Darke.*"

Chapter Twelve
The wrong man

Richard Darke instead of Charles Clancy!

Disappointment were far too weak a word to express the pang that shoots through the heart of Helen Armstrong, on discovering the mistake she has made. It is bitter vexation, commingled with a sense of shame. I or her speeches, in feigned reproach, have terribly compromised her.

She does not drop to the earth, nor show any sign of it. She is not a woman of the weak fainting sort. No cry comes from her lips—nothing to betray surprise, or even the most ordinary emotion.

As Darke stands before her with arms upraised, she simply says,—

"Well, sir; if you *are* Richard Darke, what then? Your being so matters not to me; and certainly gives you no right thus to intrude upon me. I wish to be alone, and must beg of you to leave me so."

The cool firm tone causes him to quail. He had hoped that the surprise of his unexpected appearance—coupled with his knowledge of her clandestine appointment—would do something to subdue, perhaps make her submissive.

On the contrary, the thought of the last but stings her to resentment, as he soon perceives.

His raised arms drop down, and he is about to step aside, leaving her free to pass. Though not before making an attempt to justify himself; instinct supplying a reason, with hope appended. He does so, saying,—

"If I've intruded, Miss Armstrong, permit me to apologise for it. I assure you it's been altogether an accident. Having heard you are about to leave the neighbourhood—indeed, that you start to-morrow morning—I was on the way to your father's house to say farewell. I'm sorry my coming along here, and chancing to meet you, should lay me open to the charge of intrusion. I shall still more regret, if my presence has spoiled any plans, or interfered with an appointment. Some one else expected, I presume?"

For a time she is silent—abashed, while angered, by the impudent interrogatory.

Recovering herself, she rejoins,—

"Even were it as you say, sir, by what authority do you question me? I've said I wish to be alone."

"Oh, if that's your wish, I must obey, and relieve you of my presence, apparently so disagreeable."

Saying this he steps to one side. Then continues,—

"As I've told you, I was on the way to your father's house to take leave of the family. If you're not going immediately home, perhaps I may be the bearer of a message for you?"

The irony is evident; but Helen Armstrong is not sensible of it. She does not even think of it. Her only thought is how to get disembarrassed of this man who has appeared at a moment so *mal apropos*. Charles Clancy—for he was the expected one—may have been detained by some cause unknown, a delay still possible of justification. She has a lingering thought he may yet come; and, so thinking, her eye turns towards the forest with a quick, subtle glance.

Notwithstanding its subtlety, and the obscurity surrounding them, Darke observes, comprehends it.

Without waiting for her rejoinder, he proceeds to say,—

"From the mistake you've just made, Miss Armstrong, I presume you took me for some one bearing the baptismal name of Charles. In these parts I know only one person who carries that cognomen—one Charles Clancy. If it be he you are expecting, I think I can save you the necessity of stopping out in the night air any longer. If you're staying for him you'll be disappointed; he will certainly not come."

"What mean you, Mr Darke? Why do you say that?"

His words carry weighty significance, and throw the proud girl off her guard. She speaks confusedly, and without reflection.

His rejoinder, cunningly conceived, designed with the subtlety of the devil, still further affects her, and painfully.

He answers, with assumed nonchalance,—

"Because I know it."

"How?" comes the quick, unguarded interrogatory.

"Well; I chanced to meet Charley Clancy this morning, and he told me he was going off on a journey. He was just starting when I saw him. Some affair of the heart, I believe; a little love-scrape he's got into with a pretty

Creole girl, who lives t'other side of Natchez. By the way, he showed me a photograph of yourself, which he said you had sent him. A very excellent likeness, indeed. Excuse me for telling you, that he and I came near quarrelling about it. He had another photograph—that of his Creole *chère amie*—and would insist that she is more beautiful than you. I may own, Miss Armstrong, you've given me no great reason for standing forth as your champion. Still, I couldn't stand that; and, after questioning Clancy's taste, I plainly told him he was mistaken. I'm ready to repeat the same to him, or any one, who says you are not the most beautiful woman in the State of Mississippi."

At the conclusion of his fulsome speech Helen Armstrong cares but little for the proffered championship, and not much for aught else.

Her heart is nigh to breaking. She has given her affections to Clancy—in that last letter written, lavished them. And they have been trifled with—scorned! She, daughter of the erst proudest planter in all Mississippi State, has been slighted for a Creole girl; possibly, one of the "poor white trash" living along the bayous' edge. Full proof she has of his perfidy, or how should Darke know of it? More maddening still, the man so slighting her, has been making boast of it, proclaiming her suppliance and shame, showing her photograph, exulting in the triumph obtained! "O God!"

Not in prayer, but angry ejaculation, does the name of the Almighty proceed from her lips. Along with it a scarce-suppressed scream, as, despairingly, she turns her face towards home.

Darke sees his opportunity, or thinks so; and again flings himself before her—this time on his knees.

"Helen Armstrong!" he exclaims, in an earnestness of passion—if not pure, at least heartfelt and strong—"why should you care for a man who thus mocks you? Here am I, who love you, truly—madly—more than my own life! 'Tis not too late to withdraw the answer you have given me. Gainsay it, and there need be no change—no going to Texas. Your father's home may still be his, and yours. Say you'll be my wife, and everything shall be restored to him—all will yet be well."

She is patient to the conclusion of his appeal. Its apparent sincerity stays her; though she cannot tell, or does not think, why. It is a moment of mechanical irresolution.

But, soon as ended, again returns the bitterness that has just swept through her soul—torturing her afresh.

There is no balm in the words spoken by Dick Darke; on the contrary, they but cause increased rankling.

To his appeal she makes answer, as once before she has answered him—with a single word. But now repeated three times, and in a tone not to be mistaken.

On speaking it, she parts from the spot with proud haughty step, and a denying disdainful gesture, which tells him, she is not to be further stayed.

Spited, chagrined, angry, in his craven heart he feels also cowed, subdued, crestfallen. So much, he dares not follow her, but remains under the magnolia; from whose hollow trunk seems to reverberate the echo of her last word, in its treble repetition: *"never—never—never!"*

Chapter Thirteen
The coon-hunter at home

Over the fields of Ephraim Darke's plantation a lingering ray of daylight still flickers, as Blue Bill, returning from his abandoned coon-hunt, gets back to the negro quarter. He enters it, with stealthy tread, and looking cautiously around.

For he knows that some of his fellow-slaves are aware of his having gone out "a-cooning," and will wonder at his soon return—too soon to pass without observation. If seen by them he may be asked for an explanation, which he is not prepared to give.

To avoid being called upon for it, he skulks in among the cabins; still carrying the dog under his arm, lest the latter may take a fancy to go smelling among the utensils of some other darkey's kitchen, and betray his presence in the "quarter."

Fortunately for the coon-hunter, the little "shanty" that claims him as its tenant stands at the outward extremity of the row of cabins—nearest the path leading to the plantation woodland. He is therefore enabled to reach, and re-enter it, without any great danger of attracting observation.

And as it chances, he is not observed; but gets back into the bosom of his family, no one being a bit the wiser.

Blue Bill's domestic circle consists of his wife, Phoebe, and several half-naked little "niggers," who, at his return, tackle on to his legs, and, soon as he sits down, clamber confusedly over his knees. So circumstanced, one would think he should now feel safe, and relieved from further anxiety. Far from it: he has yet a gauntlet to run.

His re-appearance so early, unexpected; his empty gamebag; the coon-dog carried under his arm; all have their effect upon Phoebe. She cannot help feeling surprise, accompanied by a keen curiosity.

She is not the woman to submit to it in silence.

Confronting her dark-skinned lord and master, with arms set akimbo, she says,—

"Bress de Lor', Bill! Wha' for you so soon home? Neider coon nor possum! An' de dog toated arter dat trange fashun! You ain't been gone more'n a hour! Who'd speck see you come back dat a way, empty-handed; nuffin, 'cep your own ole dog! 'Splain it, sah?"

Thus confronted, the coon-hunter lets fall his canine companion; which drops with a dump upon the floor. Then seats himself on a stool, but without entering upon the demanded explanation. He only says:—

"Nebba mind, Phoebe, gal; nebba you mind why I'se got home so soon. Dat's nuffin 'trange. I seed de night warn't a gwine to be fav'ble fo' trackin' de coon; so dis nigga konklood he'd leab ole cooney 'lone."

"Lookee hya, Bill!" rejoins the sable spouse, laying her hand upon his shoulder, and gazing earnestly into his eyes. "Dat ere ain't de correck explicashun. You's not tellin' me de troof!"

The coon-hunter quails under the searching glance, as if in reality a criminal; but still holds back the demanded explanation. He is at a loss what to say.

"Da's somethin' mysteerus 'bout dis," continues his better half. "You'se got a seecrit, nigga; I kin tell it by de glint ob yer eye. I nebba see dat look on ye, but I know you ain't yaseff; jess as ye use deseeve me, when you war in sich a way 'bout brown Bet."

"Wha you talkin 'bout, Phoebe? Dar's no brown Bet in de case. I swar dar ain't."

"Who sayed dar war? No, Bill, dat's all pass. I only spoked ob her 'kase ya look jess now like ye did when Bet used bamboozle ye. What I say now am dat you ain't yaseff. Dar's a cat in de bag, somewha; you better let her out, and confess de whole troof."

As Phoebe makes this appeal, her glance rests inquiringly on her husband's countenance, and keenly scrutinises the play of his features.

There is not much play to be observed. The coon-hunter is a pure-blooded African, with features immobile as those of the Sphinx. And from his colour nought can be deduced. As already said, it is the depth of its ebon blackness, producing a purplish iridescence over the epidermis, that has gained for him the sobriquet "Blue Bill."

Unflinchingly he stands the inquisitorial glance, and for the time Phoebe is foiled.

Only until after supper, when the frugality of the meal—made so by the barren chase—has perhaps something to do in melting his heart, and relaxing his tongue. Whether this, or whatever the cause, certain it is, that before going to bed, he unburdens himself to the partner of his joys, by making full confession of what he has heard and seen by the side of the cypress swamp.

He tells her, also, of the letter picked up; which, cautiously pulling out of his pocket, he submits to her inspection.

Phoebe has once been a family servant—an indoor domestic, and handmaiden to a white mistress. This in the days of youth—the halcyon days of her girlhood, in "Ole Varginny"—before she was transported west, sold to Ephraim Darke, and by him degraded to the lot of an ordinary outdoor slave. But her original owner taught her to read, and her memory still retains a trace of this early education—sufficient for her to decipher the script put into her hands.

She first looks at the photograph; as it is the first to come out of the envelope. There can be no mistaking whose likeness it is. A lady too conspicuously beautiful to have escaped notice from the humblest slave in the settlement.

The negress spends some seconds gazing upon the portrait, as she does so remarking,—

"How bewful dat young lady!"

"You am right 'bout dat, Phoebe. She bewful as any white gal dis nigga ebber sot eyes on. And she good as bewful. I'se sorry she gwine leab dis hya place. Dar's many a darkie 'll miss de dear young lady. An' won't Mass Charl Clancy miss her too! Lor! I most forgot; maybe he no trouble 'bout her now; maybe he's gone dead! Ef dat so, she miss *him*, a no mistake. She cry her eyes out."

"You tink dar war something 'tween dem two?"

"Tink! I'se shoo ob it, Phoebe. Didn't I see dem boaf down dar in de woodland, when I war out a-coonin. More'n once I seed em togedder. A young white lady an' genl'm don't meet dat way unless dar's a feelin' atween em, any more dan we brack folks. Besides, dis nigga know dey lub one noder—he know fo sartin. Jule, she tell Jupe; and Jupe hab trussed dat same seecret to me. Dey been in lub long time; afore Mass Charl went 'way to Texas. But de great Kurnel Armstrong, he don't know nuffin' 'bout it. Golly! ef he did, he shoo kill Charl Clancy; dat is, if de poor young man ain't dead arready. Le's hope 'tain't so. But, Phoebe, gal, open dat letter, an' see what de lady say. Satin it's been wrote by her. Maybe it trow some light on dis dark subjeck."

Phoebe, thus solicited, takes the letter from the envelope. Then spreading it out, and holding it close to the flare of the tallow dip, reads it from beginning to end.

It is a task that occupies her some considerable time; for her scholastic acquirements, not very bright at the best, have become dimmed by long disuse. For all, she succeeds in deciphering its contents and interpreting them to Bill; who listens with ears wide open and eyes in staring wonderment.

When the reading is at length finished, the two remain for some time silent, — pondering upon the strange circumstances thus revealed to them.

Blue Bill is the first to resume speech. He says: —

"Dar's a good deal in dat letter I know'd afore, and dar's odder points as 'pear new to me; but whether de old or de new, 'twon't do for us folk declar a single word o' what de young lady hab wrote in dat ere 'pistle. No, Phoebe, neery word must 'scape de lips ob eider o' us. We muss hide de letter, an' nebba let nob'dy know dar's sich a dockyment in our posseshun. And dar must be nuffin' know'd 'bout dis nigga findin' it. Ef dat sakumstance war to leak out, I needn't warn you what 'ud happen to me. Blue Bill 'ud catch de cowhide, —maybe de punishment ob de pump. So, Phoebe, gal, gi'e me yar word to keep dark, for de case am a dangersome, an a desprit one."

The wife can well comprehend the husband's caution, with the necessity of compliance; and the two retire to rest, in the midst of their black olive branches, with a mutual promise to be "mum."

Chapter Fourteen
Why comes he not?

Helen Armstrong goes to bed, with spiteful thoughts about Charles Clancy. So rancorous she cannot sleep, but turns distractedly on her couch, from time to time changing cheek upon the pillow.

At little more than a mile's distance from this chamber of unrest, another woman is also awake, thinking of the same man—not spitefully, but anxiously. It is his mother.

As already said, the road running north from Natchez leads past Colonel Armstrong's gate. A traveller, going in the opposite direction—that is towards the city—on clearing the skirts of the plantation, would see, near the road side, a dwelling of very different kind; of humble unpretentious aspect, compared with the grand mansion of the planter. It would be called a cottage, were this name known in the State of Mississippi—which it is not. Still it is not a log-cabin; but a "frame-house," its walls of "weather-boarding," planed and painted, its roof cedar-shingled; a style of architecture occasionally seen in the Southern States, though not so frequently as in the Northern—inhabited by men in moderate circumstances, poorer than planters, but richer, or more gentle, than the "white trash," who live in log-cabins.

Planters they are in social rank, though poor; perhaps owning a half-dozen slaves, and cultivating a small tract of cleared ground, from twenty to fifty acres. The frame-house vouches for their respectability; while two or three log structures at back—representing barn, stable, and other outbuildings—tell of land attached.

Of this class is the habitation referred to—the home of the widow Clancy.

As already known, her widowhood is of recent date. She still wears its emblems upon her person, and carries its sorrow in her heart.

Her husband, of good Irish lineage, had found his way to Nashville, the capital city of Tennessee; where, in times long past, many Irish families made settlements. There he had married her, she herself being a native Tennesseean—sprung from the old Carolina pioneer stock, that colonised the state near the end of the eighteenth century—the Robertsons, Hyneses, Hardings, and Bradfords—leaving to their descendants a patent of nobility, or at least a family name deserving respect, and generally obtaining it.

In America, as elsewhere, it is not the rule for Irishmen to grow rich; and still more exceptional in the case of Irish gentlemen. When these have wealth their hospitality is too apt to take the place of a spendthrift profuseness, ending in pecuniary embarrassment.

So was it with Captain Jack Clancy; who got wealth with his wife, but soon squandered it entertaining his own and his wife's friends. The result, a move to Mississippi, where land was cheaper, and his attenuated fortune would enable him to hold out a little longer.

Still, the property he had purchased in Mississippi State was but a poor one; leading him to contemplate a further flit into the rich red lands of North-Eastern Texas, just becoming famous as a field for colonisation. His son Charles sent thither, as said, on a trip of exploration, had spent some months in the Lone Star State, prospecting for the new home; and brought back a report in every way favourable.

But the ear, to which it was to have been spoken, could no more hear. On his return, he found himself fatherless; and to the only son there remains only a mother; whose grief, pressing heavily, has almost brought her to the grave. It is one of a long series of reverses which have sorely taxed her fortitude. Another of like heaviness, and the tomb may close over her.

Some such presentiment is in the mother's mind, on this very day, as the sun goes down, and she sits in her chamber beside a dim candle, with ear keenly bent to catch the returning footsteps of her son.

He has been absent since noon, having gone deer-stalking, as frequently before. She can spare him for this, and pardon his prolonged absence. She knows how fond he is of the chase; has been so from a boy.

But, on the present occasion, he is staying beyond his usual time. It is now night; the deer have sought their coverts; and he is not "torch-hunting."

Only one thing can she think of to explain the tardiness of his return. The eyes of the widowed mother have been of late more watchful than wont. She has noticed her son's abstracted air, and heard sighs that seemed to come from his inner heart. Who can mistake the signs of love, either in man or woman? Mrs Clancy does not. She sees that Charles has lapsed into this condition.

Rumours that seem wafted on the air—signs slight, but significant— perhaps the whisper of a confidential servant—these have given her assurance of the fact: telling her, at the same time, who has won his affections.

Mrs Clancy is neither dissatisfied nor displeased. In all the neighbourhood there is no one she would more wish to have for a daughter-in-law than Helen Armstrong. Not from any thought of the girl's great beauty, or high social standing. Caroline Clancy is herself too well descended to make much of the latter circumstance. It is the reputed noble character of the lady that influences her approval of her son's choice.

Thinking of this—remembering her own youth, and the stolen interviews with Charles Clancy's father—oft under the shadow of night— she could not, does not, reflect harshly on the absence of that father's son from home, however long, or late the hour.

It is only as the clock strikes twelve, she begins to think seriously about it. Then creeps over her a feeling of uneasiness, soon changing to apprehension. Why should he be staying out so late—after midnight? The same little bird, that brought her tidings of his love-affair, has also told her it is clandestine. Mrs Clancy may not like this. It has the semblance of a slight to her son, as herself—more keenly felt by her in their reduced circumstances. But then, as compensation, arises the retrospect of her own days of courtship carried on in the same way.

Still, at that hour the young lady cannot—dares not—be abroad. All the more unlikely, that the Armstrongs are moving off—as all the neighbourhood knows—and intend starting next day, at an early hour.

The plantation people will long since have retired to rest; therefore an interview with his sweetheart can scarce be the cause of her son's detention. Something else must be keeping him. What? So run the reflections of the fond mother.

At intervals she starts up from her seat, as some sound reaches her; each time gliding to the door, and gazing out—again to go back disappointed.

For long periods she remains in the porch, her eye interrogating the road that runs past the cottage-gate; her ear acutely listening for footsteps.

Early in the night it has been dark; now there is a brilliant moonlight. But no man, no form moving underneath it. No sound of coming feet; nothing that resembles a footfall.

One o'clock, and still silence; to the mother of Charles Clancy become oppressive, as with increased anxiety she watches and waits.

At intervals she glances at the little "Connecticut" clock that ticks over the mantel. A pedlar's thing, it may be false, as the men who come south selling "sech." It is the reflection of a Southern woman, hoping her conjecture may be true.

But, as she lingers in the porch, and looks at the moving moon, she knows the hour must be late.

Certain sounds coming from the forest, and the farther swamp, tell her so. As a backwoods woman she can interpret them. She hears the call of the turkey "gobbler." She knows it means morning.

The clock strikes two; still she hears no fall of footstep—sees no son returning!

"Where is my Charles? What can be detaining him?"

Phrases almost identical with those that fell from the lips of Helen Armstrong, but a few hours before, in a different place, and prompted by a different sentiment—a passion equally strong, equally pure!

Both doomed to disappointment, alike bitter and hard to bear. The same in cause, but dissimilar in the impression produced. The sweetheart believing herself slighted, forsaken, left without a lover; the mother tortured with the presentiment, she no longer has a son!

When, at a yet later hour—or rather earlier, since it is nigh daybreak—a dog, his coat disordered, comes gliding through the gate, and Mrs Clancy recognises her son's favourite hunting hound, she has still only a presentiment of the terrible truth. But one which to the maternal heart, already filled with foreboding, feels too like certainty.

And too much for her strength. Wearied with watching, prostrated by the intensity of her vigil, when the hound crawls up the steps, and under the dim light she sees his bedraggled body—blood as well as mud upon it—the sight produces a climax—a shock apparently fatal.

She swoons upon the spot, and is carried inside the house by a female slave—the last left to her.

Chapter Fifteen
A moonlight moving

While the widowed mother, now doubly bereft—stricken down by the blow—is still in a state of syncope, the faithful negress doing what she can to restore her, there are sounds outside unheard by either. A dull rumble of wheels, as of some heavy vehicle coming along the main road, with the occasional crack of a whip, and the sonorous "wo-ha" of a teamster.

Presently, a large "Conestoga" wagon passes the cottage-gate, full freighted with what looks like house furniture, screened under canvas. The vehicle is drawn by a team of four strong mules, driven by a negro; while at the wagon's tail, three or four other darkeys follow afoot.

The cortege, of purely southern character, has scarce passed out of sight, and not yet beyond hearing, when another vehicle comes rolling along the road. This, of lighter build, and proceeding at a more rapid rate, is a barouche, drawn by a pair of large Kentucky horses. As the night is warm, and there is no need to spring up the leathern hood—its occupants can all be seen, and their individuality made out. On the box-seat is a black coachman; and by his side a young girl whose tawny complexion, visible in the whiter moonbeams, tells her to be a mulatto. Her face has been seen before, under a certain forest tree—a magnolia—its owner depositing a letter in the cavity of the trunk. She who sits alongside the driver is "Jule."

In the barouche, behind, is a second face that has been seen under the same tree, but with an expression upon it sadder and more disturbed. For of the three who occupy the inside seats one is Helen Armstrong; the others her father, and sister. They are *en route* for the city of Natchez, the port of departure for their journey south-westward into Texas; just starting away from their old long-loved dwelling, whose gates they have left ajar, its walls desolate behind thorn.

The wagon, before, carries the remnant of the planter's property,—all his inexorable creditor allows him to take along. No wonder he sits in the barouche, with bowed head, and chin between his knees, not caring to look back. For the first time in his life he feels truly, terribly humiliated.

This, and no flight from creditors, no writ, nor pursuing sheriff, will account for his commencing the journey at so early an hour. To be seen going off in the open daylight would attract spectators around; it may be many sympathisers. But in the hour of adversity his sensitive nature shrinks from the glance of sympathy, as he would dread the stare of exultation, were any disposed to indulge in it.

But besides the sentiment, there is another cause for their night moving — an inexorable necessity as to time. The steamboat, which is to take them up Red River, leaves Natchez at sunrise. He must be aboard by daybreak.

If the bankrupt planter be thus broken-spirited, his eldest daughter is as much cast down as he, and far more unhappily reflecting.

Throughout all that night Helen Armstrong has had no sleep; and now, in the pale moonlight of the morning, her cheeks show white and wan, while a dark shadow broods upon her brow, and her eyes glisten with wild unnatural light, as one in a raging fever. Absorbed in thought, she takes no heed of anything along the road; and scarce makes answer to an occasional observation addressed to her by her sifter, evidently with the intention to cheer her. It has less chance of success, because of Jessie herself being somewhat out of sorts. Even she, habitually merry, is for the time sobered; indeed saddened at the thought of that they are leaving behind, and what may be before them. Possibly, as she looks back at the gate of their grand old home, through which they will never again go, she may be reflecting on the change from their late luxurious life, to the log-cabin and coarse fare, of which her father had forewarned them.

If so, the reflection is hers—not Helen's. Different with the latter, and far more bitter the emotion that stirs within her person, scalding her heart. Little cares she what sort of house she is hitherto to dwell in, what she will have to wear, or eat. The scantiest raiment, or coarsest food, can give no discomfort now. She could bear the thought of sheltering under the humblest roof in Texas—ay, think of it with cheerfulness—had Charles Clancy been but true, to share its shelter along with her. He has not, and that is an end of it.

Is it? No; not for her, though it may be for him. In the company of his Creole girl he will soon cease to think of her—forget the solemn vows made, and the sweet words spoken, beneath the magnolia—tree, in her retrospect seeming sadder than yew, or cypress.

Will she ever forget him? Can she? No; unless in that land, whither her face is set, she find the fabled Lethean stream. Oh! it is bitter—keenly bitter!

It reaches the climax of its bitterness, when the barouche rolling along opens out a vista between the trees, disclosing a cottage—Clancy's. Inside it sleeps the man, who has made her life a misery! Can he sleep, after what he has done?

While making this reflection she herself feels, as if never caring to close her eyelids more—except in death!

Her emotions are terribly intense, her anguish so overpowering, she can scarce conceal it—indeed does not try, so long as the house is in sight. Perhaps fortunate that her father is absorbed in his own particular sadness. But her sister observes all, guessing—nay, knowing the cause. She says nothing. Such sorrow is too sacred to be intruded on. There are times, when even a sister may not attempt consolation.

Jessie is glad when the carriage, gliding on, again enters among trees, and the little cottage of the Clancys, like their own great house, is forever lost to view.

Could the eyes of Helen Armstrong, in passing, have penetrated through the walls of that white painted dwelling—could she have rested them upon a bed with a woman laid astretch upon it, apparently dead, or dying—could she have looked on another bed, unoccupied, untouched, and been told how he, its usual occupant, was at that moment lying in the middle of a chill marsh, under the sombre canopy of cypresses—it would have caused a revulsion in her feelings, sudden, painful, and powerful as the shock already received.

There would still be sadness in her breast, but no bitterness. The former far easier to endure; she would sooner believe Clancy dead, than think of his traitorous defection.

But she is ignorant of all that has occurred; of the sanguinary scene enacted—played out complete—on the edge of the cypress swamp, and the sad one inside the house—still continuing. Aware of the one, or witness of the other, while passing that lone cottage, as with wet eyes she takes a last look at its walls, she would still be shedding tears—not of spite, but sorrow.

Chapter Sixteen
What has become of Clancy?

The sun is up—the hour ten o'clock, morning. Around the residence of the widow Clancy a crowd of people has collected. They are her nearest neighbours; while those who dwell at a distance are still in the act of assembling. Every few minutes two or three horsemen ride up, carrying long rifles over their shoulders, with powder-horns and bullet-pouches strapped across their breasts. Those already on the ground are similarly armed, and accoutred.

The cause of this warlike muster is understood by all. Some hours before, a report has spread throughout the plantations that Charles Clancy is missing from his home, under circumstances to justify suspicion of foul play having befallen him. His mother has sent messengers to and fro; hence the gathering around her house.

In the South-Western States, on occasions of this kind, it does not do for any one to show indifference, whatever his station in life. The wealthiest, as well as the poorest, is expected to take part in the administration of backwoods' justice—at times not strictly *en règle* with the laws of the land.

For this reason Mrs Clancy's neighbours, far and near, summoned or not summoned, come to her cottage. Among them Ephraim Darke, and his son Richard.

Archibald Armstrong is not there, nor looked for. Most know of his having moved away that same morning. The track of his waggon wheels has been seen upon the road; and, if the boat he is to take passage by, start at the advertised hour, he should now be nigh fifty miles from the spot, and still further departing. No one is thinking of him, or his; since no one dreams of the deposed planter, or his family, having ought to do with the business that brings them together.

This is to search for Charles Clancy, still absent from his home. The mother's story has been already told, and only the late comers have to hear it again.

In detail she narrates what occurred on the preceding night; how the hound came home wet, and wounded. Confirmatory of her speech, the animal is before their eyes, still in the condition spoken of. They can all see it has been shot—the tear of the bullet being visible on its back, having just cut through the skin. Coupled with its master's absence, this circumstance strengthens the suspicion of something amiss.

Another, of less serious suggestion, is a piece of cord knotted around the dog's neck—the loose end looking as though gnawed by teeth, and then broken off with a pluck; as if the animal had been tied up, and succeeded in setting itself free.

But why tied? And why has it been shot? These are questions that not anybody can answer.

Strange, too, in the hound having reached home at the hour it did. As Clancy went out about the middle of the day, he could not have gone to such a distance for his dog to have been nearly all night getting back.

Could he himself have fired the bullet, whose effect is before their eyes?

A question almost instantly answered in the negative; by old backwoodsmen among the mustered crowd—hunters who know how to interpret "sign" as surely as Champollion an Egyptian hieroglyph. These having examined the mark on the hound's skin, pronounce the ball that made it to have come from a *smooth-bore, and not a rifle*. It is notorious, that Charles Clancy never carried a smooth-bore, but always a rifled gun. His own dog has not been shot by him.

After some time spent in discussing the probabilities and possibilities of the case, it is at length resolved to drop conjecturing, and commence search for the missing man. In the presence of his mother no one speaks of searching for his *dead body*; though there is a general apprehension, that this will be the thing found.

She, the mother, most interested of all, has a too true foreboding of it. When the searchers, starting off, in kindly sympathy tell her to be of good cheer, her heart more truly says, she will never see her son again.

On leaving the house, the horsemen separate into two distinct parties, and proceed in different directions.

With one and the larger, goes Clancy's hound; an old hunter, named Woodley, taking the animal along. He has an idea it may prove serviceable, when thrown on its master's track—supposing this can be discovered.

Just as conjectured, the hound does prove of service. Once inside the woods, without even setting nose to the ground, it starts off in a straight run—going so swiftly, the horsemen find it difficult to keep pace with it.

It sets them all into a gallop; this continued for quite a couple of miles through timber thick and thin, at length ending upon the edge of the swamp.

Only a few have followed the hound thus far, keeping close. The others, straggling behind, come up by twos and threes.

The hunter, Woodley, is among the foremost to be in at the death; for *death* all expect it to prove. They are sure of it, on seeing the stag-hound stop beside something, as it does so loudly baying.

Spurring on towards the spot, they expect to behold the dead body of Charles Clancy. They are disappointed.

There is no body there—dead or alive. Only a pile of Spanish moss, which appears recently dragged from the trees; then thrown into a heap, and afterwards scattered.

The hound has taken stand beside it; and there stays, giving tongue. As the horsemen dismount, and get their eyes closer to the ground, they see something red; which proves to be blood. It is dark crimson, almost black, and coagulated. Still is it blood.

From under the edge of the moss-heap protrudes the barrel of a gun. On kicking the loose cover aside, they see it is a rifle—not of the kind common among backwoodsmen. But they have no need to waste conjecture on the gun. Many present identify it as the yäger usually carried by Clancy.

More of the moss being removed, a hat is uncovered—also Clancy's. Several know it as his—can swear to it.

A gun upon the ground, abandoned, discharged as they see; a hat alongside it; blood beside both—there must have been shooting on the spot—some one wounded, if not actually killed? And who but Charles Clancy? The gun is his, the hat too, and his must be the blood.

They have no doubt of its being his, no more of his being dead; the only question asked is "Where's his body?"

While those first up are mutually exchanging this interrogatory, others, later arriving, also put it in turn. All equally unable to give a satisfactory answer—alike surprised by what they see, and puzzled to explain it.

There is one man present who could enlighten them in part, though not altogether—one who comes lagging up with the last. It is Richard Darke.

Strange he should be among the stragglers. At starting out he appeared the most zealous of all!

Then he was not thinking of the dog; had no idea how direct, and soon, the instinct of the animal would lead them to the spot where he had given Clancy his death shot.

The foremost of the searchers have dismounted and are standing grouped around it. He sees them, and would gladly go back, but dares not. Defection now would be damning evidence against him. After all, what has he to fear? They will find a dead body—Clancy's—a corpse with a bullet-hole in the breast. They can't tell who fired the fatal shot—how could they? There were no witnesses save the trunks of the cypresses, and the dumb brute of a dog—not so dumb but that it now makes the woods resound with its long-drawn continuous whining. If it could but shape this into articulate speech, then he might have to fear. As it is, he need not.

Fortified with these reflections, he approaches the spot, by himself made bloody. Trembling, nevertheless, and with cheeks pale. *Not* strange. He is about being brought face to face with the man he has murdered—with his corpse!

Nothing of the kind. There is no murdered man there, no corpse! Only a gun, a hat, and some blotches of crimson!

Does Darke rejoice at seeing only this? Judging by his looks, the reverse. Before, he only trembled slightly, with a hue of pallor on his cheeks. Now his lips show white, his eyes sunken in their sockets, while his teeth chatter and his whole frame shivers as if under an ague chill!

Luckily for the assassin this tale-telling exhibition occurs under the shadow of the great cypress, whose gloomy obscurity guards against its being observed. But to counteract this little bit of good luck there chances to be present a detective that trusts less to sight, than scent. This is Clancy's dog. As Darke presents himself in the circle of searchers collected around it, the animal perceiving, suddenly springs towards him with the shrill cry of an enraged cat, and the elastic leap of a tiger!

But for Simeon Woodley seizing the hound, and holding it back, the throat of Richard Darke would be in danger.

It is so, notwithstanding.

Around the blood-stained spot there is a pause; the searchers forming a tableau strikingly significant. They have come up, to the very last lagger; and stand in attitudes expressing astonishment, with glances that speak inquiry. These, not directed to the ground, nor straying through the trees, but fixed upon Dick Darke.

Strange the antipathy of the dog, which all observe! For the animal, soon as let loose, repeats its hostile demonstrations, and has to be held off again. Surely it signifies something, and this bearing upon the object of their search? The inference is unavoidable.

Darke is well aware their eyes are upon him, as also their thoughts. Fortunate for him, that night-like shadow surrounding. But for it, his blanched lips, and craven cast of countenance, would tell a tale to condemn him at once—perhaps to punishment on the spot.

As it if, his scared condition is not unnoticed. It is heard, if not clearly seen. Two or three, standing close to him, can hear his teeth clacking like castanets!

His terror is trebly intensified—from a threefold cause. Seeing no body first gave him a shock of surprise; soon followed by superstitious awe; this succeeded by apprehension of another kind. But he had no time to dwell upon it before being set upon by the dog, which drove the more distant danger out of his head.

Delivered also from this, his present fear is about those glances regarding him. In the obscurity he cannot read them, but for all that can tell they are sternly inquisitorial. *En revanche*, neither can they read his; and, from this drawing confidence, he recovers his habitual coolness—knowing how much he now needs it.

The behaviour of the hound must not pass unspoken of. With a forced laugh, and in a tone of assumed nonchalance, he says:

"I can't tell how many scores of times that dog of Clancy's has made at me in the same way. It's never forgiven me since the day I chastised it, when it came after one of our sluts. I'd have killed the cur long ago, but spared it through friendship for its master."

An explanation plausible, and cunningly conceived; though not satisfactory to some. Only the unsuspicious are beguiled by it. However, it holds good for the time; and, so regarded, the searchers resume their quest.

It is no use for them to remain longer by the moss-heap. There they but see blood; they are looking for a body. To find this they must go farther.

One taking up the hat, another the abandoned gun, they scatter off, proceeding in diverse directions.

For several hours they go tramping among the trees, peering under the broad fan-like fronds of the saw-palmettoes, groping around the buttressed trunks of the cypresses, sending glances into the shadowed spaces between— in short, searching everywhere.

For more than a mile around they quarter the forest, giving it thorough examination. The swamp also, far as the treacherous ooze will allow them to penetrate within its *gloomy* portals—fit abode of death—place appropriate for the concealment of darkest crime.

Notwithstanding their zeal, prompted by sympathising hearts, as by a sense of outraged justice, the day's search proves fruitless—bootless. No body can be found, dead or living; no trace of the missing man. Nothing beyond what they have already obtained—his hat and gun.

Dispirited, tired out, hungry, hankering after dinners delayed, as eve approaches they again congregate around the gory spot; and, with a mutual understanding to resume search on the morrow, separate, and set off—each to his own home.

Chapter Seventeen
A bullet extracted

Not all of the searching party leave the place. Two remain, staying as by stealth. Some time before the departure of the others, these had slipped aside, and sauntered off several hundred yards, taking their horses along with them.

Halting in an out-of-the-way spot, under deepest shadow, and then dismounting, they wait till the crowd shall disperse. To all appearance impatiently, as if they wanted to have the range of the forest to themselves, and for some particular reason. Just this do they, or at least one of them does; making his design known to the other, soon as he believes himself beyond earshot of those from whom they separated.

It is the elder that instructs; who, in addition to the horse he is holding, has another animal by his side—a dog. For it is the hunter, Woodley, still in charge of Clancy's hound.

The man remaining with him is one of his own kind and calling; younger in years, but, like himself, a professional follower of the chase—by name, Heywood.

Giving his reason for the step he is taking, Woodley says, "We kin do nothin' till them greenhorns air gone. Old Dan Boone hisself kedn't take up trail, wi' sich a noisy clanjamfry aroun him. For myself I hain't hardly tried, seein' 'twar no use till they'd clar off out o' the way. And now the darned fools hev' made the thing more diffeequilt, trampin about, an' blottin' out every shadder o' sign, an everything as looks like a futmark. For all, I've tuk notice to somethin' none o' them seed. Soon's the coast is clar we kin go thar, an' gie it a more pertikler examinashun."

The younger hunter nods assent, adding a word, signifying readiness to follow his older confrère.

For some minutes they remain; until silence restored throughout the forest tells them it is forsaken. Then, leaving their horses behind, with bridles looped around branches—the hound also attached to one of the stirrups—they go back to the place, where the hat and gun were found.

They do not stay there; but continue a little farther on, Woodley leading.

At some twenty paces distance, the old hunter comes to a halt, stopping by the side of a cypress "knee"; one of those vegetable monstrosities that perplex the botanist—to this hour scientifically unexplained. In shape resembling a ham, with the shank end upwards; indeed so like to this, that the Yankee bacon-curers have been accused, by their southern customers, of covering them with canvas, and selling them for the real article!

It may be that the Mississippian backwoodsman, Woodley, could give a better account of these singular excrescences than all the closet scientists in the world.

He is not thinking of either science, or his own superior knowledge, while conducting his companion to the side of that "cypress knee." His only thought is to show Heywood something he had espied while passing it in the search; but of which he did not then appear to take notice, and said nothing, so long as surrounded by the other searchers.

The time has come to scrutinise it more closely, and ascertain if it be what he suspects it.

The "knee" in question is one which could not be palmed off for a porker's ham. Its superior dimensions forbid the counterfeit. As the two hunters halt beside it, its bulk shows bigger than either of their own bodies, while its top is at the height of their heads.

Standing in front of it, Woodley points to a break in the bark—a round hole, with edge slightly ragged. The fibre appears freshly cut, and more than cut—encrimsoned! Twenty-four hours may have elapsed, but not many more, since that hole was made. So believe the backwoodsmen, soon as setting their eyes on it.

Speaking first, Woodley asks,—

"What d'ye think o' it, Ned?"

Heywood, of taciturn habit, does not make immediate answer, but stands silently regarding the perforated spot. His comrade continues:—

"Thar's a blue pill goed in thar', which jedgin' by the size and shape o' the hole must a kum out a biggish gun barrel. An', lookin' at the red stain 'roun' its edge, that pill must a been blood-coated."

"Looks like blood, certainly."

"*It air blood*—the real red thing itself; the blood o' Charley Clancy. The ball inside thar' has first goed through his body. It's been deadened by something and don't appear to hev penetrated a great way into the timmer, for all o' that bein' soft as sapwood."

Drawing out his knife, the old hunter inserts the point of its blade into the hole, probing it.

"Jest as I sayed. Hain't entered the hul o' an inch. I kin feel the lead ludged thar'."

"Suppose you cut it out, Sime?"

"Precisely what I intend doin'. But not in a careless way. I want the surroundin' wood along wi' it. The two thegither will best answer our purpiss. So hyar goes to git 'em thegither."

Saying this, he inserts his knife-blade into the bark, and first makes a circular incision around the bullet-hole. Then deepens it, taking care not to touch the ensanguined edge of the orifice, or come near it.

The soft vegetable substance yields to his keen steel, almost as easily as if he were slicing a Swedish turnip; and soon he detaches a pear-shaped piece, but bigger than the largest prize "Jargonelle."

Holding it in his hand, and apparently testing its ponderosity, he says:

"Ned; this chunk o' timmer encloses a bit o' lead as niver kim out o' a rifle. Thar's big eends o' an ounce weight o' metal inside. Only a smooth-bore barrel ked a tuk it; an' from sech it's been dischurged."

"You're right about that," responds Heywood, taking hold of the piece of wood, and also trying its weight. "It's a smooth-bore ball—no doubt of it."

"Well, then, who carries a smooth-bore through these hyar woods? Who, Ned Heywood?"

"I know only one man that does."

"Name him! Name the damned rascal!"

"Dick Darke."

"Ye kin drink afore me, Ned. That's the skunk I war a-thinkin' 'bout, an' hev been all the day. I've seed other sign beside this—the which escaped the eyes o' the others. An' I'm gled it did: for I didn't want Dick Darke to be about when I war follerin' it up. For that reezun I drawed the rest aside—so as none o' 'em shed notice it. By good luck they didn't."

"You saw other sign! What, Sime?"

"Tracks in the mud, clost in by the edge o' the swamp. They're a good bit from the place whar the poor young fellur's blood's been spilt, an' makin' away from it. I got only a glimp at 'em, but ked see they'd been made by a man runnin'. You bet yur life o't they war made by a pair o' boots I've seen on Dick Darke's feet. It's too gloomsome now to make any thin' out o' them. So let's you an' me come back here by ourselves, at the earliest o' daybreak, afore the people git about. Then we kin gie them tracks a thorrer scrutination. If they don't prove to be Dick Darke's, ye may call Sime Woodley a thick-headed woodchuck."

"If we only had one of his boots, so that we might compare it with the tracks."

"*If!* Thar's no if. We *shall* hev one o' his boots—ay, both—I'm boun' to hev 'em."

"But how?"

"Leave that to me. I've thought o' a plan to git purssession o' the scoundrel's futwear, an' everythin' else belongin' to him that kin throw a ray o' daylight unto this darksome bizness. Come, Ned! Le's go to the widder's house, an' see if we kin say a word to comfort the poor lady—for a lady she air. Belike enough this thing'll be the death o' her. She warn't strong at best, an' she's been a deal weaker since the husban' died. Now the son's goed too—ah! Come along, an' le's show her, she ain't forsook by everybody."

With the alacrity of a loyal heart, alike leaning to pity, the young hunter promptly responds to the appeal, saying:—

"I'm with you, Woodley!"

Chapter Eighteen
"To the sheriff!"

A day of dread, pitiless suspense to the mother of Charles Clancy, while they are abroad searching for her son.

Still more terrible the night after their return—not without tidings of the missing man. Such tidings! The too certain assurance of his death—of his murder—with the added mystery of their not having been able to find his body. Only his hat, his gun, his blood!

Her grief, hitherto held in check by a still lingering hope, now escapes all trammels, and becomes truly agonising. Her heart seems broken, or breaking.

Although without wealth, and therefore with but few friends, in her hour of lamentation she is not left alone. It is never so in the backwoods of the Far West; where, under rough home-wove coats, throb hearts gentle and sympathetic, as ever beat under the finest broadcloth.

Among Mrs Clancy's neighbours are many of this kind; chiefly "poor whites,"—as scornfully styled by the prouder planters. Some half-score of them determine to stay by her throughout the night; with a belief their presence may do something to solace her, and a presentiment that ere morning they may be needed for a service yet more solemn. She has retired to her chamber—taken to her bed; she may never leave either alive.

As the night chances to be a warm one—indeed stifling hot, the men stay outside, smoking their pipes in the porch, or reclining upon the little grass plot in front of the dwelling, while within, by the bedside of the bereaved widow, are their wives, sisters, and daughters.

Needless to say, that the conversation of those without relates exclusively to the occurrences of the day, and the mystery of the murder. For this, they all believe it to have been; though utterly unable to make out, or conjecture a motive.

They are equally perplexed about the disappearance of the body; though this adds not much to the mystery.

They deem it simply a corollary, and consequence, of the other. He, who did the foul deed, has taken steps to conceal it, and so far succeeded. It remains to be seen whether his astuteness will serve against the search to be resumed on the morrow.

Two questions in chief, correlative, occupy them: "Who killed Clancy?" and "What has been the motive for killing him?"

To the former, none of them would have thought of answering "Dick Darke,"—that is when starting out on the search near noon.

Now that night is on, and they have returned from it, his name is on every lip. At first only in whispers, and guarded insinuations; but gradually pronounced in louder tone, and bolder speech—this approaching accusation.

Still the second question remains unanswered:—

"Why should Dick Darke have killed Charley Clancy?"

Even put in this familiar form it receives no reply. It is an enigma to which no one present holds the key. For none know aught of a rivalry having existed between the two men—much less a love-jealousy, than which no motive more inciting to murder ever beat in human breast.

Darke's partiality for Colonel Armstrong's eldest daughter has been no secret throughout the settlement. He himself, childishly, in his cups, long since made all scandal-mongers acquainted with that. But Clancy, of higher tone, if not more secretive habit, has kept his love-affair to himself; influenced by the additional reason of its being clandestine.

Therefore, those, sitting up as company to his afflicted parent, have no knowledge of the tender relations that existed between him and Helen Armstrong, any more than of their being the cause of that disaster for which the widow now weeps.

She herself alone knows of them; but, in the first moment of her misfortune, completely prostrated by it, she has not yet communicated aught of this to the sympathetic ears around her. It is a family secret, too sacred for their sympathy; and, with some last lingering pride of superior birth, she keeps it to herself. The time has not come for disclosing it.

But it soon will—she knows that. All must needs be told. For, after the first throes of the overwhelming calamity, in which her thoughts alone dwelt on the slain son, they turned towards him suspected as the slayer. In her case with something stronger than suspicion—indeed almost belief, based on her foreknowledge of the circumstances; these not only accounting for the crime, but pointing to the man who must have committed it.

As she lies upon her couch, with tears streaming down her cheeks, and sighs heaved from the very bottom of her breast—as she listens to the kind voices vainly essaying to console her—she herself says not a word.

Her sorrow is too deep, too absorbing, to find expression in speech. But in her thoughts are two men—before, her distracted fancy two faces—one of a murdered man, the other his murderer—the first her own son, the second that of Ephraim Darke.

Notwithstanding ignorance of all these circumstances, the thoughts of her sympathising neighbours—those in council outside—dwell upon Dick Darke; while his name is continuously upon their tongues. His unaccountable conduct during the day—as also the strange behaviour of the hound—is now called up, and commented upon.

Why should the dog have made such demonstration? Why bark at him above all the others—selecting him out of the crowd—so resolutely and angrily assailing him?

His own explanation, given at the time, appeared lame and unsatisfactory.

It looks lamer now, as they sit smoking their pipes, more coolly and closely considering it.

While they are thus occupied, the wicket-gate, in front of the cottage, is heard turning upon its hinges, and two men are seen entering the enclosure.

As these draw near to the porch, where a tallow dip dimly burns, its light is reflected from the features of Simeon Woodley and Edward Heywood.

The hunters are both well-known to all upon the ground; and welcomed, as men likely to make a little less irksome that melancholy midnight watch.

If the new-comers cannot contribute cheerfulness, they may something else, as predicted by the expression observed upon their faces, at stepping into the porch. Their demeanour shows them possessed of some knowledge pertinent to the subject under discussion, as also important.

Going close to the candle, and summoning the rest around, Woodley draws from the ample pocket of his large, loose coat a bit of wood, bearing resemblance to a pine-apple, or turnip roughly peeled.

Holding it to the light, he says: "Come hyar, fellurs! fix yar eyes on this."

All do as desired.

"Kin any o' ye tell what it air?" the hunter asks.

"A bit of tree timber, I take it," answers one.

"Looks like a chunk carved out of a cypress knee," adds a second.

"It ought," assents Sime, "since that's jest what it air; an' this child air he who curved it out. Ye kin see thar's a hole in the skin-front; which any greenhorn may tell's been made by a bullet: an' he'd be still greener in the horn as kedn't observe a tinge o' red roun' thet hole, the which air nothin' more nor less than blood. Now, boys! the bullet's yit inside the wud, for me an' Heywood here tuk care not to extract it till the proper time shed come."

"It's come now; let's hev it out!" exclaims Heywood; the others endorsing the demand.

"Thet ye shall. Now, fellurs; take partikler notice o' what sort o' *egg* hez been hatchin' in this nest o' cypress knee."

While speaking, Sime draws his large-bladed knife from its sheath; and, resting the piece of wood on the porch bench, splits it open. When cleft, it discloses a thing of rounded form and metallic lustre, dull leaden—a gun-bullet, as all expected.

There is not any blood upon it, this having been brushed off in its passage through the fibrous texture of the wood. But it still preserves its spherical shape, perfect as when it issued from the barrel of the gun that discharged, or the mould that made it.

Soon as seeing it they all cry out, "A bullet!" several adding, "The ball of a smooth-bore."

Then one asks, suggestingly:

"Who is there in this neighbourhood that's got a shooting-iron of such sort?"

The question is instantly answered by another, though not satisfactorily.

"Plenty of smooth-bores about, though nobody as I knows of hunts with them."

A third speaks more to the point, saying:—

"Yes; there's one does."

"Name him!" is the demand of many voices.

"*Dick Darke!*"

The statement is confirmed by several others, in succession repeating it.

After this succeeds silence—a pause in the proceedings—a lull ominous, not of further speech but, action.

Daring its continuance, Woodley replaces the piece of lead in the wood, just as it was before; then laying the two cleft pieces together, and tying them with a string, he returns the chunk to his pocket.

This done, he makes a sign to the chiefs of the conclave to follow him as if for further communication.

Which they do, drawing off out of the porch, and taking stand upon grass plot below at some paces distant from the dwelling.

With heads close together, they converse for a while, *sotto voce*.

Not so low, but that a title, the terror of all malefactors, can be heard repeatedly pronounced.

And also a name; the same, which, throughout all the evening has been upon their lips, bandied about, spoken of with gritting teeth and brows contracted.

Not all of those, who watch with the widow are admitted to this muttering council. Simon Woodley, who presides over it, has his reasons for excluding some. Only men take part in it who can be relied on for an emergency, such as that the hunter has before him.

Their conference closed, four of them, as if by agreement with the others, separate from the group, glide out through the wicket-gate, and on to their horses left tied to the roadside rail fence.

"Unhitching" these, they climb silently into their saddles, and as silently slip away; only some muttered words passing between them, as they ride along the road.

Among these may be heard the name of a man, conjoined to a speech, under the circumstances significant: —

"Let's straight to the Sheriff!"

Chapter Nineteen
The "Belle of Natchez"

While search is still being made for the body of the murdered man, and he suspected of the crime is threatened with a prison cell, she, the innocent cause of it, is being borne far away from the scene of its committal.

The steamboat, carrying Colonel Armstrong and his belongings, having left port punctually at the hour advertised, has forsaken the "Father of Waters," entered the Red River of Louisiana, and now, on the second day after, is cleaving the current of this ochre-tinted stream, some fifty miles from its mouth.

The boat is the "Belle of Natchez." Singular coincidence of name; since one aboard bears also the distinctive sobriquet.

Oft have the young "bloods" of the "City of the Bluffs," while quaffing their sherry cobblers, or champagne, toasted Helen Armstrong, with this appellation added.

Taking quality into account, she has a better right to it than the boat. For this, notwithstanding the proud title bestowed upon it, is but a sorry craft; a little "stern-wheel" steamer, such as, in those early days, were oft seen ploughing the bosom of the mighty Mississippi, more often threading the intricate and shallower channels of its tributaries. A single set of paddles, placed where the rudder acts in other vessels, and looking very much like an old-fashioned mill-wheel, supplies the impulsive power—at best giving but poor speed.

Nevertheless, a sort of craft with correct excuse, and fair *raison d'être*; as all know, who navigate narrow rivers, and their still narrower reaches, with trees from each side outstretching, as is the case with many of the streams of Louisiana.

Not that the noble Red River can be thus classified; nor in any sense spoken of as a narrow stream. Broad, and deep enough, for the biggest boats to navigate to Natchitoches—the butt of Colonel Armstrong's journey by water.

Why the broken planter has taken passage on the little "stern-wheeler" is due to two distinct causes. It suited him as to time, and also expense.

On the Mississippi, and its tributaries, a passage in "crack" boats is costly, in proportion to their character for "crackness." The "Belle of Natchez," being without reputation of this kind, carries her passengers at a reasonable rate.

But, indeed, something beyond ideas of opportune time, or economy, influenced Colonel Armstrong in selecting her. The same thought which hurried him away from his old home under the shadows of night, has taken him aboard a third-rate river steamboat. Travelling thus obscurely, he hopes to shun encounter with men of his own class; to escape not only observation, but the sympathy he shrinks from.

In this hope he is disappointed, and on both horns of his fancied, not to say ridiculous, dilemma. For it so chances, that the "bully" boat, which was to leave Natchez for Natchitoches on the same day with the "Belle," has burst one of her boilers. As a consequence, the smaller steamer has started on her trip, loaded down to the water-line with freight, her state-rooms and cabins crowded with passengers—many of these the best, bluest blood of Mississippi and Louisiana.

Whatever of chagrin this *contretemps* has caused Colonel Armstrong—and, it may be, the older of his daughters—to the younger it gives gladness. For among the supernumeraries forced to take passage in the stern-wheel steamer, is a man she has met before. Not only met, but danced with; and not only danced but been delighted with; so much, that souvenirs of that night, with its saltative enjoyment, have since oft occupied her thoughts, thrilling her with sweetest reminiscence.

He, who has produced this pleasant impression, is a young planter, by name Luis Dupré. A Louisianian by birth, therefore a "Creole." And without any taint of the African; else he would not be a Creole *pur sang*.

The English reader seems to need undeceiving about this, constantly, repeatedly. In the Creole, simply so-called, there is no admixture of negro blood.

Not a drop of it in the veins of Luis Dupré; else Jessie Armstrong could not have danced with him at a Natchez ball; nor would her father, fallen as he is, permit her to keep company with him on a Red River steamboat.

In this case, there is no condescension on the part of the ex-Mississippian planter. He of Louisiana is his equal in social rank, and now his superior in point of wealth, by hundreds, thousands. For Luis Dupré is one of the largest landowners along the line of Red River plantations, while his slaves number several hundred field-hands, and house domestics: the able-bodied of both, without enumerating the aged, the imbecile, and piccaninnies, more costly than profitable.

If, in the presence of such a prosperous man, Colonel Armstrong reflects painfully upon his own reduced state, it is different with his daughter Jessie.

Into her ear Luis Dupré has whispered sweet words—a speech telling her, that not only are his lands, houses, and slaves at her disposal, but along with them his heart and hand.

It is but repeating what he said on the night of the Natchez ball; his impulsive Creole nature having then influenced him to speak as he felt.

Now, on the gliding steamboat, he reiterates the proposal, more earnestly pressing for an answer.

And he gets it in the affirmative. Before the "Belle of Natchez" has reached fifty miles from the Red River's mouth, Luis Dupré and Jessie Armstrong have mutually confessed affection, clasped hands, let lips meet, and tongues swear, never more to live asunder. That journey commenced upon the Mississippi is to continue throughout life.

In their case, there is no fear of aught arising to hinder the consummation of their hopes; no stern parent to stand in the way of their life's happiness. By the death of both father and mother, Luis Dupré has long since been emancipated from parental authority, and is as much his own master as he is of his many slaves.

On the other side, Jessie Armstrong is left free to her choice; because she has chosen well. Her father has given ready consent; or at all events said enough to ensure his doing so.

The huge "high-pressure" steam craft which ply upon the western rivers of America bear but a very slight resemblance to the black, long, low—hulled leviathans that plough the briny waste of ocean. The steamboat of the Mississippi more resembles a house, two stories in height, and, not unfrequently, something of a third—abode of mates and pilots. Rounded off at stern, the structure, of oblong oval shape, is universally painted chalk-white; the second, or cabin story, having on each face a row of casement windows, with Venetian shutters, of emerald green. These also serve as outside doors to the state-rooms—each having its own. Inside ones, opposite them, give admission to the main cabin, or "saloon;" which extends longitudinally nearly the whole length of the vessel. Figured glass folding-doors cut it into three compartments; the ladies' cabin aft, the dining saloon amidships, with a third division forward, containing clerk's office and "bar," the last devoted to male passengers for smoking, drinking, and, too often, gambling. A gangway, some three feet in width, runs along the outside façade, forming a balcony to the windows of the state-rooms. It is furnished with a balustrade, called "guard-rail," to prevent careless passengers from stepping overboard. A projection of the roof, yclept "hurricane-deck," serves as an awning to this continuous terrace, shading it from the sun.

Two immense twin chimneys—"funnels" as called—tower above all, pouring forth a continuous volume of whitish wood-smoke; while a smaller cylinder—the "scape-pipe"—intermittently vomits a vapour yet whiter, the steam; at each emission with a hoarse belching bark, that can be heard reverberating for leagues along the river.

Seen from the bank, as it passes, the Mississippi steamboat looks like a large hotel, or mansion of many windows, set adrift and moving majestically—"walking the water like a thing of life," as it has been poetically described. Some of the larger ones, taking into account their splendid interior decoration, and, along with it their sumptuous table fare, may well merit the name oft bestowed upon them, of "floating palaces."

Only in point of size, some inferiority in splendour, and having a stern-wheel instead of side-paddles, does the "Belle of Natchez" differ from other boats seen upon the same waters. As them, she has her large central saloon, with ladies' cabin astern; the flanking rows of state-rooms; the casements with green jalousies; the gangway and guard-rail; the twin funnels, pouring forth their fleecy cloud, and the scape-pipe, coughing in regular repetition.

In the evening hour, after the day has cooled down, the balcony outside the state-room windows is a pleasant place to stand, saunter, or sit in. More especially that portion of it contiguous to the stern, and exclusively devoted to lady passengers—with only such of the male sex admitted as can claim relationship, or liens of a like intimate order.

On this evening—the first after leaving port—the poop deck of the little steamer is so occupied by several individuals; who stand gazing at the scene that passes like a panorama before their eyes. The hot southern sun has disappeared behind the dark belt of cypress forest, which forms, far and near, the horizon line of Louisiana; while the soft evening breeze, laden with the mixed perfumes of the *liquid ambar*, and *magnolia grandiflora*, is wafted around them, like incense scattered from a censer.

Notwithstanding its delights, and loveliness, Nature does not long detain the saunterers outside. Within is a spell more powerful, and to many of them more attractive. It is after dinner hour; the cabin tables have been cleared, and its lamps lit. Under the sheen of brilliant chandeliers the passengers are drawing together in groups, and coteries; some to converse, others to play *écarté* or *vingt-un*; here and there a solitary individual burying himself in a book; or a pair, almost as unsocial, engaging in the selfish duality of chess.

Three alone linger outside; and of these only two appear to do so with enjoyment. They are some paces apart from the third, who is now left to herself: for it is a woman. Not that they are unacquainted with her, or in any way wishing to be churlish. But, simply, because neither can spare word or thought for any one, save their two sweet selves.

It scarce needs telling who is the couple thus mutually engrossed. An easy guess gives Jessie Armstrong and Luis Dupré. The young Creole's handsome features, black eyes, brunette complexion, and dark curly hair have made havoc with the heart of Armstrong's youngest daughter; while, *en revanche*, her contrasting colours of red, blue, and gold have held their own in the amorous encounter. They are in love with one another to their finger tips.

As they stand conversing in soft whispers, the eyes of the third individual are turned towards them. This only at intervals, and with nought of jealousy in the glance. For it is Jessie's own sister who gives it. Whatever of that burn in Helen's breast, not these, nor by them, has its torch been kindled. The love that late occupied her heart has been plucked therefrom, leaving it lacerated, and lorn. It was the one love of her life, and now crushed out, can never be rekindled. If she have a thought about her sister's new-sprung happiness, it is only to measure it against her own misery—to contrast its light of joy, with the shadow surrounding herself.

But for a short moment, and with transient glance, does she regard them. Aside from any sentiment of envy, their happy communion calls up a reminiscence too painful to be dwelt upon. She remembers how she herself stood talking in that same way, with one she cannot, must not, know more. To escape recalling the painful souvenir, she turns her eyes from the love episode, and lowers them to look upon the river.

Chapter Twenty
Saved by a sister

The boat is slowly forging its course up-stream, its wheel in constant revolution, churning the ochre-coloured water into foam. This, floating behind, dances and simmers upon the surface, forming a wake-way of white tinted with red. In Helen Armstrong's eyes it has the appearance of blood-froth—such being the hue of her thoughts.

Contemplating it for a time, not pleasantly, and then, turning round, she perceives that she is alone. The lovers have stepped inside a state-room, or the ladies' cabin, or perhaps gone on to the general saloon, to take part in the sports of the evening. She sees the lights shimmering through the latticed windows, and can hear the hum of voices, all merry. She has no desire to join in that merriment, though many may be wishing her. Inside she would assuredly become the centre of an admiring circle; be addressed in courtly speeches, with phrases of soft flattery. She is aware of this, and keeps away from it. Strange woman!

In her present mood the speeches would but weary, the flattery fash her. She prefers solitude; likes better the noise made by the ever-turning wheel. In the tumult of the water there is consonance with that agitating her own bosom.

Night is now down; darkness has descended upon forest and river, holding both in its black embrace. Along with it a kindred feeling creeps over her—a thought darker than night, more sombre than forest shadows. It is that which oft prompts to annihilation; a memory of the past, which, making the future unendurable, calls for life to come to an end. The man to whom she has given her heart—its firstlings, as its fulness—a heart from which there can be no second gleanings, and she knows it—he has made light of the offering. A sacrifice grand, as complete; glowing with all the interests of her life. The life, too, of one rarely endowed; a woman of proud spirit, queenly and commanding, beyond air beautiful.

She does not think thus of herself, as, leaning over the guard-rail, with eyes mechanically bent upon the wheel, she watches it whipping the water into spray. Her thoughts are not of lofty pride, but low humiliation. Spurned by him at whose feet she has flung herself, so fondly, so rashly—

ay, recklessly—surrendering even that which woman deems most dear, and holds back to the ultimate moment of rendition—the word which speaks it!

To Charles Clancy she has spoken it. True, only in writing; but still in terms unmistakeable, and with nothing reserved. And how has he treated them? No response—not even denial! Only contemptuous silence, worse than outspoken scorn!

No wonder her breast is filled with chagrin, and her brow burning with shame!

Both may be ended in an instant. A step over the low rail—a plunge into the red rolling river—a momentary struggle amidst its seething waters—not to preserve life, but destroy it—this, and all will be over! Sadness, jealousy, the pangs of disappointed love—these baleful passions, and all others alike, can be soothed, and set at rest, by one little effort—a leap into oblivion!

Her nerves are fast becoming strung to the taking it. The past seems all dark, the future yet darker. For her, life has lost its fascinations, while death is divested of its terrors.

Suicide in one so young, so fair, so incomparably lovely; one capable of charming others, no longer to be charmed herself! A thing fearful to reflect upon.

And yet is she contemplating it!

She stands close to the rail, wavering, irresolute. It is no lingering love of life which causes her to hesitate. Nor yet fear of death, even in the horrid form, she cannot fail to see before her, spring she but over that slight railing.

The moon has arisen, and now courses across the blue canopy of sky, in full effulgence, her beams falling bright upon the bosom of the river. At intervals the boat, keeping the deeper channel, is forced close to either bank. Then, as the surging eddies set the floating but stationary logs in motion, the huge saurian asleep on them can be heard giving a grunt of anger for the rude arousing, and pitching over into the current with dull sullen plash.

She sees, and hears all this. It should shake her nerves, and cause shivering throughout her frame.

It does neither. The despair of life has deadened the dread of death—even of being devoured by an alligator!

Fortunately, at this moment, a gentle hand is laid on her shoulder, and a soft voice sounds in her ear. They are the hand and voice of her sister.

Jessie, coming out of her state-room, has glided silently up. She sees Helen prepossessed, sad, and can somewhat divine the cause. But she little suspects, how near things have been to a fatal climax, and dreams not of the diversion her coming has caused.

"Sister!" she says, in soothing tone, her arms extended caressingly, "why do you stay out here? The night is chilly; and they say the atmosphere of this Red River country is full of miasma, with fevers and ague to shake the comb out of one's hair! Come with me inside! There's pleasant people in the saloon, and we're going to have a round game at cards—*vingt-un*, or something of the sort. Come!"

Helen turns round trembling at the touch, as if she felt herself a criminal, and it was the sheriff's hand laid upon her shoulder!

Jessie notices the strange, strong emotion. She could not fail to do so. Attributing it to its remotest cause, long since confided to her, she says:—

"Be a woman, Helen! Be true to yourself, as I know you will; and don't think of him any more. There's a new world, a new life, opening to both of us. Forget the sorrows of the old, as I shall. Pluck Charles Clancy from your heart, and fling every memory, every thought of him, to the winds! I say again, be a woman—be yourself! Bury the past, and think only of the future—*of our father*!"

The last words act like a galvanic shock, at the same time soothing as balm. For in the heart of Helen Armstrong they touch a tender chord—that of filial affection.

And it vibrates true to the touch. Flinging her arms around Jessie's neck, she cries:—

"Sister; you have saved me!"

Chapter Twenty One
Seized by spectral arms

"Sister, you have saved me!"

On giving utterance to the ill-understood speech, Helen Armstrong imprints a kiss upon her sister's cheek, at the same time bedewing it with her tears. For she is now weeping—convulsively sobbing.

Returning the kiss, Jessie looks not a little perplexed. She can neither comprehend the meaning of the words, nor the strange tone of their utterance. Equally is she at a loss to account for the trembling throughout her sister's frame, continued while their bosoms stay in contact.

Helen gives her no time to ask questions.

"Go in!" she says, spinning the other round, and pushing her towards the door of the state-room. Then, attuning her voice to cheerfulness, she adds:—

"In, and set the game of *vingt-un* going. I'll join you by the time you've got the cards shuffled."

Jessie, glad to see her sister in spirits unusually gleeful, makes no protest, but glides towards the cabin door.

Soon as her back is turned, Helen once more faces round to the river, again taking stand by the guard-rail. The wheel still goes round, its paddles beating the water into bubbles, and casting the crimson-white spray afar over the surface of the stream.

But now, she has no thought of flinging herself into the seething swirl, though she means to do so with something else.

"Before the game of *vingt-un* begins," she says in soliloquy, "I've got a pack of cards to be dealt out here—among them a knave."

While speaking, she draws forth a bundle of letters—evidently old ones—tied in a bit of blue ribbon. One after another, she drags them free of the fastening—just as if dealing out cards. Each, as it comes clear, is rent right across the middle, and tossed disdainfully into the stream.

At the bottom of the packet, after the letters have been all disposed of, is something seeming different. A piece of cardboard—a portrait—in short, a *carte de visite.* It is the likeness of Charles Clancy, given her on one of those days when he flung himself affectionately at her feet.

She does not tear it in twain, as she has the letters; though at first this is nearest her intent. Some thought restraining her, she holds it up in the moon's light, her eyes for a time resting on, and closely scanning it. Painful memories, winters of them, pass through her soul, shown upon her countenance, while she makes scrutiny of the features so indelibly graven upon her heart. She is looking her last upon them—not with a wish to remember, but the hope to forget—of being able to erase that image of him long-loved, wildly worshipped, from the tablets of her memory, at once and for ever.

Who can tell what passed through her mind at that impending moment? Who could describe her heart's desolation? Certainly, no writer of romance.

Whatever resolve she has arrived at, for a while she appears to hesitate about executing it. —

Then, like an echo heard amidst the rippling waves, return to her ear the words late spoken by her sister—

"Let us think only of the future—*of our father.*"

The thought decides her; and, stepping out to the extremest limit the guard-rail allows, she flings the photograph upon the paddles of the revolving wheel, as she does so, saying—

"Away, image of one once loved—picture of a man who has proved false! Be crushed, and broken, as he has broken my heart!"

The sigh that escapes her, on letting drop the bit of cardboard, more resembles a subdued scream—a stifled cry of anguish, such as could only come from what she has just spoken of—a broken heart.

As she turns to re-enter the cabin, she appears ill-prepared for taking part, or pleasure, in a game of cards.

And she takes not either. That round of *vingt-un* is never to be played— at least not with her as one of the players.

Still half distraught with the agony through which her soul has passed— the traces of which she fancies must be observable on her face—before making appearance in the brilliantly-lighted saloon, she passes around the corner of the ladies' cabin, intending to enter her own state-room by the outside door.

It is but to spend a moment before her mirror, there to arrange her dress, the plaiting of her hair—perhaps the expression of her face—all things that to men may appear trivial, but to women important—even in the hour of sadness and despair. No blame to them for this. It is but an instinct—the primary care of their lives—the secret spring of their power.

In repairing to her toilette, Helen Armstrong is but following the example of her sex.

She does not follow it far—not even so far as to get to her looking-glass, or even inside her state-room. Before entering it, she makes stop by the door, and tarries with face turned towards the river's bank.

The boat, tacking across stream, has sheered close in shore; so close that the tall forest trees shadow her track—the tips of their branches almost touching the hurricane-deck. They are cypresses, festooned with grey-beard moss, that hangs down like the drapery of a death-bed. She sees one blighted, stretching forth bare limbs, blanched white by the weather, desiccated and jointed like the arms of a skeleton.

'Tis a ghostly sight, and causes her weird thoughts, as under the clear moonbeams the steamer sweeps past the place.

It is a relief to her, when the boat, gliding on, gets back into darkness.

Only momentary; for there under the shadow of the cypresses, lit up by the flash of the fire-flies, she sees, or fancies it, a face! It is that of a man—him latest in her thoughts—Charles Clancy!

It is among the trees high up, on a level with the hurricane-deck.

Of course it can be but a fancy? Clancy could not be there, either in the trees, or on the earth. She knows it is but a deception of her senses—an illusive vision—such as occur to clairvoyantes, at times deceiving themselves.

Illusion or not, Helen Armstrong has no time to reflect upon it. Ere the face of her false lover fades from view; a pair of arms, black, sinewy, and stiff, seem reaching towards her!

More than seem; it is a reality. Before she can stir from the spot, or make effort to avoid them, she feels herself roughly grasped around the waist, and lifted aloft into the air.

Chapter Twenty Two
Up and down

Whatever has lifted Helen Armstrong aloft, for time holds her suspended. Only for a few seconds, during which she sees the boat pass on beneath, and her sister rush out to the stern rail, sending forth a scream responsive to her own.

Before she can repeat the piercing cry, the thing grasping her relaxes its hold, letting her go altogether, and she feels herself falling, as from a great height. The sensation of giddiness is succeeded by a shock, which almost deprives her of consciousness. It is but the fall, broken by a plunge into water. Then there is a drumming in her ears, a choking in the throat; in short, the sensation that precedes drowning.

Notwithstanding her late suicidal thoughts, the instinctive aversion to death is stronger than her weariness of life, and instinctively does she strive to avert it.

No longer crying out; she cannot; her throat is filled with the water of the turbid stream. It stifles, as if a noose were being drawn around her neck, tighter and tighter. She can neither speak nor shout, only plunge and struggle.

Fortunately, while falling, the skirt of her dress, spreading as a parachute, lessened the velocity of the descent. This still extended, hinders her from sinking. As she knows not how to swim, it will not sustain her long; itself becoming weighted with the water.

Her wild shriek, with that of her sister responding—the latter still continued in terrified repetition—has summoned the passengers from the saloon, a crowd collecting on the stern-guards.

"Some one overboard!" is the cry sent all over the vessel.

It reaches the ear of the pilot; who instantly rings the stop-bell, causing the paddles to suspend revolution, and bringing the boat to an almost instantaneous stop. The strong current, against which they are contending, makes the movement easy of execution.

The shout of, "some one overboard!" is quickly followed by another of more particular significance. "It's a lady!"

This announcement intensifies the feeling of regret and alarm. Nowhere in the world more likely to do so, than among the chivalric spirits sure to be passengers on a Mississippian steamboat. Half a dozen voices are heard simultaneously asking, not "who is the lady?" but "where?" while several are seen pulling off their coats, as if preparing to take to the water.

Foremost among them is the young Creole, Dupré. He knows who the lady is. Another lady has met him frantically, exclaiming—

"'Tis Helen! She has fallen, or *leaped* overboard."

The ambiguity of expression appears strange; indeed incomprehensible, to Dupré, as to others who overhear it. They attributed it to incoherence, arising from the shock of the unexpected catastrophe.

This is its cause, only partially: there is something besides.

Confused, half-frenzied, Jessie continues to cry out:

"My sister! Save her! save her!"

"We'll try; show us where she is," respond several.

"Yonder—there—under that tree. She was in its branches above, then dropped down upon the water. I heard the plunge, but did not see her after. She has gone to the bottom. Merciful heavens! O Helen! where are you?"

The people are puzzled by these incoherent speeches—both the passengers above, and the boatmen on the under-deck. They stand as if spell-bound.

Fortunately, one of the former has retained presence of mind, and along with it coolness. It is the young planter, Dupré. He stays not for the end of her speech, but springing over the guards, swims towards the spot pointed out.

"Brave fellow!" is the thought of Jessie Armstrong, admiration for her lover almost making her forget her sister's peril.

She stands, as every one else upon the steamer, watching with earnest eyes. Hers are more; they are flashing with feverish excitement, with glances of anxiety—at times the fixed gaze of fear.

No wonder at its being so. The moon has sunk to the level of the tree-tops, and the bosom of the river is in dark shadow; darker by the bank where the boat is now drifting. But little chance to distinguish an object in the water—less for one swimming upon its surface. And the river is deep, its current rapid, the "reach" they are in, full of dangerous eddies. In addition, it is a spot infested, as all know—the favourite haunt of that hideous reptile the alligator, with the equally-dreaded gar-fish—the shark of the South-western rivers. All these things are in Jessie Armstrong's thoughts.

Amidst these dangers are the two dearest to her on earth; her sister, her lover. Not strange that her apprehension is almost an agony!

Meanwhile the steamer's boat has been manned, and set loose as quickly as could be done. It is rowed towards the spot, where the swimmer was last seen; and all eyes are strained upon it—all ears listening to catch any word of cheer.

Not long have they to listen. From the shadowed surface comes the shout, "*Saved*!"

Then, a rough boatman's voice, saying:

"All right! We've got 'em both. Throw us a rope."

It is thrown by ready hands, after which is heard the command, "Haul in!"

A light, held high upon the steamer, flashes its beams down into, the boat. Lying along its thwarts can be perceived a female form, in a dress once white, now discoloured and dripping. Her head is held up by a man, whose scant garments show similarly stained.

It is Helen Armstrong, supported by Dupré.

She appears lifeless, and the first sight of her draws anxious exclamations from those standing on the steamer. Her sister gives out an agonised cry; while her father trembles on taking her into his arms, and totters as he carries her to her state-room—believing he bears but a corpse!

But no! She breathes; her pulse beats; her lips move in low murmur; her bosom's swell shows sign of returning animation.

By good fortune there chances to be a medical man among the passengers; who, after administering restoratives, pronounces her out of danger.

The announcement causes universal joy on board the boat—crew and passengers alike sharing it.

With one alone remains a thought to sadden. It is Jessie: her heart is sore with the suspicion, that *her sister has attempted suicide*!

Chapter Twenty Three
The sleep of the assassin

On the night after killing Clancy, Richard Darke does not sleep soundly—indeed scarce at all.

His wakefulness is not due to remorse; there is no such sentiment in his soul. It comes from two other causes, in themselves totally, diametrically distinct; for the one is fear, the other love.

While dwelling on the crime he has committed, he only dreads its consequences to himself; but, reflecting on what led him to commit it, his dread gives place to dire jealousy; and, instead of repentance, spite holds possession of his heart. Not the less bitter, that the man and woman who made him jealous can never meet more. For, at that hour, he knows Charles Clancy to be lying dead in the dank swamp; while, ere dawn of the following day, Helen Armstrong will be starting upon a journey which must take her away from the place, far, and for ever.

The only consolation he draws from her departure is, that she, too, will be reflecting spitefully and bitterly as himself. Because of Clancy not having kept his appointment with her; deeming the failure due to the falsehood by himself fabricated—the story of the Creole girl.

Withal, it affords him but scant solace. She will be alike gone from him, and he may never behold her again. Her beauty will never belong to his rival; but neither can it be his, even though chance might take him to Texas, or by design he should proceed thither. To what end should he? No more now can he build castles in the air, basing them on the power of creditor over debtor. That bubble has burst, leaving him only the reflection, how illusory it has been. Although, for his nefarious purpose, it has proved weak as a spider's web, it is not likely Colonel Armstrong will ever again submit himself to be so ensnared. Broken men become cautious, and shun taking credit a second time.

And yet Richard Darke does not comprehend this. Blinded by passion, he cannot see any impossibility, and already thoughts of future proceedings begin to flit vaguely through his mind. They are too distant to be dwelt upon now. For this night he has enough to occupy heart and brain—keeping both on the rack and stretch, so tensely as to render prolonged sleep impossible.

Only for a few seconds at a time does he know the sweet unconsciousness of slumber; then, suddenly starting awake, to be again the prey of galling reflections.

Turn to which side he will, rest his head on the pillow as he may, two sounds seem ever ringing in his ears—one, a woman's voice, that speaks the denying word, "Never!"—the other, a dog's bark, which seems persistently to say, "I demand vengeance for my murdered master!"

If, in the first night after his nefarious deed, fears and jealous fancies chase one another through the assassin's soul, on the second it is different. Jealousy has no longer a share in his thoughts, fear having full possession of them. And no trifling fear of some far off danger, depending on chances and contingencies, but one real and near, seeming almost certain. The day's doings have gone all against him. The behaviour of Clancy's hound has not only directed suspicion towards him, but given evidence, almost conclusive, of his guilt; as though the barking of the dumb brute were words of truthful testimony, spoken in a witness-box!

The affair cannot, will not, be allowed to rest thus. The suspicions of the searchers will take a more definite shape, ending in accusation, if not in the actual deed of his arrest. He feels convinced of this.

Therefore, on this second night, it is no common apprehension which keeps him awake, but one of the intensest kind, akin to stark terror. For, added to the fear of his fellow man, there is something besides—a fear of God; or, rather of the Devil. His soul is now disturbed by a dread of the supernatural. He saw Charles Clancy stretched dead, under the cypress—was sure of it, before parting from the spot. Returning to it, what beheld he?

To him, more than any other, is the missing body a mystery. It has been perplexing, troubling him, throughout all the afternoon, even when his blood was up, and nerves strung with excitement. Now, at night, in the dark, silent hours, as he dwells ponderingly upon it, it more than perplexes, more than troubles—it awes, horrifies him.

In vain he tries to compose himself, by shaping conjectures based on natural causes. Even these could not much benefit him; for, whether Clancy be dead or still living—whether he has walked away from the ground, or been carried from it a corpse—to him, Darke, the danger will be almost equal. Not quite. Better, of course, if Clancy be dead, for then there will be but circumstantial evidence against, and, surely, not sufficient to convict him?

Little suspects he, that in the same hour, while he is thus distractedly cogitating, men are weighing evidence he knows not of; or that, in another hour, they will be on the march to make him their prisoner.

For all his ignorance of it, he has a presentiment of danger, sprung from the consciousness of his crime. This, and no sentiment of remorse, or repentance, wrings from him the self-interrogation, several times repeated:—

"Why the devil did I do it?"

He regrets the deed, not because grieving at its guilt, but the position it has placed him in—one of dread danger, with no advantage derived, nothing to compensate him for the crime. No wonder at his asking, in the name of the Devil, why he has done it!

He is being punished for it now; if not through remorse of conscience, by coward craven fear. He feels what other criminals have felt before—what, be it hoped, they will ever feel—how hard it is to sleep the sleep of the assassin, or lie awake on a murderer's bed.

On the last Richard Darke lies; since this night he sleeps not at all. From the hour of retiring to his chamber, till morning's dawn comes creeping through the window, he has never closed eye; or, if so, not in the sweet oblivion of slumber.

He is still turning upon his couch, chafing in fretful apprehension, when daylight breaks into his bedroom, and shows its shine upon the floor. It is the soft blue light of a southern morn, which usually enters accompanied by bird music—the songs of the wild forest warblers mingling with domestic voices not so melodious. Among these the harsh "screek" of the guinea-fowl; the more sonorous call of the turkey "gobbler;" the scream of the goose, always as in agony; the merrier cackle of the laying hen, with the still more cheerful note of her lord—Chanticleer.

All these sounds hears Dick Darke, the agreeable as the disagreeable. Both are alike to him on this morning, the second after the murder.

Far more unpleasant than the last are some other sounds which salute his ear, as he lies listening. Noises which, breaking out abruptly, at once put an end to the singing of the forest birds, and the calling of the farm-yard fowls.

They are of two kinds; one, the clattering of horses' hoofs, the other, the clack and clangour of men's voices. Evidently there are several, speaking at the same time, and all in like tone—this of anger, of vengeance!

At first they seem at some distance off, but evidently drawing nigh.

Soon they are close up to the dwelling, their voices loudly reverberating from its walls.

The assassin cannot any longer keep to his couch. Too well knows he what the noise is, his guilty heart guessing it.

Springing to his feet, he glides across the room, and approaches the window—cautiously, because in fear.

His limbs tremble, as he draws the curtain and looks out. Then almost refusing to support him: for, in the courtyard he sees a half-score of armed horsemen, and hears them angrily discoursing. One at their head he knows to be the Sheriff of the county; beside him his Deputy, and behind a brace of constables. In rear of these, two men he has reason to believe will be his most resolute accusers.

He has no time to discriminate; for, soon as entering the enclosure, the horsemen dismount, and make towards the door of the dwelling.

In less than sixty seconds after, they knock against that of his sleeping chamber, demanding admission.

No use denying them, as its occupant is well aware—not even to ask—

"Who's there?"

Instead, he says, in accent tremulous—

"Come in."

Instantly after, he sees the door thrown open, and a form filling up its outlines—the stalwart figure of a Mississippi sheriff; who, as he stands upon the threshold, says, in firm voice, with tone of legal authority:

"Richard Darke, I arrest you!"

"For what?" mechanically demands the culprit, shivering in his shirt.

"For the murder of Charles Clancy!"

Chapter Twenty Four
The coon-hunter conscience-stricken

On the night preceding Richard Darke's arrest, another man, not many rods distant, lies awake, or, at least, loses more than half his customary measure of sleep.

This is the coon-hunter. In his case the disturbing cause *is* conscience; though his crime is comparatively a light one, and should scarce rob him of his rest. It would not, were he a hardened sinner; but Blue Bill is the very reverse; and though, at times, cruel to "coony," he is, in the main, merciful, his breast overflowing with the milk of human kindness.

On the night succeeding his spoilt coon-chase, he has slept sound enough, his mind being unburdened by the confession to Phoebe. Besides, he had then no certain knowledge that a murder had been committed, or of any one being even killed. He only knew there were shots, and angry words, resembling a fight between two men; one his young master; the other, as he supposed, Charles Clancy. True, the former, rushing past in such headlong pace, seemed to prove that the affair had a tragical termination.

But of this, he, Blue Bill, could only have conjecture; and, hoping the *dénouement* might not be so bad as at first deemed, neither was he so alarmed as to let it interfere with his night's slumbers.

In the morning, when, as usual, hoe in hand, he goes abroad to his day's work, no one would suspect him of being the depository of a secret so momentous. He was always noted as the gayest of the working gang—his laugh, the loudest, longest, and merriest, carried across the plantation fields; and on this particular day, it rings with its wonted cheerfulness.

Only during the earlier hours. When, at mid-day, a report reaches the place where the slaves are at work, that a man has been murdered—this, Charles Clancy—the coon-hunter, in common with the rest of the gang, throws down his hoe; all uniting in a cry of sympathetic sorrow. For all of them know young "Massr Clancy;" respecting, many of them loving him. He has been accustomed to meet them with pleasant looks, and accost them in kindly words.

The tidings produce a painful impression upon them; and from that moment, though their task has to be continued, there is no more cheerfulness in the cotton field. Even their conversation is hushed, or carried on in a subdued tone; the hoes being alone heard, as their steel blades clink against an occasional "donick."

But while his fellow-labourers are silent through sorrow, Blue Bill is speechless from another and different cause. They only hear that young Massr Clancy has been killed—murdered, as the report says—while he knows how, when, where, and *by whom*. The knowledge gives him double uneasiness; for while sorrowing as much, perhaps more than any, for Charles Clancy's death, he has fears for his own life, with good reasons for having them.

If by any sinister chance Massr Dick should get acquainted with the fact of his having been witness to that rapid retreat among the trees, he, Blue Bill, would be speedily put where his tongue could never give testimony.

In full consciousness of his danger, he determines not to commit himself by any voluntary avowal of what he has seen and heard; but to bury the secret in his own breast, as also insist on its being so interred within the bosom of his better half.

This day, Phoebe is not in the field along with the working gang; which causes him some anxiety. The coon-hunter can trust his wife's affections, but is not so confident as to her prudence. She may say something in the "quarter" to compromise him. A word—the slightest hint of what has happened—may lead to his being questioned, and confessed; with torture, if the truth be suspected.

No wonder that during the rest of the day Blue Bill wears an air of abstraction, and hoes the tobacco plants with a careless hand, often chopping off the leaves. Fortunately for him, his fellow-workers are not in a mood to observe these vagaries, or make inquiry as to the cause.

He is rejoiced, when the boom of the evening bell summons them back to the "big house."

Once more in the midst of his piccaninnies, with Phoebe by his side, he imparts to her a renewed caution, to "keep dark on dat ere seerous subjeck."

At supper, the two talk over the events of the day—Phoebe being the narrator. She tells him of all that has happened—of the search, and such incidents connected with it as have reached the plantation of the Darkes; how both the old and young master took part in it, since having returned home. She adds, of her own observation, that Massr Dick looked "berry scared-like, an' white in de cheeks as a ole she-possum."

"Dats jess de way he oughter look," is the husband's response.

After which they finish their frugal meal, and once more retire to rest.

But on this second night, the terrible secret shared by them, keeps both from sleeping. Neither gets so much as a wink.

As morning dawns, they are startled by strange noises in the negro quarter. These are not the usual sounds consequent on the uprising of their fellow-slaves—a chorus of voices, in jest and jocund laughter. On the contrary, it is a din of serious tone, with cries that tell of calamity.

When the coon-hunter draws—back his door, and looks forth, he sees there is commotion outside; and is soon told its cause. One of his fellow-bondsmen, coming forward, says:—

"Massr Dick am arrested by de sheriff. Dey've tuk 'im for de murder ob Massr Charl Clancy."

The coon-hunter rushes out, and up to the big house.

He reaches it in time to see Richard Darke set upon a horse, and conducted away from the place, with a man on each side, guarding him. All know that he goes a prisoner.

With a sense of relief, Blue Bill hastens back to his own domicile, where lie communicates what has happened to the wife anxiously waiting.

"Phoebe, gal," he adds, in a congratulatory whisper, "dar ain't no longer so much reezun for us to hab fear. I see Sime Woodley mong de men; and dis nigger know dat he'll gub me his purtecshun, whatsomever I do. So I'se jess made up my mind to make a clean bress ob de hul ting, and tell what I heern an' see, besides deliverin' up boaf dat letter an' picter. What's yar view ob de matter? Peak plain, and doan be noways mealy-moufed 'bout it."

"My views is den, for de tellin' ob de troof. Ole Eph Darke may flog us till dar ain't a bit o' skin left upon our bare backs. I'll take my share ob de 'sponsibility, an a full half ob de noggin'. Yes, Bill, I'se willin' to do dat. But let de troof be tole—de whole troof, an' nuffin but de troof."

"Den it shall be did. Phoebe, you's a darlin'. Kiss me, ole gal. If need be, we'll boaf die togedder."

And their two black faces come in contact, as also their bosoms; both beating with a humanity that might shame whiter skins.

Chapter Twenty Five
An unceremonious search

Arrested, Richard Darke is taken to jail. This not in Natchez, but a place of less note; the Court-house town of the county, within the limits of which lie the Darke and Armstrong plantations. He is there consigned to the custody of Joe Harkness, jailer.

But few, who assisted at the arrest, accompany him to the place of imprisonment; only the Deputy, and the brace of constables.

The sheriff himself, with the others, does not leave Ephraim Darke's premises, till after having given them a thorough examination, in quest of evidence against the accused.

This duty done, without regard to the sensibilities of the owner, who follows them from room to room, now childishly crying—now frantically cursing.

Alike disregarded are his tears and oaths.

The searchers have no sympathy for him in his hour of affliction. Some even secretly rejoice at it.

Ephraim Darke is not a Southerner, *pur sang*; and, though without the slightest taint of abolitionism—indeed the very opposite—he has always been unpopular in the neighbourhood; alike detested by planter and "poor white." Many of both have been his debtors, and felt his iron hand over them, just as Archibald Armstrong.

Besides, some of these now around his house were present two days before upon Armstrong's plantation; saw his establishment broken up, his goods and chattels confiscated, his home made desolate.

Knowing by whom all this was done, with ill-concealed satisfaction, they now behold the *arcana* of Ephraim Darke's dwelling exposed to public gaze; himself humiliated, far more than the man he made homeless.

With no more ceremony than was shown in making the arrest, do the sheriff and party explore the paternal mansion of him arrested, rudely ransacking it from cellar to garret; the outbuildings as well, even to the grounds and garden.

Their search is but poorly rewarded. All they get, likely to throw light on the matter of inquiry, is Richard Darke's double-barrelled gun, with the clothes he wore on the day fatal to Clancy. On these there is no blood; but while they are looking for it, something comes under their eyes, almost equally significant of strife.

Through the coat-skirt is a hole, ragged, and recently made. Several pronounce it a bullet-hole; further declaring the ball to have been discharged from a rifle.

For certain, a singular discovery!

But like all the others that have been made, only serving to perplex them. It is rather in favour of the accused; giving colour to the idea, that between him and Clancy there has been a fight, with shots fired from both sides. The question is, "has it been a fair one?"

To negative this, a bit of adjunct evidence is adduced, which goes against the accused. The coat, with the perforated skirt, is *not* the one worn by him on the day before, when out assisting in the search; while it is that he had on, the day preceding, when Clancy came not home. Ephraim Darke's domestics, on being sternly interrogated, and aside, disclose this fact; unaware how greatly their master may desire them to keep it concealed.

Still, it is not much. A man might have many reasons for changing his coat, especially for the dress of two different days. It would be nothing, but for the conjoint circumstance of the shot through the skirt. This makes it significant.

Another item of intelligence, of still more suspicious nature, is got out of the domestics, whose stern questioners give them no chance to prevaricate. Indeed, terrified, they do not try.

Their young "Massr Dick" had on a different pair of boots the day he went out hunting, from those worn by him, when, yesterday, he went searching.

The latter are in the hands of the sheriff, but the former are missing— cannot be found anywhere, in or about the house!

All search for them proves idle. And not strange it should; since one is in the side-pocket of Sime Woodley's surtout, the other having a like lodgment in that of Ned Heywood.

The two hunters, "prospecting" apart, found the boots thickly coated with mud, concealed under a brush pile, at the bottom of the peach orchard. Even the sheriff does not know what bulges out the coat-skirts of the two backwoodsmen.

Nor is he told there or then. Sime has an object in keeping that secret to himself and his companion; he will only reveal it, when the time comes to make it more available.

The affair of the arrest and subsequent action over, the sheriff and his party retire from the plantation of Ephraim Darke, leaving its owner in a state of frenzied bewilderment.

They go direct to Mrs Clancy's cottage; not to stay there, but as a starting point, to resume the search for the body of her son, adjourned since yester-eve.

They do not tell her of Dick Darke's arrest. She is inside her chamber—on her couch—so prostrated by the calamity already known to her, they fear referring to it.

The doctor in attendance tells them, that any further revelation concerning the sad event may prove fatal to her.

Again her neighbours, now in greater number, go off to the woods, some afoot, others on horseback. As on the day preceding, they divide into different parties, and scatter in diverse directions. Though not till after all have revisited the ensanguined spot under the cypress, and renewed their scrutiny of the stains. Darker than on the day before, they now look more like ink than blood!

The cypress knee, out of which Woodley and Heywood "gouged" the smooth-bore bullet, is also examined, its position noted. Attempts are made to draw inferences therefrom, though with but indifferent success. True, it tells a tale; and, judging by the blood around the bullet-hole, which all of them have seen, a tragic one, though it cannot of itself give the interpretation.

A few linger around the place, now tracked and trodden hard by their going and coming feet. The larger number proceeds upon the search, in scattered parties of six or eight each, carrying it for as many miles around.

They pole and drag the creek near by, as others at a greater distance; penetrate the swamp as far as possible, or likely that a dead body might be carried for concealment. In its dim recesses they discover no body, living or dead, no trace of human being, nought save the solitude-loving heron, the snake-bird, and scaly alligator.

On this second day's quest they observe nothing new, either to throw additional light on the commission of the crime, or assist them in recovering the corpse.

It is but an unsatisfactory report to take back to the mother of the missing man. Perhaps better for her she should never receive it?

And she never does. Before it can reach her ear, this is beyond hearing sound. The thunder of heaven could not awake Mrs Clancy from the sleep into which she has fallen. For it is no momentary unconsciousness, but the cold insensible slumber of Death.

The long-endured agony of ill fortune, the more recent one of widowhood, and, now, this new bereavement of a lost, only son—these accumulated trials have proved too much for her woman's strength, of late fast failing.

When, at evening hour, the searchers, on their return, approach the desolated dwelling, they hear sounds within that speak of some terrible disaster.

On the night before their ears were saluted by the same, though in tones somewhat different. Then the widow's voice was lifted in lamentation; now it is not heard at all.

Whatever of mystery there may be is soon removed. A woman, stepping out upon the porch, and, raising her hand in token of attention, says, in sad solemn voice,—

"Mrs Clancy is dead!"

Chapter Twenty Six
Tell-tale tracks

"Mrs Clancy is dead!"

The simple, but solemn speech, makes an impression on the assembled backwoodsmen difficult to be described. All deem it a double-murder; her death caused by that of her son. The same blow has killed both.

It makes them all the more eager to discover the author of this crime, by its consequence twofold; and now, more than ever, do their thoughts turn towards Dick Darke, and become fixed upon him.

As the announcement of Mrs Clancy's death makes complete the events of the day, one might suppose, that after this climax, her neighbours, satisfied nothing more could be done, would return to their own homes.

This is not the custom in the backwoods of America, or with any people whose hearts beat true to the better instincts of humanity. It is only in Old world countries, under tyrannical rule, where these have been crushed out, that such selfishness can prevail.

Nothing of this around Natchez—not a spark of it in the breasts of those collected about that cottage, in which lies the corpse of a woman.

The widow will be waked by men ready to avenge her wrongs.

If friendless and forlorn while living, it is different now she is dead. There is not a man among them but would give his horse, his gun, ay, a slice of his land, to restore her to life, or bring back that of her son.

Neither being now possible, they can only show their sympathy by the punishment of him who has caused the double desolation.

It still needs to know who. After all, it may not be the man arrested and arraigned, though most think it is. But, to be fully convinced, further evidence is wanted; as also a more careful sifting of that already obtained.

As on the night before, a council is convened, the place being the bit of green sward, that, lawn-like, extends from the cottage front to the rail fence of the road. But now the number taking part in it is different. Instead of a half-score, there is nearer a half hundred. The news of the second death has been spreading meanwhile, and the added sympathy causes the crowd to increase.

In its centre soon forms a ring, an open space, surrounded by men, acknowledged as chief on such occasions. They discuss the points of the case; state such incidents and events as are known; recall all circumstances that can be remembered; and inquire into their connection with motives.

It is, in short, a jury, *standing*, not *sitting*, on the trial of a criminal case; and, with still greater difference between them and the ordinary "twelve good men and true," in that, unlike these, they are not mere dummies, with a strong inclination to accept the blandishments of the barrister, or give way to the rulings of the judge, too often wrong. On the contrary, men who, in themselves, combine the functions of all three—judge, jury, and counsel—with this triple power, inspired by a corresponding determination to arrive at the truth.

In short it is the court of "Justice Lynch" in session. Every circumstance which has a possible bearing on the case, or can throw light into its dark ambiguity, is called up and considered. The behaviour of the accused himself, coupled with that of the hound, are the strongest points yet appearing against him. Though not the only ones. The bullet extracted from the cypress knee, has been tried in the barrel of his gun, and found to fit exactly. About the other ball, which made the hole through the skirt of his coat, no one can say more than that it came out of a rifle. Every backwoodsman among them can testify to this.

A minor point against the accused man is, his having changed his clothes on the two succeeding days; though one stronger and more significant, is the fact that the boots, known to have been worn by him on the former, are still missing and cannot anywhere be found.

"Can't they, indeed?" asks Sime Woodley, in response to one, who has just expressed surprise at this.

The old hunter has been hitherto holding back; not from any want of will to assist the lynch jury in their investigation, but because, only lately arrived, he has scarce yet entered into the spirit of their proceedings.

His grief, on getting the news of Mrs Clancy's death, for a time holds him in restraint. It is a fresh sorrow; since, not only had her son been long his friend, but in like manner her husband and herself.

In loyal memory of this friendship, he has been making every effort to bring the murderer to justice; and one just ended accounts for his late arrival at the cottage. As on the day before, he and Heywood have remained behind the other searchers; staying in the woods till all these returned home. Yesterday they were detained by an affair of *bullets*—to-day it is *boots*. The same that are missing, and about which questions have just been asked, the last by Sime Woodley himself.

In answer to it he continues:—

"They not only kin be foun', but hev been. Hyar they air!"

Saying this, the hunter pulls a boot out of his pocket, and holds it up before their eyes; Heywood simultaneously exposing another—its fellow!

"That's the fut wear ye're in sarch o', I reck'n," pursues Woodley. "'T all eevents it's a pair o' boots belongin' to Dick Darke, an' war worn by him the day afore yesterday. What's more, they left thar marks down on the swamp mud, not a hunderd mile from the spot whar poor Charley Clancy hez got his death shot; an' them tracks war made not a hundred minnits from the time he got it. Now boys! what d'ye think o' the thing?"

"Where did you get the boots?" ask several, speaking at the same time.

"No matter whar. Ye kin all see we've got 'em. Time enuf to tell o' the whar an' the wharf or when it kums to a trial. Tho lookin' in yur faces, fellurs, I shed say it's kim to somethin' o' that sort now."

"*It has!*" responds one of the jury, in a tone of emphatic affirmation.

"In that case," pursues the hunter, "me an' Ned Heywood are ready to *gie* sech evidince as we've got. Both o' us has spent good part o' this arternoon collectin' it; an' now it's at the sarvice o' the court o' Judge Lynch, or any other."

"Well then, Woodley!" says a planter of respectability, who by tacit consent is representing the stern terrible judge spoken of. "Suppose the Court to be in session. Tell us all you know."

With alacrity Woodley responds to the appeal; giving his experience, along with it his suspicions and conjectures; not simply as a witness, but more like a counsel in the case. It needs not to say, he is against the accused, in his statement of facts, as the deductions he draws from them. For the hunter has long since decided within himself, as to who killed Clancy.

Heywood follows him in like manner, though with no new matter. His testimony but corroborates that of his elder confrère.

Taken together, or separately, it makes profound impression on the jurors of Judge Lynch; almost influencing them to pronounce an instant verdict, condemnatory of the accused.

If so, it will soon be followed by the sentence; this by execution, short and quick, but sternly terrible!

Chapter Twenty Seven
Additional evidence

While the Lynchers are still in deliberation, the little clock on the mantel strikes twelve, midnight; of late, not oft a merry hour in the cottage of the Clancys; but this night more than ever sad.

Its striking seems the announcement of a crisis. For a time it silences the voices of those conversing.

Scarce has the last stroke ceased to vibrate on the still night air, when a voice is heard; one that has not hitherto taken part in the deliberations. It sounds as though coming up from the road gate.

"Mass Woodley in da?" are the words spoken interrogatively; the question addressed generally to the group gathered in front of the house. "Yes: he's here," simultaneously answer several.

"Kin I peak a wud wif you, Mass Woodley?" again asks the inquirer at the wicket.

"Sartinly," says the hunter, separating from the others, and striding off towards the entrance.

"I reck'n I know that voice," he adds, on drawing near the gate. "It's Blue Bill, ain't it?"

"Hush, Mass' Woodley! For Goramity's sake doan peak out ma name. Not fo' all de worl let dem people hear it. Ef dey do, dis nigger am a dead man, shoo."

"Darn it, Bill; what's the matter? Why d'ye talk so mysteerous? Is thar anythin' wrong? Oh! now I think o't, you're out arter time. Never mind 'bout that; I'll not betray you. Say; what hev ye kim for?"

"Foller me, Mass Woodley; I tell yer all. I dasent tay hya, less some ob dem folk see me. Les' go little way from de house, into de wood groun' ober yonner; den I tell you wha fotch me out. Dis nigger hab someting say to you, someting berry patickler. Yes, Mass Woodley, berry patickler. 'Tarn a matter ob life an' def."

Sime does not stay to hear more; but, lifting the latch, quietly pushes open the gate, and passes out into the road. Then following the negro, who flits like a shadow before him, the two are soon standing among some bushes that form a strip of thicket running along the roadside.

"Now, what air it?" asks Woodley of the coon-hunter, with whom he is well acquainted—having often met him in his midnight rambles.

"Mass Woodley, you want know who kill Mass Charl Clancy?"

"Why, Bill, that's the very thing we're all talkin' 'bout, an' tryin' to find out. In coorse we want to know. But who's to tell us?"

"Dis nigger do dat."

"Air ye in airnest, Bill?"

"So much in earness I ha'n't got no chance get sleep, till I make clean bress ob de seecret. De ole ooman neider. No, Mass Woodley, Phoebe she no let me ress till I do dat same. She say it am de duty ob a Christyun man, an', as ye know, we boaf b'long to de Methodies. Darfore, I now tell ye, de man who kill Charl Clancy was my own massr—de young un—Dick."

"Bill! are you sure o' what ye say?"

"So shoo I kin swa it as de troof, de whole troof, an' nuffin but de troof."

"But what proof have ye?"

"Proof! I moas seed it wif ma own eyes. If I didn't see, I heerd it wif ma ears."

"By the 'tarnal! this looks like clar evydince at last. Tell me, Bill, o' all that you seed an' what you heern?"

"Ya, Mass Woodley, I tell you ebberyting; all de sarkunistances c'nected wif de case."

In ten minutes after, Simeon Woodley is made acquainted with everything the coon-hunter knows; the latter having given him full details of all that occurred on that occasion when his coon-chase was brought to such an unsatisfactory termination.

To the backwoodsman it brings no surprise. He has already arrived at a fixed conclusion, and Bill's revelation is in correspondence with it.

On hearing it, he but says:—

"While runnin' off, yur master let fall a letter, did he? You picked it up, Bill? Ye've gob it?"

"Hya's dat eyedentikil dockyment."

The negro hands over the epistle, the photograph inside.

"All right, Bill! I reck'n this oughter make things tol'ably clur. Now, what d'ye want me to do for yurself?"

"Lor, Mass Woodley, you knows bess. I'se needn't tell ye, dat ef ole Eph'm Darke hear wha dis nigger's been, an' gone, an' dud, de life ob Blue Bill wuldn't be wuth a ole coon-skin—no; not so much as a corn-shuck. I'se get de cowhide ebbery hour ob de day, and de night too. I'se get flog to def, sa'tin shoo."

"Yur right thar, I reck'n," rejoins the hunter; then continues, reflectingly, "Yes; you'd be sarved putty saveer, if they war to know on't. Wal, that mustn't be, and won't. So much I kin promise ye, Bill. Yur evydince wouldn't count for nuthin' in a law court, nohow. Tharfor, we won't bring ye forrad; so don't you be skeeart. I guess we shan't wan't no more testymony, as thar ain't like to be any crosskwestenin' lawyers in this case. Now; d'you slip back to yur quarters, and gi'e yurself no furrer consarn. I'll see you don't git into any trouble. May I be damned ef ye do!"

With this emphatic promise, the old bear-hunter separates from the less pretentious votary of the chase; as he does so giving the latter a squeeze of the hand, which tells him he may go back in confidence to the negro quarter, and sit, or sleep, by the side of his Phoebe, without fear.

Chapter Twenty Eight
"To the jail!"

With impatience Judge Lynch and his jurors await the hunter's return. Before his leaving them, they had well-nigh made up their minds to the verdict. All know it will be "Guilty," given unanimously. Woodley's temporary absence will not affect it. Neither the longer time allowed them for deliberation. If this cause change, it will not be to modify, but make more fixed their determination. Still others keep coming up. Like wildfire the news has spread that the mother of the murdered man is herself stricken down. This, acting as a fresh stimulus to sympathy, brings back such of the searchers as had gone home; many starting from beds to which they had betaken themselves after the day's fatigue.

It is past midnight, and the crowd collected around the cottage is greater than ever. As one after another arrives upon the ground they step across the threshold, enter the chamber of death, and look upon the corpse, whose pale face seems to make mute appeal to them for justice. After gazing on it for an instant, their anger with difficulty subdued in the solemn presence of death, each comes out muttering a resolve there shall be both justice and vengeance, many loudly vociferating it with the added emphasis of an oath.

It does not need what Simeon Woodley has in store to incite them to action. Already are they sufficiently inflamed. The furor of the mob, with its mutually maddening effect, gradually growing upon them, permeating their spirits, has reached the culminating point.

Still do they preserve sufficient calmness to wait a little longer, and hear what the hunter may have to say. They take it, he has been called from them on some matter connected with the subject under consideration. At such a time who would dare interrupt their deliberations for any trivial purpose? Although none of them has recognised Blue Bill's voice, they know it to have been that of a negro. This, however, is no reason why he should not have made some communication likely to throw new light on the affair. So, on Woodley's return, once more gathering around him, they demand to hear what it is.

He tells all that has been imparted to him; but without making known the name of his informant, or in any way compromising the brave fellow with a black skin, who has risked life itself by making disclosure of the truth.

To him the old hunter refers in a slight but significant manner. Comprehending, no one presses for more minute explanation.

"He as says all that," Woodley continues, after stating the circumstances communicated by the coon-hunter, "has guv me the letter dropped by Dick Darke; which, as I've tolt, ye, he picked up. Here air the thing itself. Preehaps it may let some new light into the matter; though I guess you'll all agree wi' me, it's clar enough a'ready."

They all do agree. A dozen voices have declared, are still declaring that. One now cries out—

"What need to talk any more? Charley Clancy's been killed—he's been murdered. An' Dick Darke's the man that did it!"

It is not from any lack of convincing evidence, but rather a feeling of curiosity, that prompts them to call for the reading of the letter, which the hunter now holds conspicuously in his hand. Its contents may have no bearing upon the case. Still it can be no harm to know what they are.

"You read it, Henry Spence! You're a scholart, an' I ain't," says Woodley, handing the letter over to a young fellow of learned look—the schoolmaster of the settlement.

Spence, stepping close up to the porch—into which some one has carried a candle—and holding the letter before the light, first reads the superscription, which, as he informs them, is in a lady's handwriting.

"To Charley Clancy" it is.

"Charles Clancy!"

Half a score voices pronounce the name, all in a similar tone—that of surprise. One interrogates,—

"Was that letter dropped by Dick Darke?"

"It was," responds Woodley, to whom the question is addressed.

"Have patience, boys!" puts in the planter, who represents Justice Lynch; "don't interrupt till we hear what's in it."

They take the hint, and remain silent.

But when the envelope is laid open, and a photograph drawn out, showing the portrait of a young lady, recognised by all as a likeness of Helen Armstrong, there is a fresh outburst of exclamations which betoken increased surprise; this stronger still, after Spence reads out the inscript upon the picture:

"Helen Armstrong—for him she loves."

The letter is addressed to Charles Clancy; to him the photograph must have been sent. A love-affair between Miss Armstrong and the man who has been murdered! A new revelation to all—startling, as pertinent to the case.—

"Go on, Spence! Give us the contents of the letter!" demands an impatient voice.

"Yes, give them!" adds another. "I reckon we're on the right track now."

The epistle is taken out of the envelope. The schoolmaster, unfolding it, reads aloud:—

"Dear Charles,—

"When we last met under the magnolia, you asked me a question. I told you I would answer it in writing. I now keep my promise, and you will find the answer underneath my own very imperfect image, which I herewith send in closed. Papa has finally fixed the day of our departure from the old home. On Tuesday next we are to set out in search of a new one. Will it ever be as dear as that we are leaving behind? The answer will depend upon—need I say whom? After reading what I have written upon the *carte*, surely you can guess. There, I have confessed all—all woman can, could, or should. In six little words I have made over to you my heart. Accept them as its surrender!

"And now, Charles, to speak of things prosaic, as in this hard world we are too oft constrained to do. On Tuesday morning—at a very early hour, I believe—a boat will leave Natchez, bound up the Red River. Upon it we travel, as far as Natchitoches. There to remain for some time, while papa is completing preparations for our farther transport into Texas, I am not certain what part of the 'Lone Star' State he will select for our future home. He speaks of a place upon some branch of the Colorado River, said to be a beautiful country; which, you, having been out there, will know all about. In any case, we are to remain for a time, a month or more, in Nachitoches; and there, *Carlos mio*, I need not tell you, there is a post-office for receiving letters, as also for delivering them. Mind, I say for *delivering* them! Before we leave for the far frontier, where there may be neither post-office nor post, I shall write you full particulars about our intended 'location'—with directions how to reach it. Need I be very minute? Or can I promise myself, that your wonderful skill as a 'tracker,' of which we've heard, will enable you to discover it? They say Love is blind. I hope, yours will not be so: else you may fail in finding the way to your sweetheart in the wilderness.

"How I go on talking, or rather writing, things I intended to say to you at our next meeting tinder the magnolia—our magnolia! Sad thought this, tagged to a pleasant expectation: for it must be our last interview under the dear old tree. Our last anywhere, until we come together again in Texas—perhaps on some prairie where there are no trees. Well; we shall then meet, I hope, never more to part; and in the open daylight, with no need either of night, or tree-shadows to conceal us. I'm sure father, humbled as he now is, will no longer object. Dear Charles, I don't think he would have done so at any time, but for his reverses. They made him think of—never mind what. I shall tell you all under the magnolia.

"And now, master mine—this makes you so—be punctual! Monday night, and ten o'clock—the old hour. Remember that the morning after? I shall be gone—long before the wild-wood songsters are singing their '*reveillé*' to awake you. Jule will drop this into our tree post-office this evening—Saturday. As you've told me you go there every day, you'll be sure of getting it in time; and once more I may listen to your flattery, as when you quoted the words of the old song, making me promise to come, saying you would 'show the night flowers their queen.'

"Ah! Charles, how easy to keep that promise! How sweet the flattery was, is, and ever will be, to yours,—

"Helen Armstrong."

"And that letter was found on Dick Darke?" questions a voice, as soon as the reading has come to an end.

"It war dropped by him," answers Woodley; "and tharfor ye may say it war found on him."

"You're sure of that, Simeon Woodley?"

"Wal, a man can't be sure o' a thing unless he sees it. I didn't see it myself wi' my own eyes. For all that, I've had proof clar enough to convince me; an' I'm reddy to stan' at the back o' it."

"Damn the letter!" exclaims one of the impatient ones, who has already spoken in similar strain; "the picture, too! Don't mistake me, boys. I ain't referrin' eyther to the young lady as wrote it, nor him she wrote to. I only mean that neither letter nor picture are needed to prove what we're all wantin' to know, an' do know. They arn't nor warn't reequired. To my mind, from the fust go off, nothin' ked be clarer than that Charley Clancy has been killed, cepting as to who killed him—murdered him, if ye will; for that's what's been done. Is there a man on the ground who can't call out the murderer?"

The interrogatory is answered by a unanimous negative, followed by the name, "Dick Darke."

And along with the answer commences a movement throughout the crowd. A scattering with threats heard—some muttered, some spoken aloud—while men are observed looking to their guns, and striding towards their horses; as they do so, saying sternly,—

"To the jail!"

In ten minutes after both men and horses are in motion moving along the road between Clancy's cottage and the county town. They form a phalanx, if not regular in line of march, terribly imposing in aspect.

Could Richard Darke, from inside the cell where he is confined, but see that approaching cavalcade, hear the conversation of those who compose it, and witness their angry gesticulations, he would shake in his shoes, with trembling worse than any ague that ever followed fever.

Chapter Twenty Nine
A scheme of colonisation

About two hundred miles from the mouth of Red River—the Red of Louisiana—stands the town of Natchitoches. The name is Indian, and pronounced as if written "Nak-e-tosh." Though never a populous place, it is one of peculiar interest, historically and ethnologically. Dating from the earliest days of French and Spanish colonisation, on the Lower Mississippi, it has at different periods been in possession of both these nations; finally falling to the United States, at the transfer of the Louisiana territory by Napoleon Bonaparte. Hence, around its history is woven much of romantic interest; while from the same cause its population, composed of many various nationalities, with their distinctive physical types and idiosyncracies of custom, offers to the eye of the stranger a picturesqueness unknown to northern towns. Placed on a projecting bluff of the river's bank, its painted wooden houses, of French Creole fashion, with "piazzas" and high-pitched roofs, its trottoirs brick-paved, and shaded by trees of sub-tropical foliage— among them the odoriferous magnolia, and *melia azedarach*, or "Pride of China,"—these, in places, completely arcading the street—Natchitoches has the orthodox aspect of a *rus in urbe*, or *urbs in rure*, whichever way you wish it.

Its porticoes, entwined with parasites, here and there show stretches of trellis, along which meander the cord-like tendrils of bignonias, aristolochias, and orchids, the flowers of which, drooping over windows and doorways, shut out the too garish sunlight, while filling the air with fragrance. Among these whirr tiny humming birds, buzz humble bees almost as big, while butterflies bigger than either lazily flout and flap about on soft, silent wing.

Such sights greet you at every turning as you make promenade through the streets of Natchitoches.

And there are others equally gratifying. Within these same trellised verandahs, you may observe young girls of graceful mien, elegantly apparelled, lounging on cane rocking-chairs, or perhaps peering coyly through the half-closed jalousies, their eyes invariably dark brown or coal black, the marble forehead above surmounted with a chevelure in hue resembling the plumage of the raven. For most of these demoiselles are descended from the old colonists of the two Latinic races; not a few with some admixture of African, or Indian. The flaxen hair, blue eyes, and blonde complexion of the Northland are only exceptional appearances in the town of Natchitoches.

Meet these same young ladies in the street, it is the custom, and *comme il faut*, to take off your hat, and make a bow. Every man who claims to be a gentleman does this deference; while every woman, with a white skin, expects it. On whichever side the privilege may be supposed to lie, it is certainly denied to none. The humblest shop clerk or artisan—even the dray-driver—may thus make obeisance to the proudest and daintiest damsel who treads the trottoirs of Natchitoches. It gives no right of converse, nor the slightest claim to acquaintanceship. A mere formality of politeness; and to presume carrying it further would not only be deemed a rudeness, but instantly, perhaps very seriously, resented.

Such is the polished town to which the Belle of Natchez has brought Colonel Armstrong, with his belongings, and from which he intends taking final departure for Texas. The "Lone Star State" lies a little beyond—the Sabine River forming the boundary line. But from earliest time of Texan settlement on the north-eastern side, Natchitoches has been the place of ultimate outfit and departure.

Here the ex-Mississippian planter has made halt, and purposes to remain for a much longer time than originally intended. For a far grander scheme of migration, than that he started out with, is now in his mind. Born upon the Belle of Natchez, it has been gradually developing itself during the remainder of the voyage, and is now complete—at least as to general design.

It has not originated with Archibald Armstrong himself, but one, whom he is soon to call son-in-law. The young Creole, Dupré, entranced with love, has nevertheless not permitted its delirium to destroy all ideas of other kind. Rather has it re-inspired him with one already conceived, but which, for some time, has been in abeyance. He, too, has been casting thoughts towards Texas, with a view to migrating thither. Of late travelling in Europe—more particularly in France—with some of whose noblest families he holds relationship, he has there been smitten with a grand idea, dictated by a spirit of ambition. In Louisiana he is only a planter among planters and though a rich one, is still not satisfied, either with the number of his negroes, or the area of his acres. In Texas, where land is comparatively low priced, he has conceived a project of colonisation, on an extended scale—in short, the founding a sort of Transatlantic *seigneurie*. For some months has this ambitious dream been brooding in his brain; and now, meeting the Mississippian planter aboard the boat and learning the latter's intentions, this, and the more tender *liens* late established between, them, have determined Louis Dupré to make his dream a reality, and become one of the migrating party. He will sell his Louisiana houses and lands, but not his slaves. These can be taken to Texas.

Scarce necessary to say, that, on thus declaring himself, he becomes the real chief of the proposed settlement. Whether showing conspicuously in front, or remaining obscurely in the rear, the capitalist controls all; and Dupré is this.

Still, though virtually the controlling spirit, apparently the power remains in the hands of Colonel Armstrong. The young Creole wishes it to appear so. He has no jealousy of him, who is soon to be his second father. Besides, there is another and substantial reason why Colonel Armstrong should assume the chieftainship of the purposed expedition. Though reduced in circumstances, the ex-Mississippian planter is held in high respect. His character commands it; while his name, known throughout all the South-west, will be sure to draw around, and rally under his standard, some of those strong stalwart men of the backwoods, equally apt with axe and rifle, without whom no settlement on the far frontier of Texas would stand a chance of either security, or success.

For it is to the far frontier they purpose going, where land can be got at government prices, and where they intend to purchase it not by the acre, but in square miles—in leagues.

Such is Dupré's design, easy of execution with the capital he can command after disposing of his Red River plantation.

And within a week after his arrival in Natchitoches, he has disposed of it; signed the deed of delivery, and received the money. An immense sum, notwithstanding the sacrifice of a sale requiring quick despatch. On the transfer being completed, the Creole holds in hand a cash capital of $200,000; in those days sufficient not only for the purchase of a large tract of territory, but enough to make the dream of a seignorial estate appear a possible reality.

Not much of the future is he reflecting upon now. If, at times, he cast a chance thought towards it, it may be to picture to himself how his blonde beauty will look as lady *suzeraine*—*chatelaine* of the castle to be erected in Texas.

In his fancy, no doubt, he figures her as the handsomest creature that ever carried keys at her belt.

If these fancies of the future are sweet, the facts of the present are even more so. Daring their sojourn in Natchitoches the life of Louis Dupré and Jessie Armstrong is almost a continuous chapter of amorous converse and dalliance; left hands mutually clasped, right ones around waists, or playing with curls and tresses; lips at intervals meeting in a touch that intoxicates the soul—the delicious drunkenness of love, from which no one need ever wish to get sober.

Chapter Thirty
News from Natchez

While thus pleasantly pass the days with Colonel Armstrong's younger daughter, to the elder they are drear and dark. No love lights up the path of *her* life, no sun shines upon it; nothing save shadow and clouds.

More than a week has elapsed since their arrival in Natchitoches, and for much of this time has she been left alone. Love, reputed a generous passion, is of all the most selfish. Kind to its own chosen, to others it can be cruel; often is, when the open exhibition of its fervid zeal recalls the cold neglect, it may be, making their misery.

Not that Jessie Armstrong is insensible to the sufferings of her sister. On the contrary, she feels for—all that sister can—on occasions tries to comfort her, by words such as she has already spoken, beseeching her to forget—to pluck the poison from out her heart.

Easy to counsel thus, for one in whose heart there is no poison; instead a honeyed sweetness, almost seraphic. She, who this enjoys can ill understand the opposite; and, Jessie, benighted with her own bliss, gives less thought to the unhappiness of Helen. Even less than she might, were it more known to her. For the proud elder sister keeps her sorrow to herself, eschewing sympathy, and scarce ever recurring to the past. On her side the younger rarely refers to it. She knows it would cause pain. Though once a reference to it has given pleasure to herself; when Helen explained to her the mystery of that midnight plunge into the river. This, shortly after its occurrence; soon as she herself came to a clear comprehension of it. It was no mystery after all. The face seen among the cypress tops was but the fancy of an overwrought brain; while the spectral arms were the forking tines of a branch, which, catching upon the boat, in rebound had caught Helen Armstrong, first raising her aloft, then letting her drop out of their innocent, but withal dangerous, embrace.

An explanation more pleasing to Jessie than she cared to let Helen know; since it gave the assurance that her sister had no thought of self-destruction. She is further comforted by the reflection, that Helen has no need to repine, and the hope it may not be for long. Some other and truer lover will replace the lost false one, and she will soon forget his falsehood. So reasons the happy heart. Indeed, judging by what she sees, Jessie Armstrong may well come to this conclusion. Already around her sister circle new suitors; a host seeking her hand. Among them the best blood of which the neighbourhood can boast. There are planters, lawyers, members of the State Assembly — one of the General Congress — and military men, young officers stationed at Fort Jessup, higher up the river; who, forsaking the lonely post, occasionally come down on a day's furlough to enjoy the delights of town life, and dip a little into its dissipations.

Before Helen Armstrong has been two weeks in Natchitoches she becomes, what for over two years she has been in Natchez — its *belle*. The "bloods" toast her at the drinking bar, and talk of her over the billiard table.

Some of them too much for their safety, since already two or three duels have occurred on her account — fortunately without fatal termination.

Not that she has given any of them cause to stand forth as her champion; for not one can boast of having been favoured even with a smile. On the contrary, she has met their approaches if not frowningly, at least with denying indifference. All suspect there is *un ver — rongeur* — a worm eating at her heart; that she suffers from a passion of the past. This does not dismay her Natchitoches adorers, nor hinder them from continuing their adoration. On the contrary it deepens it; her indifference only attracting them, her very coldness setting their hot southern hearts aflame, maddening them all the more.

She is not unconscious of the admiration thus excited. If she were, she would not be woman. But also, because being a true woman, she has no care for, and does not accept it. Instead of oft showing herself in society to receive homage and hear flattering speeches, she stays almost constantly within her chamber — a little sitting-room in the hotel, appropriated to herself and sister.

For reasons already known, she is often deprived of her sister's company; having to content herself with that of her mulatto maid.

A companion who can well sympathise; for Jule, like herself, has a canker at the heart. The "yellow girl" on leaving Mississippi State has also left a lover behind. True, not one who has proved false — far from it. But one who every day, every hour of his life, is in danger of losing it. Jupe she supposes to be still safe, within the recesses of the cypress swamp, but cannot tell how long his security may continue. If taken, she may never see him more, and can only think of his receiving some terrible chastisement. But she is sustained by the reflection, that her Jupiter is a brave fellow, and crafty as courageous; by the hope he will yet get away from that horrid hiding-place, and rejoin her, in a land where the dogs of Dick Darke can no more scent or assail him. Whatever may be the fate of the fugitive, she is sure of his devotion to herself; and this hinders her from despairing.

She is almost as much alarmed about her young mistress whom she sees grieving, day by day evidently sinking under some secret sorrow.

To her it is not much of a secret. She more than guesses at the cause; in truth, knows it, as it is known to that mistress herself. For the wench can read; and made the messenger of that correspondence carried on clandestinely, strange, if, herself a woman, she should not surmise many things beyond what could be gleaned from the superscription on the exchanged epistles.

She has surmised; but, like her mistress, something wide away from the reality. No wonder at her being surprised at what she sees in a Natchez newspaper—brought to the hotel from a boat just arrived at Natchitoches—something concerning Charles Clancy, very different from that suspected of him. She stays not to consider what impression it may produce on the mind of the young lady. Unpleasant no doubt; but a woman's instinct whispers the maid, it will not be worse than the agony her mistress is now enduring.

Entering the chamber, where the latter is alone, she places the paper in her hands, saying: "Missy Helen, here's a newspaper from Natchez, brought by a boat just arrived. There's something in it, I think, will be news to you—sad too."

Helen Armstrong stretches forth her hand, and takes hold of the sheet. Her fingers tremble, closing upon it; her whole frame, as she searches through its columns.

At the same time her eyes glow, burn, almost blaze, with a wild unnatural light—an expression telling of jealousy roused, rekindled, in a last spurt of desperation. Among the marriage notices she expects to see that of Charles Clancy with a Creole girl, whose name is unknown to her. It will be the latest chapter, climax and culminating point, of his perfidy!

Who could describe the sudden revulsion of thought; what pen depict the horror that sweeps through her soul; or pencil portray the expression of her countenance, as, with eyes glaring aghast, she rests them on a large type heading, in which is the name "Charles Clancy?"

For, the paragraph underneath tells not of his *marriage*, but his *murder*!

Not the climax of his perfidy, as expected, but of her suffering. Her bosom late burning with indignant jealousy, is now the prey of a very different passion.

Letting the paper fall to the floor, she sinks back into her chair, her heart audibly beating—threatening to beat no more.

Chapter Thirty One
Spectres in the street

Colonel Armstrong is staying at the "Planters' House," the chief hotel in the town of Natchitoches. Not a very grand establishment, nevertheless. Compared with such a princely hostelry as the "Langham" of London, it would be as a peasant's hut to a palace. Withal, in every way comfortable; and what it may lack in architectural style is made up in natural adornment; a fine effect, produced by trees surrounding and o'ershading it.

A hotel of the true Southern States type: weather-board walls, painted chalk-white, with green Venetian shutters to the windows; a raised verandah—the "piazza"—running all around it; a portion of this usually occupied by gentlemen in white linen coats, sky-blue "cottonade" pants, and Panama hats, who drink mint-juleps all day long; while another portion, furnished with cane rocking-chairs, presents a certain air of exclusiveness, which tells of its being tabooed to the sterner sex, or more particularly meant for ladies.

A pleasant snuggery this, giving a good view of the street, while its privacy is secured by a trellis, which extends between the supporting pillars, clustered with Virginia creepers and other plants trained to such service. A row of grand magnolias stands along the brick banquette in front, their broad glabrous leaves effectually fending off the sun; while at the ladies' end two large Persian lilacs, rivalling the indigenous tree both in the beauty of their leaves and the fragrance of their flowers, waft delicious odours into the windows of the chambers adjacent, ever open.

Orange-trees grow contiguous, and so close to the verandah rail, that one leaning over may pluck either their ripe golden globes, or white wax-like blossoms in all stages of expansion; these beautiful evergreens bearing fruit and flower at the same time.

A pleasant place at all hours this open air boudoir; and none more enjoyable than at night, just after sunset. For then the hot atmosphere has cooled down, and the soft southern breeze coming up from the bosom of the river, stirs the leaves of the lilacs into gentle rustling, and shakes their flower-spikes, scattering sweet incense around. Then the light from street lamps and house windows, gleaming through the foliage, mingles with that of the fire-flies crossing and scintillating like sparks in a pyrotechnic display. Then the tree-crickets have commenced their continuous trill, a sound by no means disagreeable; if it were, there is compensation in the song of the mock-bird, that, perched upon the top of some tall tree, makes the night cheerful with its ever-changing notes. Sometimes there are other sounds in this shady retreat, still more congenial to the ears of those who hear them. Oft is it tenanted by dark-eyed demoiselles, and their Creole cavaliers, who converse in the low whisperings of love, to them far sweeter than song of thrush, or note of nightingale—words speaking the surrender of a heart, with others signifying its acceptance.

To-night there is nothing of this within the vine-trellised verandah; for only two individuals occupy it, both ladies. By the light from street lamps and open casements, from moonbeams shining through the lilac leaves, from fire-flies hovering and shooting about, it can be seen that both are young, and both beautiful. Of two different types, dark and fair: for they are the two daughters of Archibald Armstrong.

As said, they are alone, nor man nor woman near. There have been others of both sexes, but all have gone inside; most to retire for the night, now getting late.

Colonel Armstrong is not in the hotel, nor Dupré. Both are abroad on the business of their colonising scheme. About this everything has been arranged, even to selection of the place. A Texan land speculator, who holds a large "grant" upon the San Saba river, opportunely chances to be in Natchitoches at the time. It is a tract of territory surrounding, and formerly belonging to, an old mission by the monks, long ago abandoned. Dupré has purchased it; and all now remaining to be done is to complete the make-up of the migrating party, and start off to take possession.

Busied with these preparations, the young Creole, and his future father-in-law, are out to a later hour than usual, which accounts for the ladies being left alone. Otherwise, one, at least, would not be long left to herself. If within the hotel, Dupré would certainly be by the side of his Jessie.

The girls are together, standing by the baluster rail, with eyes bent upon the street. They have been conversing, but have ceased. As usual, the younger has been trying to cheer the elder, still sad, though now from a far different cause. The pain at her heart is no longer that of jealousy, but pure grief, with an admixture of remorse. The Natchez newspaper has caused this change; what she read there, clearing Clancy of all treason, leaving herself guilty for having suspected him.

But, oh! such an *éclaircissement*! Obtained at the expense of a life dear to her as her own—dearer now she knows he is dead!

The newspaper has furnished but a meagre account of the murder. It bears date but two days subsequent, and must have been issued subsequent to Mrs Clancy's death, as it speaks of this event having occurred.

It would be out at an early hour that same morning.

In epitome its account is: that a man is missing, supposed to be murdered; by name, Charles Clancy. That search is being made for his body, not yet found. That the son of a well-known planter, Ephraim Darke, himself called Richard, has been arrested on suspicion, and lodged in the county jail; and, just as the paper is going to press, it has received the additional intelligence, that the mother of the murdered man has succumbed to the shock, and followed her unfortunate son to the "bourne from which no traveller returns."

The report is in the flowery phraseology usually indulged, in by the south-western journals. It is accompanied by comments and conjectures as to the motive of the crime. Among these Helen Armstrong has read her own name, with the contents of that letter addressed to Clancy, but proved to have been in the possession of Darke. Though given only in epitome — for the editor confesses not to have seen the epistle, but only had account of it from him who furnished the report — still to Helen Armstrong is the thing painfully compromising. All the world will now know the relations that existed between her and Charles Clancy. What would she care were he alive? And what need she, now he is dead?

She does not care — no. It is not this that afflicts her. Could she but bring him to life again, she would laugh the world to scorn, brave the frowns of her father, to prove herself a true woman by becoming the wife of him her heart had chosen for a husband.

"It cannot be; he is dead — gone — lost for ever!"

So run her reflections, as she stands in silence by her sister's side, their conversation for the time suspended. Oppressed by their painfulness, she retires a seep, and sinks down into one of the chairs; not to escape the bitter thoughts — for she cannot — but to brood on them alone.

Jessie remains with hands rested on the rail, gazing down into the street. She is looking for her Luis, who should now soon be returning to the hotel.

People are passing, some in leisurely promenade, others in hurried step, telling of early habits and a desire to get home.

One catching her eye, causes her to tremble; one for whom she has a feeling of fear, or rather repulsion. A man of large stature is seen loitering under the shadow of a tree, and looking at her as though he would devour her. Even in his figure there is an expression of sinister and slouching brutality. Still more on his face, visible by the light of a lamp which beams over the entrance door of the hotel. The young girl does not stay to scrutinise it; but shrinking back, cowers by the side of her sister.

"What's the matter, Jess?" asks Helen, observing her frayed aspect, and in turn becoming the supporter. "You've seen something to vex you? something of—Luis?"

"No—no, Helen. Not him."

"Who then?"

"Oh, sister! A man fearful to look at. A great rough fellow, ugly enough to frighten any one. I've met him several times when out walking, and every time it's made me shudder."

"Has he been rude to you?"

"Not exactly rude, though something like it. He stares at me in a strange way. And such horrid eyes! They're hollow, gowlish like an alligator's. I'd half a mind to tell father, or Luis, about it; but I know Luis would go wild, and want to kill the big brute. I saw him just now, standing on the side-walk close by. No doubt he's there still."

"Let me have a look at those alligator eyes."

The fearless elder sister, defiant from very despair, steps out to the rail, and leaning over, looks along the street.

She sees men passing; but no one who answers to the description given.

There is one standing under a tree, but not in the place of which Jessie has spoken; he is on the opposite side of the street. Neither is he a man of large size, but rather short and slight. He is in shadow, however, and she cannot be sure of this.

At the moment he moves off, and his gait attracts her attention; then his figure, and, finally, his face, as the last comes under the lamp-light. They attract and fix it, sending a cold shiver through her frame.

It was a fancy her thinking she saw Charles Clancy among the tree-tops. Is it a like delusion, that now shows her his assassin in the streets of Natchitoches? No; it cannot be! It is a reality; assuredly the man moving off is *Richard Darke*!

She has it on her tongue to cry "murderer!" and raise a "hue and cry;" but cannot. She feels paralysed, fascinated; and stands speechless, not stirring, scarce breathing.

Thus, till the assassin is out of sight.

Then she totters back to the side of her sister, to tell in trembling accents, how she, too, had been frayed by a *spectre in the street*!

Chapter Thirty Two
The "Choctaw Chief"

"You'll excuse me, stranger, for interruptin' you in the readin' o' your newspaper. I like to see men in the way o' acquirin' knowledge. But we're all of us here goin' to licker up. Won't you join?"

The invitation, brusquely, if not uncourteously, extended, comes from a man of middle age, in height at least six feet three, without reckoning the thick soles of his bull-skin boots—the tops of which rise several inches above the knee. A personage, rawboned, and of rough exterior, wearing a red blanket-coat; his trousers tucked into the aforesaid boots; with a leather belt buckled around his waist, under the coat, but over the haft of a bowie-knife, alongside which peeps out the butt of a Colt's revolving pistol. In correspondence with his clothing and equipment, he shows a cut-throat countenance, typical of the State Penitentiary; cheeks bloated as from excessive indulgence in drink; eyes watery and somewhat bloodshot; lips thick and sensual; with a nose set obliquely, looking as if it had received hard treatment in some pugilistic encounter. His hair is of a yellowish clay colour, lighter in tint upon the eyebrows. There is none either on his lips or jaws, nor yet upon his thick hog-like throat; which looks as if some day it may need something stiffer than a beard to protect it from the hemp of the hangman.

He, to whom the invitation has been extended, is of quite a different appearance. In age a little over half that of the individual who has addressed him; complexion dark and cadaverous; the cheeks hollow and haggard, as from sleepless anxiety; the upper lip showing two elongated bluish blotches—the stub of moustaches recently removed; the eyes coal black, with sinister glances sent in suspicious furtiveness from under a broad hat-brim pulled low down over the brow; the figure fairly shaped, but with garments coarse and clumsily fitting, too ample both for body and limbs, as if intended to conceal rather than show them to advantage.

A practised detective, after scanning this individual, taking note of his habiliments, with the hat and his manner of wearing it, would pronounce him a person dressed in disguise—this, for some good reason, adopted. A suspicion of the kind appears to be in the mind of the rough Hercules, who has invited him to "licker up;" though *he* is no detective.

"Thank you," rejoins the young fellow, lowering the newspaper to his knee, and raising the rim of his hat, as little as possible; "I've just had a drain. I hope you'll excuse me."

"Damned if we do! Not this time, stranger. The rule o' this tavern is, that all in its bar takes a smile thegither—leastwise on first meeting. So, say what's the name o' yer tipple."

"Oh! in that case I'm agreeable," assents the newspaper reader, laying aside his reluctance, and along with it the paper—at the same time rising to his feet. Then, stepping up to the bar, he adds, in a tone of apparent frankness: "Phil Quantrell ain't the man to back out where there's glasses going. But, gentlemen, as I'm the stranger in this crowd, I hope you'll let me pay for the drinks."

The men thus addressed as "gentlemen" are seven or eight in number; not one of whom, from outward seeming, could lay claim to the epithet. So far as this goes, they are all of a sort with the brutal-looking bully in the blanket-coat who commenced the conversation. Did Phil Quantrell address them as "blackguards," he would be much nearer the mark. Villainous scoundrels they appear, every one of them, though of different degrees, judging by their countenances, and with like variety in their costumes.

"No—no!" respond several, determined to show themselves gentlemen in generosity. "No stranger can stand treat here. You must drink with us, Mr Quantrell."

"This score's mine!" proclaims the first spokesman, in an authoritative voice. "After that anybody as likes may stand treat. Come, Johnny! trot out the stuff. Brandy smash for me."

The bar-keeper thus appealed to—as repulsive-looking as any of the party upon whom he is called to wait—with that dexterity peculiar to his craft, soon furnishes the counter with bottles and decanters containing several sorts of liquors. After which he arranges a row of tumblers alongside, corresponding to the number of those designing to drink.

And soon they are all drinking; each the mixture most agreeable to his palate.

It is a scene of every-day occurrence, every hour, almost every minute, in a hotel bar-room of the Southern United States; the only peculiarity in this case being, that the Natchitoches tavern in which it takes place is very different from the ordinary village inn, or roadside hotel. It stands upon the outskirts of the town, in a suburb known as the "Indian quarter;" sometimes also called "Spanish town"—both name having reference to the fact, that some queer little shanties around are inhabited by pure-blooded Indians and half-breeds, with poor whites of Spanish extraction—these last the degenerate descendants of heroic soldiers who originally established the settlement.

The tavern itself, bearing an old weather-washed swing-sign, on which is depicted an Indian in full war-paint, is known as the "Choctaw Chief," and is kept by a man supposed to be a Mexican, but who may be anything else; having for his bar-keeper the afore-mentioned "Johnny," a personage supposed to be an Irishman, though of like dubious nationality as his employer.

The Choctaw Chief takes in travellers; giving them bed, board, and lodging, without asking them any questions, beyond a demand of payment before they have either eaten or slept under its roof. It usually has a goodly number, and of a peculiar kind—strange both in aspect and manners—no one knowing whence they come, or whither bent when taking their departure.

As the house stands out of the ordinary path of town promenaders, in an outskirt scarce ever visited by respectable people, no one cares to inquire into the character of its guests, or aught else relating to it. To those who chance to stray in its direction, it is known as a sort of cheap hostelry, that gives shelter to all sorts of odd customers—hunters, trappers, small Indian traders, returned from an expedition on the prairies; along with these, such travellers as are without the means to stop at the more pretentious inns of the village; or, having the means, prefer, for reasons of their own, to put up at the Choctaw Chief.

Such is the reputation of the hostelry, before whose drinking bar stands Phil Quantrell—so calling himself—with the men to whose boon companionship he has been so unceremoniously introduced; as declared by his introducer, according to the custom of the establishment.

The first drinks swallowed, Quantrell calls for another round; and then a third is ordered, by some one else, who pays, or promises to pay for it.

A fourth "smile" is insisted upon by another some one who announces himself ready to stand treat; all the liquor, up to this time consumed, being either cheap brandy or "rot-gut" whisky.

Quantrell, now pleasantly convivial, and acting under the generous impulse the drink has produced, sings out "Champagne!" a wine which the poorest tavern in the Southern States, even the Choctaw Chief, can plentifully supply.

After this the choice vintage of France, or its gooseberry counterfeit, flows feebly; Johnny with gleeful alacrity stripping off the leaden capsules, twisting the wires, and letting pop the corks. For the stranger guest has taken a wallet from his pocket, which all can perceive to be "chock full" of gold "eagles," some reflecting upon, but saying nothing about, the singular contrast between this plethoric purse, and the coarse coat out of whose pocket it is pulled.

After all, not much in this. Within the wooden walls of the Choctaw Chief there have been seen many contrasts quite as curious. Neither its hybrid landlord, nor his bar-keeper, nor its guests are addicted to take note—or, at all events make remarks upon—circumstances which elsewhere would seem singular.

Still, is there one among the roystering crowd who does note this; as also other acts done, and sayings spoken, by Phil Quantrell in his cups. It is the Colossus who has introduced him to the jovial company, and who still sticks to him as chaperon.

Some of this man's associates, who appear on familiar footing, called him "Jim Borlasse;" others, less free, address him as "Mister Borlasse;" while still others, at intervals, and as if by a slip of the tongue, give him the title "Captain." Jim, Mister, or Captain Borlasse—whichever designation he deserve—throughout the whole debauch, keeps his bloodshot eyes bent upon their new acquaintance, noting his every movement. His ears, too, are strained to catch every word Quantrell utters, weighing its import.

For all he neither says nor does aught to tell of his being thus attentive to the stranger—at first his guest, but now a spendthrift host to himself and his party.

While the champagne is being freely quaffed, of course there is much conversation, and on many subjects. But one is special; seeming more than all others to engross the attention of the roysterers under the roof of the Choctaw Chief.

It is a murder that has been committed in the State of Mississippi, near the town of Natchez; an account of which has just appeared in the local journal of Natchitoches. The paper is lying on the bar-room table; and all of them, who can read, have already made themselves acquainted with the particulars of the crime. Those, whose scholarship does not extend so far, have learnt them at secondhand from their better-educated associates.

The murdered man is called Clancy—Charles Clancy—while the murderer, or he under suspicion of being so, is named Richard Darke, the son of Ephraim Darke, a rich Mississippi planter.

The paper gives further details: that the body of the murdered man has not been found, before the time of its going to press; though the evidence collected leaves no doubt of a foul deed having been done; adding, that Darke, the man accused of it, after being arrested and lodged in the county jail, has managed to make his escape—this through connivance with his jailer, who has also disappeared from the place. Just in time, pursues the report, to save the culprit's neck from a rope, made ready for him by the executioners of Justice Lynch, a party of whom had burst open the doors of the prison, only to find it untenanted. The paper likewise mentions the motive for the committal of the crime—at least as conjectured; giving the name of a young lady, Miss Helen Armstrong, and speaking of a letter, with her picture, found upon the suspected assassin. It winds up by saying, that no doubt both prisoner and jailer have G.T.T.—"Gone to Texas"—a phrase of frequent use in the Southern States, applied to fugitives from justice. Then follows the copy of a proclamation from the State authorities, offering a reward of two thousand dollars for the apprehension of Richard Darke, and five hundred for Joe Harkness—this being the name of the conniving prison-keeper.

While the murder is being canvassed and discussed by the *bon-vivants* in the bar-room of the Choctaw Chief—a subject that seems to have a strange fascination for them—Borlasse, who has become elevated with the alcohol, though usually a man of taciturn habit, breaks out with an asseveration, which causes surprise to all, even his intimate associates.

"Damn the luck!" he vociferates, bringing his fist down upon the counter till the decanters dance at the concussion; "I'd 'a given a hundred dollars to 'a been in the place o' that fellow Darke, whoever he is!"

"Why?" interrogate several of his confrères, in tones that express the different degrees of their familiarity with him questioned, "Why, Jim?"

"Why, Mr Borlasse?"

"Why, Captain?"

"Why?" echoes the man of many titles, again striking the counter, and causing decanters and glasses to jingle. "Why? Because that Clancy—that same Clancy—is the skunk that, before a packed jury, half o' them yellar-bellied Mexikins, in the town of Nacogdoches, swore I stole a horse from him. Not only swore it, but war believed; an' got me—me, Jim Borlasse—tied for twenty-four hours to a post, and whipped into the bargain. Yes, boys, whipped! An' by a damned Mexikin nigger, under the orders o' one o' their constables, they call algazeels. I've got the mark o' them lashes on me now, and can show them, if any o' ye hev a doubt about it. I ain't 'shamed to show 'em to *you* fellows; as ye've all got something o' the same, I guess. But I'm burnin' mad to think that Charley Clancy's escaped clear o' the vengeance I'd sworn again him. I know'd he was comin' back to Texas, him and his. That's what took him out thar, when I met him at Nacogdoches. I've been waitin' and watchin' till he shed stray this way. Now, it appears, somebody has spoilt my plans—somebody o' the name Richard Darke. An', while I envy this Dick Darke, I say damn him for doin' it!"

"Damn Dick Darke! Damn him for doin' it!" they shout, till the walls re-echo their ribald blasphemy.

The drinking debauch is continued till a late hour, Quantrell paying shot for the whole party. Maudlin as most of them have become, they still wonder that a man so shabbily dressed can command so much cash and coin. Some of them are not a little perplexed by it.

Borlasse is less so than any of his fellow-tipplers. He has noted certain circumstances that give him a clue to the explanation; one, especially, which seems to make everything clear. As the stranger, calling himself Phil Quantrell, stands holding his glass in hand, his handkerchief employed to wipe the wine from his lips, and carelessly returned to his pocket, slips out, and fails upon the floor. Borlasse stooping, picks it up, but without restoring it to its owner.

Instead, he retires to one side; and, unobserved, makes himself acquainted with a name embroidered on its corner.

When, at a later hour, the two sit together, drinking a last good-night draught, Borlasse places his lips close to the stranger's ear, whispering as if it were Satan himself who spoke, "*Your name is not Philip Quantrell: 'tis Richard Darke!*"

Chapter Thirty Three
The murderer unmasked

A rattlesnake sounding its harsh "skirr" under the chair on which the stranger is sitting could not cause him to start up more abruptly than he does, when Borlasse says:—

"Your name is not Philip Quantrell: 'tis Richard Darke!"

He first half rises to his feet, then sits down again; all the while trembling in such fashion, that the wine goes over the edge of his glass, sprinkling the sanded floor.

Fortunately for him, all the others have retired to their beds, it being now a very late hour of the night—near midnight. The drinking "saloon" of the Choctaw Chief is quite emptied of its guests. Even Johnny, the bar-keeper, has gone kitchen-wards to look after his supper.

Only Borlasse witnesses the effect of his own speech; which, though but whispered, has proved so impressive.

The speaker, on his side, shows no surprise. Throughout all the evening he has been taking the measure of his man, and has arrived at a clear comprehension of the case. He now knows he is in the company of Charles Clancy's assassin. The disguise which Darke has adopted— the mere shaving off moustaches and donning a dress of home-wove "cottonade"—the common wear of the Louisiana Creole—with slouch hat to correspond, is too flimsy to deceive Captain Jim Borlasse, himself accustomed to metamorphoses more ingenious, it is nothing new for him to meet a murderer fleeing from the scene of his crime—stealthily, disguisedly making way towards that boundary line, between the United States and Texas—the limit of executive justice.

"Come, Quantrell!" he says, raising his arm in a gesture of reassurance, "don't waste the wine in that ridikelous fashion. You and me are alone, and I reckin we understand one another. If not, we soon will—the sooner by your puttin' on no nonsensical airs, but confessin' the clar and candid truth. First, then, answer me this questyun: Air you, or air you not, Richard Darke? If ye air, don't be afeerd to say so. No humbuggery! Thar's no need for't. An' it won't do for Jim Borlasse."

The stranger, trembling, hesitates to make reply.

Only for a moment. He sees it will be of no use denying his identity. The man who has questioned him—of giant size and formidable aspect—notwithstanding the copious draughts he has swallowed, appears cool as a tombstone, and stern as an Inquisitor. The bloodshot eyes look upon him with a leer that seems to say: "Tell me a lie, and I'm your enemy."

At the same time those eyes speak of friendship; such as may exist between two scoundrels equally steeped in crime.

The murderer of Charles Clancy—now for many days and nights wandering the earth, a fugitive from foiled justice, taking untrodden paths, hiding in holes and corners, at length seeking shelter under the roof of the Choctaw Chief, because of its repute, sees he has reached a haven of safety.

The volunteered confessions of Borlasse—the tale of his hostility to Clancy, and its cause—inspire him with confidence about any revelations he may make in return. Beyond all doubt his new acquaintance stands in mud, deep as himself. Without further hesitation, he says—"I *am* Richard Darke."

"All right!" is the rejoinder. "And now, Mr Darke, let me tell you, I like your manly way of answerin' the question I've put ye. Same time, I may as well remark, 'twould 'a been all one if ye'd sayed *no*! This child hain't been hidin' half o' his life, 'count o' some little mistakes made at the beginnin' of it, not to know when a man's got into a sim'lar fix. First day you showed your face inside the Choctaw Chief I seed thar war something amiss; tho', in course, I couldn't gie the thing a name, much less know 'thar that ugly word which begins with a M. This evenin', I acknowledge, I war a bit put out— seein' you round thar by the planter's, spyin' after one of them Armstrong girls; which of them I needn't say."

Darke starts, saying mechanically, "You saw me?"

"In coorse I did—bein' there myself, on a like lay."

"Well?" interrogates the other, feigning coolness.

"Well; that, as I've said, some leetle bamboozled me. From your looks and ways since you first came hyar, I guessed that the something wrong must be different from a love-scrape. Sartint, a man stayin' at the Choctaw Chief, and sporting the cheap rig as you've got on, wan't likely to be aspirin' to sech dainty damsels as them. You'll give in, yourself, it looked a leetle queer; didn't it?"

"I don't know that it did," is the reply, pronounced doggedly, and in an assumed tone of devil-may-care-ishness.

"You don't! Well, I thought so, up to the time o' gettin' back to the tavern hyar—not many minutes afore my meetin' and askin' you to jine us in drinks. If you've any curiosity to know what changed my mind, I'll tell ye."

"What?" asks Darke, scarcely reflecting on his words.

"That ere newspaper you war readin' when I gave you the invite. I read it *afore* you did, and had ciphered out the whole thing. Puttin' six and six thegither, I could easy make the dozen. The same bein', that one of the young ladies stayin' at the hotel is the Miss Helen Armstrong spoke of in the paper; and the man I observed watchin' her is Richard Darke, who killed Charles Clancy—*yourself*!"

"I—I am—I won't—I don't deny it to you, Mr Borlasse. I am Richard Darke. I did kill Charles Clancy; though I protest against its being said I *murdered* him."

"Never mind that. Between friends, as I suppose we can now call ourselves, there need be no nice distinguishin' of tarms. Murder or manslaughter, it's all the same, when a man has a motive sech as yourn. An' when he's druv out o' the pale of what they call society, an' hunted from the settlements, he's not like to lose the respect of them who's been sarved the same way. Your bein' Richard Darke an' havin' killed Charles Clancy, in no ways makes you an enemy o' Jim Borlasse—except in your havin' robbed me of a revenge I'd sworn to take myself. Let that go now. I ain't angry, but only envious o' you, for havin' the satisfaction of sendin' the skunk to kingdom come, without givin' me the chance. An' now, Mister Darke, what do you intend doin'?"

The question comes upon the assassin with a sobering effect. His copious potations have hitherto kept him from reflecting.

Despite the thieve's confidence with which Borlasse has inspired him, this reference to his future brings up its darkness, with its dangers; and he pauses before making response.

Without waiting for it, his questioner continues:

"If you've got no fixed plan of action, and will listen to the advice of a friend, I'd advise you to become *one o' us*."

"One of you! What does that mean, Mr Borlasse?"

"Well, I can't tell you here," answers Borlasse, in a subdued tone. "Desarted as this bar-room appear to be, it's got ears for all that. I see that curse, Johnny, sneakin' about, pretendin' to be lookin' after his supper. If he knew as much about you as I do, you'd be in limbo afore you ked get into your bed. I needn't tell you thar's a reward offered; for you seed that yourself in the newspaper. Two thousand dollars for you, an' five hundred dollars for the fellow as I've seed about along wi' you, and who I'd already figured up as bein' jailer Joe Harkness. Johnny, an' a good many more, would be glad to go halves with me, for tellin' them only half of what I now know. *I* ain't goin' to betray you. I've my reasons for not. After what's been said I reckon you can trust me?"

"I can," rejoins the assassin, heaving a sigh of relief.

"All right, then," resumes Borlasse; "we understand one another. But it won't do to stay palaverin hyar any longer. Let's go up to my bedroom. We'll be safe there; and I've got a bottle of whisky, the best stuff for a nightcap. Over that we can talk things straight, without any one havin' the chance to set them crooked. Come along!"

Darke, without protest, accepts the invitation. He dares not do otherwise. It sounds more like a command. The man extending it has now full control over him; can deliver him to justice—have him dragged to a jail.

Chapter Thirty Four
"Will you be one of us?"

Once inside his sleeping apartment, Borlasse shuts the door, points out a chair to his invited guest, and plants himself upon another. With the promised bottle of whisky between them, he resumes speech.

"I've asked you, Quantrell, to be one o' us. I've done it for your own good, as you ought to know without my tellin' ye. Well; you asked me in return what that means?"

"Yes, I did," rejoins Darke, speaking without purpose.

"It means, then," continues Borlasse, taking a gulp out of his glass, "that me, an' the others you've been drinking with, air as good a set of fellows as ever lived. That we're a cheerful party, you've seen for yourself. What's passed this night ain't nowheres to the merry times we spend upon the prairies out in Texas—for it's in Texas we live."

"May I ask, Mr Borlasse, what business you follow?"

"Well; when we're engaged in regular business, it's mostly horse-catchin'. We rope wild horses, *mustangs*, as they're called; an' sometimes them that ain't jest so wild. We bring 'em into the settlements for sale. For which reason we pass by the name of *mustangers*. Between whiles, when business isn't very brisk, we spend our time in some of the Texas towns—them what's well in to'rds the Rio Grande, whar there's a good sprinklin' of Mexikins in the population. We've some rare times among the Mexikin girls, I kin assure you. You'll take Jim Borlasse's word for that, won't you?"

"I have no cause to doubt it."

"Well, I needn't say more, need I? I know, Quantrell, you're fond of a pretty face yourself, with sloe-black eyes in it. You'll see them among the Mexikin saynoritas, to your heart's content. Enough o' 'em, maybe, to make you forget the pair as war late glancin' at you out of the hotel gallery."

"Glancing at me?" exclaims Darke, showing surprise, not unmixed with alarm.

"Glancing at ye; strait custrut; them same eyes as inspired ye to do that little bit of shootin', wi' Charley Clancy for a target."

"You think she *saw* me?" asks the assassin, with increasing uneasiness.

"Think! I'm sure of it. More than saw—she recognised ye. I could tell that from the way she shot back into the shadow. Did ye not notice it yourself?"

"No," rejoins Darke, the monosyllable issuing mechanically from his lips, while a shiver runs through his frame.

His questioner, observing these signs, continues,—

"T'ike my advice, and come with us fellows to Texas. Before you're long there, the Mexikin girls will make you stop moping about Miss Armstrong. After the first *fandango* you've been at, you won't care a straw for her. Believe me, you'll soon forget her."

"Never!" exclaims Darke, in the fervour of his passion—thwarted though it has been—forgetting the danger he is in.

"If that's your detarmination," returns Borlasse, "an' you've made up your mind to keep that sweetheart in sight, you won't be likely to live long. As sure as you're sittin' thar, afore breakfast time to-morrow mornin' the town of Naketosh 'll be too hot to hold ye."

Darke starts from his chair, as if *it* had become too hot.

"Keep cool, Quantrell!" counsels the Texan. "No need for ye to be scared at what I'm sayin'. Thar's no great danger jest yet. There might be, if you were in that chair, or this room, eight hours later. I won't be myself, not one. For I may as well tell ye, that Jim Borlasse, same's yourself, has reasons for shiftin' quarters from the Choctaw Chief. And so, too, some o' the fellows we've been drinkin' with. We'll all be out o' this a good hour afore sun-up. Take a friend's advice, and make tracks along wi' us. Will you?"

Darke still hesitates to give an affirmative answer. His love for Helen Armstrong—wild, wanton passion though it be—is the controlling influence of his life. It has influenced him to follow her thus far, almost as much as the hope of escaping punishment for his crime. And though knowing, that the officers of justice are after him, he clings to the spot where she is staying, with that fascination which keeps the fox by the kennel holding the hounds. The thought of leaving her behind—perhaps never to see her again—is more repugnant than the spectre of a scaffold!

The Texan guesses the reason of his irresolution. More than this, he knows he has the means to put an end to it. A word will be sufficient; or, at most, a single speech. He puts it thus—

"If you're detarmined to stick by the apron-strings o' Miss Armstrong, you'll not do that by staying here in Naketosh. Your best place, to be *near her*, will be along *with me*."

"How so, Mr Borlasse?" questions Darke, his eyes opening to a new light. "Why do you say that?"

"You ought to know, without my tellin' you—a man of your 'cuteness, Quantrell! You say you can never forget the older of that pair o' girls. I believe you; and will be candid, too, in sayin', no more is Jim Borlasse like to forget the younger. I thought nothin' could 'a fetched that soft feelin' over me. 'Twant likely, after what I've gone through in my time. But she's done it—them blue eyes of hers; hanged if they hain't! Then, do you suppose that I'm going to run away from, and lose sight o' her and them? *No*; not till I've had her within these arms, and tears out o' them same peepers droppin' on my cheeks. That is, if she take it in the weepin' way."

"I don't understand," stammers Darke.

"You will in time," rejoins the ruffian; "that is, if you become one o' us, and go where we're a-goin'. Enough now for you to be told that, *there you will find your sweetheart!*"

Without waiting to watch the effect of his last words, the tempter continues—

"Now, Phil Quantrell, or Dick Darke, as in confidence I may call ye, are you willin' to be one o' us?"

"I am."

"Good! That's settled. An' your comrade, Harkness; I take it, he'll go, too, when told o' the danger of staying behind; not that he appears o' much account, anyway. Still, among us *mustangers*, the more the merrier; and, sometimes we need numbers to help in the surroundin' o' the horses. He'll go along, won't he?"

"Anywhere, with me."

"Well, then, you'd better step into his bedroom, and roust him up. Both of ye must be ready at once. Slip out to the stable, an' see to the saddles of your horses. You needn't trouble about settlin' the tavern bill. That's all scored to me; we kin fix the proportions of it afterward. Now, Quantrell, look sharp; in twenty minutes, time, I expect to find you an' Harkness in the saddle, where you'll see ten o' us others the same."

Saying this, the Texan strides out into the corridor, Darke preceding him. In the dimly-lighted passage they part company, Borlasse opening door after door of several bedrooms, ranged on both sides of it; into each, speaking a word, which, though only in whisper, seems to awake a sleeper as if a cannon were discharged close to his ears. Then succeeds a general shuffling, as of men hastily putting on coats and boots, with an occasional grunt of discontent at slumber disturbed; but neither talking nor angry protest. Soon, one after another, is seen issuing forth from his sleeping apartment, skulking along the corridor, out through the entrance door at back, and on towards the stable.

Presently, they fetch their horses forth, saddled and bridled. Then, leaping upon their backs, ride silently off under the shadow of the trees; Borlasse at their head, Quantrell by his side, Harkness among those behind.

Almost instantly they are in the thick forest which comes close up to the suburbs of Natchitoches; the Choctaw Chief standing among trees never planted by the hand of man.

The wholesale departure appearing surreptitious, is not unobserved. Both the tavern Boniface and his bar-keeper witness it, standing in the door as their guests go off; the landlord chuckling at the large pile of glittering coins left behind; Johnny scratching his carroty poll, and saying,—

"Be japers! they intind clearin' that fellow Quantrell out. He won't long be throubled wid that shinin' stuff as seems burnin' the bottom out av his pocket. I wudn't be surrprized if they putt both him an' 'tother fool past tillin' tales afore ayther sees sun. Will, boss, it's no bizness av ours."

With this self-consolatory remark, to which the "boss" assents, Johnny proceeds to shut and lock the tavern door. Soon after the windows of the Choctaw Chief show lightless, its interior silent, the moonbeams shining upon its shingled roof peacefully and innocently, as though it had never sheltered robber, and drunken talk or ribald blasphemy been heard under it.

So, till morning's dawn; till daylight; till the sun is o'ertopping the trees. Then is it surrounded by angry men; its wooden walls re-echoing their demand for admittance.

They are the local authorities of the district; the sheriff of Natchitoches with his *posse* of constables, and a crowd of people accompanying. Among them are Colonel Armstrong and the Creole, Dupré; these instigating the movement; indeed, directing it.

Ah knew, from yesterday's newspaper, of the murder committed near Natchez, as also of the murderer having broken jail. Only this morning have they learnt that the escaped criminal has been seen in the streets of their town. From an early hour they have been scouring these in search of him;

and, at length, reached the Choctaw Chief—the place where he should be found, if found at all.

On its doors being opened, they discover traces of him. No man named Darke has been there, but one calling himself Quantrell, with another, who went by the name of Walsh.

As, in this case, neither the landlord nor bar-keeper have any interest in screening that particular pair of their late guests, they make no attempt to do so; but, on the contrary, tell all they know about them; adding, how both went away with a number of other gentlemen, who paid their tavern bills, and took departure at an early hour of the morning.

The description of the other "gentlemen" is not so particularly given, because not so specially called for. In that of Quantrell and Walsh, Colonel Armstrong, without difficulty, identifies Richard Darke and the jailer, Joe Harkness.

He, sheriff, constables, crowd, stand with countenances expressing defeat—disappointment. They have reached the Choctaw Chief a little too late. They know nothing of Borlasse, or how he has baffled them. They but believe, that, for the second time, the assassin of Charles Clancy has eluded the grasp of justice.

Chapter Thirty Five
A ghost going its rounds

It is nearly a month since the day of Clancy's death; still the excitement caused by it, though to some extent subsided, has not died out. Curiosity and speculation are kept alive by the fact of the body not having been found. For it has not. Search has been made everywhere for miles around. Field and forest, creeks, ponds, swamp, and river, have all been traversed and interrogated, in vain. All have refused to surrender up the dead.

That Clancy is dead no one has a doubt. To say nothing of the blood spilt beside his abandoned hat and gun, with the other circumstances attendant, there is testimony of a moral nature, to many quite as convincing.

Alive he would long since have returned home, at thought of what his mother must be suffering. He was just the man to do that, as all who knew him are aware. Even wounded and crippled, if able to crawl, it would be to the side of the only woman at such a crisis he should care for.

Though it is now known that he cared for another, no one entertains a thought of his having gone off after *her*. It would not be in keeping with his character, any more than with the incidents and events that have conspired to make the mystery. Days pass, and it still remains one.

The sun rises and sets, without throwing any light upon it. Conjecture can do nothing to clear it up; and search, over and over unsuccessful, is at length abandoned.

If people still speculate upon how the body of the murdered man has been disposed of, there is no speculation as to who was his murderer, or how the latter made escape.

The treason of the jail-keeper explains this—itself accounted for by Ephraim Darke having on the previous day paid a visit to his son in the cell, and left with him a key that ere now has opened many a prison door. Joe Harkness, a weak-witted fellow, long suspected of faithlessness, was not the man to resist the temptation with which his palm had been touched.

Since that day some changes have taken place in the settlement. The plantation late Armstrong's has passed into the hands of a new proprietor— Darke having disposed of it—while the cottage of the Clancys, now ownerless, stays untenanted. Unfurnished too: for the bailiff has been there, and a bill of sale, which covered its scant plenishing, farm-stock, implements and utensils, has swept all away.

For a single day there was a stir about the place, with noise corresponding, when the chattels were being disposed of by public auction. Then the household gods of the decayed Irish gentleman were knocked down to the highest bidder, and scattered throughout the district. Rare books, pictures, and other articles, telling of refined taste, with some slight remnants of *bijouterie*, were carried off to log-cabins, there to be esteemed in proportion to the prices paid for them. In fine, the Clancy cottage, stripped of everything, has been left untenanted. Lone as to the situation in which it stands, it is yet lonelier in its desolation. Even the dog, that did such service in pointing out the criminality of him who caused all the ruin, no longer guards its enclosures, or cheers them with his familiar bark. The faithful animal, adopted by Simeon Woodley, has found a home in the cabin of the hunter.

It is midnight; an hour still and voiceless in Northern climes, but not so in the Southern. Far from it in the State of Mississippi. There the sun's excessive heat keeps Nature alert and alive, even at night, and in days of December.

Though night, it is not December, but a date nearer Spring. February is written on the heading of letters, and this, a Spring month on the Lower Mississippi, has commenced making its imprint on the forest trees. Their buds have already burst, some showing leaves fully expanded, others of still earlier habit bedecked with blossoms. Birds, too, awaking from a short winter's silence, pour forth their amorous lays, filling glade and grove with music, that does not end with the day; for the mock-bird, taking up the strain, carries it on through the hours of night; so well counterfeiting the notes of his fellow-songsters, one might fancy them awake—still singing.

Not so melodious are other voices disturbing the stillness of the Southern night. Quite the opposite are the croaking of frogs, the screeching of owls, the jerking call of tree-crickets, and the bellowing of the alligator. Still, the ear accustomed to such sounds is not jarred by them. They are but the bass notes, needed to complete the symphony of Nature's concert.

In the midst of this mélange,—the hour, as already stated, midnight—a man, or something bearing man's semblance, is seen gliding along the edge of the cypress swamp, not far from the place where Charles Clancy fell.

After skirting the mud-flat for a time, the figure—whether ghost or human—turns face toward the tract of lighter woodland, extending between the thick timber and cleared ground of the plantations.

Having traversed this, the nocturnal wayfarer comes within sight of the deserted cottage, late occupied by the Clancys.

The moonlight, falling upon his face, shows it to be white. Also, that his cheeks are pallid, with eyes hollow and sunken, as from sickness—some malady long-endured, and not yet cured. As he strides over fallen logs, or climbs fences stretching athwart his course, his tottering step tells of a frame enfeebled.

When at length clear of the woods, and within sight of the untenanted dwelling, he stops, and for a time remains contemplating it. That he is aware of its being unoccupied is evident, from the glance with which he regards it.

His familiarity with the place is equally evident. On entering the cottage grounds, which he soon after does, through, some shrubbery at the back, he takes the path leading up to the house, without appearing to have any doubt about its being the right one.

For all this he makes approach with caution, looking suspiciously around—either actually afraid, or not desiring to be observed.

There is little likelihood of his being so. At that hour all in the settlement should be asleep. The house stands remote, more than a mile from its nearest neighbour. It is empty; has been stripped of its furniture, of everything. What should any one be doing there?

What is *he* doing there? A question which would suggest itself to one seeing him; with interest added on making note of his movements.

There is no one to do either; and he continues on to the house, making for its back door, where there is a porch, as also a covered way, leading to a log-cabin—the kitchen.

Even as within the porch, he tries the handle of the door which at a touch goes open. There is no lock, or if there was, it has not been thought worth while to turn the key in it. There are no burglars in the backwoods. If there were, nothing in that house need tempt them.

Its nocturnal visitor enters under its roof. The ring of his footsteps, though he still treads cautiously, gives out a sad, solemn sound. It is in unison with the sighs that come, deep-drawn, from his breast; at times so sonorous as to be audible all over the house.

He passes from room to room. There are not many—only five of them. In each he remains a few moments, gazing dismally around. But in one— that which was the widow's sleeping chamber—he tarries a longer time; regarding a particular spot—the place formerly occupied by a bed. Then a sigh, louder than any that has preceded it, succeeded by the words, low-muttered:—

"There she must have breathed her last!"

After this speech, more sighing, accompanied by still surer signs of sorrow—sobs and weeping. As the moonbeams, pouring in through the open window, fall upon his face, their pale silvery light sparkles upon tears, streaming from hollow eyes, chasing one another down emaciated cheeks.

After surrendering himself some minutes to what appears a very agony of grief, he turns out of the sleeping chamber; passes through the narrow hall-way; and on into the porch. Not now the back one, but that facing front to the road.

On the other side of this is an open tract of ground, half cleared, half woodland; the former sterile, the latter scraggy. It seems to belong to no one, as if not worth claiming, or cultivating. It has been, in fact, an appanage of Colonel Armstrong's estate, who had granted it to the public as the site for a schoolhouse, and a common burying-ground—free to all desiring to be instructed, or needing to be interred. The schoolhouse has disappeared, but the cemetery is still there—only distinguishable from the surrounding *terrain* by some oblong elevations, having the well-known configuration of graves. There are in all about a score of them; some having a plain head-board—a piece of painted plank, with letters rudely limned, recording the name and age of him or her resting underneath.

Time and the weather have turned most of them greyish, with dates decayed, and names scarcely legible. But there is one upon which the paint shows fresh and white; in the clear moonlight gleaming like a meteor.

He who has explored the deserted dwelling, stands for a while with eyes directed on this recently erected memorial. Then, stepping down from the porch, he passes through the wicket-gate; crosses the road; and goes straight towards it, as though a hand beckoned him thither.

When close up, he sees it to be by a grave upon which the herbage has not yet grown.

The night is a cold one—chill for that Southern clime. The dew upon the withered grass of the grave turf is almost congealed into hoar frost, adding to its ghostly aspect.

The lettering upon the head-board is in shadow, the moon being on the opposite side.

But stooping forward, so as to bring his eyes close to the slab, he is enabled to decipher the inscription.

It is the simplest form of memento—only a name, with the date of death—

"Caroline Clancy,
Died January 18—"

After reading it, a fresh sob bursts from his bosom, new tears start from his eyes, and he flings himself down upon the grave. Disregarding the dew, thinking nought of the night's dullness, he stretches his arms over the cold turf, embracing it as though it were the warm body of one beloved!

For several minutes he remains in this attitude. Then, suddenly rising erect, as if impelled by some strong purpose, there comes from his lips, poured forth in wild passionate accent, the speeches:—

"Mother! dear mother! I am still living! I am here! And you, dead! No more to know—no more hear me! O God!"

They are the words of one frantic with grief, scarce knowing what he says.

Presently, sober reason seems to assert itself, and he again resumes speech; but now with voice, expression of features, attitude, everything so changed, that no one, seeing him the moment before, would believe it the same man.

Upon his countenance sternness has replaced sorrow; the soft lines have become rigid; the melancholy glance is gone, replaced by one that tells of determination—of vengeance.

Once more he glances down at the grave; then up to the sky, till the moon, coursing across high heaven, falls full upon his face. With his body slightly leaning backward, the arms along his sides, stiffly extended, the hands closed in convulsive clutch, he cries out:—

"By the heavens above—by the shade of my murdered mother, who lies beneath—I swear not to know rest, never more seek contentment, till I've punished her murderer! Night and day—through summer and winter—shall I search for him. Yes; search till I've found and chastised this man, this monster, who has brought blight on me, death to my mother, and desolation to our house! Ah! think not you can escape me! Texas, whither I know you have gone, will not be large enough to hold, nor its wilderness wide enough to screen you from my vengeance. If not found there, I shall follow you to the end of the earth—to the end of the earth, Richard Darke!"

"Charley Clancy!"

He turns as if a shot had struck him. He sees a man standing within six paces of the spot.

"Sime Woodsy!"

Chapter Thirty Six
"She is true—still true!"

The men who thus mutually pronounce each other's names are they who bear them. For it is, in truth, Charles Clancy who stands by the grave, and Simeon Woodley who has saluted him.

The surprise is all upon the side of Sime, and something more. He beholds a man all supposed to be dead, apparently returned from the tomb! Sees him in a place appropriate to resurrection, in the centre of a burying-ground, by the side of a recently made grave!

The backwoodsman is not above believing in spiritual existences, and for an instant he is under a spell of the supernatural.

It passes off on his perceiving that real flesh and blood is before him—Charles Clancy himself, and not his wraith.

He reaches this conclusion the sooner from having all along entertained a doubt about Clancy being dead. Despite the many circumstances pointing to, almost proving, his death, Woodley was never quite convinced of it. No one has taken so much trouble, or made so many efforts, to clear up the mystery. He has been foremost in the attempt to get punishment for the guilty man, as in the search for the body of his victim; both of which failed, to his great humiliation; his grief too, for he sincerely lamented his lost friend. Friends they were of no common kind. Not only had they oft hunted in company, but been together in Texas during Clancy's visit to the Lone Star State; together at Nacogdoches, where Borlasse received chastisement for stealing the horse; together saw the thief tied to the stake, Woodley being one of the stern jury who sentenced him to be whipped, and saw to the sentence being carried into execution.

The hunter had been to Natchez for the disposal of some pelts and deer-meat, a week's produce of his gun. Returning at a late hour, he must needs pass the cottage of the Clancys, his own humble domicile lying beyond. At sight of the deserted dwelling a painful throb passed through his heart, as he recalled the sad fate of those who once occupied it.

Making an effort to forget the gloomy record, he was riding on, when a figure flitting across the road arrested his attention. The clear moonlight showed the figure to be that of a man, and one whose movements betrayed absence of mind, if not actual aberration.

With the instinct habitual to the hunter Woodley at once tightened rein, coming to a stop under the shadow of the roadside trees. Sitting in his saddle he watched the midnight wanderer, whose eccentric movements continued to cause him surprise. He saw the latter walk on to the little woodland cemetery, take stand by the side of a grave, bending forward as if to read the epitaph on its painted slab. Soon after kneeling down as in prayer, then throwing himself prostrate along the earth. Woodley well knew the grave thus venerated. For he had himself assisted in digging and smoothing down the turf that covered it. He had also been instrumental in erecting the frail tablet that stood over. Who was this man, in the chill, silent hour of midnight, flinging himself upon it in sorrow or adoration?

With a feeling far different from curiosity, the hunter slipped out of his saddle, and leaving his horse behind, cautiously approached the spot. As the man upon the grave was too much absorbed with his own thoughts, he got close up without being observed; so close as to hear that strange adjuration, and see a face he never expected to look upon again. Despite the features, pale and marked with emaciation, the hollow cheeks, and sunken but glaring eyeballs, he recognised the countenance of Charles Clancy; soon as he did so, mechanically calling out his name.

Hearing his own pronounced, in response, Sime again exclaims, "Charley Clancy!" adding the interrogatory, "Is it yurself or yur shader?"

Then, becoming assured, he throws open his arms, and closes them around his old hunting associate.

Joy, at seeing the latter still alive, expels every trace of supernatural thought, and he gives way—to exuberant congratulation.

On Clancy's side the only return is a faint smile, with a few confused words, that seem to speak more of sadness than satisfaction. The expression upon his face is rather or chagrin, as if sorry at the encounter having occurred. His words are proof of it.

"Simeon Woodley," he says, "I should have been happy to meet you at any other time, but not now."

"Why, Clancy!" returns the hunter, supremely astonished at the coldness with which his warm advances have been received. "Surely you know I'm yur friend?"

"Right well I know it."

"Wal, then, believin' you to be dead—tho' I for one never felt sure o't—still thinking it might be—didn't I do all my possible to git justice done for ye?"

"You did. I've heard all—everything that has happened. Too much I've heard. O God! look there! Her grave—my murdered mother!"

"That's true. It killed the poor lady, sure enough."

"Yes; *he* killed her."

"I needn't axe who you refar to. I heerd you mention the name as I got up. We all know that Dick Darke has done whatever hez been done. We hed him put in prison, but the skunk got away from us, by the bribin' o' another skunk like hisself. The two went off thegither, an' no word's ever been since heerd 'bout eyther. I guess they've put for Texas, whar every scoundrel goes nowadays. Wal, Lordy! I'm so glad to see ye still alive. Won't ye tell me how it's all kim about?"

"In time I shall—not now."

"But why are ye displeezed at meetin' me—me that mayent be the grandest, but saitinly one o' the truest an' fastest o' yur friends?"

"I believe you are, Woodley—am sure of it. And, now that I think more of the matter, I'm not sorry at having met you. Rather am I glad of it; for I feel that I can depend upon you. Sime, will you go with me to Texas?"

"To Texas, or anywhars. In coorse I will. An' I reck'n we'll hev a good chance o' meetin' Dick Darke thar, an' then—"

"Meet him!" exclaimed Clancy, without waiting for the backwoodsman to finish his speech, "I'm sure of meeting him. I know the spot where. Ah, Simeon Woodley! 'tis a wicked world! Murderer as that man is, or supposed to be, there's a woman gone to Texas who will welcome him—receive him with open arms; lovingly entwine them around his neck. O God!"

"What woman air ye talkin' o', Clancy?"

"Her who has been the cause of all—Helen Armstrong."

"Wal; ye speak the truth partwise—but only partwise. Thar' can be no doubt o' Miss Armstrong's being the innercent cause of most o' what's been did. But as to her hevin' a likin' for Dick Darke, or puttin' them soft white arms o' hern willingly or lovingly aroun' his neck, thar you're clar off the trail—a million miles off o' it. That ere gurl hates the very sight o' the man, as Sime Woodley hev' good reason to know. An' I know, too, that she's nuts on another man—leastwise has been afore all this happened, and I reck'n still continue to be. Weemen—that air, weemen o' her kidney—ain't so changeable as people supposes. 'Bout Miss Helen Armstrong hevin' once been inclined to'ardst this other man, an' ready to freeze to him, I hev' the proof in my pocket."

"The proof! What are you speaking of?"

"A dookyment, Charley Clancy, that shed hev reached you long ago, seein' that it's got your name on it. Thar's both a letter and a pictur'. To examine 'em, we must have a clarer light than what's unner this tree, or kin be got out o' that 'ere moon. S'pose we adjern to my shanty. Thar we kin set the logs a-bleezin'. When they throw thar glint on the bit o' paper I've spoke about, I'll take long odds you won't be so down in the mouth. Come along, Charley Clancy! Ye've had a durned dodrotted deal both o' sufferin' an' sorrow. Be cheered! Sime Woodley's got somethin' thet's likely to put ye straight upright on your pins. It's only a bit o' pasteboard an' a sheet o' paper—both inside what in Natcheez they calls a enwelope. Come wi' me to the ole cabin, an' thar you kin take a squint at 'em."

Clancy's heart is too full to make rejoinder. The words of Woodley have inspired him with new hope. Health, long doubtful, seems suddenly restored to him. The colour comes back to his cheeks; and, as he follows the hunter to his hut, his stride exhibits all its old vigour and elasticity.

When the burning logs are kicked into a blaze; when by its light he reads Helen Armstrong's letter, and looks upon her photograph—on that sweet inscript intended for himself—he cries out in ecstasy,—

"Thank heaven! she is true—still true!"

No longer looks he the sad despairing invalid, but the lover—strong, proud, triumphant.

Chapter Thirty Seven
The home of the hunted slave

Throughout all these days where has Clancy been? Dead, and come to life again? Or, but half killed and recovered? Where the while hidden? And why? Questions that in quick succession occur to Simeon Woodley meeting him by his mother's grave.

Not all put then or there; but afterwards on the hunter's own hearth, as the two sit before the blazing logs, by whose light Clancy has read the letter so cheering him.

Then Woodley asks them, and impatiently awaits the answers.

The reader may be asking the same questions, and in like manner expecting reply.

He shall have it, as Woodley, not in a word or at once, but in a series of incidents, for the narration of which it is necessary to return upon time; as also to introduce a personage hitherto known but by repute—the fugitive slave, Jupiter.

"Jupe" is of the colour called "light mulatto," closely approximating to that of newly tanned leather. His features are naturally of a pleasing expression; only now and then showing fierce, when he reflects on a terrible flogging, and general ill treatment experienced, at the hands of the cruel master from whom he has absconded.

He is still but a young fellow, with face beardless; only two darkish streaks of down along the upper lip. But the absence of virile sign upon his cheeks has full compensation in a thick shock covering his crown, where the hair of Shem struggles for supremacy with the wool of Ham, and so successfully, as to result in a profusion of curls of which Apollo might be proud. The god of Beauty need not want a better form or face; nor he of Strength a set of sinews tougher, or limbs more tersely knit. Young though he may be, Jupe has performed feats of Herculean strength, requiring courage as well. No wonder at his having won Jule!

A free fearless spirit he: somewhat wild, though not heart-wicked; a good deal given to nocturnal excursions to neighbouring plantations; hence the infliction of the lash, which has finally caused his absconding from that of Ephraim Darke.

A merry jovial fellow he has been—would be still—but for the cloud of danger that hangs over him; dark as the den in which he has found a hiding-place. This is in the very heart and centre of the cypress swamp, as also in the heart and hollow of a cypress tree. No dead log, but a living growing trunk, which stands on a little eyot, not immediately surrounded by water, but marsh and mud. There is water beyond, on every side, extending more than a mile, with trees standing in and shadowing its stagnant surface.

On the little islet Nature has provided a home for the hunted fugitive—an asylum where he is safe from pursuit—beyond the scent of savage hounds, and the trailing of men almost as savage as they; for the place cannot be approached by water-craft, and is equally unapproachable by land. Even a dog could not make way through the quagmire of mud, stretching immediately around it to a distance of several hundred yards. If one tried, it would soon be snapped up by the great saurian, master of this darksome domain. Still is there a way to traverse the treacherous ground, for one knowing it, as does Darke's runaway slave. Here, again, has Nature intervened, lending her beneficent aid to the oppressed fleeing from oppression. The elements in their anger, spoken by tempest and tornado, have laid prostrate several trees, whose trunks, lying along the ooze, lap one another, and form a continuous causeway. Where there chances to be a break, human ingenuity has supplied the connecting link, making it as much as possible to look like Nature's own handiwork; though it is that of Jupiter himself. The hollow tree has given him a house ready built, with walls strong as any constructed by human hands, and a roof to shelter him from the rain. If no better than the lair of a wild beast, still is it snug and safe. The winds may blow above, the thunder rattle, and the lightning flash; but below, under the close canopy of leaves and thickly-woven parasites, he but hears the first in soft sighings, the second in distant reverberation, and sees the last only in faint phosphoric gleams. Far brighter the sparkle of insects that nightly play around the door of his dwelling.

A month has elapsed since the day when, incensed at the flogging received—this cruel as causeless—he ran away, resolved to risk everything, life itself, rather than longer endure the tyrannous treatment of the Darkes.

Though suspected of having taken refuge in the swamp, and there repeatedly sought for, throughout all this time he has contrived to baffle search. Nor has he either starved or suffered, except from solitude. Naturally of a social disposition, this has been irksome to him. Otherwise, he has comforts enough. Though rude his domicile, and remote from a market, it is sufficiently furnished and provided. The Spanish moss makes a soft couch, on which he can peacefully repose. And for food he need not be hard up, nor has he been for a single day. If it come to that, he can easily entrap an alligator, and make a meal off the tenderest part of its tail; this yielding a steak which, if not equal to best beef, is at all events eatable.

But Jupe has never been driven to diet on alligator meat too much of musky flavour. His usual fare is roast pork, with now and then broiled ham and chicken; failing which, a *fricassée* of 'coon or a *barbecue* of 'possum. No lack of bread besides—maize bread—in its various bakings of "pone," "hoe cake," and "dodger." Sometimes, too, he indulges in "Virginia biscuit," of sweetest and whitest flour.

The question is called up, Whence gets he such good things? The 'coon and 'possum may be accounted for, these being wild game of the woods, which he can procure by capture; but the other viands are domestic, and could only be obtained from a plantation.

And from one they are obtained—that of Ephraim Darke! How? Does Jupiter himself steal them? Not likely. The theft would be attended with too much danger. To attempt it would be to risk not only his liberty, but his life. He does not speculate on such rashness, feeling sure his larder will be plentifully supplied, as it has hitherto been—by a friend.

Who is he?

A question scarce requiring answer. It almost responds to itself, saying, "Blue Bill." Yes; the man who has kept the fugitive in provisions—the faithful friend and confederate—is no other than the coon-hunter.

Something more than bread and meat has Blue Bill brought to the swamp's edge, there storing them in a safe place of deposit, mutually agreed upon. Oft, as he starts forth "a-cooning," may he be observed with something swelling out his coat-pockets, seemingly carried with circumspection. Were they at such times searched, they would be found to contain a gourd of corn whisky, and beside it a plug of tobacco. But no one searches them; no one can guess at their contents—except Phoebe. To her the little matter of commissariat has necessarily been made known, by repeated drafts on her meat-safe, and calls upon her culinary skill. She has no jealous suspicion as to why her scanty store is thus almost daily depleted—no thought of its being for Brown Bet. She knows it is for "poor Jupe," and approves, instead of making protest.

Chapter Thirty Eight
An excursion by canoe

On that day when Dick Darke way-laid Charles Clancy, almost the same hour in which the strife is taking place between them, the fugitive slave is standing by the side of his hollow tree, on the bit of dry land around its roots.

His air and bearing indicate intention not to stay there long. Ever and anon he casts a glance upward, as if endeavouring to make out the time of day. A thing not easily done in that sombre spot. For he can see no sun, and only knows there is such by a faint reflection of its light scarce penetrating through the close canopy of foliage overhead. Still, this gradually growing fainter, tells him that evening is at hand.

Twilight is the hour he is waiting for, or rather some twenty minutes preceding it. For, to a minute he knows how long it will take him to reach the edge of the swamp, at a certain point to which he contemplates proceeding. It is the place of deposit for the stores he receives from the coon-hunter.

On this particular evening he expects something besides provender, and is more than usually anxious about it. Mental, not bodily food, is what he is craving. He hopes to get tidings of her, whose image is engraven upon his heart—his yellow girl, Jule. For under his coarse cotton shirt, and saddle-coloured skin, Jupe's breast burns with a love pure and passionate, as it could, be were the skin white, and the shirt finest linen.

He knows of all that is taking place in the plantations; is aware of what has been done by Ephraim Darke in the matter of the mortgage, and what is about to be done by Colonel Armstrong. The coon-hunter has kept him posted up in everything—facts and fancies, rumours and realities.

One of the last, and latest, is the intention of the Armstrongs to remove from the neighbourhood. He has already heard of this, as also their destination. It might not so much concern him, but for the implied supposition that his sweetheart will be going along with them. In fact, he feels sure of it; an assurance that, so far from causing regret, rather gives him gladness. It promises a happier future for all. Jupe, too, has had thoughts about Texas. Not that the Lone Star State is at all a safe asylum for such as he; but upon its wild borderland there may be a chance for him to escape the bondage of civilisation, by alliance with the savage! Even this idea of a freedom far off, difficult of realisation, and if realised not so delectable, has nevertheless been flitting before the mind of the mulatto. Any life but that of a slave! His purpose, modified by late events and occurrences, is likely to be altogether changed by them. His Jule will be going to Texas, along with her master and young mistresses. In the hope of rejoining her, he will go there too—as soon as he can escape to the swamp.

On this evening he expects later news, with a more particular account of what is about to be done. Blue Bill is to bring them, and direct from Jule, whom the coon-hunter has promised to see. Moreover, Jupe has a hope of being able to see her himself, previous to departure; and to arrange an interview, through the intervention of his friend, is the matter now most on his mind. No wonder, then, his scanning the sky, or its faint reflection, with glances that speak impatience.

At length, becoming satisfied it must be near night, he starts off from the eyot, and makes way along the causeway furnished by the trunks of the fallen trees. This serves him only for some two hundred yards, ending on the edge of deep water, beyond which the logs lie submerged. The last of them showing above, is the wreck of a grand forest giant, with branches undecayed, and still carrying the parasite of Spanish moss in profusion. This hanging down in streamers, scatters over the surface and dips underneath, like the tails of white horses wading knee-deep. In its midst appears something, which would escape the eye of one passing carelessly by. On close scrutiny it is seen to be a craft of rude construction—a log with the heart wood removed—in short, a canoe of the kind called "dug-out."

No surprise to the runaway slave seeing it there; no more at its seeming to have been placed in concealment. It is his own property, by himself secreted.

Gliding down through the moss-bedecked branches, he steps into it; and, after balancing himself aboard, dips his paddle into the water, and sets the dug-out adrift.

A way for a while through thick standing trunks that require many tortuous turnings to avoid them.

At length a creek is reached, a *bayou* with scarce any current; along which the canoe-man continues his course, propelling the craft up-stream. He has made way for something more than a mile, when a noise reaches his ear, causing him to suspend stroke, with a suddenness that shows alarm.

It is only the barking of a dog; but to him no sound could be more significant—more indicative of danger.

On its repetition, which almost instantly occurs, he plucks his paddle out of the water, leaving the dug-out to drift.

On his head is a wool hat of the cheap fabric supplied by the Penitentiaries of the Southern States, chiefly for negro wear. Tilting it to one side, he bends low, and listens.

Certainly a dog giving tongue—but in tone strange, unintelligible. It is a hound's bay, but not as on slot, or chase.

It is a howl, or plaintive whine, as if the animal were tied up, or being chastised!

After listening to it for some time—for it is nearly continuous—the mulatto makes remark to himself. "There's no danger in the growl of that dog. I know it nearly as well as my own voice. It's the deer-hound that belong to young Masser Clancy. He's no slave-catcher."

Re-assured he again dips his blade, and pushes on as before.

But now on the alert, he rows with increased caution, and more noiselessly than ever. So slight is the plash of his paddle, it does not hinder him from noting every sound—the slightest that stirs among the cypresses.

The only one heard is the hound's voice, still in whining, wailing note.

"Lor!" he exclaims once more, staying his stroke, and giving way to conjectures, "what can be the matter with the poor brute? There must be something amiss to make it cry; out in that strain. Hope 'taint no mischance happened its young masser, the best man about all these parts. Come what will, I'll go to the ground, an' see."

A few more strokes carries the canoe on to the place, where its owner has been accustomed to moor it, for meeting Blue Bill; and where on this evening, as on others, he has arranged his interview with the coon-hunter. A huge sycamore, standing half on land, half in the water, with long outstretching roots laid bare by the wash of the current, affords him a safe point of debarkation. For on these his footsteps will leave no trace, and his craft can be stowed in concealment.

It chances to be near the spot where the dog is still giving tongue—apparently not more than two hundred yards off.

Drawing the dug-out in between the roots of the sycamore, and there roping it fast, the mulatto mounts upon the bank. Then after standing some seconds to listen, he goes gliding off through the trees.

If cautious while making approach by water, he is even more so on the land; so long being away from it, he there feels less at home.

Guided by the yelps of the animal, that reach him in quick repetition, he has no difficulty about the direction—no need for aught save caution. The knowledge that he may be endangering his liberty—his life—stimulates him to observe this. Treading as if on eggs, he glides from trunk to trunk; for a time sheltering behind each, till assured he can reach another without being seen.

He at length arrives at one, in rear of which he remains for a more prolonged period.

For he now sees the dog—as conjectured, Clancy's deer-hound. The animal is standing, or rather crouching, beside a heap of moss, ever and anon raising its head and howling, till the forest is filled with the plaintive refrain.

For what is it lamenting? What can the creature mean? Interrogatives which the mulatto puts to himself; for there is none else to whom he may address them. No man near—at least none in sight. No living thing, save the hound itself.

Is there anything dead? Question of a different kind which now occurs, causing him to stick closer than ever to his cover behind the tree.

Still there is nought to give him a clue to the strange behaviour of the hound. Had he been there half-an-hour sooner, he need not now be racking his brain with conjectures. For he would have witnessed the strife, with all the incidents succeeding, and already known to the reader—with others not yet related, in which the hound was itself sole actor. For the animal, after being struck by Darke's bullet, did not go directly home. There could be no home where its master was not; and it knew he would not be there. In the heart of the faithful creature, while retreating, affection got the better of its fears; and once more turning, it trotted back to the scene of the tragedy.

This time not hindered from approaching the spot; the assassin—as he supposed himself—having wound up his cruel work, and hurriedly made away. Despite the shroud thrown over its master's body, the dog soon discovered it—dead, no doubt the animal believed, while tearing aside the moss with claws and teeth, and afterwards with warm tongue licking the cold face.

Believing it still, as crouched beside the seeming corpse it continues its plaintive lamentation, which yet perplexes the runaway, while alarming him.

Not for long does he listen to it. There is no one in sight, therefore no one to be feared. Certainly not Charles Clancy, nor his dog. With confidence thus restored, he forsakes his place of concealment, and strides on to the spot where the hound has couched itself. At his approach the animal starts up with an angry growl, and advances to meet him. Then, as if in the mulatto recognising a friend of its master, it suddenly changes tone, bounding towards and fawning upon him.

After answering its caresses, Jupe continues on till up to the side of the moss pile. Protruding from it he sees a human head, with face turned towards him—the lips apart, livid, and bloodless; the teeth clenched; the eyes fixed and filmy.

And beneath the half-scattered heap he knows there is a body; believes it to be dead.

He has no other thought, than that he is standing beside a corpse.

Chapter Thirty Nine
Is it a corpse?

"Surely Charl Clancy!" exclaims the mulatto as soon as setting eyes on the face. "Dead—shot—murdered!"

For a time he stands aghast, with arms upraised, and eyes staring wildly.

Then, as if struck by something in the appearance of the corpse, he mutteringly interrogates: "Is he sure gone dead?"

To convince himself he kneels down beside the body, having cleared away the loose coverlet still partially shrouding it.

He sees the blood, and the wound from which it is yet welling. He places his hand over the heart with a hope it may still be beating.

Surely it is! Or is he mistaken?

The pulse should be a better test; and he proceeds to feel it, taking the smooth white wrist between his rough brown fingers.

"It beats! I do believe it does!" are his words, spoken hopefully.

For some time he retains his grasp of the wrist. To make more sure, he tries the artery at different points, with a touch as tender, as if holding in his hand the life of an infant.

He becomes certain that the heart throbs; that there is yet breath in the body.

What next? What is he to do?

Hasten to the settlement, and summon a doctor?

He dares not do this; nor seek assistance of any kind. To show himself to a white man would be to go back into hated bondage—to the slavery from which he has so lately, and at risk of life, escaped. It would be an act of grand generosity—a self-sacrifice—more than man, more than human being is capable of. Could a poor runaway slave be expected to make it?

Some sacrifice he intends making, as may be gathered from his muttered words:

"Breath in his body, or no breath, it won't do to leave it lyin' here. Poor young gen'leman! The best of them all about these parts. What would Miss

Helen say if she see him now? What will she say when she hear o' it? I wonder who's done it? No, I don't—not a bit. There's only one likely. From what Jule told me, I thought 't would come to this, some day. Wish I could a been about to warn him. Well, it's too late now. The Devil has got the upper hand, as seem always the way. Ah! what 'll become o' Miss Armstrong? She loved him, sure as I love Jule, or Jule me."

For a time he stands considering what he ought to do. The dread spectacle has driven out of his mind all thoughts of his appointment with Blue Bell; just as what preceded hindered the coon-hunter from keeping it with him. For the latter, terrified, has taken departure from the dangerous place, and is now hastening homeward.

Only for a short while does the mulatto remain hesitating. His eyes are upon the form at his feet. He sees warm blood still oozing from the wound, and knows, or hopes, Clancy is not dead. Something must be done immediately.

"Dead or alive," he mutters. "I mustn't, shan't leave him here. The wolves would soon make bare bones of him, and the carrion crows peck that handsome face of his. They shan't either get at him. No. He's did me a kindness more'n once, it's my turn now. Slave, mulatto, nigger, as they call me, I'll show them that under a coloured skin there can be gratitude, as much as under a white one—may be more. Show them! What am I talkin' 'bout? There's nobody to see. Good thing for me there isn't. But there might be, if I stand shilly-shallying here. I mustn't a minute longer."

Bracing himself for an effort, he opens his arms, and stoops as to take up the body. Just then the hound, for some time silent, again gives out its mournful monotone—continuing the dirge the runaway had interrupted.

Suddenly he rises erect, and glances around, a new fear showing upon his face. For he perceives a new danger in the presence of the dog.

"What's to be done with it?" he asks himself. "I daren't take it along. 'Twould be sure some day make a noise, and guide the nigger-hunters to my nest—I mustn't risk that. To leave the dog here may be worse still. It'll sure follow me toatin away its master, an' if it didn't take to the water an' swim after 'twould know where the dug-out lay, an' might show them the place. I shan't make any tracks; for all that they'd suspect somethin', down the creek, an' come that way sarchin'. 'Twont do take the dog—'twont do to leave it—what *will* do?"

The series of reflections, and questions, runs rapidly as thought itself. And to the last, quick as thought, comes an answer—a plan which promises a solution of the difficulty. He thinks of killing the dog—cutting its throat with his knife.

Only for an instant is the murderous intent in his mind. In the next he changes it, saying:

"I can't do that—no; the poor brute so 'fectionate an' faithful! 'Twould be downright cruel. A'most the same as murderin' a man. I wont do it."

Another pause spent in considering; another plan soon suggesting itself.

"Ah!" he exclaims, with air showing satisfied, "I have it now. That'll be just the thing."

The "thing" thus approved of, is to tie the hound to a tree, and so leave it.

First to get hold of it. For this he turns towards the animal, and commences coaxing it nearer. "Come up, ole fella. You aint afeerd o' me. I'm Jupe, your master's friend, ye know. There's a good dog! Come now; come!"

The deer-hound, not afraid, does not flee him; and soon he has his hands upon it.

Pulling a piece of cord out of his pocket, he continues to apostrophise it, saying:

"Stand still, good dog! Steady, and let me slip this round your neck. Don't be skeeart. I'm not goin' to hang you—only to keep you quiet a bit."

The animal makes no resistance; but yields to the manipulation, believing it to be by a friendly hand, and for its good.

In a trice the cord is knotted around its neck; and the mulatto looks out for a tree to which he may attach it.

A thought now strikes him, another step calling for caution. It will not do to let the dog see him go off, or know the direction he takes; for some one will be sure to come in search of Clancy, and set the hound loose. Still, time will likely elapse; the scent will be cold, as far as the creek's edge, and cannot be lifted. With the water beyond there will be no danger.

The runaway, glancing around, espies a palmetto brake; these forming a sort of underwood in the cypress forest, their fan-shaped leaves growing on stalks that rise directly out of the earth to a height of three or four feet, covering the ground with a *chevaux de frise* of deepest green, but hirsute and spinous as hedgehogs.

The very place for his purpose. So mutters he to himself, as he conducts the dog towards it. Still thinking the same, after he has tied the animal to a palmetto shank near the middle of the brake, and there left it. He goes off, regardless of its convulsive struggles to set itself free, with accompanying yelps, by which the betrayed quadruped seems to protest against such unexpected as ill-deserved, captivity.

Not five minutes time has all this action occupied. In less than five more a second chapter is complete, by the carrying of Clancy's body—it may be his corpse—to the creek, and laying it along the bottom of the canoe.

Notwithstanding the weight of his burden, the mulatto, a man of uncommon strength, takes care to make no footmarks along the forest path, or at the point of embarkation. The ground, thickly strewn with the leaves of the deciduous *taxodium*, does not betray a trace, any more than if he were treading on thrashed straw.

Undoing the slip-knot of his painter, he shoves the canoe clear of its entanglement among the roots of the tree. Then plying his paddle, directs its course down stream, silently as he ascended, but with look more troubled, and air intensely solemnal. This continuing, while he again shoulders the insensible form, and carries it along the causeway of logs, until he has laid it upon soft moss within the cavity of the cypress—his own couch. Then, once more taking Clancy's wrist between his fingers, and placing his ear opposite the heart, he feels the pulse of the first, and listens for the beatings of the last.

A ray of joy illuminates his countenance, as both respond to his examination. It grows brighter, on perceiving a muscular movement of the limbs, late rigid and seemingly inanimate, a light in the eyes looking like life; above all, words from the lips so long mute. Words low-murmured, but still distinguishable; telling him a tale, at the same time giving its interpretation. That in this hour of his unconsciousness Clancy should in his speech couple the names of Richard Darke and Helen Armstrong is a fact strangely significant, he does the same for many days, in his delirious ravings; amid which the mulatto, tenderly nursing him, gets the clue to most of what has happened.

Clearer when his patient, at length restored to consciousness, confides everything to the faithful fellow who has so befriended him. Every circumstance he ought to know, at the same time imparting secrecy.

This, so closely kept, that even Blue Bill, while himself disclosing many an item, of news exciting the settlement, is not entrusted with one the most interesting, and which would have answered the questions on every tongue:—"What has become of Charles Clancy?" and "Where is his body?"

Clancy still in it, living and breathing, has his reasons for keeping the fact concealed. He has succeeded in doing so till this night; till encountering Simeon Woodley by the side of his mother's tomb.

And now on Woodley's own hearth, after all has been explained, Clancy once more returns to speak of the purpose he has but half communicated to the hunter.

"You say, Sime, I can depend upon you to stand by me?"

"Ye may stake yur life on that. Had you iver reezun to misdoubt me?"

"No—never."

"But, Charley, ye hain't tolt me why ye appeared a bit displeezed at meetin' me the night. That war a mystery to me."

"There was nothing in it, Sime. Only that I didn't care to meet, or be seen by, any one till I should be strong enough to carry out my purpose. It would, in all probability, be defeated were the world to know I am still alive. That secret I shall expect you to keep."

"You kin trust to me for that; an' yur plans too. Don't be afeerd to confide them to Sime Woodley. Maybe he may help ye to gettin' 'em shipshape."

Clancy is gratified at this offer of aid. For he knows that in the backwoodsman he will find his best ally; that besides his friendship tested and proved, he is the very man to be with him in the work he has cut out for himself—a purpose which has engrossed his thoughts ever since consciousness came back after his long dream of delirium. It is that so solemnly proclaimed, as he stood in the cemetery, with no thought of any one overhearing him.

He had then three distinct passions impelling him to the stern threat— three reasons, any of them sufficient to ensure his keeping it. First, his own wrongs. True the attempt at assassinating him had failed; still the criminality remained the same. But the second had succeeded. His mother's corpse was under the cold sod at his feet, her blood calling to him for vengeance. And still another passion prompted him to seek it—perhaps the darkest of all, jealousy in its direst shape, the sting from a love promised but unbestowed. For the coon-hunter had never told Jupe of Helen Armstrong's letter. Perhaps, engrossed with other cares, he had forgotten it; or, supposing the circumstance known to all, had not thought it worth communicating. Clancy, therefore, up to that hour, believed his sweetheart not only false to himself, but having favoured his rival.

The bitter delusion, now removed, does not in any way alter his determination. That is fixed beyond change, as he tells Simeon Woodley while declaring it. He will proceed to Texas in quest of the assassin—there kill him.

"The poor old place!" he says, pointing to the cottage as he passes it on return to the swamp. "No more mine! Empty—every stick sold out of it, I've heard. Well, let them go! I go to Texas."

"An' I with ye. To Texas, or anywhars, in a cause like your'n, Clancy. Sime Woodley wouldn't desarve the name o' man, to hang back on a trail like that. But, say! don't ye think we'd be more likely o' findin' the game by stayin' hyar? Ef ye make it known that you're still alive, then thar ain't been no murder done, an' Dick Darke 'll be sure to kum home agin."

"If he came what could I do? Shoot him down like a dog, as he thought he had me? That would make *me* a murderer, with good chance of being hanged for it. In Texas it is different. There, if I can meet him—. But we only lose time in talking. You say, Woodley, you'll go with me?"

"In course I've said it, and I'll do as I've sayed. There's no backin' out in this child. Besides, I war jest thinkin' o' a return to Texas, afore I seed you. An' thar's another 'll go along wi' us; that's young Ned Heywood, a friend o' your'n most as much as myself. Ned's wantin' bad to steer torst the Lone Star State. So, thar'll be three o' us on the trail o' Dick Darke."

"There will be *four* of us."

"Four! Who's the t'other, may I axe?"

"A man I've sworn to take to Texas along with me. A brave, noble man, though his skin be—. But never mind now. I'll tell you all about it by-and-by. Meanwhile we must get ready. There's not a moment to lose. A single day wasted, and I may be too late to settle scores with Richard Darke. There's some one else in danger from him—"

Here Clancy's utterance becomes indistinct, as if his voice were stifled by strong emotion.

"Some one else!" echoes Sime, interrupting; "who mout ye mean, Clancy?"

"Her."

"That air's Helen Armstrong. I don't see how she kin be in any danger from Dick Darke. Thet ere gurl hev courage enuf to take care o' herself, an' the spirit too. Besides, she'll hev about her purtectors a plenty."

"There can be no safety against an assassin. Who should know that better than I? Woodley, that man's wicked enough for anything."

"Then, let's straight to Texas!"

Chapter Forty
"Across the Sabine"

At the time when Texas was an independent Republic, and not, as now, a State of the Federal Union, the phrase, "Across the Sabine" was one of noted signification.

Its significance lay in the fact, that fugitives from States' justice, once over the Sabine, felt themselves safe; extradition laws being somewhat loose in the letter, and more so in the spirit, at any attempt made to carry them into execution.

As a consequence, the fleeing malefactor could breathe freely—even the murderer imagine the weight of guilt lifted from off his soul—the moment his foot touched Texan soil.

On a morning of early spring—the season when settlers most affect migration to the Lone Star State—a party of horsemen is seen crossing the boundary river, with faces turned toward Texas. The place where they are making passage is not the usual emigrants' crossing—on the old Spanish military road between Natchitoches and Nacogdoches,—but several miles above, at a point where the stream is, at certain seasons, fordable. From the Louisiana side this ford is approached through a tract of heavy timber, mostly pine forest, along a trail little used by travellers, still less by those who enter Texas with honest intent, or leave Louisiana with unblemished reputations.

That these horsemen belong not to either category can be told at a glance. They have no waggons, nor other wheeled vehicles, to give them the semblance of emigrants; no baggage to embarrass them on their march. Without it, they might be explorers, land speculators, surveyors, or hunters. But no. They have not the look of persons who pursue any of these callings; no semblance of aught honest or honourable. In all there are twelve of them; among them not a face but speaks of the Penitentiary—not one which does not brighten up, and show more cheerful, as the hooves of their horses strike the Texan bank of the Sabine.

While on the *terrain* of Louisiana, they have been riding fast and hard—silent, and with pent-up thoughts, as though pursuers were after. Once on the Texan side all seem relieved, as if conscious of having at length reached a haven of safety.

Then he who appears leader of the party, reining up his horse, breaks silence, saying—

"Boys! I reckon we may take a spell o' rest here. We're now in Texas, whar freemen needn't feel afeard. If thar's been any fools followin' us, I guess they'll take care to keep on t'other side o' the river. Tharfor, let's dismount and have a bit o' breakfast under the shadder o' these trees. After we've done that, we can talk about what shed be our next move. For my part, I feel sleepy as a 'possum. That ar licker o' Naketosh allers knocks me up for a day or two. This time, our young friend Quantrell here, has given us a double dose, the which I for one won't get over in a week."

It is scarcely necessary to say the speaker is Jim Borlasse, and those spoken to his drinking companions in the Choctaw Chief.

To a man, they all make affirmative response. Like himself, they too are fatigued—dead done up by being all night in the saddle,—to say nought about the debilitating effects of their debauch, and riding rapidly with beard upon the shoulder, under the apprehension that a sheriff and posse may be coming on behind. For, during the period of their sojourn in Natchitoches, nearly every one of them has committed some crime that renders him amenable to the laws.

It may be wondered how such roughs could carry on and escape observation, much more, punishment. But at the time Natchitoches was a true frontier town, and almost every day witnessed the arrival and departure of characters "queer" as to dress and discipline—the trappers and prairie traders. Like the sailor in port, when paid off and with full pockets—making every effort to deplete them—so is the trapper during his stay at a fort, or settlement. He does things that seem odd, are odd, to the extreme of eccentricity. Among such the late guests of the Choctaw Chief would not, and did not, attract particular attention. Not much was said or thought of them, till after they were gone; and then but by those who had been victimised, resignedly abandoning claims and losses with the laconic remark, "The scoundrels have G.T.T."

It was supposed the assassin of Charles Clancy had gone with them; but this, affecting the authorities more than the general public, was left to the former to deal with; and in a land of many like affairs, soon ceased to be spoken of.

Borlasse's visit to Natchitoches had not been for mere pleasure. It was business that took him thither—to concoct a scheme of villainy such as might be supposed unknown among Anglo-Saxon people, and practised only by those of Latinic descent, on the southern side of the Rio Grande.

But robbery is not confined to any race; and on the borderland of Texas may be encountered brigandage as rife and ruthless as among the mountains of the Sierra Morena, or the defiles of the Appenines.

That the Texan bandit has succeeded in arranging everything to his satisfaction may be learnt from his hilarious demeanour, with the speech now addressed to his associates:—

"Boys!" he says, calling them around after they have finished eating, and are ready to ride on, "We've got a big thing before us—one that'll beat horse-ropin' all to shucks. Most o' ye, I reckin, know what I mean; 'ceptin', perhaps, our friends here, who've just joined us."

The speaker looks towards Phil Quantrell *alias* Dick Darke, and another, named Walsh, whom he knows to be Joe Harkness, ex-jailer.

After glancing from one to the other, he continues—

"I'll take charge o' tellin' *them* in good time; an', I think, can answer for their standin' by us in the bizness. Thar's fifty thousand dollars, clar cash, at the bottom of it; besides sundries in the trinket line. The question then is, whether we'd best wait till this nice assortment of property gets conveyed to the place intended for its destination, or make a try to pick it up on the way. What say ye, fellers? Let every man speak his opinion; then I'll give mine."

"You're sure o' whar they're goin', capting?" asks one of his following. "You know the place?"

"Better'n I know the spot we're now camped on. Ye needn't let that trouble ye. An' most all o' ye know it yourselves. As good luck has it, 'taint over twenty mile from our old stampin' groun' o' last year. Thar, if we let em' alone, everythin' air sure to be lodged 'ithin less'n a month from now. Thar, we'll find the specie, trinkets, an' other fixins not forgetting the petticoats—sure as eggs is eggs. To some o' ye it may appear only a question o' time and patience. I'm sorry to tell ye it may turn out somethin' more."

"Why d'ye say that, capting? What's the use o' waitin' till they get there?"

Chapter Forty One
A repentant sinner

Nearly three weeks after Borlasse and his brigands crossed the Sabine, a second party is seen travelling towards the same river through the forests of Louisiana, with faces set for the same fording-place.

In number they are but a third of that composing the band of Borlasse; as there are only four of them. Three are on horseback, the fourth bestriding a mule.

The three horsemen are white; the mule-rider a mulatto.

The last is a little behind; the distance, as also a certain air of deference—to say nothing of his coloured skin—proclaiming him a servant, or slave.

Still further rearward, and seemingly careful to keep beyond reach of the hybrid's heels, is a large dog—a deer-hound. The individuals of this second cavalcade will be easily identified, as also the dog that accompanies it. The three whites are Charles Clancy, Simeon Woodley, and Ned Heywood; he with the tawny complexion Jupiter; while the hound is Clancy's—the same he had with him when shot down by Richard Darke.

Strange they too should be travelling, as if under an apprehension of being pursued! Yet seems it so, judging from the rapid pace at which they ride, and there anxious glances occasionally cast behind. It is so; though for very different reasons from those that affected the freebooters.

None of the white men has reason to fear for himself—only for the fugitive slave whom they are assisting to escape from slavery. Partly on this account are they taking the route, described as rarely travelled by honest men. But not altogether. Another reason has influenced their selection of it while in Natchitoches they too have put up at the Choctaw Chief; their plans requiring that privacy which an obscure hostelry affords. To have been seen with Jupiter at the Planter's House might have been for some Mississippian planter to remember, and identify, him as the absconded slave of Ephraim Darke. A *contretemps* less likely to occur at the Choctaw Chief, and there stayed they. It would have been Woodley's choice anyhow; the hunter having frequently before made this house his home; there meeting many others of his kind and calling.

On this occasion his sojourn in it has been short; only long enough for him and his travelling companions to procure a mount for their journey into Texas. And while thus occupied they have learnt something, which determined them as to the route they should take. Not the direct road for Nacogdoches by which Colonel Armstrong and his emigrants have gone, some ten days before; but a trail taken by another party that had been staying at the Choctaw Chief, and left Natchitoches at an earlier period — that they are now on.

Of this party Woodley has received information, sufficiently minute for him to identify more than one of the personages composing it. Johnny has given him the clue. For the Hibernian innkeeper, with his national habit of wagging a free tongue, has besides a sort of liking for Sime, as an antipathy towards Sime's old enemy, Jim Borlasse. The consequence of which has been a tale told in confidence to the hunter, about the twelve men late sojourning at the Choctaw Chief, that was kept back from the Sheriff on the morning after their departure. The result being, that in choice of a route to Texas, Woodley has chosen that by which they are now travelling. For he knows — has told Clancy — that by it has gone Jim Borlasse, and along with him Richard Darke.

The last is enough for Clancy. He is making towards Texas with two distinct aims, the motives diametrically opposite. One is to comfort the woman he loves, the other to kill the man he hates.

For both he is eagerly impatient; but he has vowed that the last shall be first — sworn it upon the grave of his mother.

Having reached the river, and crossed it, Clancy and his travelling companions, just as Borlasse and his, seek relaxation under the shade of the trees. Perhaps, not quite so easy in their minds. For the murderer, on entering Texas, may feel less anxiety than he who has with him a runaway slave!

Still in that solitary place — on a path rarely trodden — there is no great danger; and knowing this, they dismount and make their bivouac *sans souci*. The spot chosen is the same as was occupied by Borlasse and his band. Near the bank of the river is a spreading tree, underneath which a log affords sitting accommodation for at least a score of men. Seated on this, smoking his pipe, after a refection of corn-bread and bacon, Sime Woodley unburdens himself of some secrets he obtained in the Choctaw Chief, which up to this time he has kept back from the others.

"Boys!" he begins, addressing himself to Clancy and Heywood, the mulatto still keeping respectfully apart. "We're now on a spot, whar less'n two weeks agone, sot or stud, two o' the darndest scoundrels as iver made futmark on Texan soil. *You* know one o' 'em, Ned Heywood, but not the tother. Charley Clancy hev akwaintance wi' both, an' a ugly reccoleckshun o' them inter the bargain."

The hunter pauses in his speech, takes a whiff or two from his pipe, then resumes:—

"They've been hyar sure. From what thet fox, Johnny, tolt me, they must a tuk this trail. An' as they hed to make quick tracks arter leavin' Naketosh, they'd be tired on gettin' this fur, an' good as sartin to lay up a bit. Look! thar's the ashes o' thar fire, whar I 'spose they cooked somethin'. Thar hain't been a critter crossed the river since the big rain, else we'd a seed tracks along the way. For they started jest the day afore the rain; and that ere fire hez been put out by it. Ye kin tell by them chunks showin' only half consoomed. Yis, by the Eturnal! Roun' the bleeze o' them sticks has sot seven, eight, nine, or may be a dozen, o' the darndest cut-throats as ever crossed the Sabine; an' that's sayin' a goodish deal. Two o' them I kin swar to bein' so; an' the rest may be counted the same from their kumpny—that kumpny bein' Jim Borlasse an' Dick Darke."

After thus delivering himself, the hunter remains apparently reflecting, not on what he has said, but what they ought to do. Clancy has been all the while silent, brooding with clouded brow—only now and then showing a faint smile as the hound comes up, and licks his outstretched hand. Heywood has nothing to say; while Jupiter is not expected to take any part in the conversation.

For a time they all seem under a spell of lethargy—the lassitude of fatigue. They have ridden a long way, and need rest. They might go to sleep alongside the log, but none of them thinks of doing so, least of all Clancy. There is that in his breast forbidding sleep, and he is but too glad when Woodley's next words arouse him from the torpid repose to which he has been yielding. These are:—

"Now we've struck thar trail, what, boys, d'ye think we'd best do?"

Neither of the two replying, the hunter continues:—

"To the best of my opeenyun, our plan will be to put straight on to whar Planter Armstrong intends settin' up his sticks. I know the place 'most as well as the public squar o' Natchez. This chile intends jeinin' the ole kurnel, anyhow. As for you, Charley Clancy, we know whar ye want to go, an' the game ye intend trackin' up. Wal; ef you'll put trust in what Sime Woodley say, he sez this: ye'll find that game in the neighbourhood o' Helen Armstrong;—nigh to her as it dar' ventur'."

The final words have an inflammatory effect upon Clancy. He springs up from the log, and strides over the ground, with a wild look and strangely excited air. He seems impatient to be back in his saddle.

"In coorse," resumes Woodley, "we'll foller the trail o' Borlasse an' his lot. It air sure to lead to the same place. What they're arter 'tain't eezy to tell. Some deviltry, for sartin. They purtend to make thar livin' by ropin' wild horses? I guess he gits more by takin' them as air tame;—as you, Clancy, hev reezun to know. I hain't a doubt he'd do wuss than that, ef opportunity offered. Thar's been more'n one case o' highway robbery out thar in West Texas, on emigrant people goin' that way; an' I don't know a likelier than Borlasse to a had a hand in't. Ef Kurnel Armstrong's party wan't so strong as 'tis, an' the kurnel hisself a old campayner, I mout hev my fears for 'em. I reckin they're safe enuf. Borlasse an' his fellurs won't dar tech them. Johnny sez thar war but ten or twelve in all. Still, tho' they moutn't openly attack the waggon train, thar's jest a chance o' their hangin' on its skirts, an' stealin' somethin' from it. Ye heerd in Naketosh o' a young Creole planter, by name Dupray, who's goed wi' Armstrong, an's tuk a big count o' dollars along. Jest the bait to temp Jim Borlasse; an' as for Dick Darke, thar's somethin' else to temp him. So—"

"Woodley!" exclaims Clancy, without waiting for the hunter to conclude; "we must be off from here. For God's sake let us go!"

His comrades, divining the cause of Clancy's impatience, make no attempt to restrain him. They have rested and sufficiently refreshed themselves. There is no reason for their remaining any longer on the ground.

Rising simultaneously, each unhitches his horse, and stands by the stirrup, taking in the slack of his reins.

Before they can spring into their saddles, the deer-hound darts off from their midst—as he does so giving out a growl.

The stroke of a hoof tells them of some one approaching, and the next moment a horseman is seen through the trees.

Apparently undaunted, he comes on towards their camp ground; but when near enough to have fair view of their faces, he suddenly reins up, and shows signs of a desire to retreat.

If this be his intention, it is too late.

Before he can wrench round his horse a rifle is levelled, its barrel bearing upon his body; while a voice sounds threateningly in his ears, in clear tone, pronouncing the words,—

"Keep yur ground, Joe Harkness! Don't attempt retreetin'. If ye do, I'll send a bullet through ye sure as my name's Sime Woodley."

The threat is sufficient. Harkness—for it is he—ceases tugging upon his rein, and permits his horse to stand still.

Then, at a second command from Woodley, accompanied by; a similar menace, he urges the animal into action, and moves on towards their bivouac.

In less than sixty seconds after, he is in their midst, dismounted and down upon his knees, piteously appealing to them to spare his life.

The ex-jailor's story is soon told, and that without any reservation. The man who has connived at Richard Darke's escape, and made money by the connivance, is now more than repentant for his dereliction of duty. For he has not only been bullied by Borlasse's band, but stripped of his ill-gotten gains. Still more, beaten, and otherwise so roughly handled that he has been long trying to get quit of their company. Having stolen away from their camp—while the robbers were asleep—he is now returning along the trail they had taken into Texas, on his way back to the States, with not much left him, except a very sorry horse and a sorrowing heart.

His captors soon discover that, with his sorrow, there is an admixture of spite against his late associates. Against Darke in particular, who has proved ungrateful for the great service done him.

All this does Harkness communicate to them, and something besides.

Something that sets Clancy well-nigh crazed, and makes almost as much impression upon his fellow-travellers.

After hearing it they bound instantly to their saddles, and spur away from the spot; Harkness, as commanded, following at their horses' heels. This he does without daring to disobey; trotting after, in company with the dog, seemingly less cur than himself.

They have no fear of his falling back. Woodley's rifle, whose barrel has been already borne upon him, can be again brought to the level in an instant of time.

The thought holds him secure, as if a trail-rope attached him to the tail of the hunter's horse.

Chapter Forty Two
The prairie caravan

Picture in imagination meadows, on which scythe of mower has never cut sward, nor haymaker set foot; meadows loaded with such luxuriance of vegetation—lush, tall grass—that tons of hay might be garnered off a single acre; meadows of such extent, that in speaking of them you may not use the word acres, but miles, even this but faintly conveying the idea of their immensity; in fancy summon up such a scene, and you will have before you what is a reality in Texas.

In seeming these plains have no boundary save the sky—no limit nearer than the horizon. And since to the eye of the traveller this keeps continually changing, he may well believe them without limit at all, and fancy himself moving in the midst of a green sea, boundless as ocean itself, his horse the boat on which he has embarked.

In places this extended surface presents a somewhat monotonous aspect, though it is not so everywhere. Here and there it is pleasantly interspersed with trees, some standing solitary, but mostly in groves, copses, or belts; these looking, for all the world, like islands in the ocean. So perfect is the resemblance, that this very name has been given them, by men of Norman and Saxon race; whose ancestors, after crossing the Atlantic, carried into the colonies many ideas of the mariner, with much of his nomenclature. To them the isolated groves are "islands;" larger tracts of timber, seen afar, "land;" narrow spaces between, "straits;" and indentations along their edges "bays."

To carry the analogy further, the herds of buffalo, with bodies half buried in the tall grass, may be likened to "schools" of whales; the wild horses to porpoises at play; the deer to dolphins; and the fleet antelopes to flying-fish.

Completing the figure, we have the vultures that soar above, performing the part of predatory sea-gulls; the eagle representing the rarer frigate-bird, or albatross.

In the midst of this verdant expanse, less than a quarter of a century ago, man was rarely met; still more rarely civilised man; and rarer yet his dwelling-place. If at times a human being appeared among the prairie groves, he was not there as a sojourner—only a traveller, passing from place to place. The herds of cattle, with shaggy frontlets and humped shoulders—the droves of horses, long-tailed and with full flowing manes—the proud antlered stags, and prong-horned antelopes, were not his. He had no control over them. The turf he trod was free to them for pasture, as to him for passage; and, as he made way through their midst, his presence scarce affrighted them. He and his might boast of being "war's arbiter's," and lords of the great ocean. They were not lords of that emerald sea stretching between the Sabine River and the Rio Grande. Civilised man had as yet but shown himself upon its shores.

Since then he has entered upon, and scratched a portion of its surface; though not much, compared with its immensity. There are still grand expanses of the Texan prairie unfurrowed by the ploughshare of the colonist—almost untrodden by the foot of the explorer. Even at this hour, the traveller may journey for days on grass-grown plains, amidst groves of timber, without seeing tower, steeple, or so much as a chimney rising above the tree-tops. If he perceive a solitary smoke, curling skyward, he knows that it is over the camp-fire of some one like himself—a wayfarer.

And it may be above the bivouac of those he would do well to shun. For upon the green surface of the prairie, as upon the blue expanse of the ocean, all men met with are not honest. There be land-sharks as well as water-sharks—prairie pirates as corsairs of the sea.

No spectacle more picturesque, nor yet more pleasing, than that of an emigrant caravan *en route* over the plains. The huge waggons—"prairie ships," as oft, and not inaptly, named—with their white canvass tilts, typifying spread sails, aligned and moving along one after the other, like a *corps d'armée* on march by columns; a group of horsemen ahead, representing its vanguard; others on the flanks, and still another party riding behind, to look after strays and stragglers, the rear-guard. Usually a herd of cattle along—steers for the plough, young bullocks to supply beef for consumption on the journey, milch kine to give comfort to the children and colour to the tea and coffee—among them an old bull or two, to propagate the species on reaching the projected settlement. Not unfrequently a drove of pigs, or flock of sheep, with coops containing ducks, geese, turkeys, Guinea-fowl—perhaps a screaming peacock, but certainly Chanticleer and his harem.

A train of Texan settlers has its peculiarities, though now not so marked as in the times of which we write. Then a noted feature was the negro—his *status* a slave. He would be seen afoot, toiling on at the tails of the waggons, not in silence or despondingly, as if the march were a forced one. Footsore he might be, in his cheap "brogans" of Penitentiary fabric, and sore aweary of the way, but never sad. On the contrary, ever hilarious, exchanging jests with his fellow-pedestrians, or a word with Dinah in the wagon, jibing the teamsters, mocking the mule-drivers, sending his cachinations in sonorous ring along the moving line; himself far more mirthful than his master— more enjoying the march.

Strange it is, but true, that a lifetime of bondage does not stifle merriment in the heart of the Ethiopian. Grace of God to the sons of Ham— merciful compensation for mercies endured by them from the day Canaan was cursed, as it were a doom from the dawning of creation!

Just such a train as described is that commanded by Colonel Armstrong, *en route* towards Western Texas. Starting from Natchitoches some twenty days ago, it has reached the Colorado river, crossed it, and is now wending its way towards the San Saba, a tributary of the former stream.

It is one of the largest caravans that has yet passed over the prairies of Texas, counting between twenty and thirty "Conestoga" wagons, with several "carrioles" and vehicles of varied kind. Full fifty horsemen ride in its front, on its flank, and rear; while five times the number of pedestrians, men with black or yellow skins, keep pace with it. A proportionate number of women and children are carried in the wagons, their dusky faces peeping out from under the tilts, in contrast with the colour of the rain-bleached canvass; while other women and children of white complexion ride in the vehicles with springs.

In one of the latter—a barouche of the American build—travel two young ladies, distinguished by particular attentions. Half a dozen horsemen hover around their carriage, acting as its escort, each apparently anxious to exchange words with them. With one they can talk, jest, laugh, chatter as much as they like; but the other repels them. For the soul of the former is full of joy; that of the latter steeped in sadness.

Superfluous to say, they are Jessie and Helen Armstrong. And needless to tell why the one is gay, the other grave. Since we last saw them in the hotel of Natchitoches, no change has taken place in their hearts or their hopes. The younger of the two, Jessie, is still an expectant bride, certain soon to be a wife; and with this certainty rejoices in the future. Helen, with no such expectation, no wish for it, feeling as one widowed, grieves over the past. The former sees her lover by her side living and loving, constantly, caressingly; the latter can but think of hers as something afar off—a dream—a dread vision—a cold corpse—herself the cause of it!

Colonel Armstrong's eldest daughter is indeed sad—a prey to repining. Her heart, after receiving so many shocks, has almost succumbed to that the supremest, most painful suffering that can afflict humanity—the malady of *melancholia*. The word conveys but a faint idea of the suffering itself. Only they who have known it—fortunately but few—can comprehend the terror, the wan, wasting misery, endured by those whose nerves have given way under some terrible stroke of misfortune. 'Tis the story of a broken heart.

Byron has told us "the heart may break and brokenly live on." In this her hour of unhappiness, Helen Armstrong would not and could not believe him. It may seem strange that Jessie is still only a bride to be. But no. She remembers the promise made to her father—to share with him a home in Texas, however humble it might be. All the same, now that she knows it will be splendid; knowing, too, it is to be shared by another—her Louis. He is still but her *fiancée*; but his troth is plighted, his truthfulness beyond suspicion. They are all but man and wife; which they will be soon as the new home is reached.

The goal of their journey is to be the culminating point of Jessie's joy— the climax of her life's happiness.

Chapter Forty Three
The hand of God

Scarce any stream of South-Western Texas but runs between bluffs. There is a valley or "bottom-land," only a little elevated above the water's surface, and often submerged during inundations,—beyond this the bluffs. The valley may be a mile or more in width, in some places ten, at others contracted, till the opposing cliffs are scarce a pistol-shot apart. And of these there are frequently two or three tiers, or terraces, receding backward from the river, the crest of the last and outmost being but the edge of an upland plain, which is often sterile and treeless. Any timber upon it is stunted, and of those species to which a dry soil is congenial. Mezquite, juniper, and "black-jack" oaks grow in groves or spinneys; while standing apart may be observed the arborescent jucca—the "dragon-tree" of the Western world, towering above an underwood unlike any other, composed of *cactaceae* in all the varieties of cereus, cactus, and echinocactus. Altogether unlike is the bottom-land bordering upon the river. There the vegetation is lush and luxuriant, showing a growth of large forest timber—the trees set thickly, and matted with many parasites, that look like cables coiling around and keeping them together. These timbered tracts are not continuous, but show stretches of open between,—here little glades filled with flowers, there grand meadows overgrown with grass—so tall that the horseman riding through it has his shoulders swept by the spikes, which shed their pollen upon his coat.

Just such a bottom-land is that of the San Saba, near the river's mouth; where, after meandering many a score of miles from its source in the Llano Estacado, it espouses the Colorado—gliding softly, like a shy bride, into the embrace of the larger and stronger-flowing stream.

For a moment departing from the field of romance, and treading upon the domain of history—or it may be but legend—a word about this Colorado river may interest the reader.

Possibly, probably, almost lor certain, there is no province in all Spanish America without its "Rio Colorado." The geographer could count some scores of rivers so named—point them out on any map. They are seen in every latitude, trending in all directions, from the great Colorado of *cañon* celebrity in the north to another far south, which cuts a deep groove through the plains of Patagonia. All these streams have been so designated from the hue of their waters—muddy, with a pronounced tinge of red: this from the ochreous earth through which they have coursed, holding it in suspension.

In the Texan Colorado there is nothing of this; on the contrary, it is a clear water stream. A circumstance that may seem strange, till the explanation be given—which is, that the name is a *misnomer*. In other words, the Texan river now bearing the designation Colorado is not that so-called by the Spaniards, but their Rio Brazos; while the present Brazos is their Rio Colorado—a true red-tinted stream. The exchange of names is due to an error of the American map-makers, unacquainted with the Spanish tongue. Giving the Colorado its true name of Brazos, or more correctly "Brazos de Dios" ("The Arms of God"), the origin of this singular title for a stream presents us with a history, or legend, alike singular. As all know, Texas was first colonised by Spaniards, or Spanish Mexicans, on what might be termed the "militant missionary system." Monks were sent into the province, cross in hand, with soldiers at their back, bearing the sword. Establishments were formed in different parts of the country; San Antonio de Bejar being the ecclesiastical centre, as also the political capital. Around these the aborigines were collected, and after a fashion converted to Christianity. With the christianising process, however, there were other motives mixed up, having very little to do either with morality or religion. Comfortable subsistence, with the accumulation of wealth by the missionaries themselves, was in most instances the lure which attracted them to Texas, tempting them to risk their lives in the so-called conversion of the heathen.

The mission-houses were in the monasterial style, many of them on a grand scale—mansions in fact, with roomy refectories, and kitchens to correspond; snug sitting and sleeping-chambers; well-paved courts and spacious gardens attached. Outside the main building, sometimes forming part of it, was a church, or *capilla*; near by the *presidio*, or barrack for their military protectors; and beyond, the *rancheria*, or village of huts, the homes of the new-made neophytes.

No great difficulty had the fathers in thus handsomely housing themselves. The converts did all the work, willingly, for the sake and in the name of the "Holy Faith," into which they had been recently inducted. Nor did their toil end with the erection of the mission-buildings. It was only transferred to a more layical kind; to the herding of cattle, and tillage of the surrounding land; this continued throughout their whole lives—not for their own benefit, but to enrich those idle and lazy friars, in many cases men of the most profligate character. It was, in fact, a system of slavery, based upon and sustained by religious fanaticism. The result as might be expected—failure and far worse. Instead of civilising the aborigines of

America, it has but brutalised them the more—by eradicating from their hearts whatever of savage virtue they had, and implanting in its place a debasing bigotry and superstition.

Most American writers, who speak of these missionary establishments, have formed an erroneous estimate of them. And, what is worse, have given it to the world. Many of these writers are, or were, officers in the United States army, deputed to explore the wild territories in which the missions existed. Having received their education in Roman Catholic seminaries, they have been inducted into taking a too lenient view of the doings of the "old Spanish padres;" hence their testimony so favourable to the system.

The facts are all against them; these showing it a scheme of *villeinage*, more oppressive than the European serfdom of the Middle Ages. The issue is sufficient proof of this. For it was falling to pieces, long before the Anglo-Saxon race entered into possession of the territory where it once flourished. The missions are now in a state of decadence, their buildings fast falling into decay; while the red man, disgusted at the attempt to enslave, under the clock of christianising him, has returned to his idolatry, as to his savage life.

Several of these *misiones* were established on the San Saba river; one of which for a considerable period enjoyed a prosperous existence, and numbered among its neophytes many Indians of the Lipan and Comanche tribes.

But the tyranny of their monkish teachers by exactions of tenths and almost continuous toil—themselves living in luxurious ease, and without much regard to that continence they inculcated—at length provoked the suffering serfs to revolt. In which they were aided by those Indians who had remained unconverted, and still heretically roamed around the environs. The consequence was that, on a certain day when the hunters of the *mision* were abroad, and the soldiers of the *presidio* alike absent on some expedition, a band of the outside idolaters, in league with the discontented converts, entered the mission-building, with arms concealed under their ample cloaks of buffalo skin. After prowling about for a while in an insolent manner, they at length, at a given signal from their chief, attacked the proselytising *padres*, with those who adhered to them; tomahawked and scalped all who came in their way.

Only one monk escaped—a man of great repute in those early times of Texas. Stealing off at the commencement of the massacre, he succeeded in making his way down the valley of the San Saba, to its confluence with the Colorado. But to reach an asylum of safety it was necessary for him to cross the latter stream; in which unfortunately there was a freshet, its current so swollen that neither man nor horse could ford it.

The *padre* stood upon its bank, looking covetously across, and listening in terror to the sounds behind; these being the war-cries of the pursuing Comanches.

For a moment the monk believed himself lost. But just then the arm of God was stretched forth to save him. This done in a fashion somewhat difficult to give credence to, though easy enough for believers in Holy Faith. It was a mere miracle; not stranger, or more apocryphal, than we hear of at this day in France, Spain, or Italy. The only singularity about the Texan tale is the fact of its not being original; for it is a pure piracy from Sacred Writ — that passage of it which relates to the crossing of the Red Sea by Moses and his Israelites.

The Spanish monk stood on the river's bank, his eyes fixed despairingly on its deep rapid-running current, which he knew he could not cross without danger of being drowned. Just at this crisis he saw the waters separate; the current suddenly stayed, and the pebbly bed showing dry as a shingle!

Tucking his gown under his girdle, he struck into the channel; and, no doubt, making good time — though the legend does not speak of this — he succeeded in planting his sandalled feet, dry shod, on the opposite shore! So far the Texan story closely corresponds with the Mosaic. Beyond, the incidents as related, are slightly different. Pharaoh's following host was overwhelmed by the closing waters. The pursuing Comanches did not so much as enter the charmed stream; which, with channel filled up, as before, was running rapidly on. They were found next morning upon the bank where they had arrived in pursuit, all dead, all lying at full stretch along the sward, their heads turned in the same direction, like trees struck down by a tornado!

Only the Omnipotent could have done this. No mortal hand could make such a *coup*. Hence the name which the Spaniards bestowed upon the present Colorado, *Brazos de Dios* — the "Hand of God." Hence also the history, or rather fable, intended to awe the minds of the rebellious redskins, and restore them to Christanity, or serfdom.

Which it did not; since from that day the *misiones* of San Saba remained abandoned, running into ruin.

It is to one of these forsaken establishments Colonel Armstrong is conducting his colony; his future son-in-law having purchased the large tract of territory attached to it.

To that spot, where more than a century ago the monks made halt, with cross borne conspicuously in one hand, and sword carried surreptitiously in the other, there is now approaching a new invasion — that of axe and rifle — neither ostentatiously paraded, but neither insidiously concealed.

Chapter Forty Four
A cloud on the cliffs

After a long toilsome journey through Eastern Texas, the emigrant train has reached the San Saba, and is working its way up-stream. Slowly, for the bottom-land is in some places heavily timbered, and the road requires clearing for the waggons.

The caravan has entered the valley on the left, or northern, bank of the river, while its point of destination is the southern; but a few miles above its confluence with the Colorado is a ford, by which the right side may be reached at low water. Luckily it is now at its lowest, and the waggons are got across without accident, or any great difficulty.

Once on the southern side, there is nothing to obstruct or further delay them. Some ten miles above is the abandoned mission-house, which they expect to reach that day, before going down of the sun.

With perhaps one exception, the emigrants are all happy, most of them in exuberant spirits. They are nearing a new home, having long ago left the old one behind; left also a thousand cankering cares,—many of them more than half a life spent in struggles and disappointments. In the untried field before them there is hope; it may be success and splendour; a prospect like the renewing of life's lease, the younger to find fresh joys, the older to grow young again.

For weeks has the San Saba mission-house been the theme of their thoughts, and topic of discourse. They will re-people the deserted dwelling, restore it to its pristine splendour; bring its long neglected fields under tillage—out of them make fortunes by the cultivation of cotton.

There is no cloud to darken the horizon of their hopes. The toilsome journey is nearly at an end, and rejoicingly they hail its termination. Whether their train of white tilted wagons winds its way under shadowing trees, or across sunlit glades, there is heard along its line only joyous speech and loud hilarious laughter.

So go they on, regardless about the future, or only thinking of it as full of bright promise. Little do they dream how it may be affected by something seen upon the cliffs above, though not seen by them. At the point they have now reached, the bottom-land is several miles wide, with its bordering of grim bluffs rising on either flank, and running far as eye can see. On the left side, that they have just forsaken, not upon the river's bank, but the cliff far back, is a cloud. No darkness of the sky, or concentration of unsubstantial vapour. But a gathering on the earth, and of men; who, but for their being on horseback, might be mistaken for devils. In Satan's history the horse has no part; though, strange to say, Satan's sons are those who most affect friendship for the noble animal. Of the horsemen seen hovering above the San Saba there are in all twenty; most of them mounted upon mustangs, the native steed of Texas, though two or three bestride larger and better stock, the breed of the States.

All appear Indians, or if there be white man among them, he must have been sun-tanned beyond anything commonly seen. In addition to their tint of burnt umber, they are all garishly painted; their faces escutcheoned with chalk-white, charcoal-black, and vermillion-red. Of their bodies not much can be seen. Blankets of blue and scarlet, or buffalo robes, shroud their shoulders; while buckskin breeches and leggings wrap their lower limbs; mocassins encasing their feet. In addition to its dress, they wear the usual Indian adornments. Stained eagle-plumes stand tuft-like out of their raven-black hair, which, in trailing tresses, sweeps back over the hips of their horses; while strings of peccaries' teeth and claws of the grizzly bear fall over their breasts in bountiful profusion.

It is true, they are not in correct fighting costume. Nor would their toilet betoken them on the "war-trail." But the Texan Indian does not always dress warrior-fashion, when he goes forth upon a predatory excursion. More rarely when on a mere pilfering maraud, directed against some frontier settlement, or travelling party of whites. On such occasions he does not intend fighting, but rather shuns it. And, as thieving is more congenial to him, he can steal as cleverly and adroitly in a buckskin hunting-shirt, as with bare arms.

The Indians in question number too few for a war party. At the same time, their being without women is evidence they are on no errand of peace. But for the arms carried, they might be mistaken for hunters. They have spears and guns, some of them "bowie" knives and pistols; while the Indian hunter still believes in the efficacy of the silent arrow.

In their armour, and equipment there are other peculiarities the ordinary traveller might not comprehend, but which to the eye of an old prairie man would be regarded as suspicious. Such an one would at once pronounce them a band of *prairie pirates*, and of the most dangerous kind to be encountered in all the territory of Texas.

Whoever they may be, and whatever their design, their behaviour is certainly singular. Both by their looks and gestures it can be told they are watching the waggon train, and interested in its every movement; as also taking care not to be themselves observed by those belonging to it. To avoid this they keep back from the crest of the escarpment; so far, it would not be possible to see them from any part of the bottom-land below.

One of their number, afoot, goes closer to the cliff's edge, evidently sent there by the others as a sort of moving vidette. Screened by the cedars that form its *crinière*, he commands a view of the river valley below, without danger of being himself seen from it.

At short intervals he passes back a pace or two, and gesticulates to the others. Then returning to the cliff's edge, he continues on as before.

These movements, apparently eccentric, are nevertheless of grave import. The man who makes them, with those to whom they are made, must be watching the travellers with the intention of waylaying them.

Afar off are the waggons, just distinguishable as such by their white canvas tilts—the latter in contrast with the surface of vivid green over which they are progressing. Slowly crawling along, they bear similitude to a string of gigantic *termites* bent on some industrial excursion. Still the forms of mounted men—at least forty in number, can be distinguished. Some riding in front of the train, some in its rear, and others alongside of it. No wonder the twenty savage men, who pursue the parallel line along the cliff, are taking care not to approach it too nearly. One would suppose that from such a strong travelling party their chance of obtaining plunder would seem to them but slight. And yet they do not appear to think so. For as the caravan train tardily toils on up the bottom-land, they too move along the upper plain at a like rate of speed, their scout keeping the waggons in sight, at intervals, as before, admonishing them of every movement.

And they still continue watching the emigrant train until the sun sinks low—almost to the horizon. Then they halt upon a spot thickly beset with cedar trees—a sort of promontory projecting over the river valley.

On its opposite side they can see the waggons still slowly creeping along, though now not all in motion. Those in the lead have stopped; the others doing likewise, as, successively, they arrive at the same place.

This in front of a large building, just discernible in the distance, its outlines with difficulty traceable under the fast gathering gloom of the twilight.

But the savages who survey it from the bluff have seen that building before, and know all about it; know it to be one of the abandoned *misiones* of San Saba; as, also, why those vehicles are now coming to a stop before its walls.

While watching these, but few words are exchanged between them, and only in an under tone. Much or loud talk would not be in keeping with their Indian character. Still enough passes in their muttered speeches—observable also in the expression of their features—for any one hearing the first, or seeing the last, to predict danger to the colony of Colonel Armstrong. If looks count for aught, or words can be relied on the chances seem as if the old San Saba mission-house, long in ruins, may remain so yet longer.

Chapter Forty Five
A suspicious surveillance

The ancient monastery, erst the abode of Spanish monks, now become the dwelling-place of the ci-devant Mississippi planter, calls for a word of description.

It stands on the right side of the river, several hundred yards from the bank, on a platform slightly elevated above the general level of the surrounding *terrain*.

The site has been chosen with an eye to the pleasant and picturesque—that keen look-out towards temporal enjoyment, which at all times, and in all countries, has characterised these spiritual teachers of the heathen.

Its elevated position gives it command of a fine prospect, at the same time securing it against the danger of inundation, when the river is in flood.

In architectural style the mission-building itself does not much differ from that of most Mexican country houses—called *haciendas*.

Usually a grand quadrangular structure, with an uncovered court in the centre, the *patio*; around which runs a gallery or corridor, communicating with the doors of the different apartments.

But few windows face outside; such as there are being casements, unglazed, but protected by a *grille* of iron bars set vertically—the *reja*. In the centre of its front *façade* is a double door, of gaol-like aspect, giving admittance to the passage-way, called *saguan*; this of sufficient capacity to admit a waggon with its load, intended for those grand old coaches that lumbered along our own highways in the days of Dick Turpin, and in which Sir Charles Grandison used luxuriously to ride. Vehicles of the exact size, and pattern, may be seen to this day crawling along the country roads of modern Mexico—relics of a grandeur long since gone.

The *patio* is paved with stone flags, or tesselated tiles; and, where a head of water can be had, a fountain plays in the centre, surrounded by orange-trees, or other evergreens, with flowering-plants in pots. To rearward of this inner court, a second passage-way gives entrance to another, and larger, if not so sumptuously arrayed; this devoted to stables, store-rooms, and other domestic offices. Still farther back is the *huerta*, or garden.

That attached to the ancient monastery is an enclosure of several acres in extent, surrounded by a high wall of *adobes*; made to look still higher from being crested with a palisade of the organ cactus. Filled with fruit trees and flowering shrubs, these once carefully cultivated, but for long neglected, now cover the walks in wild luxuriance. Under their shade, silently treading with sandalled feet, or reclining on rustic benches, the Texan friars used to spend their idle hours, quite as pleasantly as their British brethren of Tintern and Tewkesbury. Oft have the walls of the San Saba mission-house echoed their "ha, ha!" as they quaffed the choicest vintage of Xeres, and laughed at jests ribald as any ever perpetrated in a pot-house. Not heard, however, by the converted heathen under their care; nor intended to be. For them there were dwellings apart; a collection of rude hovels, styled the *rancheria*. These were screened from view by a thick grove of evergreen trees; the *padres* not relishing a too close contact with their half-naked neophytes, who were but their *peons*—in short their slaves. In point of fact, it was the feudal system of the Old World transported to the New; with the exception that the manorial lords were monks, and the *villeins* savage men. And the pretence at proselytising, with its mongrel mixture of Christianity and superstition, did not make this Transatlantic *villeinage* a whit less irksome to endure. Proof, that the red-skinned serfs required the iron hand of control is found in the *presidio*, or soldier's barrack—standing close by—its ruin overlooking those of the *rancheria*. They who had been conquered by the Cross, still needed the sword to keep them in subjection, which, as we have seen, it finally failed to do.

Several of the huts still standing, and in a tolerable state of repair, have supplied shelter to the new settlers; most of whom have taken up their abode in them. They are only to serve as temporary residences, until better homes can be built. There is no time for this now. The spring is on, and the cotton-seed must be got into the ground, to the neglect of everything else.

Colonel Armstrong himself, with his daughters and domestics, occupies the old mission-building, which also gives lodgment to Luis Dupré and his belongings. For the young planter is now looked upon as a member of the Armstrong family, and it wants but a word from one in holy orders to make him really so. And such an one has come out with the colonists. The marriage ceremony is but deferred until the cotton-seed be safe under the soil. Then there will be a day of jubilee, such as has never been seen upon the San Saba; a *fiesta*, which in splendour will eclipse anything the Spanish monks, celebrated for such exhibitions, have ever got up, or attempted.

But "business before pleasure" is the adage of the hour; and, after a day or two given to rest, with the arrangement of household affairs, the real work of colonising commences. The little painted ploughs, transported from the States, are set to soiling their paint, by turning up the fertile clod of the San Saba valley, which has so long lain fallow; while the seed of the cotton-plant is scattered far and wide over hundreds—ay, thousands of acres.

Around the ancient mission is inaugurated a new life, with scenes of industry, stirring as those presided over by the *padres*.

Is it sure of being as prosperous, or more likely to be permanent?

One confining his view to the valley—regarding only the vigorous activity there displayed—would answer this question in the affirmative.

But he who looks farther off—raising his eyes to the bluff on the opposite side of the river, fixing them on that spot where the Indians made halt—would hesitate before thus prognosticating. In the dusky cohort he might suspect some danger threatening the new settlement.

True, the savages are no longer there. After seeing the waggons one after another becoming stationary, like vultures deprived of a carrion repast, they moved away. But not far. Only about five miles, to a grove of timber standing back upon the plain, where they have made a more permanent camp.

Two alone are left upon the cliff's edge; evidently to act as videttes. They keep watch night and day, one always remaining awake. Especially during the night hours do they appear on the alert—with eyes bent on the far off mission-buildings—watching the window-lights that steadily shine, and the torches that flit to and fro. Watching for something not yet seen. What can it be?

And what is the design of these painted savages, who look more like demons than men? Is it to attack the new colony, plunder, and destroy it?

Regarding their numbers, this would seem absurd. They are in all only twenty; while the colonists count at least fifty fighting men. No common men either; but most of them accustomed to the use of arms; many backwoodsmen, born borderers, staunch as steel. Against such, twenty Indians—though the picked warriors of the warlike Comanche tribe—would stand no chance in fair open fight. But they may not mean this; and their intent be only stealing?

Or they may be but a pioneer party—the vanguard of a greater force?

In any case, their behaviour is singularly suspicious. Such manoeuvring can mean no good, but may be fraught with evil to Colonel Armstrong and his colonists.

For several successive days is this surveillance maintained, and still nothing seems to come of it. The party of savages remains encamped in the timber at back; while the two sentinels keep their place upon the promontory; though now and then going and coming, as before.

But on a certain night they forsake their post altogether, as if their object has been attained, and there is no need to keep watch any more.

On this same night, a man might be seen issuing out of the mission-building, and making away from its walls. He is not seen, nevertheless. For it is the hour of midnight, and all have retired to rest—the whole household seemingly wrapt in profoundest slumber. Moreover, the man slips out stealthily, through the backdoor; thence across the second courtyard, and along a narrow passage leading into the garden. Having reached this, he keeps on down the centre walk, and over the wall at bottom, through which there chances to be a breach. All these mysterious movements are in keeping with the appearance of the man. For his countenance shows cunning of no ordinary kind. At first glance, and under the moonlight, he might be mistaken for a mulatto. But, though coloured, he is not of this kind. His tawny skin shows a tinge of red, which tells of Indian, rather than African blood. He is, in truth, a *mestizo*—half Spaniard or Mexican, the other half being the aboriginal race of America.

It is a breed not always evil-disposed, still less frequently ill-featured; and, so far as looks go, the individual in question might claim to be called handsome. He has a plenteous profusion of dark curly hair, framing a countenance by no means common. A face of oval form, regular features, the nose and chin markedly prominent, a pair of coal black eyes, with a well-defined crescent over each. Between his lips are teeth, sound and of ivory whiteness, seeming whiter in contrast with a pair of jet black moustaches.

Taking his features singly, any of them might be pronounced comely. And yet the *tout ensemble* is not pleasing. Despite physical beauty, there is something in the man's face that appears repulsive, and causes shrinking in the heart of the beholder. Chiefly is it his eyes that seem to produce this effect; their glance inspiring fear, such as one feels while being gazed at by an adder.

Not always can this sinister look be observed. For the *mestizo*, when face to face with his superiors, has the habit of holding his eyes averted—cast down, as if conscious of having committed crime, or an intention to commit it.

Most with whom he comes in contact are impressed with the idea, that he either has sinned, or intends sinning; so all are chary of giving him confidence.

No—not all. There is one exception: one man who has trusted, and still continues to trust him—the young planter, Dupré. So far, that he has made him his man of confidence—head-servant over all the household. For it need scarce be told, that the real master of the house is he who rendered it habitable, by filling it with furniture and giving it a staff of servants. Colonel Armstrong is but its head through courtesy due to age, and the respect shown to a future father-in-law.

Why the Creole puts such trust in Fernand—the *mestizo's* name—no one can clearly comprehend. For he is not one of those domestics, whose integrity has been tested by long years of service. On the contrary, Dupré has never set eyes on him, till just before leaving Nachitoches.

While organising the expedition, the half-blood had presented himself, and offered to act as its guide—professing acquaintance with that section of Texas whither the colony was to be conducted. But long before reaching their destination, Dupré had promoted him to a higher and more lucrative post—in short, made him his "major-domo."

Colonel Armstrong does not object. He has not the right. Still less, anybody else. Outsiders only wonder and shake their heads; saying, in whispers, that the thing is strange, and adding, "No good can come of it."

Could any of them observe the *mestizo* at this midnight hour, skulking away from the house; could they follow and watch his further movements, they might indulge in something more than a surmise about his fidelity; indeed, be convinced he is a traitor.

After getting about half-a-mile from the mission walls, he makes stop on the edge of attract of timber lying between—its outer edge, open towards the river's bank, and the bluffs beyond.

There, crouching down by the side of a flat stone, he pours some gunpowder upon it, from a horn taken out of his pocket.

This done, he draws forth a box of lucifer matches; scrapes one across the stone, and sets the powder ablaze.

It flashes up in bright glare, illumining the darkness around.

A second, time he repeats this manoeuvre; a third, and a fourth; and on, till, for the tenth time, powder has been burnt.

Then turning away from the spot, he makes back towards the dwelling-house, entering it by the way he went out, and stealthily as before.

No one within its walls has been witness to the pyrotechnic display.

For all, it has not been unobserved. The Indian videttes, stationed on the far-off bluff, see it. See, and furthermore, seem to accept it as a signal—a cue for action. What but this could have caused them to spring upon the backs of their horses, forsake their post of observation, and gallop off to the bivouac of their comrades; which they do, soon as noting that the tenth flash is not followed by another?

Surely must it be a signal, and preconcerted?

In the life of the prairie savage fire plays a conspicuous part. It is his telegraph, by which he can communicate with far off friends, telling them where an enemy is, and how or when he should be "struck." A single spark, or smoke, has in it much of meaning. A flash may mean more; but ten following in succession were alphabet enough to tell a tale of no common kind—one, it may be, predicting death.

Chapter Forty Six
A suspected servant

Now fairly inaugurated, the new colony gives promise of a great success; and the colonists are congratulating themselves.

None more than their chief, Colonel Armstrong. His leaving Mississippi has been a lucky move; so far all has gone well; and if the future but respond to its promise, his star, long waning, will be once more in the ascendant. There is but one thought to darken this bright dream: the condition of his eldest daughter. Where all others are rejoicing, there is no gladness for her. Sombre melancholy seems to have taken possession of her spirit, its shadow almost continuously seated on her brow. Her eyes tell of mental anguish, which, affecting her heart, is also making inroad on her health. Already the roses have gone out of her cheeks, leaving only lilies; the pale flowers foretelling an early tomb.

The distressing symptoms do not escape the fond father's observation. Indeed he knows all about them, now knowing their cause. Only through the Natchez newspapers was he first made aware of that secret correspondence between his daughter and Clancy. But since she has confessed all—how her heart went with her words; is still true to what she then said. The last an avowal not needed: her pallid cheeks proclaiming it. The frank confession, instead of enraging her father, but gives him regret, and along with it self-reproach. But for his aristocratic pride, with some admixture of cupidity, he would have permitted Clancy's addresses to his daughter. With an open honourable courtship, the end might have been different—perhaps less disastrous. It could not have been more.

He can now only hope, that time, the great soother of suffering hearts, may bring balm to hers. New scenes in Texas, with thoughts arising therefrom, may throw oblivion over the past. And perchance a new lover may cause the lost one to be less painfully remembered. Several aspirants have already presented themselves; more than one of the younger members of the colony having accompanied it, with no view of making fortunes by the cultivation of cotton, but solely to be beside Helen Armstrong.

Her suitors one and all will be disappointed. She to whom they sue is not an ordinary woman; nor her affections of the fickle kind. Like the eagle's mate, deprived of her proud lord, she will live all her after life in lone solitude—or die. She has lost her lover, or thinks so, believing Clancy dead; but the love still burns within her bosom, and will, so long as her life may last. Colonel Armstrong soon begins to see this, and despairs of the roses ever again returning to the cheeks of his elder daughter.

It would, no doubt, be different were the blighted heart that of his younger. With her the Spanish proverb, "*un clavo saca otro clavo*," might have meaning. By good fortune, Jessie needs no nail to drive out another. Her natural exuberance of spirits grown to greater joy from the hopes that now halo her young life, is flung over the future of all. Some compensation for her sister's sadness—something to cheer their common father. There is also the excitement attendant on the industries of the hour—the cares of the cotton-planting, with speculations about the success of the crop—these, with a hundred like thoughts and things, hinder him from so frequently recurring to, or so long dwelling on, that which can but cruelly distress.

It is the night succeeding that in which the mestizo made his private pyrotechnic display; and Colonel Armstrong with his future son-in-law is seated in the former refectory of the mission, which they have converted into a decent dining-room.

They are not alone, or, as in French phraseology better expressed, *chez eux mêmes*. Six or seven of their fellow-colonists of the better class share the saloon with them—these being guests whom they have invited to dinner.

The meal is over, the hour touching ten, the ladies have retired from the table, only the gentlemen remain, drinking choice claret, which Dupré, a sort of Transatlantic Lucullus, has brought with him from his Louisiana wine bins.

Armstrong himself, being of Scotch ancestry, has the national preference for whisky punch; and a tumbler of this beverage—the best in the world—stands on the table before him. His glass has been filled three times, and is as often emptied.

It need not be said, at this moment he is not sad. After three tumblers of whisky toddy no man can help being hilarious; and so is it with Colonel Armstrong. Seated at the head of his dining-table, the steaming punch before him, he converses with his guests, gay as the gayest. For a time their conversation is on general topics; but at length changes to one more particular. Something said has directed their attention to a man, who waited upon them at table, now no longer in the room.

The individual thus honoured is Dupré's confidential servant Fernand; who, as already said, is house-steward, butler, *factotum* of affairs generally.

As is usual with such grand dignitaries, he has withdrawn simultaneously with the removal of the tablecloth, leaving a deputy to look to the decanting of the wine. Therefore, there is nothing remarkable in his disappearance; nor would aught be observed about it, but for a remark made by one of the guests during the course of conversation. A young surgeon, who has cast in his lot with the new colony, is he who starts the topic, thus introducing it:—

"Friend Dupré, where did you get that fellow Fernand? I don't remember having seen him on your Louisiana plantation."

"I picked him up in Natchitoches while we were organising. You know I lost my old major-domo last fall by the yellow fever. It took him off while we were down in New Orleans. Fernand, however, is his superior in every sense; can keep plantation accounts, wait at table, drive a carriage, or help in a hunt. He's a fellow of wonderful versatility; in short, a genius. And what is rare in such a combination of talents, he is devoted to his duties—a very slave to them."

"What breed may your admirable Crichton be?" asks another of the guests, adding: "He looks a cross between Spaniard and Indian."

"Just what he is," answers the young planter; "at least says so. By his own account his father was a Spaniard, or rather a Mexican, and his mother an Indian of the Seminole tribe. His real name is Fernandez; but for convenience I've dropped the final syllable."

"It's a bad sort of mixture, that between Spaniard and Seminole, and not improved by the Spaniard being a Mexican," remarks he who made the inquiry.

"I don't like his looks," observes a third speaker.

Then all around the table wait to hear what Wharton, the young surgeon, has to say. For it is evident, from his way of introducing the subject, he either knows or suspects something prejudicial to the character of the major-domo. Instead of going on to explain, he puts a second interrogatory—

"May I ask, M. Dupré, whether you had any character with him?"

"No, indeed," admits the master. "He came to me just before we left Natchitoches asking for an engagement. He professed to know all about Texas, and offered to act as a guide. As I had engaged guides, I didn't want him for that when he said any other place would do. Seeing him to be a smart sort of fellow, which he certainly has proved, I engaged him to look after my baggage. Since, I've found him useful in other ways, and have given him full charge of everything—even to entrusting him with the care of my modest money chest."

"In doing that," rejoins the surgeon, "I should say you've acted somewhat imprudently. Excuse me, M. Dupré, for making the observation."

"Oh, certainly," is the planter's frank reply. "But why do you say so, Mr Wharton? Have you any reason to suspect his honesty?"

"I have; more than one."

"Indeed! Let us hear them all."

"Well; in the first place I don't like the look of the man, nor ever did since the day of our starting. Since I never set eyes on him before, I could have had no impression to prejudice me against him. I admit that, judging by physiognomy, any one may be mistaken; and I shouldn't have allowed myself to be led by that. In this case, however, a circumstance has contributed to shaping my judgment; in fact, deciding me in the opinion, that your fellow Fernand is not only dishonest, but something worse than a thief."

"Worse than a thief!" is the simultaneous echo from all sides of the table, succeeded by a universal demand for explanation.

"Your words have a weighty sound, doctor," is Colonel Armstrong's way of putting it. "We are anxious to hear what they mean."

"Well," responds Wharton, "you shall know why I've spoken them, and what's led me to suspect this fellow Fernand. You can draw your own conclusions, from the premises I put before you. Last night at a late hour—near midnight—I took a fancy into my head to have a stroll towards the river. Lighting a weed, I started out. I can't say exactly how far I may have gone; but I know that the cigar—a long 'Henry Clay'—was burnt to the end before I thought of turning back. As I was about doing so, I heard a sound, easily made out to be the footsteps of a man, treading the firm prairie turf. As it chanced just then, I was under a pecan-tree that screened me with its shadow; and I kept my ground without making any noise.

"Shortly after, I saw the man whose footfall I had heard, and recognised him as M. Dupré's head-servant. He was coming up the valley, toward the house here, as if returning from some excursion. I mightn't have thought much of that, but for noticing, as he passed me, that he didn't walk erect or on the path, but crouchingly, among the trees skirting it.

"Throwing away the stump of my cigar, I set out after him, treading stealthily as he. Instead of entering by the front, he went round the garden, all the way to its rear; where suddenly I lost sight of him. On arriving at the spot where he had disappeared, I saw there was a break in the wall. Through that, of course, he must have passed, and entered the mission-building at the back. Now, what are we to make of all this?"

"What do you make of it, doctor?" asks Dupré.

"Give us your own deductions!"

"To say the truth, I don't know what deductions to draw, I confess myself at fault; and cannot account for the fellow's movements; though I take you'll all acknowledge they were odd. As I've said, M. Dupré, I didn't from the first like your man of versatile talents; and I'm now more than ever distrustful of him. Still I profess myself unable to guess what he was after last night. Can any of you, gentlemen?"

No one can. The singular behaviour of Dupré's servant is a puzzle to all present. At the same time, under the circumstances, it has a serious aspect.

Were there any neighbouring settlement, the man might be supposed returning from a visit to it; entering stealthily, from being out late, and under fear of rebuke from his master. As there are no such neighbours, this theory cannot be entertained.

On the other hand, there has been no report of Indians having been seen in proximity to the place. If there had, the mestizo's conduct might be accounted for, upon an hypothesis that would certainly cause apprehension to those discussing it.

But no savages have been seen, or heard of; and it is known that the Southern Comanches—the only Indians likely to be there encountered—are in treaty of peace with the Texan Government. Therefore, the nocturnal excursion of the half-blood could not be connected with anything of this kind.

His singular, and seemingly eccentric, behaviour, remains an unsolved problem to the guests around the table; and the subject is eventually dropped their conversation changing to other and pleasanter themes.

Chapter Forty Seven
Opposite emblems

Pleasure has not been the sole purpose for which Colonel Armstrong is giving his little dinner party, else there would have been ladies invited along with the gentlemen. It is rather a re-union to talk over the affairs of the colony; hence the only ladies present were the daughters of the host. And, for the same reason, these have retired from the table at an early hour, betaking themselves to the *sala* of the old monastery, their sitting and drawing-room. This, though an ample apartment, is anything but a pleasant one; never much affected by the monks, who in their post-prandial hours, preferred sticking to the refectory. A hasty attempt has been made to modernise it; but the light furniture of French Creole fabric, brought along from Louisiana, ill accords with its heavy style of architecture, while its decayed walls and ceilings *lezardée*, give it a gloomy dismal look, all the more from the large room being but dimly lit up. As it is not a drawing-room party, the ladies expect that for a long while, if not all evening, they will be left alone in it. For a time they scarce know how to employ themselves. With Helen, amusement is out of the question. She has flung herself into a *fauteuil*, and sits in pensive attitude; of late, alas! become habitual to her.

Jessie, taking up her guitar, commences a song, the first that occurs to her, which chances to be "Lucy Neal," a negro melody, at the time much in vogue on the plantations of the South. She has chosen the pathetic strain without thought of the effect it may produce upon her sister. Observing it to be painful she abruptly breaks off, and with a sweep of her fingers across the guitar strings, changes to the merrier refrain of "Old Dan Tucker." Helen, touched by the delicate consideration, rewards it with a faint smile. Then, Jessie rattles on through a *mélange* of negro ministrelsy, all of the light comical kind, her only thought being to chase away her sister's despondency.

Still is she unsuccessful. Her merry voice, her laughter, and the cheerful tinkle of the guitar strings, are all exerted in vain. The sounds so little in consonance with Helen's thoughts seem sorely out of place in that gloomy apartment; whose walls, though they once echoed the laughter of roystering friars, have, no doubt, also heard the sighs of many a poor *peon* suffering chastisement for disobedience, or apostacy.

At length perceiving how idle are her efforts, the younger sister lays aside her guitar, at the same time starting to her feet, and saying:—"Come, Helen! suppose we go outside for a stroll? That will be more agreeable than moping in this gloomsome cavern. There's a beautiful moonlight, and we ought to enjoy it."

"If you wish, I have no objections. Where do you intend strolling to?"

"Say the garden. We can take a turn along its walks, though they are a little weedy. A queer weird place it is—looks as if it might be haunted. I shouldn't wonder if we met a ghost in it—some of the old monks; or it might be one of their victims. 'Tis said they were very cruel, and killed people—ay, tortured them. Only think of the savage monsters! True, the ones that were here, as I've heard, got killed themselves in the end—that's some satisfaction. But it's all the more reason for their ghosts being about. If we should meet one, what would you do?"

"That would depend on how he behaved himself."

"You're not afraid of ghosts, Helen! I know you're not."

"I was when a child. Now I fear neither the living nor the dead. I can dare both, having nought to make me care for life—"

"Come on!" cries Jessie, interrupting the melancholy train of reflection, "Let us to the garden. If we meet a monk in hood and cowl, I shall certainly—"

"Do what?"

"Run back into the house fast as feet can carry me. Come along!"

Keeping up the jocular bravado, the younger sister leads the way out. Arm-in-arm the two cross the *patio*, then the outer courtyard, and on through a narrow passage communicating with the walled enclosure at back; once a grand garden under careful cultivation, still grand in its neglect.

After entering it, the sisters make stop, and for a while stand surveying the scene. The moon at full, coursing through a cloudless sky, flings her soft light upon gorgeous flowers with corollas but half-closed, in the sultry southern night giving out their fragrance as by day. The senses of sight and smell are not the only ones gratified; that of hearing is also charmed with the song of the *czentzontle*, the Mexican nightingale. One of these birds perched upon a branch, and pouring forth its love-lay in loud passionate strain, breaks off at sight of them. Only for a short interval is it silent; then resuming its lay, as if convinced it has nought to fear from such fair intruders. Its song is not strange to their ears, though there are some notes they have not hitherto heard. It is their own mocking-bird of the States, introducing into its mimic minstrelsy certain variations, the imitations of sounds peculiar to Texas.

After having listened to it for a short while, the girls move on down the centre walk, now under the shadow of trees, anon emerging into the moonlight; which shimmering on their white evening robes, and reflecting the sparkle of their jewellery, produces a pretty effect.

The garden ground slopes gently backward; and about half-way between the house and the bottom wall is, or has been, a fountain. The basin is still there, and with water in it, trickling over its edge. But the jet no longer plays, and the mason-work shows greatly dilapidated. So also the seats and statues around, some of the latter yet standing, others broken off, and lying alongside their pedestals.

Arriving at this spot, the sisters again stop, and for a time stand contemplating the ruins; the younger making a remark, suggested by a thought of their grandeur gone.

"Fountains, statues, seats under shade trees, every luxury to be got out of a garden! What Sybarites the Holy Fathers must have been!"

"Truly so," assents Helen. "They seem to have made themselves quite comfortable; and whatever their morals, it must be admitted they displayed good taste in landscape gardening, with an eye on good living as well. They must have been very fond of fruit, and a variety of it—judging by the many sorts of trees they've planted."

"So much the better for us," gleefully replies Jessie. "We shall have the benefit of their industry, when the fruit season comes round. Won't it be a grand thing when we get the walks gravelled, these statues restored, and that fountain once more in full play. Luis has promised me it shall be done, soon as the cotton crop is in. Oh! it will be a Paradise of a place!"

"I like it better as it is."

"You do. Why?"

"Ah! that *you* cannot understand. You do not know—I hope never will—what it is to live only in the past. This place has had a past, like myself, once smiling; and now like me all desolation."

"O sister! do not speak so. It pains me—indeed it does. Besides your words only go half-way. As you say, it's had a smiling past, and's going to have a smiling future. And so will you sis. I'm determined to have it all laid out anew, in as good style as it ever was—better. Luis shall do it—must, *when he marries, me*—if not before."

To the pretty bit of bantering Helen's only answer is a sigh, with a sadder expression, as from some fresh pang shooting through her heart. It is even this; for, once again, she cannot help contrasting her own poor position with the proud one attained by her sister. She knows that Dupré is in reality master of all around, as Jessie will be mistress, she herself little better than their dependant. No wonder the thought should cause her humiliation, or that, with a spirit imperious as her's, she should feel it acutely. Still, in her crushed heart there is no envy at her sister's good fortune. Could Charles Clancy come to life again, now she knows him true—were he but there to share with her the humblest hut in Texas, all the splendours, all the grandeurs of earth, could not add to that happiness, nor give one emotion more.

After her enthusiastic outburst, to which there has been no rejoinder, Jessie continues on toward the bottom of the garden, giving way to pleasant fancies, dreams of future designs, with her fan playfully striking at the flowers as she passes them.

In silence Helen follows; and no word is exchanged between them till they reach the lower end; when Jessie, turning round, the two are face to face. The place, where they have stopped is another opening with seats and statues, admitting the moonlight. By its bright beam the younger sister sees anguish depicted on the countenance of the older.

With a thought that her last words have caused or contributed to this, she is about to add others that may remove it. But before she can speak, Helen makes a gesture that holds her silent.

Near the spot where they are standing two trees overshadow the walk, their boughs meeting across it. Both are emblematic—one symbolising the most joyous hour of existence, the other its saddest. They are an orange, and a cypress. The former is in bloom, as it always is; the latter only in leaf, without a blossom on its branches.

Helen, stepping between them, and extending an arm to each, plucks from the one a sprig, from the other a flower. Raising the orange blossom between her white fingers, more attenuated than of yore, she plants it amid Jessie's golden tresses. At the same time she sets the cypress sprig behind the plaits of her own raven hair; as she does so, saying:—

"That for you, sister—this for me. We are now decked as befits us—as we shall both soon be—*you for the bridal, I for the tomb!*"

The words, seeming but too prophetic, pierce Jessie's heart as arrow with poisoned barb. In an instant, her joy is gone, sunk into the sorrow of her sister. Herself sinking upon that sister's bosom, with arms around her neck, and tears falling thick and fast over her swan-white shoulders.

Never more than now has her heart overflowed with compassion, for never as now has Helen appeared to suffer so acutely. As she stood, holding in one hand the symbol of bright happy life, in the other the dark emblem of death, she looked the very personification of sorrow. With her magnificent outline of form, and splendid features, all the more marked in their melancholy, she might have passed for its divinity. The ancient sculptors would have given much for such a model, to mould the statue of Despair.

Chapter Forty Eight
A blank day

On the frontier every settlement has its professional hunter. Often several, seldom less than two or three; their *métier* being to supply the settlers with meat and game—venison, the standing dish—now and then bear hams, much relished—and, when the place is upon prairie-land, the flesh of the antelope and buffalo. The wild turkey, too—grandest of all game birds—is on the professional hunter's list for the larder; the lynx and panther he will kill for their pelts; but squirrels, racoons, rabbits, and other such "varmints," he disdains to meddle with, leaving them to the amateur sportsman, and the darkey.

Usually the professional votary of Saint Hubert is of solitary habit, and prefers stalking alone. There are some, however, of more social inclining, who hunt in couples; one of the pair being almost universal a veteran, the other a young man—as in the case of Sime Woodley and Ned Heywood. By the inequality of age the danger of professional jealousy is avoided; the younger looking up to his senior, and treating him with the deference due to greater knowledge and experience.

Just such a brace of professionals has come out with the Armstrong colony—their names, Alec Hawkins and Cris Tucker—the former an old bear-hunter, who has slain his hundreds; the latter, though an excellent marksman, in the art of *vénerie* but a tyro compared with his partner.

Since their arrival on the San Saba, they have kept the settlement plentifully supplied in meat; chiefly venison of the black-tailed deer, with which the bottom-land abounds. Turkeys, too, in any quantity; these noble birds thriving in the congenial climate of Texas, with its nuts and berry-bearing trees.

But there is a yet nobler game, to the hunting of which Hawkins and his younger associate aspire; both being eager to add it to the list of their trophies. It is that which has tempted many an English Nimrod to take three thousand miles of sea voyage across the Atlantic, and by land nearly as many more—the buffalo. Hawkins and Tucker, though having quartered the river bottom, for ten miles above and below the mission-building, have as yet come across none of these grand quadrupeds, nor seen "sign" of them.

This day, when Armstrong has his dinner party, the hunters bethink themselves of ascending to the upper plain, in the hope of there finding the game so much desired.

The place promising best is on the opposite side of the valley, to reach which the river must be crossed.

There are two fords at nearly equal distances from the old mission-house, one about ten miles above, the other as many below. By the latter the waggons came over, and it is the one chosen by the hunters.

Crossing it, they continue on to the bluffs rising beyond, and ascend these through a lateral ravine, the channel of a watercourse—which affords a practicable pass to the plain. On reaching its summit they behold a steppe to all appearance; illimitable, almost as sterile as Saara itself. Treeless save a skirting of dwarf cedars along the cliff's edge, with here and there a *motte* of black-jack oaks, a cluster of cactus plants, or a solitary yucca of the arborescent species—the *palmilla* of the Mexicans.

Withal, not an unlikely place to encounter the cattle with; hunched backs, and shaggy shoulders. None are in sight; but hoping they soon will be the hunters launch out upon the plain.

Till near night they scout around, but without seeing any buffalo.

The descending sun warns them it is time to return home; and, facing for the bluff, they ride back towards it. Some three or four hundred yards from the summit of the pass is a *motte* of black-jacks, the trees standing close, in full leaf, and looking shady. As it is more than fifteen miles to the mission, and they have not eaten since morning, they resolve to make halt, and have a sneck. The black-jack grove is right in their way, its shade invites them, for the sun is still sultry. Soon they are in it, their horses tied to trees, and their haversacks summoned to disgorge. Some corn-bread and bacon is all these contain; but, no better refection needs a prairie hunter, nor cares for, so long he has a little distilled corn-juice to wash it down, with a pipe of tobacco to follow. They have eaten, drunk, and are making ready to smoke, when an object upon the plain attracts their attention. Only a cloud of dust, and far off—on the edge of the horizon. For all that a sign significant. It may be a "gang" of buffaloes, the thing they have been all day vainly searching for.

Thrusting the pipes back into their pouches, they grasp their guns, with eyes eagerly scanning the dust-cloud. At first dim, it gradually becomes darker. For a whiff of wind has blown the "stoor" aside, disclosing not a drove of buffaloes, but instead a troop of horses, at the same time showing them to have riders on their backs, as the hunters can perceive Indians.

Also that the troop is coming towards them, and advancing at such rapid pace, that in less than twenty minutes after being descried, it is close to the clump of black-jacks. Fortunately for Alec Hawkins and Oris Tucker, the Indian horsemen have no intention to halt there, or rest themselves under the shadow of the copse. To all appearance they are riding in hot haste, and with a purpose which carries them straight towards the pass. They do not even stop on arrival at its—summit; but dash down the ravine, disappearing suddenly as though they had dropped into a trap!

It is some time before the two hunters have recovered from their surprise, and can compare notes about what they have seen, with conjectures as to its bearing. They have witnessed a spectacle sufficiently alarming,—a band of fierce-looking savages, armed with spear and tomahawk—some carrying guns—all plumed and painted, all alike terrible in aspect.

Quick the apparition has passed before their eyes, as suddenly disappearing. The haste in which the Indians rode down the ravine tells of their being bent on some fore-arranged purpose that calls for early execution. It may be murder, or only plunder; and the men may be Comanches—as in every likelihood they are.

"They're a ugly-looking lot," says Hawkins, after seeing them file past. "If there were a hundred, instead o' twenty, I'd predict some danger to our new settlement. They appear to be going that way—at all events they are bound for the river bottom, and the lower crossing. We must follow them, Oris, an' see if we can make out what's their game. The red devils mayn't mean downright robbery, but like enough they intend stealin'. Hitch up, and let's after em'."

In a trice the two hunters are in their saddles; and proceeding to the summit of the pass, look down at the valley below. Not carelessly, but cautiously. Hawkins is an old campaigner, has fought Indians before, and knows how to deal with them.

Keeping himself and horse under cover of the cedars, after instructing his comrade to do the same, he reconnoitres the bottom-land, before attempting to descend to it.

As expected, he sees the Indians making for the ford. At the point between the San Saba, and either of its bluffs is a breadth of some four miles, part open meadow land, the other part, contiguous to the river overgrown with heavy timber. Into this the red horsemen are riding, as the two hunters reach the summit of the pass, the latter arriving just in time to see their last files disappear among the trees. It is their cue to descend also, which they do, without further delay.

Hastening down the ravine and on to the river ford, they discover that the Indians have crossed it. The tracks of their horses are on both banks. Beyond, the hunters cannot tell which way they have taken. For though still only twilight it is dark as night under the thick standing trees; and he keenest eye could not discover a trail.

Thus thrown off, they have no choice but continue on to the settlement.

Beaching this at a rather late hour, they do not enter the mission-building nor yet any of the huts of the *rancheria*. Their own residence is a tent, standing in the grove between; and to it they betake themselves. Once under canvass their first thought is supper, and they set about cooking it. Though they have brought back no buffalo meat a twenty pound turkey "gobbler" has been all day dangling at the horn of Hawkins' saddle—enough for a plentiful repast.

Oris, who acts as cook, sets to plucking the bird, while Hawkins commences kindling a fire outside the tent. But before the fagots are ablaze, the old hunter, all along abstracted, becomes fidgetty, as if troubled with the reflection of having neglected some duty he ought to have done.

Abruptly breaking off, and pitching aside the sticks, he says:—"This wont do, Cris, nohow. I've got a notion in my head there's something not right about them Indyens. I must up to the house an' tell the Colonel. You go on, and get the gobbler roasted. I'll be back by the time its ready."

"All right," rejoins Tucker, continuing to make the feathers fly. "Don't stay if you expect any share of this bird. I'm hungry enough to eat the whole of it myself."

"You needn't fear for my stayin'. I'm just as sharp set as yourself."

So saying, Hawkins strides out of the tent, leaving his comrade to continue the preparations for their repast.

From the hunter's tent, the house is approached by a narrow path, nearly all the way running through timber. While gliding silently along it, Hawkins comes suddenly to a stop.

"Seems to me I heard a cry," he mutters to himself; "seems, too, as 'twar a woman's voice."

After listening awhile, without hearing it repeated, he adds:

"I reckon, 'twar only the skirl o' them tree-crickets. The warm night makes 'em chirp their loudest."

Listening a little longer, he becomes convinced it was but the crickets he heard, and keeps on to the house.

Chapter Forty Nine
Waiting the word

To all appearance Fernand's fireworks are about to bear fruit, this likely to be bitter. As the sky, darker after the lightning's flash, a cloud is collecting over the new settlement, which threatens to sweep down upon it in a rain storm of ruin. What but they could have caused this cloud; or, at all events, given a cue for the time of its bursting.

It appears in the shape of a cohort of dusky horsemen, painted and plumed. No need to say, they are the same that were seen by Hawkins and Tucker.

Having crossed the river at its lower ford, where so far the hunters saw their tracks, there losing them, the savages continued on. Not by the main road leading to the mission, but along a path which deflects from it soon after leaving the river's bank. A narrower trace, indeed the continuation of that they had been following all along—the transverse route across the bottom-land from bluff to bluff, on both sides ascending to the steppe.

But though they came down on one side, they went not up on the other. Instead, having reached the nether bluff, they turned sharp along its base, by another and still narrower trace, which they knew would take them up to the mission-building. A route tortuous, the path beset with many obstacles; hence their having spent several hours in passing from the ford to the mission-house, though the distance between is barely ten miles.

No doubt they have good reason for submitting to the irksome delay caused by the difficult track, as also for the cautious manner in which they have been coming along it. Otherwise, they would certainly have chosen the direct road running nearer the river's bank.

While Colonel Armstrong, and his friends, are enjoying themselves in the refectory of the ancient mission-house, in the midst of their laughing hilarity, the painted cavaliers have been making approach, and are now halted, within less than half-a-mile from its walls. In such fashion as shows, they do not intend a long stay in their stopping place. Not a saddle is removed, or girth untightened; while the bridles, remaining on their horses' heads, are but used as halters to attach them to the trees.

The men have dismounted, but not to form camp, or make bivouac. They kindle no fires, nor seem caring to cook, or eat. They drink, however; several of them taking flasks from their saddle pouches, and holding them to their heads bottom upward. Nothing strange in this. The Texan Indian, whether Comanche, Kiowa, or Lipan, likes his fire-water as much as a white man, and as constantly carries it along with him. The only peculiarity about these is that, while quaffing, they do not talk in the Indian tongue, but English of the Texan idiom, with all its wild swearing!

The place where they have halted is a bit of glade-ground, nearly circular in shape, only half-encompassed by timber, the other half being an embayment of the bluffs, twin to those on the opposite side of the river bottom. It is shaded three-quarters across by the cliff, the moon being behind this. The other quarter, on the side of the trees, is brilliantly lit up by her beams, showing the timber thick and close along its edge, to all appearance impassable as the *façade* of rugged rock frowning from the opposite concave of the enclosed circle. Communicating with this are but two paths possible for man or horse, and for either only in single file. One enters the glade coming up the river bottom along the base of the bluff; the other debouches at the opposite end, still following the cliff's foot. By the former the Indians have entered; but by the latter it is evident they intend going out, as their eyes are from time to time turned towards it, and their gestures directed that way. Still they make no movement for resuming their march, but stand in gathered groups, one central and larger than the rest. In its midst is a man by nearly the head taller than those around him: their chief to a certainty. His authority seems acknowledged by all who address him, if not with deference, in tone and speech telling they but wait for his commands, and are willing to obey them. He, himself, appears waiting for something, or somebody else, before he can issue them, his glance continually turning towards the point where the path leads out upwards.

Impatiently, too, as ever and anon he pulls out a watch and consults it as, to the time. Odd to see a savage so engaged; above all possessed of a repeater! Still the Indians of to-day are different from those of days past, and have learnt many of the white man's ways—even to wearing watches. The man in question seems to know all about it; and has his reasons for being particular as to the hour. He is evidently acting upon a preconcerted plan, with the time fixed and fore-arranged. And evident also that ten is the hour awaited; for, while in the act of examining his dial, the old mission clock, restored to striking, tolls just so many times; and, before the boom of its cracked bell has ceased rolling in broken reverberation through the trees, he thrusts the watch hurriedly into his fob. Then stands in expectant attitude, with eyes upon the embouchure of the upper path, scanning it more eagerly than ever. There is a strange coincidence between the strokes of the clock and the flashes of Fernanda powder—both numbering the same. Though not strange to the leader of the savage troop. He knows what it is—comprehends the significance of the signal—for signal it has been. A dread one, too, foreboding danger to innocent people. One who could behold this savage band, scrutinise the faces of those composing it, witness the fierce wicked flashes from their eyes, just as the clock is striking, would send up a prayer for the safety of Colonel Armstrong and his colonists.

If further informed as to who the savages are, the prayer would sure be succeeded by the reflection—"Heaven help his daughters! If God guard not, a fearful fate will be theirs—a destiny worse than death!"

Chapter Fifty
An uncanny skulker

Still within the garden are the young girls—still standing under the shadow of the two trees that furnished the contrasting symbols,—unconscious of danger near. Helen's speech, suggesting such painful sequence, has touched her sister to the quick, soon as spoken, afflicting also herself; and for a time they remain with entwined arms and cheeks touching—their tears flowing together. But Jessie's sobs are the louder, her grief greater than that she has been endeavouring to assuage.

Helen perceiving it, rises to the occasion; and, as oft before, in turn becomes the comforter; their happiness and misery like scales vibrating on the beam.

"Don't cry so, Jess. Be a good girl, now. You're a little simpleton, and I a big one. 'Twas very wrong of me to say what I did. Be it forgotten, and let's hope we may yet both be happy."

"Oh, if I could but think that!"

"Think it, then. You *are* happy, and I—shall try to be. Who knows what time may do—that and Texas? Now, my little Niobe, dry up your tears. Mine are all gone, and I feel in first rate spirits. I do indeed."

She is not sincere in what she says, and but counterfeits cheerfulness to restore that of her sister.

She has well-nigh succeeded, when a third personage appears upon the scene, causing a sudden change in their thoughts, turning these into a new and very different channel.

He whose appearance produces such effect—for it is a man—seems wholly unconscious of the influence he has exerted; indeed, is so.

When first observed, he is coming down the central walk; which, though wide, is partially shadowed by trees. And in their shadow he keeps, clinging to it, as if desirous to shun observation. His step declares it; not bold this, nor regardless, but skulking, with tread catlike; while every now and then he casts a backward glance, as if in fear of some one being behind. Just that which hinders him from seeing those who are in front.

The girls are still standing together, with hands joined—luckily on one of the side-walks, and like himself in shadow—though very near to having separated, and one, at least, rushing out into the light at first sound of his footstep. For to Jessie it gave joy, supposing it that of her Luis. Naturally expecting him to join her, she was almost sure of its being he.

Only for an instant. The tread was too light for a man marching with honest intent, and the step too shuffling to be that of the young planter. So whispered Helen.

Soon they see it is not he, but his major-domo.

Both are annoyed, some little irritated, at being thus intruded upon. At such a time, in the midst of sacred emotions, all the more by a man they both instinctively dislike. For Fernand is not a favourite with either.

Then the idea occurs, he may be coming to seek them, sent with some message from the house, and if so, they can excuse him. Concluding his errand to be this, they await it, in silence.

They are quite mistaken, and soon perceive it. An honest messenger would not be moving as he. While passing the open ground by the ruined waterworks, the moon falls full upon his face, which wears an expression anything but innocent, as they can both see. Besides, his gestures also betray guilt; for he is skulking, and casting glances back.

"What can it mean?" whispers Jessie into Helen's ear; who replies by placing a finger on her lips, and drawing her sister into deeper shadow.

Silent both stand, not stirring, scarce breathing. One seeing, might easily mistake them for statues—a Juno and a Venus. Fortunately Fernand does not see, else he might scrutinise them more closely. He is too much absorbed about his own affair, whatever it be, to think of any one loitering there at that time of the night.

Where the main garden-walk meets the one going along the bottom, is another open space, smaller than that around the fountain, still sufficient to let in the light of the moon. Here also have been seats and statues; the latter lying shattered, as if hashed to the earth by the hand of some ruthless iconoclast. Just opposite, is a breach in the wall; the mud bricks, crumbled into clods forming a *talus* on each face of it.

Arriving at this, the *mestizo* makes stop. Only for an instant, long enough to give a last glance up the garden.

Apparently satisfied, that he is not followed nor observed, he scrambles up the slope and down on the opposite side, where he is lost to the view of the sisters; who both stand wondering—the younger sensibly trembling.

"What on earth is the fellow after?" asks Helen, whose speech comes first.

"What, indeed?" echoes Jessie.

"A question, sister, you should be better able to answer than I. He is the trusted servant of M. Dupré; and he, I take it, has told you all about him."

"Not a word has he. He knows that I don't like the man, and never did from the first. I've intimated as much to him more than once."

"That ought to have got Master Fernand his discharge. Your Luis will surely not keep him, if he knows it's disagreeable to you?"

"Well, perhaps he wouldn't if I were to put it in that way. I haven't done so yet. I only hinted that the man wasn't altogether to my liking; especially made so much of as Luis makes of him. You must know, dear Helen, my future lord and master is of a very trusting nature; far too much, I fear, for some of the people now around him. He has been brought up like all Creoles, without thought for the morrow. A sprinkling of Yankee cuteness wouldn't do him any harm. As for this fellow, he has insinuated himself into Luis's confidence in some way that appears quite mysterious. It even puzzles our father; though he's said nothing much about it. So far he appears satisfied, because the man has proved capable, and, I believe, very useful to them in their affairs. For my part I've been mystified by him all along, and not less now. I wonder what he can be after. Can you not give a guess?"

"Not the slightest; unless it be theft. Do you think it's that?"

"I declare I don't know."

"Is there anything he could be carrying off from the house, with the intention of secreting it outside? Some of your Luis's gold for instance, or the pretty jewels he has given you?"

"My jewels! No; they are safe in their case; locked up in my room, of which I've the key with me. As for Luis's gold, he hasn't much of that. All the money he possesses—quite fifty thousand dollars, I believe—is in silver. I wondered at his bringing it out here in that heavy shape, for it made a whole waggon-load of itself. He's told me the reason, however; which is, that among Indians and others out here on the frontier, gold is not thought so much of as silver."

"It can't be silver Fernand is stealing—if theft it be. He would look more loaded, and couldn't have gone so lightly over that wall."

"Indeed, as you say, he went skipping over it like a grasshopper."

"Rather say gliding like a snake. I never saw a man whose movements more resembled the Devil in serpent shape—except one."

The thought of this one, who is Richard Darke, causes Helen Armstrong to suspend speech; at the same time evoking a sigh to the memory of another one—Charles Clancy.

"Shall we return into the house?" asks Jessie, after a pause.

"For what purpose?"

"To tell Luis of what we've seen; to warn him about Fernand."

"If we did the warning would be unheeded. I fear Monsieur Dupré will remain unconvinced of any intended treachery in his trusted servant, until something unpleasant occur; it may be something disastrous. After all, you and I, Jess, have only our suspicions, and may be wronging the fellow. Suppose we stay a little longer, and see what comes of it. No doubt, he'll soon return from his mysterious promenade, and by remaining, we may find out what he's been after. Shall we wait for him? You're not afraid, are you?"

"A little, I confess. Do you know, Helen, this Fernand gives me the same sort of feeling I had at meeting that big fellow in the streets of Natchitoches. At times he glares at me just in the same way. And yet the two are so different."

"Well, since no harm came of your Nachitoches bogie, it's to be hoped there won't any from this one. If you have any fear to stay, let us go in. Only my curiosity is greatly excited by what we've seen, and I'd like to know the end of it. If we don't discover anything, it can do no harm. And if we do— say; shall we go, or try?"

"I'm not afraid now. You make me brave, sister. Besides, we may find out something Luis ought to know."

"Then let us stay."

Having resolved to await the coming back of the half-blood, and watch his further movements, the sisters bethink them of seeking a safer place for observation; one where there will be less danger of being themselves seen.

It is to Helen the idea occurs.

"On his return," she says, "he might stray along this way, and not go up the centre walk. Therefore we had better conceal ourselves more effectually. I wonder he didn't see us while passing out. No doubt he would have done so, but for looking so anxiously behind, and going at such a rapid rate. Coming back he may not be so hurried; and should he sight us, then an end to our chance of finding out what he's up to. Where's the best place to play spy on him?"

The two look in different directions, in search of an appropriate spot.

There can be no difficulty in finding such. The shrubbery, long unpruned, grows luxuriantly everywhere, screening the *façade* of the wall along its whole length.

Near by is an arbour of evergreens, thickly overgrown with a trellis of trailing plants.

They know of this shady retreat; have been in it before that night. Now, although the moon is shining brightly, its interior, arcaded over by dense foliage, is in dark shadow—dark as a cavern. Once inside it, eye cannot see them from without.

"The very place," whispers Helen; and they commence moving towards it.

To reach the arbour it is necessary for them to return to the main walk, and pass the place where the bottom wall is broken down; a ruin evidently caused by rude intruders, doubtless the same savages who made the mission desolate. The talus extending to the path, with its fringe of further scattered clods, requires them to step carefully so as to avoid stumbling.

They go hand in hand, mutually supporting one another.

Their white gossamer dresses, floating lightly around them as they glide silently along, give them a resemblance to sylphs, or wood-nymphs, all the more as they emerge into the moonlight.

To complete the sylvan picture, it seems necessary there should be satyrs, or wood-demons, as well.

And such in reality there are, not a great way off. These, or something closely resembling them. No satyrs could show in more grotesque guise than the forms at that moment moving up to the wall, on its opposite side.

Gliding on, the sisters have arrived before the gap. Some instinct, perhaps curiosity, tempts them to take a look through it, into the shadowy forest beyond; and for some time, as under a spell of fascination, they stand gazing into its dark, mysterious depths.

They see nought save the sparkle of fire-flies; and hear nothing but the usual noises of the Southern night, to which they have been from infancy accustomed.

But as they are about moving on again, a sound salutes their ear— distinguishable as a footstep. Irregular and scrambling, as of one stepping among the broken bricks. Simultaneously a man is seen making his way over the wall.

"Fernand!"

No use for them now to attempt concealment; no good can come of it. He has seen them.

Nor does he any longer seem desirous of shunning observation. On the contrary, leaping down from the rampart, he comes straight towards them; in an instant presenting himself face to face, not with the nimble air of a servant, but the demeanour of one who feels himself master, and intend to play tyrant. With the moon shining full upon his tawny face, they can distinguish the play of its features. No look of humility, nor sign of subservience there. Instead, a bold, bullying expression, eyes emitting a lurid light, lips set in a satanic smile, between them teeth gleaming like a tiger's! He does not speak a word. Indeed, he has not time; for Helen Armstrong anticipates him. The proud girl, indignant at what she sees, too fearless to be frightened, at once commences chiding him.

In words bold and brave, so much that, if alone, the scoundrel might quail under their castigation. But he is not alone, nor does he allow her to continue.

Instead, he cries out, interrupting, his speech not addressed to her, but some one behind:—

"Bring hither the serapes! Quick, or—"

He himself is not permitted to finish what he intended saying; or, if so, his last words are unheard; drowned by a confused noise of rushing and rumbling, while the gap in the garden wall is suddenly closed, as if by enchantment. It is at first filled by a dark mass, seemingly compact, but soon separating into distinct forms.

The sisters, startled, terrified, have but time to give out one wild cry—a shriek. Before either can utter a second, brawny arms embrace them; blinds are thrown over their faces; and, half stifled, they feel themselves lifted from their feet, and borne rudely and rapidly away!

Chapter Fifty One
Locked in

At that same moment, when the red Sabines are carrying off his daughters, Colonel Armstrong is engaged, with his fellow-colonists, in discussing a question of great interest to all. The topic is sugar—the point, whether it will be profitable to cultivate it in their new colony. That the cane can be grown there all know. Both soil and climate are suitable. The only question is, will the produce pay, sugar being a bulky article in proportion to its price, and costly in transport through a territory without railroads, or steam communication.

While the discussion is at its height a new guest enters the room; who, soon as inside, makes a speech, which not only terminates the talk about sugar, but drives all thought of it out of their minds.

A speech of only four words, but these of startling significance: "*There are Indians about!*" 'Tis Hawkins who speaks, having entered without invitation, confident the nature of his news will hold him clear of being deemed an intruder.

And it does. At the word "Indians," all around the table spring up from their seats, and stand breathlessly expectant of what the hunter has further to communicate. For, by his serious air, they are certain there must be something more.

Colonel Armstrong alone asks, the old soldier showing the presence of mind that befits an occasion of surprise.

"Indians about? Why do you say that, Hawkins? What reason have you to think so?"

"The best o' reasons, colonel. I've seed them myself, and so's Cris Tucker along with me."

"Where?"

"Well, there's a longish story to tell. If you'll have patience, I'll make it short as possible."

"Go on!—tell it!"

The hunter responds to the demand; and without wasting words in detail, gives an epitome of his day's doings, in company with Cris Tucker. After describing the savage troop, as first seen on the upper plain, how he and his comrade followed them across the river bottom, then over the ford, and there lost their trail, he concludes his account, saying:

"Where they went afterward, or air now, 'taint possible for me to tell. All I can say is, what I've sayed already: *there are Indians about.*"

Of itself enough to cause anxiety in the minds of the assembled planters; which it does, to a man making them keenly apprehensive of danger.

All the more from its being their first alarm of the kind. For, while travelling through Eastern Texas, where the settlements are thick, and of old standing, the savages had not evens been thought of. There was no chance of seeing any there. Only, on drawing nigh to the Colorado, were Indians likely to be encountered; though it did not necessarily follow that the encounter should be hostile. On the contrary, it ought to be friendly; since a treaty of peace had for some time been existing between the Comanches and Texans.

For all this, Colonel Armstrong, well acquainted with the character of the red men, in war as in peace, had not relied altogether on their pacific promises. He knew that such contracts only bind the savage so long as convenient to him, to be broken whenever they become irksome. Moreover, a rumour had reached the emigrants that, although the great Comanche nation was itself keeping the treaty, there were several smaller independent tribes accustomed to make "maraud" upon the frontier settlements, chiefly to steal horses, or whatever chanced in their way.

For this reason, after entering the territory where such pillagers might be expected, the old soldier had conducted his expedition as if passing through an enemy's country. The waggons had been regularly *corralled,* and night guards kept—both camp sentinels and outlying pickets.

These rules had been observed up to the hour of arrival at their destination. Then, as the people got settled down in their respective domiciles, and nothing was heard of any Indians in that district, the discipline had been relaxed—in fact, abandoned. The colonists, numbering over fifty white men—to say nothing of several hundred negro slaves—deemed themselves strong enough to repel any ordinary assault from savages. They now considered themselves at home; and, with the confidence thus inspired, had ceased to speculate, on being molested by Indian enemies, or any others.

For this reason the suspicious movements of Dupré's half-breed servant, as reported by the young surgeon, had failed to make more than a passing impression on those around the dining-table; many of them treating it as an eccentricity.

Now, after hearing Hawkins, they think differently. It presents a serious aspect, is, in truth, alarmingly suggestive of treason.

The half-blood inside the house may be in correspondence with full-blooded Indians outside, for some scheme of thieving or burglary.

The thought of either is sufficient to excite Colonel Armstrong's guests, and all are on foot ready to take action.

"Dupré, call in your half-breed!" says the Colonel, directing it. "Let us hear what the fellow has to say for himself."

"Tell Fernand to come hither," commands the Creole, addressing himself to one of the negro lads waiting at table. "Tell him to come instantly!"

The boy hastens off to execute the order; and is several minutes before making re-appearance.

During the interval, they continue to discuss the circumstances that have so suddenly turned up; questioning Hawkins, and receiving from him minuter details of what he and his comrade have seen.

The additional matter made known but excites them the more, further intensifying their apprehensions.

They're at their keenest, as the darkey re-enters the room with the announcement that Fernand is not to be found!

"What do you mean, boy?" thunders Dupré, in a voice that well-nigh takes away the young negro's wits. "Is he not in the house?"

"Dat's jess what he aint, Mass Looey. De Spanish Indyin's no whar inside dis buildin'. We hab sarch all oba de place; call out his name in de store-rooms, an' de coatyard, an' de cattle closure—ebbery wha we tink of. We shout loud nuf for him to hyeer, ef he war anywha 'bout. He haint gib no answer. Sartin shoo he no inside o' dis 'tablishment."

The young planter shows dismay. So also the others, in greater or less degree, according to the light in which each views the matter.

For now on the minds of all is an impression, a presentiment, that there is danger at the bottom of Fernand's doings—how near they know not.

At any other time his absence would be a circumstance not worth noting. He might be supposed on a visit to some of the huts appropriated to the humbler families of the colonist fraternity. Or engaged outside with a mulatto "wench," of whom there are several, belonging to Dupré's extensive slave-gang, far from ill-favoured.

Fernand is rather a handsome fellow, and given to gaiety; which, under ordinary circumstances, would account for his absenting himself from the house, and neglecting his duties as its head-servant. But after what the young surgeon has seen—above all the report just brought in by Hawkins— his conduct will not convey this trivial interpretation. All in the room regard it in a more serious light—think the *mestizo* is a traitor.

Having come to this general conclusion, they turn towards the table, to take a last drink, before initiating action.

Just as they get their glasses in hand, the refectory door is once more opened; this time with a hurried violence that causes them to start, as though a bombshell had rolled into the room.

Facing towards it, they see it is only the negro boy, who had gone out again, re-entering. But now with fear depicted on his face, and wild terror gleaming from his eyes; the latter awry in their sockets, with little beside the whites seen!

Their own alarm is not much less than his, on hearing what he has to say. His words are,—

"Oh, Mass Kurnel! Mass Looey! Gemmen all! De place am full ob Indyin sabbages! Dar outside in de coatyard, more'n a thousan' ob um; an' murderin' ebbery body!"

At the dread tidings, glasses drop from the hands holding them, flung down in fear, or fury. Then all, as one man, make for the door, still standing open as in his scare the negro lad left it.

Before they can reach it, his words are too fully confirmed. Outside they see painted faces, heads covered with black hanging hair, and plumes bristling above. Only a glimpse they get of these, indistinct through the obscurity. But if transitory, not the less terrible—not less like a tableau in some horrid dream—a glance into hell itself.

The sight brings them to a stand; though, but for an instant. Then, they rush on towards the doorway, regardless of what may await them outside.

Outside they are not permitted to pass. Before they can reach the door, it is shut to with a loud clash; while another but slighter sound tells of a key turning in the wards, shooting a bolt into its keeper.

"Locked in, by God!" exclaims Hawkins, the rest involuntarily echoing his wild words; which are succeeded by a cry of rage as from one throat, though all have voice in it. Then silence, as if they were suddenly struck dumb.

For several moments they remain paralysed, gazing in one another's faces in mute despairing astonishment. No one thinks of asking explanation, or giving it. As by instinct, all realise the situation—a surprise, an Indian attack. No longer the future danger they have been deeming probable, but its dread present reality!

Short while do they stand irresolute. Hawkins, a man of herculean strength, dashes himself against the door, in hopes of heaving it from its hinges. Others add their efforts.

All idle. The door is of stout timber—oaken—massive as that of a jail; and, opening inward, can only be forced along with its posts and lintels.— These are set in the thick wall, embedded, firm as the masonry itself.

They rush to the windows, in hope of getting egress there.

Equally to be disappointed, baffled. The strong, iron bar resist every effort to break or dislodge them. Though weakened with decaying rust, they are yet strong enough to sustain the shock of shoulders, and the tug of arms.

"Trapped, by the Eternal!" despairingly exclaims the hunter. "Yes, gentlemen, we're caged to a certainty."

They need not telling. All are now aware of it—too well. They see themselves shut in—helplessly, hopelessly imprisoned.

Impossible to describe their thoughts, or depict their looks, in that anguished hour. No pen, or pencil, could do justice to either. Outside are their dear ones; near, but far away from any hope of help, as if twenty miles lay between. And what is being done to them? No one asks—none likes to tempt the answer; all guessing what it would be, dreading to hear it spoken. Never did men suffer emotions more painfully intense, passions more heartfelt and harrowing; not even the prisoners of Cawnpore, or the Black Hole of Calcutta.

They are in darkness now—have been from the moment of the door being closed. For, expecting to be fired at from the outside, they had suddenly extinguished the lights. They wonder there has been no shooting, aware that the Comanches carry fire-arms. But as yet there has been no report, either of pistol, or gun!

They hear only voices—which they can distinguish as those of the house-Servants—male and female—all negroes or mulattoes. There are shrieks, intermingled with speeches, the last in accent of piteous appealing; there is moaning and groaning. But where are the shouts of the assailants? Where the Indian yell—the dread slogan of the savage? Not a stave of it is heard—nought that resembles a warwhoop of Comanches!

And soon is nothing heard. For the shrieks of the domestics have ceased, their cries coming suddenly, abruptly to an end, as if stifled by blows bringing death.

Inside the room is a death-like stillness; outside the same.

Chapter Fifty Two
Massacre without mercy

Pass to the scene outside, than which none more tragical in the history of Texan colonisation.

No need to tell who the Indians are that have shown their faces at the dining-room door, shutting and locking it. They are those seen by Hawkins and Tucker—the same Dupré's traitorous servant has conducted through the gap in the garden wall; whence, after making seizure of the girls, they continued on to the house, the half-blood at their head.

Under his guidance they passed through the cattle corral, and into the inner court. Till entering this they were not observed. Then the negro lad, sent in search of Fernand, seeing them, rushed back for the refectory.

With all his haste, as already known, too late in giving the alarm. Half-a-dozen of the foremost, following, were at the dining-room door almost soon as he, while others proceeding to the front entrance, closed the great gate, to prevent any one escaping that way.

In the courtyard ensues a scene, horrible to behold. The domestics frightened, screaming, rushing to and fro, are struck down with tomahawks, impaled upon spears, or hacked and stabbed with long-bladed knives. At least a half-score of these unhappy creatures fall in the fearful slaughter. Indiscriminate as to age or sex: for men, women, and children are among its victims.

Their shrieks, and piteous appeals, are alike disregarded. One after another they are struck, or hewn down, like saplings by the *macheté*. A scene of red carnage, resembling a *saturnalia* of demons, doing murder!

Short as terrible; in less than ten minutes after its commencement it is all over. The victims have succumbed, their bleeding bodies lie along the pavement. Only those domestics have escaped, who preserved enough presence of mind to get inside rooms, and barricade the doors behind them.

They are not followed; for despite the red murder already done, the action ensuing, tells of only robbery intended.

This evident from the way the savages now go to work. Instead of attempting to reach those they have imprisoned within the dining-room, they place two of their number to stand guard by its door; another pair going on to the gate entrance. These steps taken, the rest, with Fernand still conducting, hurry along the corridor, towards a room which opens at one of its angles. It is the chamber Dupré has chosen for his sleeping apartment, and where he has deposited his treasure. Inside it his cash, at least fifty thousand dollars, most of it in silver, packed in stout boxes.

Fernand carries the key, which he inserts into its lock. The door flies open, and the half-blood enters, closely followed by those who appear all Indians. They go in with the eagerness of tigers springing upon prey, or more like the stealthiness of cats.

Soon they come out again, each bearing a box, of diminutive size, but weight sufficient to test his strength.

Laying these down, they re-enter the room, and return from it similarly loaded.

And so they go and come, carrying out the little boxes, until nearly a score are deposited upon the pavement of the courtyard.

The abstraction of the specie completed, the sentries set by the dining-room door, as also those sent to guard the entrance-gate, are called off; and the band becomes reunited by the treasure, as vultures around a carcass.

Some words are exchanged in undertone. Then each, laying hold of a box—there is one each for nearly all of them—and poising it upon his shoulders, strides off out of the courtyard.

Silently, and in single file, they pass across the cattle corral, on into the garden, down the central walk, and out through the gap by which they came in.

Then on to the glade where they have left their horses.

These they remount, after balancing the boxes upon their saddle-bows, and there securing them with trail-ropes.

Soon as in the saddle they move silently, but quickly away; the half-blood going along with them.

He, too, has a horse, the best in the troop—taken from the stable of the master he has so basely betrayed, so pitilessly plundered.

And that master at the moment nearly mad! Raging frantically around the room where they are left confined, nearly all the others frantic as he. For scarce any of them who has not like reason.

In the darkness groping, confusedly straying over the floor, stunned and stupified, they reel like drunken men; as they come in contact tremblingly interrogating one another as to what can have occurred.

By the silence outside it would seem as if everybody were murdered, massacred—coloured servants within the house, colonists without—all!

And what of Colonel Armstrong's own daughters? To their father it is a period of dread suspense—an agony indescribable. Much longer continued it would drive him mad. Perhaps he is saved from insanity by anger—by thoughts of vengeance, and the hope of living to accomplish it.

While mutually interrogating, one starts the suggestion that the whole affair may be a *travestie*—a freak of the younger, and more frolicksome members of the colonist fraternity. Notwithstanding its improbability, the idea takes, and is entertained, as drowning men catch at straws.

Only for an instant. The thing is too serious, affecting personages of too much importance, to be so trifled with. There are none in the settlement who would dare attempt such practical joking with its chief—the stern old soldier, Armstrong. Besides, the sounds heard outside were not those of mirth, mocking its opposite. The shouts and shrieks had the true ring of terror, and the accents of despair.

No. It could not be anything of a merrymaking, but what they at first supposed it—a tragedy.

Their rage returns, and they think only of revenge. As before, but to feel their impotence. The door, again tried, with all their united strength, refuses to stir from its hinges. As easily might they move the walls. The window railings alike resist their efforts; and they at length leave off, despairingly scattering through the room.

One alone remains, clinging to the window bars. It is Hawkins. He stays not with any hope of being able to wrench them off. He has already tested the strength of his arms, and found it insufficient. It is that of his lungs he now is determined to exert, and does so, shouting at the highest pitch of his voice.

Not that he thinks there is any chance of its being heard at the *rancheria*, nearly a half-mile off, with a grove of thick timber intervening. Besides, at that late hour the settlers will be asleep.

But in the grove between, and nearer, he knows there is a tent; and inside it a man who will be awake, if not dead—his comrade, Cris Tucker.

In the hope Cris may still be in the land of the living, Hawkins leans against the window bars and, projecting his face outward, as far as the jawbones will allow, he gives utterance to a series of shouts, interlarded with exclamations, that in the ears of a sober Puritan would have sounded terribly profane.

Chapter Fifty Three
A horrid spectacle

On a log outside the tent sits Cris Tucker, with the fire before him, kindled for cooking the turkey. The bird is upon a spit suspended above the blaze. A fat young "gobbler," it runs grease at every pore, causing the fire to flare up. Literally is it being broiled by its own grease, and is now well-nigh done brown.

Perceiving this, Tucker runs his eyes inquiringly along the path leading towards the mission, at the same time setting his ears to listen. What can be keeping his comrade, who promised so soon to be back?

"Promises are like pie-crust," says Cris in soliloquy; "Old Hawk aint keeping his, and I guess aint goin' to. I heard they war to have a big dine up there the night. So I suppose the colonel's axed him in for a glass o' his whiskey punch. Hawk's jest the one to take it—a dozen, if they insist. Well, there's no reason I should wait supper any longer. I'm 'most famished as it is. Besides, that bird's gettin' burnt."

Rising up from the log, he takes the turkey off the spit, and carries it inside the tent. Then dishing, he sets it upon the table; the dish a large platter of split wood rudely whittled into oblong oval shape, the table a stump with top horizontally hewn, over which the tent has been erected.

Placing a "pone" of corn-bread, and some salt alongside, he sits down; though not yet to commence eating. As certainly his comrade should now soon be back, he will give him ten minutes' grace.

The position is agreeable, at the same time having its drawbacks. The odour pervading the tent is delicious; still there is the sense of taste to be satisfied, and that of smell but provokes it. The savoury aroma of the roast turkey is keenly appetising, and Cris can't hold out much longer. Time passes, and no sign of Hawkins returning. Tucker's position becomes intolerable; the bird is getting cold, its juices drying up, the repast will be spoilt.

Besides, his comrade has not kept faith with him. In all probability he has eaten supper at the house, and at that moment is enjoying a jorum of whisky punch, quite forgetful of him. Tucker. Cris can stand it no longer;

and, drawing out his knife, he takes the turkey by the leg, and cuts a large slice from its breast.

This eaten, another slice of breast is severed and swallowed. Then a wing is carved off, and lastly a leg, which he polishes to the smoothness of a drumstick.—

The young hunter, now no longer ravenous, proceeds more leisurely, and completes his repast by tranquilly chewing up the gizzard, and after it the liver—the last a tit-bit upon the prairies, as in a Strasburg *paté*.

Washing all down with a gourd of whisky and water, he lights his pipe; and, seated by the mangled remains of the gobbler, commences smoking.

For a time the inhaled nicotine holds him tranquil; though not without wondering why his comrade is so long in patting in an appearance.

When over two hours have elapsed, his wonder becomes changed to anxiety. Not strange it should, recalling the reason why he has been left alone.

This increasing to keen apprehension, he can no longer stay within the tent. He will go up to the house, and find out what is detaining Hawkins.

Donning his skin cap, and stepping out into the open air, he starts off towards the mission-building.

Less than ten minutes' walking brings him to its walls, by their main front entrance.

There he pauses, surprised at the stillness surrounding the place. It is profound, unnatural.

For some moments he remains in front of the massive pile, looking at it, and listening. Still no sound, within or without.

True, it is time for the inmates to be a-bed.

But if so, where is Hawkins? He may be drinking, but surely not sleeping within!

In any case, Cris deems it his duty to look him up; and with this intent determines to enter.

He is not on terms of social equality with those who occupy the mission; still, under the circumstances, he cannot be considered intruding.

He sees that the great door is closed, but the wicket is ajar; presumptive proof of Hawkins being inside. There are no lights in the front windows, but, as Cris knows, those of the dining-room open backward.

Hesitating no longer, he steps under the arched portal, passes on through the *saguan*, and once more emerges into moonlight within the *patio*.

There, suddenly stopping, he stands aghast. For he beholds a sight that almost causes his hair to crisp up, and raise the cap from his head.

Down into the hollow quadrangle—enclosed on every side, except that towards heaven—the moonbeams are falling in full effulgence. By their light he sees forms lying along the pavement in every possible position. They are human bodies—men and boys, among them some whose drapery declares them to be women. They are black, brown, or yellow; but all spotted and spattered with red—with blood! Fresh, but fast freezing in the chill night air, it is already darkened, almost to the hue of ink.

The hunter turns faint, sick, as he contemplates this hecatomb of corpses. A spectacle far more fearful than any ever witnessed upon battle-field. There men lie in death from wounds given, as received under the grand, if delusive, idea of glory. Those Cris Tucker sees must have been struck down by the hand of the assassin!

For a time he stands gazing upon them, scarce knowing what to do.

His first impulse is to turn back, rush out of the courtyard, and away altogether from the place.

But a thought—a loyal thought or instinct, stays him. Where is Hawkins? His body may be among the rest—Cris is almost sure it will be found there—and affection for his friend prompts him to seek for it. There may still be breath in it—a spark of departing life, capable of being called back.

With this hope, however faint, he commences searching among the corpses.

The spectacle, that has sickened, makes his step feeble. He staggers as he passes among the prostrate forms, at times compelled to stride over them.

He examines one after another, bending low down to each—lower where they lie in shadow, and it is more difficult to distinguish their features.

Going the round of the courtyard, he completes the scrutiny of all. Living or dead, Hawkins is not among them.

Nor is there the body of any white man, or woman. The stricken victims are of every age, and both sexes. But all, male as female, are negroes or mulattoes—the slaves of the establishment. Many of them he recognises; knows them to be the house-servants.

Where are their masters? Where everybody? What terrible tragedy has occurred to leave such traces behind? The traces of murder—of wholesale slaughter!

Who have been the murderers, and where are they now? Where is Hawkins?

To the young hunter these self-asked interrogatories occur in quick succession; along with the last a sound reaching his ears which causes him to start, and stand listening acutely for its repetition. It seemed a human voice, as of a man in mortal agony shouting for succour. Faint, as if far off, away at the back of the building.

Continuing to listen, Tucker hears it again, this time recognising the voice of Hawkins.

He does not stay to conjecture why his comrade should be calling in accents of appeal. That they are so is enough for him to hasten to his aid. Clearly the cry comes from outside; and, soon as assured of this, Tucker turns that way, leaps lightly over the dead bodies, glides on along the saguan, and through the open wicket.

Outside he stops, and again listens, waiting for the voice to direct him, which it does.

As before he hears it, shouting for help, now sure it is Hawkins who calls. And sure, also, that the cries come from the eastern side of the building.

Towards this Tucker rushes, around the angle of the wall, breaking through the bushes like a chased bear.

Nor does he again stop till he is under a window, from which the shouts appear to proceed.

Looking up he sees a face, with cheeks pressing distractedly against the bars; at the same time hearing himself hailed in a familiar voice.

"Is't you, Cris Tucker? Thank the Almighty it is!"

"Sartin it's me," Hawkins. "What does it all mean?"

"Mean? That's more'n I can tell; or any o' us inside here; though there's big ends o' a dozen. We're shut up, locked in, as ye see. Who's done it you ought to know, bein' outside. Han't you seen the Indians?"

"I've seen no Indians; but their work I take it. There's a ugly sight round t'other side."

"What sight, Oris? Never mind—don't stay to talk. Go back, and get something to break open the door of this room. Quick, comrade, quick!"

Without stayin' for further exchange of speech, the young hunter hurries back into the *patio* as rapidly as he had quitted it; and laying hold of a heavy beam, brings it like a battering-ram, against the dining-room door.

Massive as this is, and strongly hung upon its hinges, it yields to his strength.

When at length laid open, and those inside released, they look upon a spectacle that sends a thrill of horror through their hearts.

In the courtyard lie ten corpses, all told. True they are but the dead bodies of slaves—to some beholding them scarce accounted as human beings. Though pitied, they are passed over without delay; the thoughts, as the glances, of their masters going beyond, in keen apprehension for the fate of those nearer and dearer.

Escaped from their imprisonment, they rush to and fro, like maniacs let out of a madhouse. Giving to the dead bodies only a passing glance, then going on in fear of finding others by which they will surely stay; all the time talking, interrogating, wildly gesticulating, now questioning Oris Tucker, now one another; in the confusion of voices, some heard inquiring for their wives, some their sisters or sweethearts, all with like eagerness; hopefully believing their dear ones still alive, or despairingly thinking them dead; fearing they may find them with gashed throats and bleeding breasts, like those lying along the flagstones at their feet.

The spectacle before their eyes, appalling though it be, is nought to that conjured up in their apprehensions. What they see may be but a forecast, a faint symbol, of what ere long they may be compelled to look upon.

And amid the many voices shouting for wife, sister, or sweetheart, none so loud, or sad, as that of Colonel Armstrong calling for his daughters.

Chapter Fifty Four
Riding double

With Colonel Armstrong's voice in tone of heartrending anguish, goes up that of Dupré calling the names "Helen! Jessie!"

Neither gets response. They on whom they call cannot hear. They are too far off; though nearer, it would be all the same; for both are at the moment hooded like hawks. The serapes thrown over their heads are still on them, corded around their necks, so closely as to hinder hearing, almost stifle their breathing.

Since their seizure nearly an hour has elapsed, and they are scarce yet recovered from the first shock of surprise, so terrible as to have stupified them. No wonder! What they saw before being blinded, with the rough treatment received, were enough to deprive them of their senses.

From the chaos of thought, as from a dread dream, both are now gradually recovering. But, alas! only to reflect on new fears—on the dark future before them. Captive to such captors—red ruthless savages, whose naked arms, already around, have held them in brawny embrace—carried away from home, from all they hold dear, into a captivity seeming hopeless as horrid—to the western woman especially repulsive, by songs sung over her cradle, and tales told throughout her years of childhood—tales of Indian atrocity.

The memory of these now recurring, with the reality itself, not strange that for a time their thoughts, as their senses, are almost paralysed.

Slowly they awake to a consciousness of their situation. They remember what occurred at the moment of their being made captive; how in the clear moonlight they stood face to face with Fernand, listened to his impertinent speeches, saw the savages surrounding them; then, suddenly blinded and seeing no more, felt themselves seized, lifted from their feet, carried off, hoisted a little higher, set upon the backs of horses, and there tied, each to a man already mounted. All these incidents they remember, as one recalls the fleeting phantasmagoria of a dream. But that they were real, and not fanciful, they now too surely know; for the hoods are over their heads, the horses underneath; and the savages to whom they were strapped still there, their bodies in repulsive contact with their own!

That there are only two men, and as many horses, can be told by the hoof-strokes rebounding from the turf; the same sounds proclaiming it a forest path through thick timber, at intervals emerging into open ground, and again entering among trees.

For over an hour this continues; during all the while not a word being exchanged between the two horsemen, or if so, not heard by their captives.

Possibly they may communicate with one another by signs or whispers; as for most part the horses have been abreast, going in single file only where the path is narrow.

At length a halt; of such continuance, as to make the captives suppose they have arrived at some place where they are to pass the remainder of the night. Or it may be but an obstruction; this probable from their hearing a sound, easily understood—the ripple of running water. They have arrived upon the bank of a river.

The San Saba, of course; it cannot be any other. Whether or not, 'tis the same to them. On the banks of the San Saba they are now no safer, than if it were the remotest stream in all the territory of Texas.

Whatever be the river whose waters they can hear coursing past, their guards, now halted upon its bank, have drawn their horses' heads together, and carry on a conversation. It seems in a strange tongue; but of this the captives cannot be sure, for it is in low tone—almost a whisper—the words indistinguishable amid the rush of the river's current. If heard, it is not likely they would understand. The two men are Indians, and will talk in the Indian tongue. For this same reason they need have no fear of freely conversing with one another, since the savages will be equally unable to comprehend what they say.

To Helen this thought first presents itself; soon as it does, leading her to call, though timidly and in subdued tone, "Jess!"

She is answered in the same way, Jessie saying, "Helen, I hear you."

"I only wanted to say a word to cheer you. Have courage. Keep up your heart. It looks dark now; but something may may arise up to save us."

Chapter Fifty Five
Tired travellers

The lower crossing of the San Saba, so frequently referred to, calls for topographical description.

At this point the stream, several hundred yards wide, courses in smooth, tranquil current, between banks wooded to the water's edge. The trees are chiefly cottonwoods, with oak, elm, tulip, wild China, and pecan interspersed; also the *magnolia grandiflora*; in short, such a forest as may be seen in many parts of the Southern States. On both sides of the river, and for some distance up and down, this timbered tract is close and continuous, extending nearly a mile back from the banks; where its selvedge of thinner growth becomes broken into glades, some of them resembling flower gardens, others dense thickets of the *arundo gigantea*, in the language of the country, "cane-brakes." Beyond this, the bottom-land is open meadow, a sea of green waving grass—the *gramma* of the Mexicans—which, without tree or bush, sweeps in to the base of the bluffs. On each side of the crossing the river is approached by a path, or rather an avenue-like opening in the timber, which shows signs of having been felled; doubtless, done by the former proprietors of the mission, or more like, the soldiers who served its garrison; a road made for military purposes, running between the *presidio* itself and the town of San Antonio de Bejar. Though again partially overgrown, it is sufficiently clear to permit the passage of wheeled vehicles, having been kept open by roving wild horses, with occasionally some that are tamed and ridden—by Indians on raid.

On its northern side the river is approached by two distinct trails, which unite before entering the wooded tract—their point of union being just at its edge. One is the main road coming from the Colorado; the other only an Indian trace, leading direct to the bluffs and the high land above them. It was by the former that Colonel Armstrong's train came up the valley, while the latter was the route taken by Hawkins and Tucker in their bootless excursion after buffalo.

On the same evening, when the hunters, returning from their unsuccessful search, repassed the ford, only at a later hour, a party of horsemen is seen approaching it—not by the transverse trace, but the main up-river road. In all there are five of them; four upon horseback, the fifth riding a mule. It is the same party we have seen crossing the Sabine — Clancy and his comrades — the dog still attached to it, the ex-jailer added. They are travelling in haste — have been ever since entering the territory of Texas. Evidence of this in their steeds showing jaded, themselves fatigued. Further proof of it in the fact of their being now close to the San Saba ford, within less than a week after Armstrong's party passing over, while more than two behind it at starting from the Sabine.

There has been nothing to delay them along the route — no difficulty in finding it. The wheels of the loaded waggons, denting deep in the turf, have left a trail, which Woodley for one could take up on the darkest hour of the darkest night that ever shadowed a Texan prairie. It is night now, about two hours after sundown, as coming up the river road they enter the timber, and approach the crossing place. When within about fifty yards of the ford at a spot where the path widens, they pull up, Woodley and Clancy riding a little apart from the others, as if to hold consultation whether they shall proceed across the stream, or stay where they are for the night.

Clancy wishes to go forward, but Woodley objects, urging fatigue, and saying: —

"It can't make much diff'rence now, whether we git up thar the night, or take it leezyurly in the cool o' the mornin'. Since you say ye don't intend showin' yourself 'bout the mission buildin', it'll be all the better makin' halt hyar. We kin steal nearer; an' seelect a campin' place at the skreek o' day jest afore sun-up. Arter thet me an' Ned 'll enter the settlement, an' see how things stand."

"Perhaps you're right," responds Clancy, "If you think it better for us to halt here, I shan't object; though I've an idea we ought to go on. It may appear very absurd to you, Sime, but there's something on my mind — a sort of foreboding."

"Forebodin' o' what?"

"In truth I can't tell what or why. Yet I can't get it out of my head that there's some danger hanging over — "

He interrupts himself, holding back the name — Helen Armstrong. For it is over her he fancies danger may be impending. No new fancy either; but one that has been afflicting him all along, and urging him so impatiently onward. Not that he has learnt anything new since leaving the Sabine. On its banks the ex-jailer discharged his conscience in full, by confessing all he could. At most not much; since his late associates, seeing the foolish fellow he was, had never made him sharer in their greatest secret. Still he had heard and reported enough to give Clancy good reason for uneasiness.

"I kin guess who you're alludin' to," rejoins Woodley, without waiting for the other to finish, "an' ef so, yur forebodin', as ye call it, air only a foolish notion, an' nothin' more. Take Sime Woodley's word for it, ye'll find things up the river all right."

"I hope so."

"Ye may be sure o't. Kalklate, ye don't know Planter Armstrong's well's I do, tho' I admit ye may hev a better knowledge o' one that bears the name. As for the ole kurnel hisself, this chile's kampayned wi' him in the Cherokee wars, an' kin say for sartin he aint a-goin' to sleep 'ithout keepin' one o' his peepers skinned. Beside, his party air too strong, an' the men composin' it too exparienced, to be tuk by surprise, or attacked by any enemy out on these purayras, whether red Injuns or white pirates. Ef thar air danger it'll come arter they've settled down, an' growed unsurspishus. Then thar mout be a chance o' circumventin' them. But then we'll be thar to purvent it. No fear o' our arrivin' too late. We'll get up to the ole mission long afore noon the morrow, whar ye'll find, what ye've been so long trackin' arter, soun' an' safe. Trust Sime Woodley for that."

The comforting words tranquillise Clancy's fears, at the same time checking his impatience. Still is he reluctant to stay, and shows it by his answer.

"Sime, I'd rather we went on."

"Wal, ef ye so weesh it, on let's go. Your the chief of this party an' kin command. For myself I'm only thinkin' or them poor, tired critters."

The hunter points to the horses, that for the last hour have been dragging their limbs along like bees honey-laden.

"To say nothin' o' ourselves," he adds, "though for my part I'm riddy to keep on to the Rio Grand, if you insist on goin' thar."

Notwithstanding his professed willingness, there is something in the tone of Sime's speech which contradicts it—just a *soupçon* of vexation.

Perceiving it, Clancy makes rejoinder with the delicacy becoming a gentleman. Though against his will and better judgment, his habitual belief in, and reliance on Woodley's wisdom, puts an end to his opposition; and in fine yielding, he says:—

"Very well; we shall stay. After all, it can't make much difference. A truce to my presentiments. I've often had such before, that came to nothing. Hoping it may be the same now, we'll spend our night this side the river."

"All right," responds the backwoodsman. "An' since it's decided we're to stay, I see no reezun why we shedn't make ourselves as comfortable as may be unner the circumstances. As it so chances, I know this hyar San Saba bottom 'most as well as that o' our ole Massissip. An' ef my mem'ry don't mistake, thar's a spot not far from hyar that'll jest suit for us to camp in. Foller me; I'll find it."

Saying this, he kicks his heels against the ribs of his horse, and compels the tired steed once more into reluctant motion, the rest riding after in silence.

Chapter Fifty Six
Spectral equestrians

But a short distance from where the travellers made stop, a side trace leads to the left, parallel to the direction of the river. Into this Woodley strikes, conducting the others.

It is so narrow they cannot go abreast, but in single file.

After proceeding thus for some fifty yards, they reach a spot where the path widens, debouching upon an open space—a sort of terrace that overhangs the channel of the stream, separated from it by a fringe of low trees and bushes.

Pointing to it, Sime says:—

"This chile hev slep on that spread o' grass, some'at like six yeern ago, wi' nothin' to disturb his rest 'ceptin the skeeters. Them same seems nasty bad now. Let's hope we'll git through the night 'ithout bein' clar eat up by 'em. An', talkin' o' eatin', I reckin we'll all be the better o' a bit supper. Arter thet we kin squat down an' surrender to Morpheus."

The meal suggested is speedily prepared, and, soon as despatched, the "squatting" follows.

In less than twenty minutes after forsaking the saddle, all are astretch along the ground, their horses "hitched" to trees, themselves seemingly buried in slumber—bound in its oblivious embrace.

There is one, however, still awake—Clancy.

He has slept but little any night since entering the territory of! Texas. On this he sleeps not at all—never closes eye—cannot. On the contrary, he turns restlessly on his grassy couch, fairly writhing with the presentiment he has spoken of, still upon him, and not to be cast off.

There are those who believe in dreams, in the reality of visions that appear to the slumbering senses. To Clancy's, awake, on this night, there seems a horrid realism, almost a certainty, of some dread danger. And too certain it is. If endowed with the faculty of clairvoyance, he would know it to be so—would witness a series of incidents at that moment occurring up the river—scarce ten miles from the spot where he is lying—scenes that would cause him to start suddenly to his feet, rush for his horse, and ride off, calling upon his companions to follow. Then, plunging into the river without fear of the ford, he would gallop on towards the San Saba mission, as if the house were in names, and he only had the power to extinguish them.

Not gifted with second-sight, he does not perceive the tragedy there being enacted. He is only impressed with a prescience of some evil, which keeps him wide awake, while the others around are asleep; soundly, as he can tell by their snoring.

Woodley alone sleeps lightly; the hunter habituated, as he himself phrases it, "allers to do the possum bizness, wi' one eye open."

He has heard Clancy's repeated shiftings and turnings, coupled with involuntary exclamations, as of a man murmuring in his dreams. One of these, louder than the rest, at length startling, causes Woodley to enquire what his comrade wants; and what is the matter with him.

"Oh, nothing," replies Clancy; "only that I can't sleep—that's all."

"Can't sleep! Wharfore can't ye? Sure ye oughter be able by this time. Ye've had furteeg enuf to put you in the way o' slumberin' soun' as a hummin' top."

"I can't to-night, Sime."

"Preehaps ye've swallered somethin', as don't sit well on your stummuk! Or, it may be, the klimat o' this hyar derrict. Sartin it do feel a leetle dampish, 'count o' the river fog; tho', as a general thing, the San Sabre bottom air 'counted one o' the healthiest spots in Texas. S'pose ye take a pull out o' this ole gourd o' myen. It's the best Monongaheely, an' for a seedimentary o' the narves thar ain't it's eequal to be foun' in any drug-shop. I'll bet my bottom dollar on thet. Take a suck, Charley, and see what it'll do for ye."

"It would have no effect. I know it wouldn't. It isn't nervousness that keeps me awake—something quite different."

"Oh!" grunts the old hunter, in a tone that tells of comprehension. "Something quite diff'rent? I reck'n I kin guess what thet somethin' air—the same as keeps other young fellurs awake—thinkin' o' thar sweethearts. Once't in the arms o' Morpheous, ye'll forgit all about your gurl. Foller my deevice; put some o' this physic inside yur skin, an' you'll be asleep in the shakin' o' a goat's tail."

The dialogue comes to a close by Clancy taking the prescribed physic.

After which he wraps his blanket around him, and once more essays to sleep.

As before, he is unsuccessful. Although for a while tranquil and courting slumber, it will not come. He again tosses about; and at length rises to his feet, his hound starting up at the same time.

Woodley, once more awakened, perceives that the potion has failed of effect, and counsels his trying it again.

"No," objects Clancy; "'tis no use. The strongest soporific in the world wouldn't give me sleep this night. I tell you, Sime, I have a fear upon me."

"Fear o' what?"

"That we'll be too late."

The last words, spoken solemnly, tell of apprehension keenly felt— whether false, or prophetic.

"That air's all nonsense," rejoins Woodley, wishing to reason his comrade out of what he deems an idle fancy. "The height o' nonsense. Wheesh!"

The final exclamation, uttered in an altered tone, is accompanied by a start—the hunter suddenly raising his head from the saddle on which it rests. Nor has the act any relation to his previous speeches. It comes from his hearing a sound, or fancying he hears one. At the same instant, the hound pricks up its ears, giving utterance to a low growl.

"What is't, I wonder?" interrogates Woodley, in a whisper, placing himself in a kneeling posture, his eyes sharply set upon the dog.

Again the animal jerks its ears, growling as before.

"Take clutch on the critter, Charley! Don't let it gie tongue."

Clancy lays hold of the hound, and draws it against his knees, by speech and gesture admonishing it to remain silent.

The well-trained animal sees what is wanted; and, crouching down by its master's feet, ceases making demonstration.

Meanwhile Woodley has laid himself flat along the earth, with ear close to the turf.

There is a sound, sure enough; though not what he supposed he had heard just before. That was like a human voice—some one laughing a long way off. It might be the "too-who-ha" of the owl, or the bark of a prairie wolf. The noise now reaching his ears is less ambiguous, and he has no difficulty in determining its character. It is that of water violently agitated— churned, as by the hooves of horses.

The Death Shot | 239

Clancy, standing erect, hears it, too.

The backwoodsman does not remain much longer prostrate; only a second to assure himself whence the sound proceeds. It is from the ford. The dog looked that way, on first starting up; and still keeps sniffing in the same direction.

Woodley is now on his feet, and the two men standing close together, intently listen.

They have no need to listen long; for their eyes are above the tops of the bushes that border the river's bank, and they see what is disturbing the water.

Two horses are crossing the stream. They have just got clear of the timber's shadow on the opposite side, and are making towards mid-water.

Clancy and Woodley, viewing them from higher ground, can perceive their forms, in *silhouette*, against the shining surface.

Nor have they any difficulty in making out that they are mounted. What puzzles them is the manner. Their riders do not appear to be anything human!

The horses have the true equine outline; but they upon their backs seem monsters, not men; their bodies of unnatural breadth, each with two heads rising above it!

There is a haze overhanging the river, as gauze thrown over a piece of silver plate. It is that white filmy mist which enlarges objects beyond their natural size, producing the mystery of *mirage*. By its magnifying effect the horses, as their riders, appear of gigantic dimensions; the former seeming Mastodons, the latter Titans bestriding them!

Both appear beings not of Earth, but creatures of some weird wonder-world—existences not known to our planet, or only in ages past!

Chapter Fifty Seven
Planning a capture

Speechless with surprise, the two men stand gazing at the odd apparition; with something more than surprise, a supernatural feeling, not unmingled with fear. Such strange unearthly sight were enough to beget this in the stoutest hearts; and, though none stouter than theirs, for a time both are awed by it.

Only so long as the spectral equestrians were within the shadow of the trees on the opposite side. But soon as arriving at mid-stream the mystery is at an end; like most others, simple when understood. Their forms, outlined against the moonlit surface of the water, show a very natural phenomenon—two horses carrying double.

Woodley is the first to announce it, though Clancy has made the discovery at the same instant of time.

"Injuns!" says the backwoodsman, speaking in a whisper. "Two astride o' each critter. Injuns, for sure. See the feathers stickin' up out o' their skulls! Them on the krupper look like squaws; though that's kewrous too. Out on these Texas parayras the Injun weemen hez generally a hoss to theirselves, an' kin ride 'most as well as the men. What seem queerier still is thar bein' only two kupple; but maybe there's more comin' on ahint. An' yet thar don't appear to be. I don't see stime o' anythin' on tother side the river. Kin you?"

"No. I think there's but the two. They'd be looking back if there were others behind. What ought we to do with them?"

"What every white man oughter do meetin' Injuns out hyar—gie 'em a wide berth: that's the best way."

"It may not in this case; I don't think it is."

"Why?"

"On my word, I scarce know. And yet I have an idea we ought to have a word with them. Likely they've been up to the settlement and will be able to tell us something of things there. As you know, Sime, I'm anxious to hear about—"

"I know all that. Wal, ef you're so inclined, let it be as ye say. We kin eezy stop 'em, an' hear what they've got to say for theirselves. By good luck, we've the devantage o' 'em. They're bound to kum 'long the big trail. Tharfor, ef we throw ourselves on it, we'll intercep' an' take 'em as in a trap. Jess afore we turned in hyar, I noticed a spot whar we kin ambuskade."

"Let us do so; but what about these?" Clancy points to the other three, still seemingly asleep. "Hadn't we better awake them? At all events, Heywood: we may need him."

"For that matter, no. Thar's but two buck Injuns. The does wont count for much in a skrimmage. Ef they show thar teeth I reckin we two air good for uglier odds than that. Howsomever, it'll be no harm to hev Ned. We kin roust him up, lettin' Harkness an' the mulattar lie. Ye'es; on second thinkin' it'll be as well to hev him along. Ned! Ned!"

The summons is not spoken aloud, but in a whisper, Woodley stooping down till his lips touch Heywood's ear. The young hunter hearing him, starts, then sits up, and finally gets upon his feet, rubbing his eyes while erecting himself. He sees at once why he has been awakened. A glance cast upon the river shows him the strangely ridden horses; still visible though just entering the tree-shadow on its nether bank.

In a few hurried words Woodley makes known their intention; and for some seconds the three stand in consultation, all having hold of their rifles.

They do not deem it necessary to rouse either the ex-jailer or Jupiter. It is not advisable, in view of the time that would be wasted. Besides, any noise, now, might reach the ears of the Indians, who, if alarmed, could still retreat to the opposite side, and so escape. Woodley, at first indifferent about their capture, has now entered into the spirit of it. It is just possible some information may be thus obtained, of service to their future designs. At all events, there can be no harm in knowing why the redskins are travelling at such an untimely hour.

"As a gen'ral rule," he says, "Tair best let Injuns go thar own way when thar's a big crowd thegitter. When thar aint, as it chances hyar, it may be wisest to hev a leetle palaver wi' them. They're putty sure to a been arter some diviltry anyhow. 'S like 's not this lot's been a pilferin' somethin' from the new settlement, and air in the act o' toatin' off thar plunder. Ef arter gruppin' 'em, we find it aint so, we kin let go again, an' no dammidge done. But first, let's examine 'em, an' see."

"Our horses?" suggests Heywood, "oughtn't we to take them along?"

"No need," answers Woodley. "Contrarywise, they'd only hamper us. If the redskins make to rush past, we kin eezy shoot down thar animals, an' so stop 'em. Wi' thar squaws along, they ain't like to make any resistance. Besides, arter all, they may be some sort that's friendly to the whites. Ef so, 'twould be a pity to kill the critters. We kin capter 'em without sheddin' thar blood."

"Not a drop of it," enjoins Clancy, in a tone of authority. "No, comrades. I've entered Texas to spill blood, but not that of the innocent — not that of Indians. When it comes to killing I shall see before me — . No matter; you know whom I mean."

"I guess we do," answers Woodley. "We both o' us understand your feelins, Charley Clancy; ay, an' respect 'em. But let's look sharp. Whilst we stan' palaverin the Injuns may slip past. They've arready reech'd the bank, an' — Quick, kum along!"

The three are about starting off, when a fourth figure appears standing erect. It is Jupiter. A life of long suffering has made the mulatto a light sleeper, and he has been awake all the time they were talking. Though they spoke only in whispers, he has heard enough to suspect something about to be done, in which there may be danger to Clancy. The slave, now free, would lay down his life for the man who has manumitted him.

Coming up, he requests to be taken along, and permitted to share their exploit, however perilous.

As there can be no great objection, his request is granted, and he is joined to the party.

But this necessitates a pause, for something to be considered. What is to be done with the ex-jailer? Though not strictly treated as a prisoner, still all along they have been keeping him under surveillance. Certainly, there was something strange in his making back for the States, in view of what he might there expect to meet for his misdemeanour; and, considering this, they have never been sure whether he may not still be in league with the outlaws, and prove twice traitor.

Now that they are approaching the spot where events may be expected, more than ever is it thought necessary to keep an eye on him.

It will not do to leave him alone, with their horses. What then?

While thus hesitating, Woodley cuts the Gordian knot by stepping straight to where Harkness lies, grasping the collar of his coat, and rudely arousing him out of his slumber, by a jerk that brings him erect upon his feet. Then, without waiting word of remonstrance from the astonished man, Sime hisses into his ear: —

"Kum along, Joe Harkness! Keep close arter us, an' don't ask any questyuns. Thar, Jupe; you take charge o' him!"

At this, he gives Harkness a shove which sends him staggering into the arms of the mulatto.

The latter, drawing a long stiletto-like knife, brandishes it before the ex-jailer's eyes, as he does so, saying:

"Mass Harkness; keep on afore me; I foller. If you try leave the track look-out. This blade sure go 'tween your back ribs."

The shining steel, with the sheen of Jupiter's teeth set in stern determination, is enough to hold Harkness honest, whatever his intent. He makes no resistance, but, trembling, turns along the path.

Once out of the glade, they fall into single file, the narrow trace making this necessary; Woodley in the lead; Clancy second, holding his hound in leash; Heywood third; Harkness fourth; Jupiter with bared knife-blade bringing up the rear.

Never marched troop having behind it a more inexorable file-closer, or one more determined on doing his duty.

Chapter Fifty Eight
Across the ford

No need to tell who are the strange equestrians seen coming across the river; nor to say, that those on the croup are not Indian women, but white ones—captives. The reader already knows they are Helen and Jessie Armstrong.

Had Charles Clancy or Sime Woodley but suspected this at the time, they would not have waited for Heywood, or stood dallying about the duplicity of Harkness. Instead, they would have rushed right on to the river, caring little what chances might be against them. Having no suspicion of its being ought save two travelling redskins, accompanied by their squaws, they acted otherwise.

The captives themselves know they are not in charge of Indians. After hearing that horrid laughter they are no longer in doubt. It came from the throats of white men: for only such could have understood the speeches that called it forth.

This discovery affords them no gratification, but the opposite. Instead of feeling safer in the custody of civilised men, the thought of it but intensifies their fears. From the red savage, *pur sang*, they might look for some compassion; from the white one they need not expect a spark of it.

And neither does; both have alike lost heart and sunk into deepest dejection. Never crossed Acheron two spirits more despairing—less hopeful of happiness beyond.

They are silent now. To exchange speech would only be to tempt a fresh peal of that diabolical laughter yet ringing in their ears. Therefore, they do not speak a word—have not since, nor have their captors. They, too, remain mute, for to converse, and be heard, would necessitate shouting. The horses are now wading knee-deep, and the water, in continuous agitation, makes a tumultuous noise; its cold drops dashed back, clouting against the blankets in which the forms of the captives are enfolded.

Though silent, these are busy with conjectures. Each has her own about the man who is beside her. Jessie thinks she is sharing the saddle with the traitor, Fernand. She trembles at recalling his glances from time to time cast upon her—ill-understood then, too well now. And now in his power, soon to be in his arms! Oh, heavens—it is horror.—Something like this she exclaims, the wild words wrung from her in her anguish. They are drowned by the surging noise.

Almost at the same instant, Helen gives out an ejaculation. She, too, is tortured with a terrible suspicion about him whose body touches her own. She suspects him to be one worse than traitor; is almost sure he is an assassin!

If so, what will be her fate? Reflecting on it, no wonder she cries out in agony, appealing to heaven—to God!

Suddenly there is silence, the commotion in the water having ceased. The hoofs strike upon soft sand, and soon after with firmer rebound from the bank.

For a length or two the horses strain upward; and again on level ground are halted, side by side and close together. The man who has charge of Helen, speaking to the other, says:—

"You'd better go ahead, Bill. I aint sure about the bye-path to the big tree. I've forgotten where it strikes off. You know, don't you?"

"Yes, lootenant; I guess I kin find where it forks."

No thought of Indians now—nor with Jessie any longer a fear of Fernand. By his speech, the man addressed as Bill cannot be the half-blood. It is something almost to reassure her. But for Helen—the other voice! Though speaking in undertone, and as if with some attempt at disguise, she is sure of having heard it before; then with distrust, as now with loathing. She hears it again, commanding:—"Lead on!"

Bill does not instantly obey, but says in rejoinder:—

"Skuse me, lootenant, but it seems a useless thing our goin' up to the oak. I know the Cap' sayed we were to wait for them under it. Why cant we just as well stay heer? 'Taint like they'll be long now. They wont dally a minute, I know, after they've clutched the shiners, an' I guess they got 'em most as soon as we'd secured these pair o' petticoats. Besides they'll come quicker than we've done, seeing as they're more like to be pursooed. It's a ugly bit o' track 'tween here an' the big tree, both sides thorny bramble that'll tear the duds off our backs, to say nothin' o' the skin from our faces. In my opinion we oughter stay where we air till the rest jeins us."

"No," responds the lieutenant, in tone more authoritative, "We mustn't remain here. Besides, we cant tell what may have happened to them. Suppose they have to fight for it, and get forced to take the upper crossing. In that case—"

The speaker makes pause, as if perceiving a dilemma.

"In that case," interpolates the unwilling Bill, "we'd best not stop heer at all, but put straight for head-quarters on the creek. How d'ye incline to that way of it?"

"Something in what you say," answers the lieutenant. Then adding, after a pause, "It isn't likely they'll meet any obstruction. The half-breed Indian said he had arranged everything clear as clock-work. They're safe sure to come this way, and 'twont do for us to go on without them. Besides, there's a reason you appear not to think of. Neither you nor I know the trail across the upper plain. We might get strayed there, and if so, we'd better be in hell?"

After the profane utterance succeeds a short interval of silence, both men apparently cogitating. The lieutenant is the first to resume.

"Bosley," he says, speaking in a sage tone, and for the first time addressing the subordinate by his family name. "On the prairies, as elsewhere, one should always be true to a trust, and keep it when one can. If there were time, I could tell you a curious story of one who tried but couldn't. It's generally the wisest way, and I think it's that for us now. We might make a mess of it by changing from the programme understood— which was for us to wait under the oak. Besides I've got a reason of my own for being there a bit—something you can't understand, and don't need telling about. And time's precious too; so spin ahead, and find the path."

"All right," rejoins the other, in a tone of assumed resignation. "Stayin' or goin's jest the same to me. For that matter I might like the first way best. I kin tell ye I'm precious tired toatin this burden at my back, beauty though she be; an' by remainin' heer I'll get the sooner relieved. When Cap' comes he'll be wantin' to take her off my hands; to the which I'll make him welcome as the flowers o' May."

With his poetical wind-up, the reluctant robber sets his horse in motion, and leads on. Not far along the main road. When a few yards from the ford, he faces towards a trail on his left, which under the shadow is with difficulty discernible. For all this, he strikes into it with the confidence of one well acquainted with the way.

Along it they advance between thick standing trees, the path arcaded over by leafy branches appearing as dark as a tunnel. As the horses move on, the boughs, bent forward by their breasts, swish back in rebound, striking against the legs of their riders; while higher up the hanging *llianas*, many of them beset with spines, threaten to tear the skin from their faces.

Fortunately for the captives, theirs are protected by the close-woven serapes. Though little care they now: thorns lacerating their cheeks were but trivial pain, compared to the torture in their souls. They utter no complaint, neither speaking a word. Despair has stricken them dumb; for, moving along that darksome path, they feel as martyrs being conducted to stake or scaffold.

Chapter Fifty Nine
A Foiled Ambuscade

Almost at the same instant the double-mounted steeds are turning off the main road, Woodley and those with him enter upon it; only at a point further away from the ford.

Delayed, first in considering what should be done with Harkness, and afterwards by the necessity of going slowly, as well as noiselessly along the narrow trace, they have arrived upon the road's edge just in time to be too late.

As yet they are not aware of this, though Woodley has his apprehensions; these becoming convictions, after he has stood for a time listening, and hears no sound, save that of the water, which comes in hoarse hiss between the trees, almost deafening the ear. For at this point the stream, shallowing, runs in rapid current over a pebbly bed, here and there breaking into crests.

Woodley's fear has been, that before he and his companions reach the road, the Indians might get past. If so, the chances of taking them will be diminished perhaps gone altogether. For, on horseback, they would have an advantage over those following afoot; and their capture could only be effected by the most skilful stalking, as such travellers have the habit of looking behind.

The question is—Have they passed the place, where it was intended to waylay them?

"I don't think they hev," says Woodley, answering it. "They have hardly hed time. Besides 'tain't nat'ral they'd ride strait on, jest arter kimmin' acrosst the river. It's a longish wade, wi' a good deal o' work for the horses. More like they've pulled up on reachin' the bank, an' air thar breathin' the critters a bit."

None of the others offering an opinion, he adds—

"Thur's a eezy way to make sure, an' the safest, too. Ef they've good by hyar, they can't yet be very far off. Ridin' as they air they won't think o' proceedin' at a fast pace. Therefore, let's take a scout 'long the road outwards. Ef they're on it, we'll soon sight 'em, or we may konklude they're behind on the bank o' the river. They're bound to pass this way, ef they hain't arready. So we'll eyther overtake, or meet 'em when returnin', or what mout be better'n both, ketch 'em a campin' by the water's edge. In any case our surest way air first to follow up the road. Ef that prove a failure, we kin 'bout face, an' back to the river."

"Why need we all go?" asks Heywood. "Supposing the rest of you stay here, while I scout up the road, and see whether they've gone along it."

"What ud be the use o' that?" demands Sime. "S'posin' ye did, an' sighted 'em, ye ain't goin' to make thar capture all o' yourself. Look at the time lost whiles ye air trottin' back hyar to tell us. By then, they'd get out into the clear moonlight, whar ther'd be no chance o' our comin' up to them without thar spyin' us. No, Ned: your idee won't do. What do you think, Charley?"

"That your plan seems best. You're sure there's no other way for them to pass out from the river?"

"This chile don't know o' any, ceptin' this trace we've ourselves kum off o'."

"Then, clearly, our best plan is first to try along the road—all together."

"Let's on, then!" urges Woodley. "Thar's no time to waste. While we stan' talkin' hyar, them redskins may ride to the jumpin'-off place o' creashun."

So saying, the hunter turns face to the right, and goes off at a run, the others moving in like manner behind him.

After proceeding some two or three hundred yards, they arrive at a place where the trees, standing apart, leave an open space between. There a saddle-like hollow intersects the road, traversing it from side to side. It is the channel of a rivulet when raining; but now nearly dry, its bed a mortar of soft mud. They had crossed it coming in towards the river, but without taking any notice of it, further than the necessity of guiding their tired steeds to guard against their stumbling. It was then in darkness, the twilight just past, and the moon not risen. Now that she is up in mid heaven, it is flooded by her light, so that the slightest mark in the mud can be clearly distinguished.

Running their eyes over its surface, they observe tracks they have not been looking for, and more than they have reason to expect. Signs to cause them surprise, if not actual alarm. Conspicuous are two deep parallel ruts, which they know have been made by the wheels of the emigrant wagons. A shower of rain, since fallen, has not obliterated them; only washed off their sharp angles, having done the same with the tracks of the mule teams between, and those of the half hundred horses ridden alongside, as also the hoof-marks of the horned cattle driven after.

It is not any of these that gives them concern. But other tracks more recent, made since the ram—in fact, since the sun lose that same morning—made by horses going towards the river, and with riders on their backs. Over twenty in all, without counting their own; some of them shod, but most without iron on the hoof. To the eyes of Sime Woodley—to Clancy's as well—these facts declare themselves at a single glance; and they only dwell upon further deductions. But not yet. For while scanning the slough they see two sets of horse tracks going in the opposite direction—outward from the river. Shod horses, too; their hoof-prints stamped deep in the mud, as if both had been heavily mounted.

This is a matter more immediate. The redskins, riding double, have gone past. If they are to be overtaken, nor a moment must be spent thinking of aught else.

Clancy has risen erect, ready to rush on after them. So Heywood and the rest. But not Woodley, who, still stooping over the slough, seems unsatisfied. And soon he makes a remark, which not only restrains the others, but causes an entire change in their intention.

"They aint fresh," he says, speaking of the tracks last looked at. "Thet is, they hain't been made 'ithin the hour. Tharfor, it can't be them as hev jest crossed the stream. Take a squint at 'em, Charley."

Clancy, thus called upon, lowering his eyes, again looks at the tracks. Not for long. A glance gives him evidence that Woodley is right. The horses which made these outgoing tracks cannot be the same seen coming across.

And now, the others being more carefully scrutinised, these same two are discovered among them, with the convexity of the hoof turned towards the river!

In all this there is strangeness, though it is not the time to inquire into it. That must be left till later. Their only thought now is, where are the Indians; for they have certainly not come on along the road.

"Boys!" says Woodley, "we've been makin' a big roundabout 'ithout gainin' a great deal by it. Sartin them redskins hev stopped at the river, an' thar mean squatting for the remainder o' this night. That'll suit our purpiss to a teetotum. We kin capter 'em in thar camp eezier than on the backs o' thar critters. So, let's go right on an' grup 'em!"

With this he turns, and runs back along the road, the others keeping close after.

In ten minutes more they are on the river's bank, where it declined to the crossing. They see no Indians there—no human creatures of any kind— nor yet any horses!

Chapter Sixty
"The Live-Oak"

At a pace necessarily slow, from the narrowness of the path and its numerous obstructions, the painted robbers, with their captives, have continued on; reaching their destination about the time Clancy and his comrades turned back along the ford road.

From this they are now not more than three hundred yards distant, halted in the place spoken of as a rendezvous.

A singular spot it is—one of those wild forest scenes by which nature oft surprises and delights her straying worshipper.

It is a glade of circular shape, with a colossal tree standing in its centre,—a live-oak with trunk full forty feet in girth, and branches spreading like a banyan. Though an evergreen, but little of its own foliage can be seen, only here and there a parcel of leaves at the extremity of a protruding twig; all the rest, great limbs and lesser branches, shrouded under Spanish moss, this in the moonlight showing white as flax.

Its depending garlands, stirred by the night breeze, sway to and fro, like ghosts moving in a minuet; when still, appearing as the water of a cataract suddenly frozen in its fall, its spray converted into hoar frost, the jets to gigantic icicles.

In their midst towers the supporting stem, thick and black, its bark gnarled and corrugated as the skin of an alligator.

This grim Titan of the forest, o'ertopping the other trees like a giant among men, stands alone, as though it had commanded them to keep their distance. And they seem to obey. Nearer than thirty yards to it none grow, nor so much as an underwood. It were easy to fancy it their monarch, and them not daring to intrude upon the domain it has set apart for itself.

With the moon now in the zenith, its shadow extends equally on all sides of its huge trunk, darkening half the surface of the glade—the other half in light, forming an illuminated ring around it. There could be no mistaking it for other than the "big tree," referred to in the dialogue between the two robbers; and that they recognise it as such is evident by their action. Soon as sighting it, they head straight towards its stem, and halting, slip down out of their saddles, having undone the cords by which the captives were attached to them.

When dismounted, the lieutenant, drawing Bosley a step or two apart, says: —

"You stay here, Bill, and keep your prisoner company. I want a word with mine before our fellows come up, and as it's of a private nature, I'm going to take her to the other side of the tree."

The direction is given in tone so low the captives cannot hear it; at the same time authoritatively, to secure Bill's obedience. He has no intention of refusing it. On the contrary, he responds with alacrity: —"All right. I understand." This spoken as if implying consent to some sinister purpose on the part of his superior. Without further words, the lieutenant lays hold of his horse's rein, and leads the animal round to the other side of the live-oak, his captive still in the saddle. Thus separated, the two men are not only out of each other's sight, but beyond the chance of exchanging speech. Between them is the buttressed trunk many yards in breadth, dark and frowning as the battlements of a fortress. Besides, the air is filled with noises, the skirling of tree-crickets, and other sounds of animated nature that disturb the tranquillity of the southern night. They could only communicate with one another by shouting at the highest pitch of their voices. Just now they have no need, and each proceeds to act for himself.

Bosley, soon as left alone with his captive, bethinks him what he had best do with her. He knows he must treat her tenderly, even respectfully. He has had commands to this effect from one he dare not disobey. Before starting, his chief gave him instructions, to be carried out or disregarded at peril of his life. He has no intention to disobey them—indeed, no inclination. A stern old sinner, his weakness is not woman—perhaps for this very reason selected for the delicate duty now intrusted to him. Instead of paying court to his fair captive, or presuming to hold speech with her, he only thinks how he can best discharge it to the satisfaction of his superior. No need to keep her any longer on the horse. She must be fatigued; the attitude is irksome, and he may get blamed; for not releasing her from it. Thus reflecting, he flings his arms around her, draws her down, and lays her gently along the earth.

Having so disposed of her, he pulls out his pipe, lights it, and commences smoking, apparently without, further thought of the form at his feet. That spoil is not for him.

But there is another, upon which he has set his mind. One altogether different from woman. It is Dupré's treasure, of which he is to have his share; and he speculates how much it will come to on partition. He longs to feast his eyes with a sight of the shining silver of which there has been so much talk among the robbers; and grand expectations excited; its value as I usual exaggerated.

Pondering upon it, he neither looks at his captive, nor thinks of her. His glances are toward the river ford, which he sees not, but I hears; listening amid the water's monotone for the plunging of horses hoofs. Impatiently, too, as between the puffs from his pipe, he ever and anon utters a grunt of discontent at the special duty imposed upon him, which may hinder him from getting his full share of the spoils.

Unlike is the behaviour of him on the other side of the oak. He, too, has dismounted his captive, and laid her along the ground. But not to stand idly over. Instead, he leaves her, and walks away from the spot, having attached his horse to the trunk of the tree, by hooking the bridle-rein over a piece of projecting bark. He has no fear that she will make her escape, or attempt it. Before parting he has taken precautions against that, by lashing her limbs together.

All this without saying a word—not even giving utterance to an exclamation!

In like silence he leaves her, turning his face toward the river, and striking along a trace that conducts to it.

Though several hundred yards from the ford, the bank is close by; for the path by which they approached the glade has been parallel to the trend of the stream. The live-oak overlooks it, with only a bordering of bushes between.

Through this runs a narrow trace made by wild animals, the forest denizens that frequent the adjacent timber, going down to their drinking place.

Parting the branches, that would sweep the plumed tiara from his head, the lieutenant glides along it, not stealthily, but with confidence, and as if familiar with the way. Once through the thicket, he sees the river broad and bright before him: its clear tranquil current in contrast with the dark and stormy passions agitating his own heart. He is not thinking of this, nor is there any sentiment in his soul, as he pauses by the side of the stream. He has sought it for a most prosaic purpose—to wash his face. For this he has brought with him a piece of soap and a rag of cotton cloth, taken out of a haversack carried on the pommel of his saddle.

Stepping down the slope, he stoops to perform his ablutions. In that water-mirror many a fierce ugly face has been reflected but never one fiercer or uglier than his, under its garish panoply of paint. Nor is it improved, when this, sponged off shows the skin to be white; on the contrary, the sinister passions that play upon his features would better become the complexion of the savage.

Having completed his lavatory task, he throws soap and rag into the river; then, turning, strides back up the bank. At its summit he stops to readjust his plumed head-dress, as he does so, saying in soliloquy:—

"I'll give her a surprise, such as she hasn't had since leaving the States. I'd bet odds she'll be more frightened at my face now, than when she saw it in the old garden. She didn't recognise it then; she will now. And now for her torture, and my triumph: for the revenge I've determined to take. Won't it be sweet!"

At the close of his exultant speech, he dives into the dark path, and gliding along it, soon re-enters the glade.

He perceives no change, for there has been none.

Going on to her from whom he had separated, he again places himself by her recumbent form, and stands gazing upon, gloating over it, like a panther whose prey lies disabled at its feet, to be devoured at leisure.

Only an instant stays he in this attitude; then stooping till his head almost touches hers, he hisses into her ear:—

"So, Helen, at length and at last, I have you in my power, at my mercy, sure, safe, as ever cat had mouse! Oh! it is sweet—sweet—sweet!"

She has no uncertainty now. The man exclaiming sweet, is he who has caused all her life's bitterness. The voice, no longer disguised, is that of Richard Darke!

Chapter Sixty One
A ruffian triumphant

Wild thoughts has Helen Armstrong, thus apostrophised, with not a word to say in return. She knows it would be idle; but without this, her very indignation holds her dumb—that and despair.

For a time he, too, is silent, as if surrendering his soul to delightful exultation.

Soon he resumes speech in changed tone, and interrogatively:—"Do you know who's talking to you? Or must I tell you, Nell? You'll excuse familiarity in an old friend, won't you?" Receiving no response, he continues, in the same sneering style: "Yes, an old friend, I say it; one you should well remember, though it's some time since we met, and a good way from here. To assist your recollection, let me recall an incident occurring at our last interview. Perhaps 'twill be enough to name the place and time? Wall, it was under a magnolia, in the State of Mississippi; time ten o'clock of night, moonlight, if I rightly remember, as now. It matters not the day of the month being different, or any other trivial circumstance, so long as the serious ones are so. And they are, thank God for it! Beneath the magnolia I knelt at your feet, under this tree, which is a live-oak, you lie at mine."

He pauses, but not expecting reply. The woman, so tortured speaks not; neither stirs she. The only *motion* visible throughout her frame is the swell and fall of her bosom—tumultuously beating.

He who stands, over well knows it is throbbing in pain. But no compassion has he for that; on the contrary, it gives gratification; again drawing from him the exultant exclamation—"Sweet—sweet!"

After another interval of silence, he continues, banteringly as before:

"So, fair Helen, you perceive how circumstances have changed between us, and I hope you'll have the sense to suit yourself to the change. Beneath the Mississippian tree you denied me: here under the Texan, you'll not be so inexorable—will you?"

Still no response.

"Well; if you won't vouchsafe an answer, I must be content to go without it; remembering the old saw—'Silence consents.' Perhaps, ere long your tongue will untie itself; when you've got over grieving for him who's gone—your great favourite, Charley Clancy. I take it, you've heard of his death; and possibly a report, that some one killed him. Both stories are true; and, telling you so, I may add, no one knows better than myself; since 'twas I sent the gentleman to kingdom come—Richard Darke."

On making the fearful confession, and in boastful emphasis, he bends lower to observe its effect. Not in her face, still covered with the serape, but her form, in which he can perceive a tremor from head to foot. She shudders, and not strange, as she thinks:—

"He murdered *him*. He may intend the same with *me*. I care not now."

Again the voice of the self-accused assassin:

"You know me now?"

She is silent as ever, and once more motionless; the convulsive spasm having passed. Even the beating of her heart seems stilled.

Is she dead? Has his fell speech slain her? In reality it would appear so.

"Ah, well;" he says, "you won't recognise me? Perhaps you will after seeing my face. Sight is the sharpest of the senses, and the most reliable. You shall no longer be deprived of it. Let me take you to the light."

Lifting, he carries her out to where the moonbeams meet the tree's shadow, and there lays her along. Then dropping to his knees, he draws out something that glistens. Two months before he stooped over the prostrate form of her lover, holding a photograph before his eyes—her own portrait. In her's he is about to brandish a knife!

One seeing him in this attitude would suppose he intended burying its blade in her breast. Instead, he slits open the serape in front of her face, tossing the severed edges back beyond her cheeks.

Her features exposed to the light, show wan and woeful; withal, lovely as ever; piquant in their pale beauty, like those of some rebellious nun hating the hood, discontented with cloister and convent.

As she sees him stooping beside, with blade uplifted, she feels sure he designs killing her. But she neither shrinks, nor shudders now. She even wishes him to end her agony with a blow. Were the knife in her own hand, she would herself give it.

It is not his intention to harm her that way. Words are the weapons by which he intends torturing her. With these he will lacerate her heart to its core.

For he is thinking of the time when he threw himself at her feet, and poured forth his soul in passionate entreaty, only to have his passion spurned, and his pride humiliated. It is her turn to suffer humiliation, and he has determined she shall. Recalling his own, every spark of pity, every pulsation of manhood, is extinguished within him. The cup of his scorned love has become a chalice filled with the passion of vengeance.

Sheathing the knife, he says:

"I've been longing for a good look at you. Now that I've got it, I should say you're pretty as ever, only paler. That will come right, and the roses return to your cheeks, in this recuperative climate of Texas; especially in the place where I intend taking you. But you hav'nt yet looked at my face. It's just had a washing for your sake. Come give it a glance! I want you to admire it, though it may not be quite so handsome as that of Charley Clancy."

She averts her eyes, instinctively closing them.

"Oh, well, you won't? Never mind, now. There's a time coming when you'll not be so coy, and when I shan't any longer kneel supplicating you. For know, Nell, you're completely in my power, and I can command, do with you what I will. I don't intend any harm, nor mean to be at all unkind. It'll be your own fault if you force me to harshness. And knowing that, why shouldn't there be truce between us? What's the use of fretting about Clancy? He's dead as a door nail, and your lamenting won't bring him to life again. Better take things as they are, and cheer up. If you've lost one sweetheart, there's another left, who loves you more than ever did he. I do, Helen Armstrong; by God, I do!"

The ruffian gives emphasis to his profane assertion, by bending before her, and laying his hand upon his heart.

Neither his speech nor attitude moves her. She lies as ever, still, silent. Wrapped in the Mexican blanket—whose pattern of Aztec design bears striking resemblance to the hieroglyphs of Egypt—this closed and corded round her figure, she might easily be mistaken for a mummy, one of Pharaoh's daughters taken out of the sarcophagus in which for centuries she has slept. Alone, the face with its soft white skin, negatives the comparison: though it appears bloodless, too. The eyes tell nought; their lids are closed, the long dark lashes alone showing in crescent curves. With difficulty could one tell whether she be asleep, or dead.

Richard Darke does not suppose she is either; and, incensed at receiving no reply, again apostrophises her in tone more spiteful than ever. He has lost control of his temper, and now talks unfeelingly, brutally, profanely.

"Damn you!" he cries. "Keep your tongue in your teeth, if you like. Ere long I'll find a way to make it wag; when we're man and wife, as we shall soon be—after a fashion. A good one, too, practised here upon the prairies of Texas. Just the place for a bridal, such as ours is to be. The nuptial knot tied, according to canons of our own choice, needing no sanction of church, or palaver of priests, to make it binding."

The ruffian pauses in his ribald speech. Not that he has yet sated his vengeance, for he intends continuing the torture of his victim unable to resist. He has driven the arrow deep into her heart, and leaves it to rankle there.

For a time he is silent, as if enjoying his triumph—the expression on his countenance truly satanic. It is seen suddenly to change, apprehension taking its place, succeeded by fear.

The cause: sounds coming from the other side of the tree; human voices!

Not those of Bosley, or his captive; but of strange men speaking excitedly!

Quick parting from his captive, and gliding up to the trunk, he looks cautiously around it.

In the shadow he sees several figures clustering around Bosley and his horse; then hears names pronounced, one which chills the blood within his veins—almost freezing it.

He stands transfixed; cowering as one detected in an act of crime, and by a strong hand held in the attitude in which caught! Only for a short while thus; then, starting up, he rushes to regain his horse, jerks the bridle from the back, and drags the animal in the direction of his captive. Tossing her upon the pommel of the saddle, he springs into it. But she too has heard names, and now makes herself heard, shouting, "Help—help!"

Chapter Sixty Two
"Help! Help!"

Baulked in their attempt to ambuscade the supposed Indians, Clancy and his companions thought not of abandoning the search for them. On the contrary, they continued it with renewed eagerness, their interest excited by the unexplained disappearance of the party.

And they have succeeded in finding it, for it is they who surround Bosley, having surprised him unsuspectingly puffing away at his pipe. How they made approach, remains to be told.

On reaching the river's bank, and there seeing nought of the strange equestrians, their first feeling was profound astonishment. On Woodley's part, also, some relapse to a belief in the supernatural; Heywood, to a certain degree, sharing it.

"Odd it air!" mutters Sime, with an ominous shake of the head. "Tarnashun odd! Whar kin they hev been, an' whar hev they goed?"

"Maybe back, across the river?" suggests Heywood.

"Unpossible. Thar ain't time. They'd be wadin' now, an' we'd see 'em. No. They're on this side yit, if anywhar on airth; the last bein' the doubtful."

"Supposin' they've taken the trace we came by? They might while we were up the road?"

"By the jumpin' Jeehosofat!" exclaims Woodley, startled by this second suggestion, "I never thought o' that. If they hev, thar's our horses, an' things. Let's back to camp quick as legs kin take us."

"Stay!" interposes Clancy, whose senses are not confused by any unearthly fancies. "I don't think they could have gone that way. There may be a trail up the bank, and they've taken it. There must be, Sime. I never knew a stream without one."

"Ef there be, it's beyont this child's knowledge. I hain't noticed neery one. Still, as you say, sech is usooal, ef only a way for the wild beasts. We kin try for it."

"Let us first make sure whether they came out here at all. We didn't watch them quite in to the shore."

Saying this, Clancy steps down to the water's edge, the others with him.

They have no occasion to stoop. Standing erect they can see hoof-marks, conspicuous, freshly made, filled with water that has fallen from the fetlocks.

Turning, they easily trace them up the shelving bank; but not so easily along the road, though certain they continue that way. It is black as pitch beneath the shadowing trees. Withal, Woodley is not to be thus baffled. His skill as a tracker is proverbial among men of his calling; moreover, he is chagrined at their ill success so far; and, but for there being no time, the ex-jailer, its cause, would catch it. He does in an occasional curse, which might be accompanied by a cuff, did he not keep well out of the backwoodsman's way.

Dropping on all fours, Sime feels for hoof-prints of the horses that have just crossed, groping in darkness. He can distinguish them from all others by their being wet. And so does, gaining ground, bit by bit, surely if slowly.

But Clancy has conceived a more expeditious plan, which he makes known, saying:

"No need taking all that trouble, Sime. You may be the best trailer in Texas; and no doubt you are, for a biped: still here's one can beat you."

"Who?" asks the backwoodsman, rising erect, "show me the man."

"No man," interrupts the other with a smile. "For our purpose something better. There stands your competitor."

"You're right; I didn't think o' the dog. He'll do it like a breeze. Put him on, Charley!"

"Come, Brasfort!" says Clancy, apostrophising the hound, while lengthening the leash, and setting the animal on the slot. "You tell us where the redskin riders have gone."

The intelligent creature well understands what is wanted, and with nose to the ground goes instantly off. But for the check string it would soon outstrip them for its eager action tells it has caught scent of a trail.

At first lifting it along the ford road, but only for a few yards. Then abruptly turning left, the dog is about to strike into the timber, when the hand of the master restrains it.

The instinct of the animal is no longer needed. They perceive the embouchure of a path, that looks like the entrance to a cave, dark and forbidding as the back door of a jail. But surely a trace leading in among the trees, which the plumed horsemen have taken.

After a second or two spent in arranging the order of march, they also take it, Clancy now assuming command.

They proceed with caution greater than ever; more slowly too, because along a path, dark, narrow, unknown, shaggy with thorns. They have to grope every inch of their way; all the while in surprise at the Indians having chosen it. There must be a reason, though none of them can think what it is.

They are not long left to conjectures. A light before their eyes throws light upon the enigma that has been baffling their brains. There is a break in the timber, where the moonbeams fall free to the earth.

Gliding on, silently, with undiminished caution, they arrive on the edge of an opening, and there make stop, but inside the underwood that skirts it.

Clancy and Woodley stand side by side, crouchingly; and in this attitude interrogate the ground before them.

They see the great tree, with its white shroud above, and deep obscurity beneath—the moonlit ring around it. But at first nothing more, save the fire-flies scintillating in its shadow.

After a time, their eyes becoming accustomed to the cross light, they see something besides; a group of figures close in to the tree's trunk, apparently composed of horses and men. They can make out but one of each, but they take it there are two, with two women as well. While scanning the group, they observe a light larger and redder than that emitted by the winged insects. Steadier too; for it moves not from its place. They might not know it to be the coal upon a tobacco pipe, but for the smell of the burning "weed" wafted their way.

Sniffing it, Sime says:

"That's the lot, sure; tho' thar appears but the half o't. I kin only make out one hoss, an' one man, wi' suthin' astreetch long the groun—one o' the squaws in coorse. The skunk on his feet air smokin'. Strange they hain't lit a fire! True 'tain't needed 'ceptin' for the cookin' o' thar supper. Maybe they've hed it, an' only kim hyar to get a spell o' sleep. But ef thet's thar idee why shed yon 'un be stannin' up. Wal; I guess, he's doin' sentry bizness, the which air allers needcessary out hyar. How shell we act, Charley? Rush right up an' tackle 'em? That's your way, I take it."

"It is—why not?"

"Because thar's a better—leastwise a surer to prevent spillin' thar blood. Ye say, you don't want that?"

"On no account. If I thought there was a likelihood of it, I'd go straight back to our camp, and leave them alone. They may be harmless creatures, on some innocent errand. If it prove so, we musn't molest them."

"Wal; I'm willin', for thet," rejoins Woodley, adding a reservation, "Ef they resist, how are we to help it? We must eyther kill, or be kilt."

There is reason in this, and Clancy perceives it. While he is cogitating what course to take, Woodley, resuming speech, points it out.

"'Thar's no use for us to harm a hair on thar beads, supposin' them to be innercent. For all thet, we shed make sure, an' take preecaushin in case o' them cuttin' up ugly. It air allers the best way wi redskins."

"How do you propose, Sime?"

"To surround 'em. Injuns, whether it be bucks or squaws, air slickery as eels. It's good sixty yurds to whar they're squatted yonner. Ef we push strait torst 'em, they'll see us crossin' that bit o' moonshine, an' be inter the timmer like greased lightnin' through the branches o' a gooseberry bush. Tho' out o' thar seddles now, an' some o' 'em streetched 'long the airth, apparently sleepin', they'd be up an' off in the shakin' o' a goat's tail. Tharefor, say I, let's surround 'em."

"If you think that the better way," rejoins Clancy, "let us. But it will take time, and call for the greatest caution. To get around the glade, without their seeing us, we must keep well within the timber. Through that underwood it won't be easy. On second thoughts, Sime, I'm inclined to chance it the other way. They can't possibly escape us. If they do take to their horses, they couldn't gallop off beyond reach of our rifles. We can easily shoot their animals down. Besides, remember there's two to get mounted on each. We may as well run right up, and determine the thing at once. I see no difficulty."

"Wheesht!" exclaims Woodley, just as Clancy ceases speaking.

"What is it? Do you hear anything, Sime?"

"Don't you, Charley?"

Clancy sets himself to listen, but at first hears nothing, save the usual sounds of the forest, of which it is now full. A spring night, a sultry one, the tree-crickets are in shrillest cry, the owls and goatsuckers joining in the chorus.

But in the midst of its continuous strain there is surely a sound, not animal, but human? Surely the voice of a man?

After a time, Clancy can distinguish it.

One is talking, in tone not loud, but with an accent which appears to be that of boasting or triumph. And the voice is not like an Indian's, while exclamations, at intervals uttered, are certainly such as could only proceed from the lips of a white man.

All this is strange, and causes astonishment to the travellers—to Clancy something more. But before he has time to reflect upon, or form conjectures about it, he hears that which compels him to cast aside every restraint of prudence; and springing forward, he signals the others to follow him.

They do, without a word; and in less than twenty seconds' time, they have entered the shadowed circle, and surrounded the group at which they have been so long gazing.

Only three figures after all! A man, a horse, with what may be woman, but looks less like one living than dead!

The man, Indian to all appearance, thus taken by surprise, plucks the pipe from between his teeth. It is struck out of his hand, the sparks flying from it, as Woodley on one side and Heywood the other, clutching, drag him toward the light.

When the moon shines on it, they behold a face which both have seen before.

Under its coating of charcoal and chalk they might not recognise it, but for the man making himself known by speech, which secures his identification. For he, too, sees a familiar face, that of Simeon Woodley; and under the impression he is himself recognised, mechanically pronounces the backwoodsman's name.

"Bill Bosley!" shouts the astonished Sime, "Good Lord! Painted Injun! What's this for? Some devil's doings ye're arter as ye allers war. Explain it, Bill! Tell the truth 'ithout preevaricashun. Ef ye lie, I'll split your thrapple like I wud a water-millyun."

"Sime Woodley! Ned Heywood! Joe Harkness!" gaspingly ejaculates the man, as in turn the three faces appear before him. "God Almighty! what's it mean?"

"We'll answer that when we've heern *your* story. Quick, tell it."

"I can't; your chokin' me. For God's sake, Heywood, take your hand off my throat. O Sime! sure you don't intend killin' me?—ye won't, ye won't."

"That depends—"

"But I aint to blame. Afore heaven, I swear I aint. You know that, Harkness? You heard me protest against their ugly doin's more than once.

In this business, now, I'm only actin' under the captin's order. He sent me 'long with the lootenant to take care of—"

"The lieutenant!" interrupts Clancy. "What name?"

"Phil Quantrell, we call him; though I guess he's got another—"

"Where is he?" inquires Clancy, tortured with a terrible suspicion.

"He went t'other side the tree, takin' the young lady along."

At that moment comes a cry from behind the oak—a woman's voice calling "Help! help!"

Clancy stays not to hear more, but rushes off with the air of a man struck with sudden phrenzy!

On turning the trunk, he sees other forms, a horse with man mounted, a woman before him he endeavours to restrain, who, struggling, thirsts for succour.

It is nigh, though near being too late. But for a fortunate circumstance, it would be. The horse, headed towards the forest, is urged in that direction. But, frayed by the conflict on his back, he refuses to advance; instead, jibbing and rearing, he returns under the tree.

Clancy, with rifle raised, is about to shoot the animal down. But at thought of danger to her calling "help!" he lowers his piece; and rushing in, lays hold of the bridle-rein. This instantly let go, to receive in his arms the woman, released from the ruffian's grasp, who would otherwise fall heavily to the earth.

The horse, disembarrassed, now obeying the rein, shoots out from under the oak, and headed across the moonlit belt makes straight for the timber beyond.

In the struggle Clancy has let go his gun, and now vainly gropes for it in the darkness. But two others are behind, with barrels that bear upon the retreating horseman. In an instant all would be over with him, but for Clancy himself; who, rushing between, strikes up the muzzles, crying:—

"Don't shoot, Sime! Hold your fire, Heywood! His life belongs to me!"

Strange forbearance; to the backwoodsmen, incomprehensible! But they obey; and again Richard Darke escapes chastisement for two great crimes he intended, but by good fortune failed to accomplish.

Chapter Sixty Three
An oath to be kept

No pen could portray the feelings of Helen Armstrong, on recognising her rescuer. Charles Clancy alive! Is she dreaming? Or is it indeed he whose arms are around, folding her in firm but tender embrace? Under the moonbeams, that seem to have suddenly become brighter, she beholds the manly form and noble features of him she believed dead, his cheeks showing the hue of health, his eyes late glaring in angry excitement, now glowing with the softer light of love. Yes: it is indeed her lover long mourned, living, breathing, beautiful as ever!

She asks not if he be still true, that doubt has been long since dissipated. It needs not his presence there, nor what he has just done, to reassure her.

For a time she asks no questions; neither he. Both are too absorbed with sweet thoughts to care for words. Speech could not heighten their happiness, in the midst of caresses and kisses.

On his side there is no backwardness now; on hers no coyness, no mock modesty. They come together not as at their last interview, timid sweethearts, but lovers emboldened by betrothal. For she knows, that he proposed to her; as he, that her acceptance was sent, and miscarried. It has reached him nevertheless; he has it upon his person now—both the letter and portrait. About the last are his first words. Drawing it out, and holding it up to the light, he asks playfully:

"Helen; was it meant fo' me?"

"No," she evasively answers, "it was meant for me."

"Oh! the likeness, yes; but the inscript—these pleasant words written underneath?"

"Put it back into; our pocket, Charles. And now tell me all. Am I dreaming? Or is it indeed reality?"

No wonder she should so exclaim. Never was transformation quicker, or more complete. But a few seconds before she was, as it were, in the clutches of the devil; now an angel is by her side, a seraph with soft wings to shelter, and strong arms to protect her. She feels as one, who, long lingering at the door of death, has health suddenly and miraculously restored, with the prospect of a prolonged and happy life.

Clancy replies, by again flinging his arms around, and rapturously kissing her: perhaps thinking it the best answer he can give. If that be not reality, what is?

Jessie has now joined them, and after exchanged congratulations, there succeed mutual inquiries and explanations. Clancy has commenced giving a brief account of what has occurred to himself, when he is interrupted by a rough, but kindly voice; that of Sime, saying:—

"Ye kin tell them all that at some other time, Charley; thar aint a minnit to be throwed away now." Then drawing Clancy aside, speaking so as not to be heard by the others. "Thar's danger in dallyin' hyar. I've jest been puttin' thet jail bird, Bosley, through a bit o' catechism; an' from what he's told me the sooner we git out o' hyar the better. Who d'ye spose is at the bottom o' all this? I needn't ask ye; ye're boun to guess. I kin see the ugly brute's name bulgin' out yur cheeks."

"Borlasse!"

"In course it's he. Bosley's confessed all. Ked'nt well help it, wi' my bowie threetenin' to make a red stream run out o' him. The gang—thar's twenty o' 'em all counted—goed up to the Mission to plunder it—a sort o' burglarious expedishun; Borlasse hevin' a understandin' wi' a treetur that's inside—a sort o' sarvint to the Creole, Dupray, who only late engaged him. Wal; it seems they grupped the gurls, as they war makin' for the house—chanced on 'em outside in the garden. Bosley an' the other hev toated 'em this far, an' war wait in for the rest to come on wi' the stolen goods. They may be hyar at any minnit; an', wi' Jim Borlasse at thar head, I needn't tell ye what that means. Four o' us agin twenty—for we can't count on Harkness— it's ugly odds. We'd hev no show, howsomever. It 'ud end in their again grabbin' these pretty critters, an' 's like 's not end our own lives."

Clancy needs no further speech to convince him of the danger. After what has occurred, an encounter with the robbers would, indeed, be disastrous. Richard Darke, leagued with Jim Borlasse, a noted pirate of the prairies; their diabolical plans disclosed, and only defeated by the merest accident of circumstances.

"You're right, Sime. We mustn't be caught by the scoundrels. As you say, that would be the end of everything. How are we to avoid them?"

"By streakin' out o' hyar quick as possible."

"Do you propose our taking to the timber, and lying hid till they go past?"

"No. Our better plan 'll be to go on to the Mission, an' get thar soon's we kin."

"But we may meet them in the teeth?"

"We must, ef we take the main road up tother side—pretty sure to meet 'em. We shan't be sech fools. I've thought o' all that, an' a way to get clear of the scrape."

"What way?"

"That road we kim in by, ye see, leads on'ard up the bank this side. I reckin' it goes to the upper crossin', the which air several miles above the buildin's. We kin take it, an' foller it without any fear o' encounterin' them beauties. I've sent Jupe and Harkness to bring up the hosses. Ned's tother side the tree in charge o' Bosley."

"You've arranged it right. Nothing could be better. Take the trail up this side. I can trust you for seeing them safe into their father's arms—if he still live."

Woodley wonders at this speech. He is about to ask explanation, when Clancy adds, pointing to the elder sister—

"I want a word with her before parting. While you are getting ready the horses—"

"Before partin'!" interrupts Sime with increased surprise, "Surely you mean goin' along wi' us?"

"No, I don't."

"But why, Charley?"

"Well, I've something to detain me here."

"What somethin'?"

"You ought to know without my telling you."

"Dog-goned ef I do."

"Richard Darke, then."

"But he's goed off; ye don't intend follerin' him?"

"I do—to the death. If ever I had a fixed determination in my life, 'tis that."

"Wal, but you won't go all by yerself! Ye'll want some o' us wi' ye?"

"No."

"Not me, nor Ned?"

"Neither. You'll both be needed to take care of them."

Clancy nods towards the sisters, adding:—

"You'll have your hands full enough with Bosley and Harkness. Both will need looking after—and carefully. Jupe I'll take with me."

Woodley remonstrates, pointing out the danger of the course his comrade intends pursuing. He only yields as Clancy rejoins, in a tone of determination, almost command:—

"You must do as I tell you, Sime; go on to the Mission, and take them with you. As for me, I've a strong reason for remaining behind by myself; a silly sentiment some might call it, though I don't think you would."

"What is't? Let's hear it, an' I'll gie ye my opeenyun strait an' square."

"Simply, that in this whole matter from first to last, I've een making mistakes. So many, it's just possible my courage may be called in question; or; if not that, my ability. Now, do you understand me?"

"Darned ef I do."

"Well; a man must do something to prove himself worthy of the name; at least one deed during his lifetime. There's one I've got to do—must do it, before I can think of anything else."

"That is?"

"*Kill Richard Darke,* As you know, I've sworn it, and nothing shall come between me and my oath. No, Sime, not even she who stands yonder; though I can't tell how it pains me to separate from her, now."

"Good Lord! that will be a painful partin'! Poor gurl! I reckin her heart's been nigh broke arready. She hasn't the peach colour she used to hev. It's clean faded out o' her cheeks, an' what your goin' to do now aint the way to bring it back agin."

"I cannot help it, Sime. I hear my mother calling me. Go, now! I wish it; I insist upon it!"

Saying this, he turns towards Helen Armstrong to speak a word, which he knows will be sad as was ever breathed into the ear of woman.

Chapter Sixty Four
A wild farewell

On Clancy and the hunter becoming engaged in their serious deliberation, the sisters also exchange thoughts that are troubled. The first bright flash of joy at their release from captivity, with Helen's added gratification, is once more clouded over, as they think of what may have befallen their father. Now, knowing who the miscreants are, their hearts are heavy with apprehension. Jessie may, perhaps, feel it the more, having most cause—for her dread is of a double nature. There is her affianced, as well as her father!

But for Helen there is also another agony in store, soon to be suffered. Little thinks she, as Clancy coming up takes her hand, that the light of gladness, which so suddenly shone into her heart, is to be with like suddenness extinguished; and that he who gave is about to take it away. Gently leading her apart, and leaving Jessie to be comforted by Sime, he says—

"Dearest! we've arranged everything for your being taken back to the Mission. The brave backwoodsmen, Woodley and Heywood, will be your escort. Under their protection you'll have nothing to fear. Either would lay down his life for you or your sister. Nor need you be uneasy about your father. From what this fellow, Bosley, says, the ruffians only meant robbery, and if they have not been resisted it will end in that only. Have courage, and be cheered; you'll find your father as you left him."

"And you?" she asks in surprise. "Do you not go with us?"

He hesitates to make answer, fearing the effect. But it must be made; and he at length rejoins, appealingly:

"Helen! I hope you won't be aggrieved, or blame me for hat I am going to do."

"What?"

"Leave you."

"Leave me!" she exclaims, her eyes interrogating his in wild bewilderment.

"Only for a time, love; a very short while."

"But why any time? Charles; you are surely jesting with me?"

"No, indeed. I am in earnest. Never more in my life, and never more wishing I were not. Alas! it is inevitable!"

"Inevitable! I do not understand. What do you mean?"

With her eyes fixed oh his, in earnest gaze, she anxiously awaits his answer.

"Helen Armstrong!" he says, speaking in a tone of solemnity that sounds strange, almost harsh despite its gentleness; "you are to me the dearest thing on earth. I need not tell you that, for surely you know it. Without you I should not value life, nor care to live one hour longer. To say I love you, with all my heart and soul, were but to repeat the assurance I've already given you. Ah! now more than ever, if that were possible; now that I know how true you've been, and what you've suffered for my sake. But there's another—one far away from here, who claims a share of my affections—"

She makes a movement interrupting him, her eyes kindling up with an indescribable light, her bosom rising and falling as though stirred by some terrible emotion.

Perceiving her agitation, though without suspecting its cause, he continues:

"If this night more than ever I love you, this night greater than ever is my affection for her. The sight of that man, with the thought I've again permitted him to escape, is fresh cause of reproach—a new cry from the ground, commanding me to avenge my murdered mother."

Helen Armstrong, relieved, again breathes freely. Strange, but natural; in consonance with human passions. For it was jealousy that for the moment held sway in her thoughts. Ashamed of the suspicion, now known to be unworthy, she makes an effort to conceal it, saying in calm tone—

"We have heard of your mother's death."

"Of her murder," says Clancy, sternly, and through set teeth. "Yes; my poor mother was murdered by the man who has just gone off. He won't go far, before I overtake him. I've sworn over her grave, she shall be avenged; his blood will atone for her's. I've tracked him here, shall track him on; never stop, till I stand over him, as he once stood over me, thinking—. But I won't tell you more. Enough, for you to know why I'm now leaving you. I must—I must!"

Half distracted, she rejoins:—

"You love your mother's memory more than you love me!"

Without thought the reproach escapes—wrung from her in her agony. Soon as made, she regrets, and would recall it. For she sees the painful effect it has produced.

He anticipates her, saying:—

"You wrong me, Helen, in word, as in thought. Such could not be. The two are different. You should know that. As I tell you, I've sworn to avenge my mother's death—sworn it over her grave. Is that not an oath to be kept? I ask—I appeal to you!"

Her hand, that has still been keeping hold of his, closes upon it with firmer grasp, while her eyes become fixed upon him in look more relying than ever.

The selfishness of her own passion shrinks before the sacredness of that inspiring him, and quick passes away. With her love is now mingled admiration. Yielding to it, she exclaims:

"Go—go! Get the retribution you seek. Perhaps 'tis right. God shielding you, you'll succeed, and come back to me, true as you've been to your mother. If not, I shall soon be dead."

"If not, you may know I am. Only death can hinder my return. And now, for a while, farewell!"

Farewell! And so soon. Oh! it is afflicting! So far she has borne herself with the firmness derived from a strong, self-sustaining nature. But hearing this word—wildest of all—she can hold out no longer. Her strength gives way, and flinging herself on his breast, she pours forth a torrent of tears.

"Come, Helen!" he says, kissing them from her cheeks, "be brave, and don't fear for me. I know my man, and the work cut out for me. By sheer carelessness I've twice let him have his triumph over me. But he won't the third time. When we next meet 'twill be the last hour of his life. Something whispers this—perhaps the spirit of my mother? Keep up your courage, sweet! Go back with Sime, who'll see you safe into your father's arms. When there, you can offer up a prayer for my safety, and if you like, one for the salvation of Dick Darke's soul. For sure as I stand here, ere another sun has set it will go to its God."

With these solemn words the scene ends, only one other exchanged between them—the wild "Farewell!"

This in haste, for at the moment Woodley comes forward, exclaiming:—

"Be quick, Charley! We must git away from hyar instanter. A minuit more in this gleed, an' some o' us may niver leave it alive."

Jupiter and Harkness have brought up the horses, and are holding them in readiness. Soon they are mounted, Heywood taking Jessie on his croup, Helen having a horse to herself—that late belonging to Bosley—while the latter is compelled to share the saddle with Harkness.

Heywood leads off; the suspected men ordered to keep close after; while Woodley reserves the rear-guard to himself and his rifle. Before parting, he spurs alongside Clancy, and holds out his hand, saying:—

"Gi'e me a squeeze o' yur claws, Charley. May the Almighty stan' your frien' and keep you out o' Ole Nick's clutches. Don't hev' any dubiousness 'bout us. Tho' we shed kum across Satan hisself wi' all his hellniferous host, Sime Woodley 'll take care o' them sweet gurls, or go to grass trying." With this characteristic wind-up, he puts the spur to his horse, and closes upon the rest already parted from the spot.

Alone remain under the live-oak, Clancy and the mulatto, with horse, hound, and mule.

Varied the emotions in Clancy's mind, as he stands looking after; but all dark as clouds coursing across a winter's sky. For they are all doubts and fears; that most felt finding expression in the desponding soliloquy.

"I may never see her again!"

As the departing cavalcade is about to enter among the trees, and the floating drapery of her dress is soon to pass out of sight, he half repents his determination, and is almost inclined to forego it.

But the white skirt disappears, and the dark thought returning, becomes fixed as before. Then, facing towards Jupiter, he directs:—

"Mount your mule, Jupe. We've only one more journey to make; I hope a short one. At its end we'll meet your old master, and you'll see him get what he deserves—his *death shot!*"

Chapter Sixty Five
For the rendezvous

Stillness is again restored around the crossing of the San Saba, so far as it has been disturbed by the sound of human voices. Nature has resumed her reign, and only the wild creatures of her kingdom can be heard calling, in tones that tell not of strife.

But for a short while does this tranquillity continue. Soon once more upon the river's bank resound rough voices, and rude boisterous laughter, as a band of mounted men coming from the Mission side, spur their horses down into its channel, and head to go straight across. While under the shadow of the fringing timber, no one could tell who these merry riders are; and, even after they have advanced into the open moonlight, it would be difficult to identify them. Seeing their plumed heads with their parti-coloured complexions, a stranger would set them down as Indians; while a Texan might particularise their tribe, calling them Comanches. But one who is no stranger to them—the reader—knows they are not Indians of any kind, but savages who would show skins of a tripe colour, were the pigment sponged off. For it is the band of Borlasse.

They have brought their booty thus far, *en route* for their rendezvous.

Gleeful they are, one and all. Before them on their saddle-bows, or behind on the croups, are the boxes of silver coin; enough, as they know, to give them a grand spree in the town of San Antonio, whither they intend proceeding in due time.

But first for their lair, where the spoil is to be partitioned, and a change made in their toilet; there to cast off the costume of the savage, and resume the garb of civilisation.

Riding in twos across the river, on reaching its bank they make halt. There is barely room for all on the bit of open ground by the embouchure of the ford road; and they get clumped into a dense crowd—in its midst their chief, Borlasse, conspicuous from his great bulk of body.

"Boys!" he says, soon as all have gained the summit of the slope, and gathered around him, "it ain't no use for all o' us going to where I told

Quantrell an' Bosley to wait. The approach to the oak air a bit awkward; therefore, me an' Luke Chisholm 'll slip up thar, whiles the rest o' ye stay hyar till we come back. You needn't get out of your saddles. We won't be many minutes, for we mustn't. They'll be a stirrin' at the Mission, though not like to come after us so quick, seeing the traces we've left behind. That'll be a caution to them, I take it. And from what our friend here says," Borlasse nods to the half-blood, Fernand, who is seen seated on horseback beside him, "the settlers can't muster over forty fightin' men. Calculatin' there's a whole tribe o' us Comanches, they'll be too scared to start out all of a suddint. Besides, they'll not find that back trail by the bluff so easy. I don't think they can before mornin'. Still 'twont do to hang about hyar long. Once we get across the upper plain we're safe. They'll never set eyes on these Indyins after. Come, Luke! let you an' me go on to the oak, and pick up the stragglers. An' boys! see ye behave yourselves till we come back. Don't start nail, or raise lid, from any o' them boxes. If there's a dollar missin', I'll know it; an' by the Eternal—well, I guess, you understan' Jim Borlasse's way wi' treeturs."

Leaving this to be surmised, the robber chief spurs out from their midst, with the man he has selected to accompany him; the rest, as enjoined, remaining.

Soon he turns into the up-river trace, which none of those who have already travelled it, knew as well as he. Despite his greater size, neither its thorns, nor narrowness, hinders him from riding rapidly along it. He is familiar with its every turn and obstruction, as is also Chisholm. Both have been to the big oak before, time after time; have bivouacked, slept under it, and beside booty. Approaching it now for a different purpose, they are doomed to disappointment. There is no sign of creature beneath its shade— horse, man, or woman!

Where is Quantrell? Where Bosley? What has become of them, and their captives?

They are not under the oak, or anywhere around it. They are nowhere!

The surprise of the robber chief instantly changes to anger. For a suspicion flashes across his mind, that his late appointed lieutenant has played false to him.

He knows that Richard Darke has only been one of his band by the exigency of sinister circumstances; knows, also, of the other, and stronger lien that has kept Clancy's assassin attached to their confederacy—his love for Helen Armstrong. Now that he has her—the sister too—why may he not have taken both off, intending henceforth to cut all connection with the prairie pirates? Bosley would be no bar. The subordinate might remain faithful, and to the death; still Quantrell could kill him.

It is all possible, probable; and Borlasse, now better acquainted with the character of Richard Darke, can believe it so. Convinced of his lieutenant's treachery, he rages around the tree like a tiger deprived of its prey.

Little cares he what has become of Darke himself, or Helen Armstrong. It is Jessie he misses; madly loving her in his course carnal fashion. He had hoped to have her in his arms, to carry her on to the rendezvous, to make her his wife in the same way as Darke threatened to do with her sister.

Fortunately for both, the sky has become clouded, and the moon is invisible; otherwise he might see that the ground has been trodden by a half-dozen horses, and discover the direction these have taken. Though Simeon Woodley, with his party, is now a good distance off, it would still be possible to overtake them, the robbers being well mounted and better knowing the way. Woe to Helen and Jessie Armstrong were the moon shining, as when they parted from that spot!

Neither Borlasse nor his confederate have a thought that any one has been under the oak, save Quantrell, Bosley, and the captives. How could they? And now they think not that these have been there; for, calling their names aloud, they get no response. Little do the two freebooters dream of the series of exciting incidents that in quick succession, and so recently, have occurred in that now silent spot. They have no suspicion of aught, save that Bosley has betrayed his trust, Phil Quantrell instigating him, and that both have forsaken the band, taking the captives along.

At thought of their treachery Borlasse's fury goes beyond bounds, and he stamps and storms.

To restrain him, Chisholm says, suggestingly, "Like as not, Cap', they're gone on to head-quarters. I guess, when we get there we'll find the whole four."

"You think so?"

"I'm good as sure of it. What else could they do, or would they? Quantrell darn't go back to the States, with that thing you spoke of hangin' over him. Nor is he like to show himself in any o' the settlements of Texas. And what could the two do by themselves out on the wild prairie?"

"True; I reckon you're about right, Luke. In any case we musn't waste more time here. It's getting well on to morning and by the earliest glint of day the settlers 'll take trail after us. We must on to the upper plain."

At this he heads his horse back into the narrow trail; and, hurrying along it, rejoins his followers by the ford.

Soon as reaching them, he gives the command for immediate march; promptly obeyed, since every robber in the ruck has pleasant anticipation of what is before, with ugly recollection of what is, and fears of what may be, behind him.

Chapter Sixty Six
A scouting party

Throughout all this time, the scene of wild terror, and frenzied excitement, continues to rage around the Mission. Its walls, while echoing voices of lamentation, reverberate also the shouts of revenge.

It is some time ere the colonists can realise the full extent of the catastrophe, or be sure it is at an end. The gentlemen, who dined with Colonel Armstrong, rushing back to their own homes in fearful anticipation, there find everything, as they left it; except that their families and fellow settlers are asleep. For all this, the fear does not leave their hearts. If their houses are not aflame, as they expected to see them—if their wives and children are not butchered in cold blood—they know not how soon this may be. The Indians—for Indians they still believe them—would not have attacked so strong a settlement, unless in force sufficient to destroy it. The ruin, incomplete, may still be impending. True, the interlude of inaction is difficult to understand; only intelligible, on the supposition that the savages are awaiting an accession to their strength, before they assault the *rancheria*. They may at the moment be surrounding it?

Under this apprehension, the settlers are hastily, and by loud shouts, summoned from their beds. Responding to the rude arousal, they are soon out of them, and abroad; the women and children frantically screaming; the men more calm; some of them accustomed to such surprises, issuing forth armed, and ready for action.

Soon all are similarly prepared, each with gun, pistol, and knife borne upon his person.

After hearing the tale of horror brought from the Mission-building, they hold hasty council as to what they should do.

Fear for their own firesides restrains them from starting off; and some time elapse before they feel assured that the *rancheria* will not be attacked, and need defending.

Meanwhile, they despatch messengers to the Mission; who, approaching it cautiously, find no change there.

Colonel Armstrong is still roaming distractedly around, searching for his daughters, Dupré by his side, Hawkins and Tucker assisting in the search.

The girls not found, and the frantic father settling down to the conviction that they are gone—lost to him forever!

Oh! the cruel torture of the truth thus forced upon him! His children carried off captive, that were enough. But to such captivity! To be the associates of savages, their slaves, their worse than slaves—ah! a destiny compared with which death were desirable.

So reasons the paternal heart in this supreme moment of its affliction.

Alike, distressed is he, bereaved of his all but bride. The young Creole is well-nigh beside himself. Never has he known such bitter thoughts; the bitterest of all—a remembrance of something said to him by his betrothed that very day. A word slight but significant, relating to the half-blood, Fernand; a hint of some familiarity in the man's behaviour towards her, not absolute boldness, but presumption: for Jessie did not tell all. Still enough to be now vividly recalled to Dupré's memory, with all that exaggeration the circumstances are calculated to suggest to his fancy and fears. Yes; his trusted servant has betrayed him, and never did master more repent a trust, or suffer greater pain by its betrayal.

The serpent he warmed has turned and stung him, with sting so venomous as to leave little of life.

Within and around the Mission-building are other wailing voices, besides those of its owners. Many of the domestics have like cause for lamentation, some even more. Among the massacred, still stretched in their gore, one stoops over a sister; another sees his child; a wife weeps by the side of her husband, her hot tears mingling with his yet warm blood; while brother bends down to gaze into the eyes of brother, which, glassy and sightless, cannot reciprocate the sorrowing glance!

It is not the time to give way to wild grief. The occasion calls for action, quick, immediate. Colonel Armstrong commands it; Dupré urges it. Soon as their first throes of surprise and terror have subsided, despair is replaced by anger, and their thoughts turn upon retaliation.

All is clear now. Those living at the *rancheria* have not been molested. The savages have carried off Dupré's silver. Despoiled of his far more precious treasure, what recks he of that? Only as telling that the object of the attacking party was robbery more than murder; though they have done both. Still it is certain, that, having achieved their end, they are gone off with no intention to renew the carnage of which all can see such sanguinary traces. Thus reasoning, the next thought is pursuit.

As yet the other settlers are at the *rancheria*, clinging to their own hearths, in fear of a fresh attack, only a few having come up to the Mission, to be shocked at what they see there.

But enough for Dupré's purpose; which receives the sanction of Colonel Armstrong, as also that of the hunters, Hawkins and Tucker.

It is decided not to wait till all can be ready; but for a select party to start off at once, in the capacity of scouts; these to take up the trail of the savages, and send back their report to those coming after.

To this Colonel Armstrong not only gives consent, but deems it the most prudent course, and likeliest to secure success. Despite his anxious impatience, the strategy of the old soldier tells him, that careless haste may defeat its chances.

In fine, a scouting party is dispatched, Hawkins at its head as guide, the Creole commanding.

Armstrong himself remains behind, to organise the main body of settlers getting ready for pursuit.

Chapter Sixty Seven
A straying traveller

A man on horseback making his way through a wood. Not on road, or trodden path, or trace of any kind. For it is a tract of virgin forest, in which settler's axe has never sounded, rarely traversed by ridden horse; still more rarely by pedestrian.

He, now passing through it, rides as fast as the thick standing trunks, and tangle of undergrowth will allow. The darkness also obstructs him; for it is night. Withal he advances rapidly, though cautiously; at intervals glancing back, at longer ones, delaying to listen, with chin upon his shoulder.

His behaviour shows fear; so, too, his face. Here and there the moonbeams shining through breaks in the foliage, reveal upon his features bewilderment, as well as terror. By their light he is guiding his course, though he does not seem sure of it. The only thing appearing certain is, that he fears something behind, and is fleeing from it.

Once he pauses, longer than usual; and, holding his horse in check, sits listening attentively. While thus halted, he hears a noise, which he knows to be the ripple of a river. It seems oddly to affect him, calling forth an exclamation, which shows he is dissatisfied with the sound.

"Am I never to get away from it? I've been over an hour straying about here, and there's the thing still—not a quarter of a mile off, and timber thick as ever. I thought that last shoot would have taken me out of it. I must have turned somewhere. No help for it, but try again."

Making a half-face round, he heads his horse in a direction opposite to that from which comes the sound of the water. He has done so repeatedly, as oft straying back towards the stream. It is evident he has no wish to go any nearer; but a strong desire to get away from it.

This time he is successful. The new direction followed a half-mile further shows him clear sky ahead, and in a few minutes more he is at the forest's outmost edge. Before him stretches an expanse of plain altogether treeless, but clothed with tall grass, whose culms stirred by the night breeze, and silvered by the moonbeams, sway to and fro, like the soft tremulous wavelets of a tropic sea; myriads of fire-flies prinkling among the spikes, and emitting a gleam, as phosphorescent *medusae,* make the resemblance complete.

The retreating horseman has no such comparison in his thoughts, nor any time to contemplate Nature. The troubled expression in his eyes, tells he is in no mood for it. His glance is not given to the grass, nor the brilliant "lightning bugs," but to a dark belt discernible beyond, apparently a tract of timber, similar to that he has just traversed. More carefully scrutinised, it is seen to be rocks, not trees; in short a continuous line of cliff, forming the boundary of the bottom-land.

He viewing it, well knows what it is, and intends proceeding on to it. He only stays to take bearings for a particular place, at which he evidently aims. His muttered words specify the point.

"The gulch must be to the right. I've gone up-river all the while. Confound the crooked luck! It may throw me behind them going back; and how am I to find my way over the big plain! If I get strayed there—Ha! I see the pass now; yon sharp shoulder of rock—its there."

Once more setting his horse in motion, he makes for the point thus identified. Not now in zig-zags, or slowly—as when working his way through the timber—but in a straight tail-on-end gallop, fast as the animal can go.

And now under the bright moonbeams it may be time to take a closer survey of the hastening horseman. In garb he is Indian, from the mocassins on his feet to the fillet of stained feathers surmounting his head. But the colour of his skin contradicts the idea of his being an aboriginal. His face shows white, but with some smut upon it, like that of a chimney-sweep negligently cleansed. And his features are Caucasian, not ill-favoured, except in their sinister expression; for they are the features of Richard Darke.

Knowing it is he, it will be equally understood that the San Saba is the stream whose sough is so dissonant in his ears, as also, why he is so anxious to put a wide space between himself and its waters. On its bank he has heard a name, and caught sight of him bearing it—the man of all others he has most fear. The backwoodsman who tracked him in the forests of Mississippi, now trailing him upon the prairies of Texas, Simeon Woodley ever pursuing him! If in terror he has been retreating through the trees, not less does he glide over the open ground. Though going in a gallop, every now and then, as before, he keeps slewing round in the saddle and gazing back with apprehensiveness, in fear he may see forms issuing from the timber's edge, and coming on after.

None appear, however; and, at length, arriving by the bluffs base, he draws up under its shadow, darker now, for clouds are beginning to dapple the sky, making the moon's light intermittent. Again, he appears uncertain about the direction he should take; and seated in his saddle, looks inquiringly along the façade of the cliff, scrutinising its outline.

Not long before his scrutiny is rewarded. A dark disc of triangular shape, the apex inverted, proclaims a break in the escarpment. It is the embouchure of a ravine, in short the pass he has been searching for, the same already known to the reader. Straight towards it he rides, with the confidence of one who has climbed it before. In like manner he enters between its grim jaws, and spurs his horse up the slope under the shadow of rocks overhanging right and left. He is some twenty minutes in reaching its summit, on the edge of the upland plain. There he emerges into moonlight; for Luna has again looked out.

Seated in his saddle he takes a survey of the bottom-land below. Afar off, he can distinguish the dark belt of timber, fringing the river on both sides, with here and there a reach of water between, glistening in the moon's soft light like molten silver. His eyes rest not on this, but stray over the open meadow, land in quest of something there.

There is nothing to fix his glance, and he now feels safe, for the first time since starting on that prolonged retreat.

Drawing a free breath he says, soliloquising:—

"No good my going farther now. Besides I don't know the trail, not a foot farther. No help for it but stay here till Borlasse and the boys come up. They can't be much longer, unless they've had a fight to detain them; which I don't think at all likely, after what the half-blood told us. In any case some of them will be this way. Great God! To think of Sime Woodley being here! And after me, sure, for the killing of Clancy! Heywood, too, and Harkness along with them! How is that, I wonder? Can they have met my old jailer on the way, and brought him back to help in tracing me? What the devil does it all mean? It looks as if the very Fates were conspiring for my destruction.

"And who the fellow that laid hold of my horse? So like Clancy! I could swear 'twas he, if I wasn't sure of having settled him. If ever gun-bullet gave a man his quietus, mine did him. The breath was out of his body before I left him.

"Sime Woodley's after me, sure! Damn the ugly brute of a backwoodsman! He seems to have been created for the special purpose of pursuing me?

"And she in my power, to let her so slackly go again! I may never have another such chance. She'll get safe back to the settlements, there to make mock of me! What a simpleton I've been to let her go alive! I should have driven my knife into her. Why didn't I do it? Ach!"

As he utters the harsh exclamation there is blackness on his brow, and chagrin in his glance; a look, such as Satan may have cast back at Paradise on being expelled from it.

With assumed resignation, he continues:—

"No good my grieving over it now. Regrets won't get her back. There may be another opportunity yet. If I live there shall be, though it cost me all my life to bring it about."

Another pause spent reflecting what he ought to do next. He has still some fear of being followed by Sime Woodley. Endeavouring to dismiss it, he mutters:—

"'Tisn't at all likely they'd find the way up here. They appeared to be afoot. I saw no horses. They might have them for all that. But they can't tell which way I took through the timber, and anyhow couldn't track me till after daylight. Before then Borlasse will certainly be along. Just possible he may come across Woodley and his lot. They'll be sure to make for the Mission, and take the road up t'other side. A good chance of our fellows encountering them, unless that begging fool, Bosley, has let all out. Maybe they killed him on the spot? I didn't hear the end of it, and hope they have."

With this barbarous reflection he discontinues his soliloquy, bethinking himself, how he may best pass the time till his comrades come on. At first he designs alighting, and lying down: for he has been many hours in the saddle, and feels fatigued. But just as he is about to dismount, it occurs to him the place is not a proper one. Around the summit of the pass, the plain is without a stick of timber, not even a bush to give shade or concealment, and of this last he now begins to recognise the need. For, all at once, he recalls a conversation with Borlasse, in which mention was made of Sime Woodley; the robber telling of his having been in Texas before, and out upon the San Saba—the very place where now seen! Therefore, the backwoodsman will be acquainted with the locality, and may strike for the trail he has himself taken. He remembers Sime's reputation as a tracker; he no longer feels safe. In the confusion of his senses, his fancy exaggerates his fears, and he almost dreads to look back across the bottom-land.

Thus apprehensive, he turns his eyes towards the plain, in search of a better place for his temporary bivouac, or at all events a safer one. He sees it. To the right, and some two or three hundred yards off is a *motte* of timber, standing solitary on the otherwise treeless expanse. It is the grove of black-jacks, where Hawkins and Tucker halted that same afternoon.

"The very place!" says Richard Darke to himself, after scrutinising it. "There I'll be safe every way; can see without being seen. It commands a view of the pass, and, if the moon keep clear, I'll be able to tell who comes up, whether friends or foes."

Saying this, he makes for the *motte*.

Reaching it, he dismounts, and, drawing the rein over his horse's head, leads the animal in among the trees.

At a short distance from the grove's edge is a glade. In this he makes stop, and secures the horse, by looping the bridle around a branch.

He has a tin canteen hanging over the horn of his saddle, which he lifts off. It is a large one,—capable of holding a half-gallon. It is three parts full, not of water, but of whisky. The fourth part he has drunk during the day, and earlier hours of the night, to give him courage for the part he had to play. He now drinks to drown his chagrin at having played it so badly. Cursing his crooked luck, as he calls it, he takes a swig of the whisky, and then steps back to the place where he entered among the black-jacks. There taking stand, he awaits the coming of his confederates.

He keeps his eyes upon the summit of the pass. They cannot come up without his seeing them, much less go on over the plain.

They must arrive soon, else he will not be able to see them. For he has brought the canteen along, and, raising it repeatedly to his lips, his sight is becoming obscured, the equilibrium of his body endangered.

As the vessel grows lighter, so does his head; while his limbs refuse to support the weight of his body, which oscillates from side to side.

At length, with an indistinct perception of inability to sustain himself erect, and a belief he would feel better in a recumbent attitude, he gropes his way back to the glade, where, staggering about for a while, he at length settles down, dead drunk. In ten seconds he is asleep, in slumber so profound, that a cannon shot—even the voice of Simeon Woodley—would scarce awake him.

Chapter Sixty Eight
"Brasfort"

"Brasfort has caught scent!"

The speech comes from one of two men making their way through a wood, the same across which Richard Darke has just retreated. But they are not retreating as he; on the contrary pursuing, himself the object of their pursuit. For they two men are Charles Clancy, and Jupiter.

They are mounted, Clancy on his horse—a splendid animal—the mulatto astride the mule.

The hound is with them, not now trotting idly after, but in front, with nose to the earth. They are on Darke's trail. The animal has just struck, and is following it, though not fast. For a strap around its neck, with a cord attached, and held in Clancy's hand, keeps it in check, while another buckled about its jaws hinders it from giving tongue. Both precautions show Clancy's determination to take pains with the game he is pursuing, and not again give it a chance to get away. Twice has his mother's murderer escaped him. It will not be so a third time.

They are trailing in darkness, else he would not need assistance from the dog. For it is only a short while since his separation from the party that went on to the Mission. Soon as getting into their saddles, Clancy and his faithful follower struck into the timber, at the point where Darke was seen to enter, and they are now fairly on his tracks. In the obscurity they cannot see them; but the behaviour of the hound tells they are there.

"Yes; Brasfort's on it now," says Clancy, calling the animal by a name long ago bestowed upon it.

"He's on it strong, Jupe. I can tell by the way he tugs upon the string."

"All right, Masser Charle. Give him plenty head. Let him well out. Guess we can keep up with him. An' the sooner we overtake the nigger whipper, the better it be for us, an' the worser for him. Pity you let him go. If you'd 'lowed Mass Woodley to shoot down his hoss—"

"Never mind about that. You'll see himself shot down ere long, or—"

"Or what, masser?"

"Me!"

"Lor forbid! If I ever see that, there's another goes down long side you; either the slave-catcher or the slave."

"Thanks, my brave fellow! I know you mean it. But now to our work; and let us be silent. He may not have gone far, and's still skulking in this tract of timber. If so, he stands a chance to hear us. Speak only in a whisper."

Thus instructed, Jupe makes a gesture to signify compliance; Clancy turning his attention to the hound.

By this, Brasfort is all eagerness, as can be told by the quick vibration of his tail, and spasmodic action of the body. A sound also proceeds from his lips, an attempt at baying; which, but for the confining muzzle would make the forest echoes ring around. Stopped by this his note can be heard only a short distance off, not far enough for them to have any fear. If they but get so near the man they are in chase of, they will surely overtake him.

In confidence the trackers keep on; but obstructed by the close standing trunks, with thick underwood between, they make but slow progress. They are more than an hour in getting across the timbered tract; a distance that should not have taken quarter the time.

At length, arriving on its edge, they make stop; Clancy drawing back the dog. Looking across the plain he sees that, which tells him the instinct of the animal will be no longer needed — at least for a time.

The moon, shining upon the meadow grass, shows a list differently shaded; where the tall culms have been bent down and crushed by the hoof of some heavy quadruped, that has made its way amidst them. And recently too, as Clancy, skilled in tracking, can tell; knowing, also, it is the track of Dick Darke's horse.

"You see it?" he says, pointing to the lighter shaded line. "That's the assassin's trail. He's gone out here, and straight across the bottom. He's made for the bluff yonder. From this he's been putting his animal to speed; gone in a gallop, as the stretch between the tracks show. He may go that way, or any other, 'twill make no difference in the end. He fancies himself clever, but for all his cleverness he'll not escape me now."

"I hope not, Masser Charle; an' don't think he will; don't see how he can."

"He can't."

For some time Clancy is silent, apparently absorbed in serious reflection. At length, he says to his follower: —

"Jupe, my boy, in your time you have suffered much yourself, and should know something of what it is to feel vengeful. But not a vengeance like mine. That you can't understand, and perhaps may think me cruel."

"You, Masser Charle!"

"I don't remember ever having done a harsh thing in my life, or hurt to anyone not deserving it."

"I am sure you never did, masser."

"My dealing with this man may seem an exception. For sure as I live, I'll kill him, or he shall kill me."

"There'd be no cruelty in that. He deserve die, if ever man did."

"He shall. I've sworn it—you know when and where. My poor mother sent to an untimely grave! Her spirit seems now speaking to me—urging me to keep my oath. Let us on!"

They spur out into the moonlight, and off over the open plain, the hound no longer in the lead. His nose is not needed now. The slot of Darke's galloping horse is so conspicuous they can clearly see it, though going fast as did he.

Half an hour at this rapid pace, and they are again under shadow. It is that of the bluff, so dark they can no longer make out the hoof-marks of the retreating horseman.

For a time they are stayed, while once more leashing the hound, and setting it upon the scent.

Brasfort lifts it with renewed spirit; and, keeping in advance, conducts them to an opening in the wall of rock. It is the entrance to a gorge going upward. They can perceive a trodden path, upon which are the hoof-prints of many horses, apparently an hundred of them.

Clancy dismounts to examine them. He takes note, that they are of horses unshod; though there are some with the iron on. Most of them are fresh, among others of older date. Those recently made have the convexity of the hoof turned towards the river. Whoever rode these horses came down the gorge, and kept on for the crossing. He has no doubt, but that they are the same, whose tracks were observed in the slough, and at the ford—now known to have been made by the freebooters. As these have come down the glen, in all likelihood they will go up it in return.

The thought should deter him from proceeding farther in that direction.

But it does not. He is urged on by his oath—by a determination to keep it at all cost. He fancies Darke cannot be far ahead, and trusts to overtaking, and settling the affair, before his confederates come up.

Reflecting thus, he enters the ravine, and commences ascending its slope, Jupiter and Brasfort following.

On reaching the upland plain, they have a different light around, from that below on the bottom-land. The moon is clouded over, but her silvery sheen is replaced by a gloaming of grey. There are streaks of bluish colour, rose tinted, along the horizon's edge. It is the dawn, for day is just breaking.

At first Clancy is gratified by a sight, so oft gladdening hearts. Daylight will assist him in his search.

Soon, he thinks otherwise. Sweeping his eyes over the upland plain, he sees it is sterile and treeless. A thin skirting of timber runs along the bluff edge; but elsewhere all is open, except a solitary grove at no great distance off.

The rendezvous of the robbers would not be there, but more likely on the other side of the arid expanse. Noting a trail which leads outwards, he suspects the pursued man to have taken it. But to follow in full daylight may not only defeat all chance of overtaking him, but expose them to the danger of capture by the freebooters coming in behind.

Clancy casts his eye across the plain, then back towards the bottom-land. He begins to repent his imprudence in having ventured up the pass. But now to descend might be more dangerous than to stay. There is danger either way, and in every direction. So thinking, he says:

"I fear, Jupe, we've been going too fast, and it may be too far. If we encounter these desperadoes, I needn't tell you we'll be in trouble. What ought we to do, think you?"

"Well Masser Charle, I don't jest know. I'se a stranger on these Texas prairies. If 'twar in a Massissip swamp, I might be better able to advise. Hyar I'se all in a quandairy."

"If we go back we may meet them in the teeth. Besides, I shan't—can't now. I must keep on, till I've set eyes on Dick Darke."

"Well, Masser Charle, s'pose we lie hid durin' the day, an' track him after night? The ole dog sure take up the scent for good twenty-four hours to come. There's a bunch of trees out yonner, that'll give us a hidin' place; an' if the thieves go past this way, we sure see 'em. They no see us there."

"But if they go past, it will be all over. I could have little hope of finding him alone. Along with them he would—"

Clancy speaks as if in soliloquy.

Abruptly changing tone, he continues: —

"No, Jupe; we must go on, now. I'll take the risk, if you're not afraid to follow me."

"Masser Charle, I ain't afraid. I'se told you I follow you anywhere—to death if you need me die. I'se tell you that over again."

"And again thanks, my faithful friend! We won't talk of death, till we've come up with Dick Darke. Then you shall see it one way or other. He, or I, hasn't many hours to live. Come, Brasfort! you're wanted once more."

Saying this, he lets the hound ahead, still keeping hold of the cord.

Before long, Brasfort shows signs that he has again caught scent. His ears crisp up, while his whole body quivers along the spinal column from neck to tail. There is a streak of the bloodhound in the animal; and never did dog of this kind make after a man, who more deserved hunting by a hound.

Chapter Sixty Nine
Shadows behind

When once more upon the trail of the man he intends killing, Clancy keeps on after his hound, with eager eyes watching every movement of the animal. That Brasfort is dead upon the scent can be told by his excited action, and earnest whimpering.

All at once he is checked up, his master drawing him back with sudden abruptness.

The dog appears surprised at first, so does Jupiter. The latter, looking round, discovers the cause: something which moves upon the plain, already observed by Clancy. Not clearly seen, for it is still dark.

"What goes yonder?" he asks, eagerly scanning it, with hands over his eyes.

"It don't go, Masser Charle, whatever it is. Dat thing 'pears comin'."

"You're right. It is moving in this direction. A dust-cloud; something made it. Ah! horses! Are there men on their backs? No. Bah! it's but a drove of mustangs. I came near taking them for Comanches; not that we need care. Just now the red gentry chance to be tied by a treaty, and are not likely to harm us. We've more to fear from fellows with white skins. Yes, the wild horses are heading our way; scouring along as if all the Indians in Texas were after them. What does that signify? Something, I take it."

Jupiter cannot say. He is, as he has confessed, inexperienced upon the prairies, ill understanding their "sign." However well acquainted with the craft of the forest, up in everything pertaining to timber, upon the treeless plains of Texas, an old prairie man would sneeringly pronounce him a "greenhorn."

Clancy, knowing this, scarce expects reply; or, if so, with little hope of explanation.

He does not wait for it, having himself discovered why the wild horses are going at such a rate. Besides the dust stirred up by their hooves, is another cloud rising in the sky beyond. The black belt just looming along the horizon proclaims the approach of a "norther." The scared horses are heading southward, in the hope to escape it.

They come in full career towards the spot where the two have pulled up—along a line parallel to the trend of the cliff, at some distance from its edge. Neighing, snorting, with tossed manes, and streaming tails, they tear past, and are soon wide away on the other side.

Clancy keeping horse and hound in check, waits till they are out of sight. Then sets Brasfort back upon the scent, from which he so unceremoniously jerked him.

Though without dent of hoof on the dry parched grass, the hound easily retakes it, straining on as before.

But he is soon at fault, losing it. They have come upon the tracks of the mustangs, these having spoiled the scent—killed it.

Clancy, halting, sits dissatisfied in the saddle; Jupiter sharing his dissatisfaction.

What are they to do now? The mulatto suggests crossing the ground trodden by the mustangs, and trying on the other side.

To this Clancy consents. It is the only course that seems rational.

Again moving forward, they pass over the beaten turf; and, letting Brasfort alone, look to him. The hound strikes ahead, quartering.

Not long till the vibration of his tail tells he is once more on the scent.

Now stiffer than ever, and leading in a straight line. He goes direct for the copse of timber, which is now only a very short distance off.

Again Clancy draws the dog in, at the same time reining up his horse.

Jupe has done the same with his mule; and both bend their eyes upon the copse—the grove of black-jack oaks—scanning it with glances of inquiry. If Clancy but knew what is within, how in a glade near its centre, is the man they are seeking, he would no longer tarry for Brasfort's trailing, but letting go the leash altogether, and leaping from his horse, rush in among the trees, and bring to a speedy reckoning him, to whom he owes so much misery.

Richard Darke dreams not of the danger so near him. He is in a deep sleep—the dreamless, helpless slumber of intoxication.

But a like near danger threatens Clancy himself, of which he is unconscious. With face towards the copse, and eyes eagerly scrutinising it, he thinks not of looking behind.

By the way his hound still behaves, there must be something within the grove. What can it be? He does not ask the question. He suspects— is, indeed, almost certain—his enemy is that something. Muttering to the mulatto, who has come close alongside, he says:—

"I shouldn't wonder, Jupe, if we've reached our journey's end. Look at Brasfort! See how he strains! There's man or beast among those black-jacks—both I take it."

"Looks like, masser."

"Yes; I think we'll there find what we're searching for. Strange, too, his making no show. I can't see sign of a movement."

"No more I."

"Asleep, perhaps? It won't do for us to go any nearer, till sure. He's had the advantage of me too often before. I can't afford giving it again. Ha! what's that?"

The dog has suddenly slewed round, and sniffs in the opposite direction. Clancy and Jupe, turning at the same time, see that which draws their thoughts from Richard Darke, driving him altogether out of their minds.

Their faces are turned towards the east, where the Aurora reddens the sky, and against its bright background several horsemen are seen *en silhouette*, their number each instant increasing. Some are already visible from crown to hoof; others show only to the shoulders; while the heads of others can just be distinguished surmounting the crest of the cliff. In the spectacle there is no mystery, nor anything that needs explanation. Too well does Charles Clancy comprehend. A troop of mounted men approaching up the pass, to all appearance Indians, returning spoil-laden from a raid on some frontier settlement. But in reality white men, outlawed desperadoes, the band of Jim Borlasse, long notorious throughout South-Western Texas.

One by one, they ascend *en échelon*, as fiends through a stage-trap in some theatric scene, showing faces quite as satanic. Each, on arriving at the summit, rides into line alongside their leader, already up and halted. And on they come, till nineteen can be counted upon the plain.

Clancy does not care to count them. There could be nothing gained by that. He sees there are enough to make resistance idle. To attempt it were madness.

And must he submit? There seems no alternative.

There is for all that; one he is aware of—flight. His horse is strong and swift. For both these qualities originally chosen, and later designed to be used for a special purpose—pursuit. Is the noble animal now to be tried in a way never intended—retreat?

Although that dark frowning phalanx, at the summit of the pass, would seem to answer "yes," Clancy determines "no." Of himself he could still escape—and easily. In a stretch over that smooth plain, not a horse in their troop would stand the slightest chance to come up with him, and he could soon leave all out of sight. But then, he must needs also leave behind the faithful retainer, from whose lips has just issued a declaration of readiness to follow him to the death.

He cannot, will not; and if he thinks of flight, it is instinctively, and but for an instant; the thought abandoned as he turns towards the mulatto, and gives a glance at the mule. On his horse he could yet ride away from the robbers, but the slow-footed hybrid bars all hope for Jupiter. The absconding slave were certain to be caught, now; and slave or free, the colour of his skin would ensure him cruel treatment from the lawless crew.

But what better himself taken? How can he protect poor Jupe, his own freedom—his life—equally imperilled? For he has no doubt but that Borlasse will remember, and recognise, him. It is barely twelve months since he stood beside that whipping-post in the town of Nacogdoches, and saw the ruffian receive chastisement for the stealing of his horse—the same he is now sitting upon. No fear of the horse-thief having forgotten that episode of his life.

He can have no doubt but that Borlasse will retaliate; that this will be his first thought, soon as seeing him. It needs not for the robber chief to know what has occurred by the big oak; that Bosley is a prisoner, Quantrell a fugitive, their prisoners released, and on their way back to the Mission. It is not likely he does know, as yet. But too likely he will soon learn. For Darke will be turning up ere long, and everything will be made clear. Then to the old anger of Borlasse for the affair of the scourging, will be added new rage, while that of Darke himself will be desperate.

In truth, the prospect is appalling; and Charles Clancy, almost as much as ever in his life, feels that life in peril.

Could he look into the courtyard of the San Saba Mission, and see what is there, he might think it even more so. Without that, there is sufficient to shake his resolution about standing his ground; enough to make him spur away from the spot, and leave Jupiter to his fate.

"No—never!" he mentally exclaims, closing all reflection. "As a coward I could not live. If I must die, it shall be bravely. Fear not, Jupe! We stand or fall together!"

Chapter Seventy
Surrounded and disarmed

Borlasse, riding at the head of his band, has been the first to arrive at the upper end of the gorge.

Perceiving some figures upon the plain, he supposes them to be Quantrell and Bosley with the captives. For his face is toward the west, where the sky is still night-shadowed, and he can but indistinctly trace the outlines of horses and men. As their number corresponds to that of his missing comrades, he has no thought of its being other than they. How could he, as none other are likely to be encountered there?

Congratulating himself on his suspicions of the lieutenant's defection proving unfounded, and that he will now clutch the prize long coveted, he gives his horse the spur, and rides gaily out of the gorge.

Not till then does he perceive that the men before him are in civilised costume, and that but one is on horseback, the other bestriding a mule. And they have no captives, the only other thing seen beside them being a dog!

They are not Quantrell and Bosley!

"Who can they be?" he asks of Chisholm, who has closed up behind him.

"Hanged if I know, cap. Judgin' by their toggery, they must be whites; though 'gainst that dark sky one can't make sure about the colour of their hides. A big dog with them. A couple of trappers I take it; or, more likely, Mexican mustangers."

"Not at all likely, Luke. There's none o' them 'bout here—at least I've not heard of any since we came this side the Colorado. Cannot be that. I wonder who—"

"No use wonderin', cap. We can soon settle the point by questioning them. As there's but the two, they'll have to tell who they are, or take the consequences."

By this, the other robbers have come up out of the ravine. Halted in a row, abreast, they also scan the two figures in front, interrogating one another as to who and what they are. All are alike surprised at men there, mounted or afoot; more especially white men, as by their garb they must be. But they have no apprehension at the encounter, seeing there are so few.

The chief, acting on Chisholm's suggestion, moves confidently forward, the others, in like confidence, following.

In less than sixty seconds they are up to the spot occupied by Clancy and Jupiter.

Borlasse can scarce believe his eyes; and rubs them to make sure they are not deceiving him. If not they, something else has been—a newspaper report, and a tale told by one confessing himself a murderer, boastfully proclaiming it. And now, before him is the murdered man, on horseback, firmly seated in the saddle, apparently in perfect health!

The desperado is speechless with astonishment—only muttering to himself:—"What the devil's this?"

Were the question addressed to his, comrades, they could not answer it; though none of them share his astonishment, or can tell what is causing it. All they know is that two men are in their midst, one white, the other a mulatto, but who either is they have not the slightest idea. They see that the white man is a handsome young fellow—evidently a gentleman—bestriding a steed which some of them already regard with covetous glances; while he on the mule has the bearing of a body-servant.

None of them has ever met or seen Clancy before, nor yet the fugitive slave. Their leader alone knows the first, too much of him, though nothing of the last. But no matter about the man of yellow skin. He with the white one is his chief concern.

Recovering from his first surprise, he turns his thoughts towards solving the enigma. He is not long before reaching its solution. He remembers that the newspaper report said: "the body of the murdered man has not been found." Ergo, Charles Clancy hasn't been killed after all; for there he is, alive, and life-like as any man among them; mounted upon a steed which Jim Borlasse remembers well—as well as he does his master. To forget the animal would be a lapse of memory altogether unnatural. There are weals on the robber's back,—a souvenir of chastisement received for stealing that horse,—scars cicatrised, but never to be effaced.

Deeper still than the brand on his body has sunk the record into his soul. He was more than disappointed—enraged—on hearing that Richard Darke had robbed him of a premeditated vengeance. For he knew Clancy was again returning to Texas, and intended taking it on his return. Now, discovering he has not been forestalled, seeing his prosecutor there, unexpectedly in his power, the glance he gives to him is less like that of man than demon.

His followers take note that there is a strangeness in his manner, but refrain from questioning him about it. He seems in one of his moods, when they know it is not safe to intrude upon, or trifle with him. In his belt he carries a "Colt," which more than once has silenced a too free-speaking subordinate.

Having surrounded the two strangers, in obedience to his gesture, they await further instructions how to deal with them.

His first impulse is to make himself known to Clancy; then indulge in an ebullition of triumph over his prisoner. Put a thought restraining him, he resolves to preserve his incognito a little longer. Under his Indian travestie he fancies Clancy cannot, and has not, recognised him. Nor is it likely he would have done so, but for the foreknowledge obtained through Bosley. Even now only by his greater bulk is the robber chief distinguishable among his subordinates, all their faces being alike fantastically disfigured.

Drawing back behind his followers, he whispers some words to Chisholm, instructing him what is to be done, as also to take direction of it.

"Give up yer guns!" commands the latter, addressing himself to the strangers.

"Why should we?" asks Clancy.

"We want no cross-questionin', Mister. 'Tain't the place for sech, nor the time, as you'll soon larn. Give up yer guns! Right quick, or you'll have them taken from ye, in a way you won't like."

Clancy still hesitates, glancing hastily around the ring of mounted men. He is mad at having permitted himself to be taken prisoner, for he knows he is this. He regrets not having galloped off while there was yet time. It is too late now. There is not a break in the enfilading circle through which he might make a dash. Even if there were, what chance ultimately to escape? None whatever. A score of guns and pistols are around him, ready to be discharged should he attempt to stir from the spot. Some of them are levelled, their barrels bearing upon him. It would be instant death, and madness in him to seek it so. He but says:—

"What have we done, that you should disarm us? You appear to be Indians, yet talk the white man's tongue. In any case, and whoever you are, we have no quarrel with you. Why should you wish to make us prisoners?"

"We don't do anything of the sort. That would be wastin' wishes. You're our pris'ners already."

It is Chisholm who thus facetiously speaks, adding in sterner tone:—

"Let go yer guns, or, by God! we'll shoot you out of your saddles. Boys! in upon 'em, and take their weepuns away!"

At the command several of the robbers spring their horses forward, and, closing upon Clancy, seize him from all sides; others serving Jupiter the same. Both see that resistance were worse than folly—sheer insanity—and that there is no alternative but submit.

Their arms are wrested from them, though they are allowed to retain possession of their animals. That is, they are left in their saddles—compelled to stay in them by ropes rove around their ankles, attaching them to the stirrup-leathers.

Whatever punishment awaits them, that is not the place where they are to suffer it. For, soon as getting their prisoners secured, the band is again formed into files, its leader ordering it to continue the march, so unexpectedly, and to him satisfactorily, interrupted.

Chapter Seventy One
A pathless plain

The plain across which the freebooters are now journeying, on return to what they call their "rendyvoo," is one of a kind common in South-western Texas. An arid steppe, or table-land, by the Mexicans termed *mesa*; for the most part treeless, or only with such arborescence as characterises the American desert. "Mezquite," a name bestowed on several trees of the acacia kind, "black-jack," a dwarfed species of oak, with *Prosopis, Fouquiera*, and other spinous shrubs, are here and there found in thickets called "chapparals," interspersed with the more succulent vegetation of *cactus* and *agave*, as also the *yucca*, or dragon-tree of the Western Hemisphere.

In this particular section of it almost every tree and plant carries thorns. Even certain grasses are armed with prickly spurs, and sting the hand that touches them; while the reptiles crawling among them are of the most venomous species; scorpions and centipedes, with snakes having ossified tails, and a frog furnished with horns! The last, however, though vulgarly believed to be a batrachian, is in reality a lizard—the *Agama cornuta*.

This plain, extending over thirty miles from east to west, and twice the distance in a longitudinal direction, has on one side the valley of the San Saba, on the other certain creeks tributary to the Colorado. On one of these the prairie pirates have a home, or haunt, to which they retire only on particular occasions, and for special purposes. Under circumstances of this kind they are now *en route* for it.

Its locality has been selected with an eye to safety, which it serves to perfection. A marauding party pursued from the lower settlements of the Colorado, by turning up the valley of the San Saba, and then taking across the intermediate plain, would be sure to throw the pursuers off their tracks, since on the table-land none are left throughout long stretches where even the iron heel of a horse makes no dent in the dry turf, nor leaves the slightest imprint. At one place in particular, just after striking this plain from the San Saba side, there is a broad belt, altogether without vegetation or soil upon its surface, the ground being covered with what the trappers call "cut-rock," presenting the appearance of a freshly macadamised road. Extending for more than a mile in width, and ten times as much lengthways, it is a tract no traveller would care to enter on who has any solicitude about the hooves of his horse. But just for this reason is it in every respect suitable to the prairie pirates. They may cross it empty-handed, and recross laden with spoil, without the pursuers being able to discover whence they came, or whither they have gone.

Several times has this happened; settlers having come up the Colorado in pursuit of a marauding party—supposed to be Comanche Indians— tracked them into the San Saba bottom-land, and on over the bluff—there to lose their trail, and retire disheartened from the pursuit.

Across this stony stretch proceed the freebooters, leaving no more trace behind, than one would walking on a shingled sea-beach.

On its opposite edge they make stop to take bearings. For although they have more than once passed that way before, it is a route which always requires to be traversed with caution. To get strayed on the inhospitable steppe would be attended with danger, and might result in death.

In clear weather, to those acquainted with the trail, there is little chance of losing it. For midway between the water courses runs a ridge, bisecting the steppe in a longitudinal direction; and on the crest of this is a tree, which can be seen from afar off on either side. The ridge is of no great elevation, and would scarce be observable but for the general level from which it rises, a mere comb upon the plain, such as is known northward by the term *coteau de prairie*—a title bestowed by trappers of French descent.

The tree stands solitary, beside a tiny spring, which bubbles out between its roots. This, trickling off, soon sinks into the desert sand, disappearing within a few yards of the spot where it has burst forth.

In such situation both tree and fountain are strange; though the one will account for the other, the former being due to the latter. But still another agency is needed to explain the existence of the tree. For it is a "cottonwood"—a species not found elsewhere upon the same plain; its seed no doubt transported thither by some straying bird. Dropped by the side of the spring in soil congenial, it has sprouted up, nourished, and become a tall tree. Conspicuous for long leagues around, it serves the prairie pirates as a finger-post to direct them across the steppe; for by chance it stands right on their route. It is visible from the edge of the pebble-strewn tract, but only when there is a cloudless sky and shining sun. Now, the one is clouded, the other unseen, and the tree cannot be distinguished.

For some minutes the robbers remain halted, but without dismounting. Seated in the saddle, they strain their eyes along the horizon to the west.

The Fates favour them; as in this world is too often the case with wicked men, notwithstanding many saws to the contrary. The sun shoots from behind a cloud, scattering his golden gleams broad and bright over the surface of the plain. Only for an instant, but enough to show the cottonwood standing solitary on the crest of the ridge.

"Thank the Lord for that glimp o' light!" exclaims Borlasse, catching sight of the tree, "Now, boys; we see our beacon, an' let's straight to it. When we've got thar I'll show ye a bit of sport as 'll make ye laugh till there wont be a whole rib left in your bodies, nor a button on your coats—if ye had coats on."

With this absurd premonition he presses on—his scattered troop reforming, and following.

Chapter Seventy Two
The prairie stocks

Silent is Clancy, sullen as a tiger just captured and encaged. As the moments pass, and he listens to the lawless speech of his captors, more than ever is he vexed with himself for having so tamely submitted to be taken.

Though as yet no special inhumanity has been shown him, he knows there will ere long. Coarse jests bandied between the robbers, whispered innuendoes, forewarn him of some fearful punishment about to be put upon him. Only its nature remains unknown.

He does not think they intend killing him outright. He has overheard one of his guards muttering to the other, that such is not the chiefs intention, adding some words which make the assurance little consolatory. "Worse than death" is the fragment of a sentence borne ominously to his ears.

Worse than death! Is it to be torture?

During all this time Borlasse has not declared himself, or given token of having recognised his prisoner. But Clancy can tell he has done so. He saw it in the Satanic glance of his eye as they first came face to face. Since, the robber has studiously kept away from him, riding at the head of the line, the prisoners having place in its centre.

On arrival at the underwood, all dismount; but only to slake their thirst, as that of their horses. The spring is unapproachable by the animals; and leathern buckets are called into requisition. With these, and other marching apparatus, the freebooters are provided. While one by one the horses are being watered, Borlasse draws off to some distance, beckoning Chisholm to follow him; and for a time the two seem engaged in earnest dialogue, as if in discussion. The chief promised his followers a spectacle,—a "bit of sport," as he facetiously termed it. Clancy has been forecasting torture, but in his worst fear of it could not conceive any so terrible as that in store for him. It is in truth a cruelty inconceivable, worthy a savage, or Satan himself. Made known to Chisholm, though hardened this outlaw's heart, he at first shrinks from assisting in its execution—even venturing to remonstrate.

But Borlasse is inexorable. He has no feelings of compassion for the man who was once the cause of his being made to wince under the whip. His vengeance is implacable; and will only be satisfied by seeing Clancy suffer all that flesh can. By devilish ingenuity he has contrived a scheme to this intent, and will carry it out regardless of consequences.

So says he, in answer to the somewhat mild remonstrance of his subordinate.

"Well, cap," rejoins the latter, yielding, "if you're determined to have it that way, why, have it. But let it be a leetle privater than you've spoke o'. By makin' it a public spectacle, an' lettin' all our fellars into your feelins, some o' 'em mightn't be so much amused. An some might get to blabbin' about it afterwards, in such a way as to breed trouble. The originality an' curiousness o' the thing would be sure to 'tract attention, an' the report o't would run through all Texas, like a prairie on fire. 'Twould never sleep as long's there's a soger left in the land; and sure as shootin' we'd have the Rangers and Regulators hot after us. Tharfore, if you insist on the bit o' interment, take my advice, and let the ceremony be confined to a few friends as can be trusted wi' a secret."

For some seconds Borlasse is silent, pondering upon what Chisholm has said. Then responds:—

"Guess you're about right, Luke. I'll do as you suggest. Best way will be to send the boys on ahead. There's three can stay with us we can trust— Watts, Stocker, and Driscoll. They'll be enough to do the grave-digging. The rest can go on to the rendezvous. Comrades!" he adds, moving back towards his men, who have just finished watering their horses, "I spoke o' some sport I intended givin' you here. On second thinkin' it'll be better defarred till we get to head-quarters. So into your saddles and ride on thar— takin' the yeller fellow along wi' ye. The other I'll look after myself. You, Luke Chisholm, stay; with Watts, Stocker, and Driscoll. I've got a reason for remaining here a little longer. We'll soon be after, like enough overtake ye 'fore you can reach the creek. If not, keep on to camp without us. An', boys; once more I warn ye about openin' them boxes. I know what's in them to a dollar. Fernand! you'll see to that."

The half-blood, of taciturn habit, nods assent, Borlasse adding:—

"Now, you damned rascals! jump into your saddles and be off. Take the nigger along. Leave the white gentleman in better company, as befits him."

With a yell of laughter at the coarse sally, the freebooters spring upon their horses. Then, separating Clancy from Jupe, they ride off, taking the latter. On the ground are left only the chief, Chisholm, and the trio chosen to assist at some ceremony, mysteriously spoken of as an "interment."

After all it is not to be there. On reflection, Borlasse deems the place not befitting. The grave he is about to dig must not be disturbed, nor the body he intends burying disinterred.

Though white traveller never passes that solitary tree, red ones sometimes seek relaxation under its shade. Just possible a party of Comanches may come along; and though savages, their hearts might still be humane enough to frustrate the nefarious scheme of a white man more savage than they. To guard against such contingency Borlasse has bethought him of some change in his programme, which he makes known to Chisholm, saying:—

"I won't bury him here, Luke. Some strayin' redskin might come along, and help him to resurrection. By God! he shan't have that, till he hears Gabriel's trumpet. To make sure we must plant him in a safer place."

"Can we find safer, cap?"

"Certainly we can."

"But whar?"

"Anywhare out o' sight of here. We shall take him to some distance off, so's they can't see him from the spring. Up yonder'll do."

He points to a part of the plain northward, adding:—

"It's all alike which way, so long's we go far enough."

"All right!" rejoins Chisholm, who has surrendered his scruples about the cruelty of what they intend doing, and only thinks of its being done without danger.

"Boys!" shouts Borlasse to the men in charge of Clancy, "bring on your prisoner! We're going to make a leetle deflection from the course—a bit o' a pleasure trip—only a short un."

So saying, he starts off in a northerly direction, nearly at right angles to that they have been hitherto travelling.

After proceeding about a mile, the brigand chief, still riding with Chisholm in the advance, comes to a halt, calling back to the others to do the same—also directing them to dismount their prisoner.

Clancy is unceremoniously jerked out of his saddle; and, after having his arms pinioned, and limbs lashed together, laid prostrate along the earth. This leaves them free for the infernal task, they are now instructed to perform. One only, Watts, stays with the prisoner; the other two, at the chiefs command, coming on to where he and Chisholm have halted. Then all four cluster around a spot he points out, giving directions what they are to do.

With the point of his spear Borlasse traces a circle upon the turf, some twenty inches in diameter; then tells them to dig inside it.

Stocker and Driscoll draw their tomahawks, and commence hacking at the ground; which, though hard, yields to the harder steel of hatchets manufactured for the cutting of skulls. As they make mould, it is removed by Chisholm with the broad blade of his Comanche spear.

As all prairie men are accustomed to making *caches*, they are expert at this; and soon sink a shaft that would do credit to the "crowing" of a South African Bosjesman. It is a cylinder full five feet in depth, with a diameter of less than two. Up to this time its purpose has not been declared to either Stocker, or Driscoll, though both have their conjectures. They guess it to be the grave of him who is lying along the earth—his living tomb!

At length, deeming it deep enough, Borlasse commands them to leave off work, adding, as he points to the prisoner: "Now, plant your saplin'! If it don't grow there it ought to."

The cold-blooded jest extorts a smile from the others, as they proceed to execute the diabolical order.

And they do it without show of hesitation—rather with alacrity. Not one of the five has a spark of compassion in his breast—not one whose soul is unstained with blood.

Clancy is dragged forward, and plunged feet foremost into the cavity. Standing upright, his chin is only an inch or two above the surface of the ground. A portion of the loose earth is pushed in, and packed around him, the ruffians trampling it firm. What remains they kick and scatter aside; the monster, with horrible mockery, telling them to make a "neat job of it."

During all this time Brasfort has been making wild demonstrations, struggling to free himself, as if to rescue his master. For he is also bound, tied to the stirrup of one of the robber's horses. But the behaviour of the faithful animal, instead of stirring them to compassion, only adds to their fiendish mirth.

The interment complete, Borlasse makes a sign to the rest to retire; then, placing himself in front, with arms akimbo, stands looking Clancy straight in the face. No pen could paint that glance. It can only be likened to that of Lucifer.

For a while he speaks not, but in silence exults over his victim. Then, bending down and tossing back his plumed bonnet, he asks, "D'ye know me, Charley Clancy?"

Receiving no reply, he continues, "I'll lay a hundred dollars to one, ye will, after I've told ye a bit o' a story, the which relates to a circumstance as happened jest twelve months ago. The scene o' that affair was in the public square o' Nacodosh, whar a man was tied to a post an—"

"Whipped at it, as he deserved."

"Ha!" exclaims Borlasse, surprised, partly at being recognised, but as much by the daring avowal. "You do remember that little matter? And me too?"

"Perfectly; so you may spare yourself the narration. You are Jim Borlasse, the biggest brute and most thorough scoundrel in Texas."

"Curse you!" cries the ruffian enraged, poising his spear till its point almost touches Clancy's head, "I feel like driving this through your skull."

"Do so!" is the defiant and desperate rejoinder. It is what Clancy desires. He has no hope of life now. He wishes death to come at once, and relieve him from the long agony he will otherwise have to endure.

Quick catching this to be his reason, Borlasse restrains himself, and tosses up the spear, saying:—

"No, Mister; ye don't die that eesy way—not if I know it. You and yours kept me two days tied like a martyr to the stake, to say nothin' of what came after. So to make up for't I'll give you a spell o' confinement that'll last a leetle longer. You shall stay as ye are, till the buzzarts peck out your eyes, an' the wolves peel the skin from your skull—ay, till the worms go crawlin' through your flesh. How'll ye like that, Charley Clancy?"

"There's no wolf or vulture on the prairies of Texas ugly as yourself. Dastardly dog!"

"Ah! you'd like to get me angry? But you can't. I'm cool as a cowkumber—aint I? Your dander's up, I can see. Keep it down. No good your gettin' excited. I s'pose you'd like me to spit in your face. Well, here goes to obleege ye."

At this he stoops down, and does as said. After perpetrating the outrage, he adds:—

"Why don't ye take out your handkercher an' wipe it off. It's a pity to see such a handsome fellow wi' his face in that fashion. Ha! ha! ha!"

His four confederates, standing apart, spectators of the scene, echo his fiendish laughter.

"Well, well, my proud gentleman;" he resumes, "to let a man spit in your face without resentin' it! I never expected to see you sunk so low. Humiliated up to the neck—to the chin! Ha! ha! ha!"

Again rings out the brutal cachinnation, chorused by his four followers.

In like manner the monster continues to taunt his helpless victim; so long, one might fancy his spite would be spent, his vengeance sated.

But no—not yet. There is still another arrow in his quiver—a last shaft to be shot—which he knows will carry a sting keener than any yet sent.

When his men have remounted, and are ready to ride off, he returns to Clancy, and, stooping, hisses into his ear:—

"Like enough you'll be a goodish while alone here, an' tharfore left to your reflections. Afore partin' company, let me say somethin' that may comfort you. *Dick Darke's got your girl; 'bout this time has her in his arms!*"

Chapter Seventy Three
Helpless and hopeless

"O God!"

Charles Clancy thus calls upon his Maker. Hitherto sustained by indignation, now that the tormentor has left him, the horror of his situation, striking into his soul in all its dread reality, wrings from him the prayerful apostrophe.

A groan follows, as his glance goes searching over the plain. For there is nothing to gladden it. His view commands the half of a circle—a great circle such as surrounds you upon the sea; though not as seen from the deck of a ship, but by one lying along the thwarts of a boat, or afloat upon a raft.

The robbers have ridden out of sight, and he knows they will not return. They have left him to die a lingering death, almost as if entombed alive. Perhaps better he were enclosed in a coffin; for then his sufferings would sooner end.

He has not the slightest hope of being succoured. There is no likelihood of human creature coming that way. It is a sterile waste, without game to tempt the hunter, and though a trail runs across it, Borlasse, with fiendish forethought, has placed him so far from this, that no one travelling along it could possibly see him. He can just descry the lone cottonwood afar off, outlined against the horizon like a ship at sea. It is the only tree in sight; elsewhere not even a bush to break the drear monotony of the desert.

He thinks of Simeon Woodley, Ned Heywood, and those who may pursue the plunderers of the settlement. But with hopes too faint to be worth entertaining. For he has been witness to the precautions taken by the robbers to blind their trail, and knows that the most skilled tracker cannot discover it. Chance alone could guide the pursuit in that direction, if pursuit there is to be. But even this is doubtful. For Colonel Armstrong having recovered his daughters, and only some silver stolen, the settlers may be loath to take after the thieves, or postpone following them to some future time. Clancy has no knowledge of the sanguinary drama that has been enacted at the

Mission, else he would not reason thus. Ignorant of it, he can only be sure, that Sime Woodley and Ned Heywood will come in quest of, but without much likelihood of their finding them. No doubt they will search for days, weeks, months, if need be; and in time, but too late, discover—what? His head—

"Ha!"

His painful reflections are interrupted by that which but intensifies their painfulness: a shadow he sees flitting across the plain.

His eyes do not follow it, but, directed upward, go in search of the thing which is causing it. "A vulture!"

The foul bird is soaring aloft, its black body and broad expanded wings outlined against the azure sky. For this is again clear, the clouds and threatening storm having drifted off without bursting. And now, while with woe in his look he watches the swooping bird, well knowing the sinister significance of its flight, he sees another, and another, and yet another, till the firmament seems filled with them.

Again he groans out, "O God!"

A new agony threatens, a new horror is upon him. Vain the attempt to depict his feelings, as he regards the movements of the vultures. They are as those of one swimming in the sea amidst sharks. For, although the birds do not yet fly towards him, he knows they will soon be there. He sees them sailing in spiral curves, descending at each gyration, slowly but surely stooping lower, and coming nearer. He can hear the swish of their wings, like the sough of an approaching storm, with now and then a raucous utterance from their throats—the signal of some leader directing the preliminaries of the attack, soon to take place.

At length they are so close, he can see the ruff around their naked necks, bristled up; the skin reddened as with rage, and their beaks, stained with bloody flesh of some other banquet, getting ready to feast upon his. Soon he will feel them striking against his skull, pecking out his eyes. O, heavens! can horror be felt further?

Not by him. It adds not to his, when he perceives that the birds threatening to assail him will be assisted by beasts. For he now sees this. Mingling with the shadows flitting over the earth, are things more substantial—the bodies of wolves. As with the vultures, at first only one; then two or three; their number at each instant increasing, till a whole pack of the predatory brutes have gathered upon the ground.

Less silent than their winged allies—their competitors, if it come to a repast. For the coyote is a noisy creature, and those now assembling around Clancy's head—a sight strange to them—give out their triple bark, with its prolonged whine, in sound so lugubrious, that, instead of preparing for attack, one might fancy them wailing a defeat.

Clancy has often heard that cry, and well comprehends its meaning. It seems his death-dirge. While listening to it no wonder he again calls upon God—invokes Heaven to help him!

Chapter Seventy Four
Coyote Creek

A stream coursing through a cañoned channel whose banks rise three hundred feet above its bed. They are twin cliffs that front one another, their *façades* not half so far apart. Rough with projecting points of rock, and scarred by water erosion, they look like angry giants with grim visages frowning mutual defiance. In places they approach, almost to touching; then, diverging, sweep round the opposite sides of an ellipse; again closing like the curved handles of callipers. Through the spaces thus opened the water makes its way, now rushing in hoarse torrent, anon gently meandering through meadows, whose vivid verdure, contrasting with the sombre colour of the enclosing cliffs, gives the semblance of landscape pictures set in rustic frame.

The traveller who attempts to follow the course of the stream in question will have to keep upon the cliffs above: for no nearer can he approach its deeply-indented channel. And here he will see only the sterile treeless plain; or, if trees meet his eye, they will be such as but strengthen the impression of sterility—some scrambling mezquite bushes, clumps of cactaceae, perhaps the spheroidal form of a melocactus, or yucca, with its tufts of rigid leaves— the latter resembling bunches of bayonets rising above the musket "stacks" on a military parade ground.

He will have no view of the lush vegetation that enlivens the valley a hundred yards below the hoofs of his horse. He will not even get a glimpse of the stream itself; unless by going close to the edge of the precipice, and craning his neck over. And to do this, he must needs diverge from his route to avoid the transverse rivulets, each trickling down the bed of its own deep-cut channel.

There are many such streams in South-Western Texas; but the one here described is that called *Arroyo de Coyote*—Anglice, "Coyote Creek"—a tributary of the Colorado.

In part it forms the western boundary of the table-land, already known to the reader, in part intersecting it. Approaching it from the San Saba side, there is a stretch of twenty miles, where its channel cannot be reached, except by a single lateral ravine leading down to it at right angles, the entrance to which is concealed by a thick chapparal of thorny mezquite trees. Elsewhere, the traveller may arrive on the bluff's brow, but cannot go down to the stream's edge. He may see it far below, coursing among trees of every shade of green, from clearest emerald to darkest olive, here in straight reaches, there sinuous as a gliding snake. Birds of brilliant plumage flit about through the foliage upon its banks, some disporting themselves in its pellucid wave; some making the valley vocal with their melodious warblings, and others filling it with harsh, stridulous cries. Burning with thirst, and faint from fatigue, he will fix his gaze on the glistening water, to be tortured as Tantalus, and descry the cool shade, without being able to rest his weary limbs beneath it.

But rare the traveller, who ever strays to the bluffs bounding Coyote Creek: rarer still, those who have occasion to descend to the bottom-land through which it meanders.

Some have, nevertheless, as evinced by human sign observable upon the stream's bank, just below where the lateral ravine leads down. There the cliffs diverging, and again coming near, enclose a valley of ovoidal shape, for the most part overgrown with pecan-trees. On one side of it is a thick umbrageous grove, within which several tents are seen standing. They are of rude description, partly covered by the skins of animals, partly scraps of old canvas, here and there eked out with a bit of blanket, or a cast coat. No one would mistake them for the tents of ordinary travellers, while they are equally unlike the wigwams of the nomadic aboriginal. To whom, then, do they appertain?

Were their owners present, there need be no difficulty in answering the question. But they are not. Neither outside, nor within, is soul to be seen. Nor anywhere near. No human form appears about the place; no voice of man, woman, or child, reverberates through the valley. Yet is there every evidence of recent occupation. In an open central space, are the ashes of a huge fire still hot, with fagots half-burnt, and scarce ceased smoking; while within the tents are implements, utensils, and provisions—bottles and jars of liquor left uncorked, with stores of tobacco unconsumed. What better proof that they are only temporarily deserted, and not abandoned? Certainly their owners, whether white men or Indians, intend returning to them.

It need scarce be told who these are. Enough to say, that Coyote Creek is the head-quarters of the prairie pirates, who assaulted the San Saba settlement.

Just as the sun is beginning to decline towards the western horizon, those of them sent on ahead arrive at their rendezvous; the chief, with Chisholm and the other three, not yet having come up.

On entering the encampment, they relieve their horses of the precious loads. Then unsaddling, turn them into a "corral" rudely constructed among the trees. A set of bars, serving as a gate, secures the animals against straying.

This simple stable duty done, the men betake themselves to the tents, re-kindle the fire, and commence culinary operations. By this, all are hungry enough, and they have the wherewithal to satisfy their appetites. There are skilful hunters among them, and the proceeds of a chase, that came off before starting out on their less innocent errand, are seen hanging from the trees, in the shape of bear's hams and haunches of venison. These taken down, are spitted, and soon frizzling in the fire's blaze; while the robbers gather around, knives in hand, each intending to carve for himself.

As they are about to commence their Homeric repast, Borlasse and the others ride up. Dismounting and striding in among the tents, the chief glances inquiringly around, his glance soon changing to disappointment. What he looks for is not there! "Quantrell and Bosley," he asks, "ain't they got here?"

"No, capting," answers one. "They hain't showed yet."

"And you've seen nothin' of them?"

"Nary thing."

His eyes light up with angry suspicion. Again doubts he the fidelity of Darke, or rather is he now certain that the lieutenant is a traitor.

Uttering a fearful oath, he steps inside his tent, taking Chisholm along with him.

"What can it mean, Luke?" he asks, pouring out a glass of brandy, and gulping it down.

"Hanged if I can tell, cap. It looks like you was right in supposin' they're gin us the slip. Still it's queery too, whar they could a goed, and wharf ore they should."

"There's nothing so strange about the wherefore; that's clear enough to me. I suspected Richard Darke, *alias* Phil Quantrell, would play me false some day, though I didn't expect it so soon. He don't want his beauty brought here, lest some of the boys might be takin' a fancy to her. That's one reason, but not all. There's another—to a man like him 'most as strong. He's rich, leastaways his dad is, an' he can get as much out o' the old 'un as he wants,—will have it all in time. He guesses I intended squeezin' him; an' thar he was about right, for I did. I'd lay odds that's the main thing has moved him to cut clear o' us."

"A darned mean trick if it is. You gied him protection when he was chased by the sheriffs, an' now—"

"Now, he won't need it; though he don't know that; can't, I think. If he but knew he ain't after all a murderer! See here, Luke; he may turn up yet. An' if so, for the life o' ye, ye mustn't tell him who it was we dibbled into the ground up thar. I took care not to let any of them hear his name. You're the only one as knows it."

"Ye can trust me, cap. The word Clancy won't pass through my teeth, till you gie me leave to speak it."

"Ha!" exclaims Borlasse, suddenly struck with an apprehension. "I never thought of the mulatto. He may have let it out?"

"He mayn't, however!"

"If not, he shan't now. I'll take care he don't have the chance."

"How are ye to help it? You don't intend killin' him?"

"Not yet; thar's a golden *egg* in that goose. His silence can be secured without resortin' to that. He must be kep' separate from the others."

"But some o' them 'll have to look after him, or he may cut away from us."

"Fernandez will do that. I can trust him with Clancy's name,—with anything. Slip out, Luke, and see if they've got it among them. If they have, it's all up, so far as that game goes. If not, I'll fix things safe, so that when we've spent Monsheer Dupré's silver, we may still draw cheques on the bank of San Antonio, signed Ephraim Darke."

Chisholm obeying, brings back a satisfactory report.

"The boys know nothin' o' Clancy's name, nor how we disposed o' him. In coorse, Watts, Stocker, an' Driscoll, haint sayed anything 'bout that. They've told the rest we let him go, not carin' to keep him; and that you only wanted the yellow fellow to wait on ye."

"Good! Go again, and fetch Fernandez here."

Chisholm once more turns out of the tent, soon after re-entering it, the half-blood behind him.

"Nandy," says Borlasse; calling the latter by a name mutually understood. "I want you to take charge of that mulatto, and keep him under your eye. You musn't let any of the boys come nigh enough to hold speech wi' him. You go, Luke, and give them orders they're not to." Chisholm retires.

"And, Nandy, if the nigger mentions any name—it may be that of his master—mind you it's not to be repeated to any one. You understand me?"

"I do, *capitan*."

"All serene. I know I can depend on ye. Now, to your duty."

Without another word, the taciturn mestizo glides out of the tent, leaving Borlasse alone. Speaking to himself, he says:—

"If Quantrell's turned traitor, thar's not a corner in Texas whar he'll be safe from my vengeance. I'll sarve the whelp as I've done 'tother,—a hound nobler than he. An' for sweet Jessie Armstrong, he'll have strong arms that can keep her out o' mine. By heavens! I'll hug her yet. If not, hell may take me!"

Thus blasphemously delivering himself, he clutches at the bottle of brandy, pours out a fresh glass, and drinking it at a gulp, sits down to reflect on the next step to be taken.

Chapter Seventy Five
A Transformation

Night has spread its sable pall over the desert plain, darker in the deep chasm through which runs Coyote Creek. There is light enough in the encampment of the prairie pirates; for the great fire kindled for cooking their dinners still burns, a constant supply of resinous pine-knots keeping up the blaze, which illuminates a large circle around. By its side nearly a score of men are seated in groups, some playing cards, others idly carousing. No one would suppose them the same seen there but a few hours before; since there is not the semblance of Indian among them. Instead, they are all white men, and wearing the garb of civilisation; though scarce two are costumed alike. There are coats of Kentucky jeans, of home-wove copperas stripe, of blanket-cloth in the three colours, red, blue, and green; there are blouses of brown linen, and buckskin dyed with dogwood ooze; there are Creole jackets of Attakapas "cottonade," and Mexican ones of cotton velveteen. Alike varied is the head, leg, and foot-wear. There are hats of every shape and pattern; pantaloons of many a cut and material, most of them tucked into boots with legs of different lengths, from ankle to mid-thigh. Only in the under garment is there anything like uniformity; nine out of ten wearing shirts of scarlet flannel—the fashion of the frontier.

A stranger entering the camp now, would suppose its occupants to be a party of hunters; one acquainted with the customs of South-Western Texas, might pronounce them *mustangers*—men who make their living by the taking and taming of wild horses. And if those around the fire were questioned about their calling, such would be the answer.—In their tents are all the paraphernalia used in this pursuit; lassoes for catching the horses; halters and hobbles for confining them; bits for breaking, and the like; while close by is a "corral" in which to keep the animals when caught.

All counterfeit! There is not a real mustanger among these men, nor one who is not a robber; scarce one who could lay his hand upon his heart, and say he has not, some time or other in his life, committed murder! For though changed in appearance, since last seen, they are the same who entered the camp laden with Luis Dupré's money—fresh from the massacre of his slaves. The transformation took place soon as they snatched a hasty meal. Then all hurried down to the creek, provided with pieces of soap; and plunging in, washed the paint from their hands, arms, and faces.

The Indian costume has not only been cast aside, but secreted, with all its equipments.

If the encampment were searched now, no stained feathers would be found; no beads or belts of wampum; no breech-clouts, bows, or quivers; no tomahawks or spears. All have been "cached" in a cave among the rocks; there to remain till needed for some future maraud, or massacre.

Around their camp-fire the freebooters are in full tide of enjoyment. The dollars have been divided, and each has his thousands. Those at the cards are not contented, but are craving more. They will be richer, or poorer. And soon; playing "poker" at fifty dollars an "ante."

Gamesters and lookers on alike smoke, drink, and make merry. They have no fear now, not the slightest apprehension. If pursued, the pursuers cannot find the way to Coyote creek. If they did, what would they see there? Certainly not the red-skinned savages, who plundered the San Saba mission, but a party of innocent horse hunters, all Texans. The only one resembling an Indian among them is the half-breed — Fernand. But he is also so metamorphosed, that his late master could not recognise him. The others have changed from red men to white; in reverse, he has become to all appearance a pure-blooded aboriginal.

Confident in their security, because ignorant of what has taken place under the live-oak, they little dream that one of their confederates is in a situation, where he will be forced to tell a tale sure to thwart their well-constructed scheme, casting it down as a house of cards. Equally are they unaware of the revelation which their own prisoner, the mulatto, could make. They suppose him and his master to be but two travellers encountered by accident, having no connection with the San Saba settlers. Borlasse is better informed about this, though not knowing all. He believes Clancy to have been *en route* for the new settlement, but without having reached it. He will never reach it now.

In hope of getting a clearer insight into many things still clouded, while his followers are engaged at their games, he seeks the tent to which Jupiter has been consigned, and where he is now under the surveillance of the half-blood, Fernand.

Ordering the mestizo to retire, he puts the prisoner through a course of cross-questioning.

The mulatto is a man of no ordinary intelligence. He had the misfortune to be born a slave, with the blood of a freeman in his veins; which, stirring him to discontent with his ignoble lot, at length forced him to become a fugitive. With a subtlety partly instinctive, but strengthened by many an act of injustice, he divines the object of the robber captain's visit.

Not much does the latter make of him, question as he may. Jupe knows nothing of any Phil Quantrell, or any Richard Darke. He is the slave of the young gentleman who has been separated from him. He makes no attempt to conceal his master's name, knowing that Borlasse is already acquainted with Clancy, and must have recognised him. They were on their way to join the colony of Colonel Armstrong, with a party from the States. They came up from the Colorado the night before, camping in the San Saba bottom, where he believes them to be still. Early in the morning, his master left the camp for a hunt, and the hound had tracked a bear up the gully. That was why they were on the upper plain; they were trying for the track of the bear, when taken.

The mulatto has no great liking for his master, from whom he has had many a severe flogging. In proof he tells the robber chief to turn up his shirt, and see how his back has been scored by the cowhide. Borlasse—does so; and sure enough there are the scars, somewhat similar to those he carries himself.

If not pity, the sight begets a sort of coarse sympathy, such as the convict feels for his fellow; an emotion due to the freemasonry of crime. Jupiter takes care to strengthen it, by harping on the cruelty of his master—more than hinting that he would like to leave him, if any other would but buy him. Indeed he'd be willing to run away, if he saw the chance.

"Don't trouble yerself 'bout that," says the bandit, 'as the interview comes near its end, "maybe, I'll buy ye myself. At all events, Mister Clancy ain't likely to flog you any more. How'd ye like *me* for yer master?"

"I'd be right glad, boss."

"Are ye up to takin' care of horses?"

"That's just what Masser Clancy kept me for."

"Well; he's gone on to the settlement without you. As he's left you behind that careless way, ye can stay with us, an' look after my horse. It's the same ye've been accustomed to. I swopped with your master 'fore we parted company."

Jupe is aware that Clancy's splendid steed is in the camp. Through a chink in the tent he saw the horse ridden in, Borlasse on his back; wondering why his master was not along, and what they had done with him. He has no faith in the tale told him, but a fear it is far otherwise. It will not do to show this, and concealing his anxiety, he rejoins:—

"All right, masser. I try do my best. Only hope you not a gwine where we come cross Masser Clancy. If he see me, he sure have me back, and then I'se get the cowhide right smart. He flog me dreadful."

"You're in no danger. I'll take care he never sets eye on you again.

"Here, Nandy!" he says to the mestizo, summoned back. "You can remove them ropes from your prisoner. Give him somethin' to eat and drink. Treat him as ye would one o' ourselves. He's to be that from this time forrard. Spread a buffler skin, an' get him a bit o' blanket for his bed. Same time, for safety's sake, keep an eye on him."

The caution is spoken *sotto voce*, so that the prisoner may not hear it. After which, Borlasse leaves the two together, congratulating himself on the good speculation he will make, not by keeping Jupe to groom his horse, but selling him as a slave to the first man met willing to purchase him.

In the fine able-bodied mulatto, he sees a thousand dollars cash—soon as he can come across a cotton-planter.

Chapter Seventy Six
Mestizo and mulatto

While their chief has been interrogating his prisoner, the robbers around the fire have gone on with their poker-playing, and whisky drinking.

Borlasse joining in the debauch, orders brandy to be brought out of his tent, and distributed freely around. He drinks deeply himself; in part to celebrate the occasion of such a grand stroke of business done, but as much to drown his disappointment at the captives not yet having come in.— The alcohol has its effect; and ere long rekindles a hope, which Chisholm strengthens, saying, all will yet be well, and the missing ones turn up, if not that night, on the morrow.

Somewhat relieved by this expectation, Borlasse enters into the spirit of the hour, and becomes jovial and boisterous as any of his subordinates. The cards are tossed aside, the play abandoned; instead, coarse stories are told, and songs sung, fit only for the ears of such a God-forsaken crew.

The saturnalia is brought to a close, when all become so intoxicated they can neither tell story nor sing song. Then some stagger to their tents, others dropping over where they sit, and falling fast asleep.

By midnight there is not a man of them awake, and the camp is silent, save here and there a drunken snore disturbing its stillness.

The great central fire, around which some remain lying astretch, burns on, but no longer blazes. There is no one to tend it with the pitchy pine-knots. Inside the tents also, the lights are extinguished—all except one. This, the rude skin sheiling which shelters the mestizo and mulatto. The two half-bloods, of different strain, are yet awake, and sitting up. They are also drinking, hobnobbing with one another.

Fernand has supplied the liquor freely and without stint. Pretending to fraternise with the new confederate, he has filled the latter's glass at least a half-score of times, doing the same with his own. Both have emptied them with like rapidity, and yet neither seems at all overcome. Each thinks the other the hardest case at a drinking bout he has ever come across; wondering he is not dead drunk, though knowing why he is himself sober. The Spanish moss plucked from the adjacent trees, and littering the tent floor, could tell—if it had the power of speech.

Jupiter has had many a whiskey spree in the woods of Mississippi, but never has he encountered a *convive* who could stand so much of it, and still keep his tongue and seat. What can it mean? Is the mestizo's stomach made of steel?

While perplexed, and despairing of being able to get Fernand intoxicated, an explanation suggests itself. His fellow tippler may be shamming, as himself?

Pretending to look out of the tent, he twists his eyes away so far, that, from the front, little else than their whites can be seen. But enough of the retina is uncovered to receive an impression from behind; this showing the mestizo tilting his cup, and spilling its contents among the moss!

He now knows he is being watched, as well as guarded. And of his vigilant sentinel there seems but one way to disembarrass himself.

As the thought of it flits across his brain, his eyes flash with a feverish light, such as when one intends attacking by stealth, and with the determination to kill. For he must either kill the man by his side, or give up what is to himself worth more than such a life—his own liberty.

It may be his beloved master yet lives, and there is a chance to succour him. If dead, he will find his body, and give it burial. He remembers the promise that morning mutually declared between them—to stand and fall together—he will keep his part of it. If Clancy has fallen, others will go down too; in the end, if need be, himself. But not till he has taken, or tried to take, a terrible and bloody vengeance. To this he has bound himself, by an oath sworn in the secret recesses of his heart.

Its prelude is nigh, and the death of the Indian half-breed is to initiate it. For the fugitive slave knows the part this vile caitiff has played, and will not scruple to kill him; the less that it is now an inexorable necessity. He but waits for the opportunity—has been seeking it for some time.

It offers at length. Turning suddenly, and detecting the mestizo in his act of deception, he asks laughingly why he should practice such a trick. Then stooping forward, as if to verify it, his right arm is seen to lunge out with something that glitters in his hand. It is the blade of a bowie-knife.

In an instant the arm is drawn back, the glittering gone off the blade, obliterated by blood! For it has been between the ribs, and through the heart of the mestizo; who, slipping from his seat, falls to the floor, without even a groan!

Grasping Clancy's gun, which chances to be in the tent, and then blowing out the light, the mulatto moves off, leaving but a dead body behind him.

Once outside, he looks cautiously around the encampment, scanning the tents and the ground adjacent to them. He sees the big fire still red, but not flaming. He can make out the forms of men lying around it—all of them, for him fortunately, asleep.

Stepping, as if on eggs, and keeping as much as possible in shadow, he threads his way through the tents until he is quite clear of the encampment. But he does not go directly off. Instead, he makes a circuit to the other side, where Brasfort is tied to a tree. A cut of his red blade releases the hound, that follows him in silence, as if knowing it necessary.

Then on to the corral where the horses are penned up.

Arriving at the fence he finds the bars, and there stopping, speaks some words in undertone, but loud enough to be heard by the animals inside. As if it were a cabalistic speech, one separates from the rest, and comes towards him. It is the steed of Clancy. Protruding its soft muzzle over the rail, it is stroked by the mulatto's hand, which soon after has hold of the forelock. Fortunately the saddles are close by, astride the fence, with the bridles hanging to the branches of a tree. Jupiter easily recognises those he is in search of, and soon has the horse caparisoned.

At length he leads the animal not mounting till he is well away from the camp. Then, climbing cautiously into the saddle, he continues on, Brasfort after; man, horse, and hound, making no more noise, than if all three were but shadows.

Chapter Seventy Seven
A strayed traveller

Pale, trembling, with teeth chattering, Richard Darke awakes from his drunken slumber.

He sees his horse tied to the tree, as he left him, but making violent efforts to get loose. For coyotes have come skulking around the copse, and their cry agitates the animal. It is this that has awakened the sleeper.

He starts to his feet in fear, though not of the wolves. Their proximity has nought to do with the shudder which passes through his frame. It comes from an apprehension he has overslept himself, and that, meanwhile, his confederates have passed the place.

It is broad daylight, with a bright sun in the sky; though this he cannot see through the thick foliage intervening. But his watch will tell him the time. He takes it out and glances at the dial. The hands appear not to move!

He holds it to his ear, but hears no ticking. Now, he remembers having neglected to wind it up the night before. It has run down!

Hastily returning it to his pocket, he makes for open ground, where he may get a view of the sun. By its height above the horizon, as far as he can judge it should be about nine of the morning. This point, as he supposes, settled, does not remove his apprehension, on the contrary but increases it. The returning marauders would not likely be delayed so late? In all probability they have passed.

How is he to be assured? A thought strikes him: he will step out upon the plain, and see if he can discern their tracks. He does so, keeping on to the summit of the pass. There he finds evidence to confirm his fears. The loose turf around the head of the gorge is torn and trampled by the hoofs of many horses, all going off over the plain. The robbers have returned to their rendezvous!

Hastening back to his horse, he prepares to start after.

Leading the animal to the edge of the copse, he is confronted by what sends a fresh thrill of fear through his heart. The sun is before his face, but not as when he last looked at it. Instead of having risen higher, it is now nearer the horizon!

"Great God!" he exclaims, as the truth breaks upon him. "It's setting, not rising; evening 'stead of morning!"

Shading his eye with spread palm, he gazes at the golden orb, in look bewildered. Not long, till assured, the sun is sinking, and night nigh.

The deduction drawn is full of sinister sequence. More than one starts up in his mind to dismay him. He is little acquainted with the trail to Coyote Creek, and may be unable to find it. Moreover, the robbers are certain of being pursued, and Sime Woodley will be one of the pursuers; Bosley forced to conduct them, far as he can. The outraged settlers may at any moment appear coming up the pass!

He glances apprehensively towards it, then across the plain.

His face is now towards the sun, whose lower limb just touches the horizon, the red round orb appearing across the smooth surface, as over that of a tranquil sea.

He regards it, to direct his course. He knows that the camping place on Coyote Creek is due west from where he is.

And at length, having resolved, he sets his foot in the stirrup, vaults into the saddle, and spurs off, leaving the black-jack grove behind him.

He does not proceed far, before becoming uncertain as to his course. The sun goes down, leaving heaven's firmament in darkness, with only some last lingering rays along its western edge. These grow fainter and fainter, till scarce any difference can be noted around the horizon's ring.

He now rides in doubt, guessing the direction. Scanning the stars he searches for the Polar constellation. But a mist has meanwhile sprung up over the plain, and, creeping across the northern sky, concealed it.

In the midst of his perplexity, the moon appears; and taking bearings by this, he once more makes westward.

But there are cumulus clouds in the sky; and these, ever and anon drifting over the moon's disc, compel him to pull up till they pass.

At length he is favoured with a prolonged interval of light, during which he puts his animal to its best speed, and advances many miles in what he supposes to be the right direction. As yet he has encountered no living creature, nor object of any kind. He is in hopes to get sight of the solitary tree; for beyond it the trail to Coyote Creek is easily taken.

While scanning the moonlit expanse he descries a group of figures; apparently quadrupeds, though of what species he cannot tell. They appear too large for wolves, and yet are not like wild horses, deer, or buffaloes.

On drawing nearer, he discovers them to be but coyotes; the film, refracting the moon's light, having deceived him as to their size.

What can they be doing out there? Perhaps collected around some animal they have hunted down, and killed—possibly a prong-horn antelope? It is not with any purpose he approaches them. He only does so because they are in the line of his route. But before reaching the spot where they are assembled, he sees something to excite his curiosity, at the same time, baffling all conjecture what it can be. On his coming closer, the jackals scatter apart, exposing it to view; then, loping off, leave it behind them. Whatever it be, it is evidently the lure that has brought the predatory beasts together. It is not the dead body of deer, antelope, or animal of any kind; but a thing of rounded shape, set upon a short shank, or stem.

"What the devil is it?" he asks himself, first pausing, and then spurring on towards it. "Looks lor all the world like a man's head!"

At that moment, the moon emitting one of her brightest beams, shows the object still clearer, causing him to add in exclamation, "By heavens, it is a head!"

Another instant and he sees a face, which sends the blood back to his heart, almost freezing it in his veins.

Horror stricken he reins up, dragging his horse upon the haunches; and in this attitude remains, his eyes rolling as though they would start from their sockets. Then, shouting the words, "Great God, Clancy!" followed by a wild shriek, he wrenches the horse around, and mechanically spurs into desperate speed.

In his headlong flight he hears a cry, which comes as from out the earth—his own name pronounced, and after it, the word "murderer!"

Chapter Seventy Eight
Hours of agony

Out of the earth literally arose that cry, so affrighting Richard Darke; since it came from Charles Clancy. Throughout the live-long day, on to the mid hours of night, has he been enduring agony unspeakable.

Alone with but the companionship of hostile creatures—wolves that threaten to gnaw the skin from his skull, and vultures ready to tear his eyes out of their sockets.

Why has he not gone mad?

There are moments when it comes too near this, when his reason is well-nigh unseated. But manfully he struggles against it; thoughtfully, with reliance on Him, whose name he has repeated and prayerfully invoked. And God, in His mercy, sends something to sustain him—a remembrance. In his most despairing hour he recalls one circumstance seeming favourable, and which in the confusion of thought, consequent on such a succession of scenes, had escaped him. He now remembers the other man found along with Darke under the live-oak. Bosley will be able to guide a pursuing party, and with Woodley controlling, will be forced to do it. He can lead them direct to the rendezvous of the robbers; where Clancy can have no fear but that they will settle things satisfactorily. There learning what has been done to himself, they would lose no time in coming after him.

This train of conjecture, rational enough, restores his hopes, and again he believes there is a chance of his receiving succour. About time is he chiefly apprehensive. They may come too late?

He will do all he can to keep up; hold out as long as life itself may last.

So resolved, he makes renewed efforts to fight off the wolves, and frighten the vultures.

Fortunately for him the former are but coyotes, the latter turkey buzzards both cowardly creatures, timid as hares, except when the quarry is helpless. They must not know he is this; and to deceive them he shakes his head, rolls his eyes, and shouts at the highest pitch of his voice. But only at intervals, when they appear too threateningly near. He knows the necessity of economising his cries and gestures. By too frequent repetition they might cease to avail him.

Throughout the day he has the double enemy to deal with. But night disembarrasses him of the birds, leaving only the beasts.

He derives little benefit from the change; for the coyotes, but jackals in daylight, at night become wolves, emboldened by the darkness. Besides, they have been too long gazing at the strange thing, and listening to the shouts which have proceeded from it, without receiving hurt or harm, to fear it as before. The time has come for attack.

Blending their unearthly notes into one grand chorus they close around, finally resolved to assault it.

And, again, Clancy calls upon God—upon Heaven, to help him.

His prayer is heard; for what he sees seems an answer to it. The moon is low down, her disc directly before his face, and upon the plain between a shadow is projected, reaching to his chin. At the same time, he sees what is making it—a man upon horseback! Simultaneously, he hears a sound—the trampling of hoofs upon the hard turf.

The coyotes catching it, too, are scared, changing from their attitude of attack, and dropping tails to the ground. As the shadow darkening over them tells that the horseman is drawing nigh, they scatter off in retreat.

Clancy utters an ejaculation of joy. He is about to hail the approaching Norseman, when a doubt restrains him.

"Who can it be?" he asks himself with mingled hope and apprehension. "Woodley would not be coming in that way, alone? If not some of the settlers, at least Heywood would be along with him? Besides, there is scarce time for them to have reached the Mission and returned. It cannot be either. Jupiter? Has he escaped from the custody of the outlawed crew?"

Clancy is accustomed to seeing the mulatto upon a mule. This man rides a horse, and otherwise looks not like Jupiter. It is not he. Who, then?

During all this time the horseman is drawing nearer, though slowly. When first heard, the tramp told him to be going at a gallop; but he has slackened speed, and now makes approach, apparently with caution, as if reconnoitring. He has descried the jackals, and comes to see what they are gathered about. These having retreated, Clancy can perceive that the eyes of the stranger are fixed upon his own head, and that he is evidently puzzled to make out what it is.

For a moment the man makes stop, then moves on, coming closer and closer. With the moon behind his back, his face is in shadow, and cannot be seen by Clancy. But it is not needed for his identification. The dress and figure are sufficient. Cut sharply against the sky is the figure of a plumed savage; a sham one Clancy knows, with a thrill of fresh despair, recognising Richard Darke.

It will soon be all over with him now; in another instant his hopes, doubts, fears, will be alike ended, with his life. He has no thought but that Darke, since last seen, has been in communication with Borlasse; and from him learning all, has, returned for the life he failed to take before.

Meanwhile the plumed horseman continues to approach, till within less than a length of his horse. Then drawing bridle with a jerk, suddenly comes to a stop. Clancy can see, that he is struck with astonishment—his features, now near enough to be distinguished, wearing a bewildered look. Then hears his own name called out, a shriek succeeding; the horse wheeled round, and away, as if Satan had hold of his tail!

For a long time is heard the tramp of the retreating horse going in full fast gallop—gradually less distinct—at length dying away in the distance.

Chapter Seventy Nine
An unexpected visitor

To Clancy there is nothing strange in Darke's sudden and terrified departure. With the quickness of thought itself, he comprehends its cause. In their encounter under the live-oak, in shadow and silence, his old rival has not recognised him. Nor can he since have seen Borlasse, or any of the band. Why he is behind them, Clancy cannot surmise; though he has a suspicion of the truth. Certainly Darke came not there by any design, but only chance-conducted. Had it been otherwise, he would not have gone off in such wild affright.

All this Clancy intuitively perceives, on the instant of his turning to retreat. And partly to make this more sure, though also stirred by indignation he cannot restrain, he eends forth that shout, causing the scared wretch to flee faster and farther.

Now that he is gone, Clancy is again left to his reflections, but little less gloomy than before. From only one does he derive satisfaction. The robber chief must have lied. Helen Armstrong has not been in the arms of Richard Darke.—He may hope she has reached her home in safety.

All else is as ever, and soon likely to be worse. For he feels as one who has only had a respite, believing it will be but short. Darke will soon recover from his scare. For he will now go to the rendezvous, and there, getting an explanation of what has caused it, come back to glut his delayed vengeance, more terrible from long accumulation.

Will the wolves wait for him?

"Ha! there they are again!"

So exclaims the wretched man, as he sees them once more making approach.

And now they draw nigh with increased audacity, their ravenous instincts but strengthened by the check. The enemy late dreaded has not molested them, but gone off, leaving their prey unprotected. They are again free to assail, and this time will surely devour it.

Once more their melancholy whine breaks the stillness of the night, as they come loping up one after another. Soon all are re-assembled round the strange thing, which through their fears has long defied them. More familiar, they fear it less now.

Renewing their hostile demonstration, they circle about it, gliding from side to side in *chassez-croissez*, as through the mazes of a cotillon. With forms magnified under the moonlight, they look like werewolves dancing around a "Death's Head,"—their long-drawn lugubrious wails making appropriate music to the measure!

Horror for him who hears, hearing it without hope. Of this not a ray left now, its last lingering spark extinguished, and before him but the darkness of death in all its dread certainty—a death horrible, appalling!

Putting forth all his moral strength, exerting it to the utmost, he tries to resign himself to the inevitable.

In vain. Life is too sweet to be so surrendered. He cannot calmly resign it, and again instinctively makes an effort to fright off his hideous assailants. His eyes rolling, scintillating in their sockets—his lips moving—his cries sent from between them—are all to no purpose now. The coyotes come nearer and nearer. They are within three feet of his face. He can see their wolfish eyes, the white serrature of their teeth, the red panting tongues; can feel their fetid breath blown against his brow. Their jaws are agape. Each instant he expects them to close around his skull!

Why did he shout, sending Darke away? He regrets having done it. Better his head to have been crushed or cleft by a tomahawk, killing him at once, than torn while still alive, gnawed, mumbled over, by those frightful fangs threatening so near! The thought stifles reflection. It is of itself excruciating torture. He cannot bear it much longer. No man could, however strong, however firm his faith in the Almighty. Even yet he has not lost this. The teachings of early life, the precepts inculcated by a pious mother, stand him in stead now. And though sure he must die, and wants death to come quickly, he nevertheless tries to meet it resignedly, mentally exclaiming:—

"Mother! Father! I come. Soon shall I join you. Helen, my love! Oh, how I have wronged you in thus throwing my life away! God forgive—"

His regrets are interrupted, as if by God Himself. He has been heard by the All-Merciful, the Omnipotent; for seemingly no other hand could now succour him. While the prayerful thoughts are still passing through his mind, the wolves suddenly cease their attack, and he sees them retiring with closed jaws and fallen tails! Not hastily, but slow and skulkingly; ceding the ground inch by inch, as though reluctant to leave it.

What can it mean?

Casting his eyes outward, he sees nothing to explain the behaviour of the brutes, nor account for their changed demeanour.

He listens, all ears, expecting to hear the hoof-stroke of a horse—the same he late saw reined up in front of him, with Richard Darke upon his back. The ruffian is returning sooner than anticipated.

There is no such sound. Instead, one softer, which, but for the hollow cretaceous rock underlying the plain and acting as a conductor, would not be conveyed to his ears. It is a pattering as of some animal's paws, going in rapid gait. He cannot imagine what sort of creature it may be; in truth he has no time to think, before hearing the sound close behind his head, the animal approaching from that direction. Soon after he feels a hot breath strike against his brow, with something still warmer touching his cheek. It is the tongue of a dog!

"Brasfort!"

Brasfort it is, cowering before his face, filling his ears with a soft whimpering, sweet as any speech ever heard. For he has seen the jackals retreat, and knows they will not return. His strong stag-hound is more than a match for the whole pack of cowardly creatures. As easily as it has scattered, can it destroy them.

Clancy's first feeling is one of mingled pleasure and surprise. For he fancies himself succoured, released from his earth-bound prison, so near to have been his grave.

The glad emotion is alas! short-lived; departing as he perceives it to be only a fancy, and his perilous situation, but little changed or improved. For what can the dog do for him? True he may keep off the coyotes, but that will not save his life. Death must come all the same. A little later, and in less horrid shape, but it must come. Hunger, thirst, one or both will bring it, surely if slowly.

"My brave Brasfort! faithful fellow!" he says apostrophising the hound; "You cannot protect me from them. But how have you got here?"

The question is succeeded by a train of conjecture, as follows:—

"They took the dog with them. I saw one lead him away. They've let him loose, and he has scented back on the trail? That's it. Oh! if Jupiter were but with him! No fear of their letting him off—no."

During all this time Brasfort has continued his caresses, fondling his master's head, affectionately as a mother her child.

Again Clancy speaks, apostrophising the animal.

"Dear old dog! you're but come to see me die. Well; it's something to have you here—like a friend beside the death-bed. And you'll stay with me long as life holds out, and protect me from those skulking creatures? I know you will. Ah! You won't need to stand sentry long. I feel growing fainter. When all's over you can go. I shall never see her more; but some one may find, and take you there. She'll care for, and reward you for this fidelity."

The soliloquy is brought to a close, by the hound suddenly changing attitude. All at once it has ceased its fond demonstrations, and stands as if about to make an attack upon its master's head! Very different the intent. Yielding to a simple canine instinct, from the strain of terrier in its blood, it commences scratching up the earth around his neck!

For Clancy a fresh surprise, as before mingled with pleasure. For the hound's instinctive action shows him a chance of getting relieved, by means he had never himself thought of.

He continues talking to the animal, encouraging it by speeches it can comprehend. On it scrapes, tearing up the clods, and casting them in showers behind.

Despite the firmness with which the earth is packed, the hound soon makes a hollow around its master's neck, exposing his shoulder—the right one—above the surface. A little more mould removed, and his arm will be free. With that his whole body can be extricated by himself.

Stirred by the pleasant anticipation, he continues speaking encouragement to the dog. But Brasfort needs it not, working away in silence and with determined earnestness, as if knowing that time was an element of success.

Clancy begins to congratulate himself on escape, is almost sure of it, when a sound breaks upon his ear, bringing back all his apprehensions. Again the hoof-stroke of a horse!

Richard Darke is returning!

"Too late, Brasfort!" says his master, apostrophising him in speech almost mechanical, "Too late your help. Soon you'll see me die."

Chapter Eighty
A Resurrectionist

"Surely the end has come!"

So reflects Clancy, as with keen apprehension he listens to the tread of the approaching horseman. For to a certainty he approaches, the dull distant thud of hooves gradually growing more distinct. Nor has he any doubt of its being the same steed late reined up in front of him, the fresh score of whose calkers are there within a few feet of his face.

The direction whence comes the sound, is of itself significant; that in which Darke went off. It is he returning—can be no other.

Yes; surely his end has come—the last hour of his life. And so near being saved! Ten minutes more, and Brasfort would have disinterred him.

Turning his eyes downward, he can see the cavity enlarged, and getting larger. For the dog continues to drag out the earth, as if not hearing, or disregarding the hoof-stroke. Already its paws are within a few inches of his elbow.

Is it possible for him to wrench out his arm! With it free he might do something to defend himself. And the great stag-hound will help him.

With hope half resuscitated, he makes an effort to extricate the arm, heaving his shoulder upward. In vain.—It is held as in a vice, or the clasp of a giant. There is *no* alternative—he must submit to his fate. And such a fate! Once more he will see the sole enemy of his life, his mother's murderer, standing triumphant over him; will hear his taunting speeches—almost a repetition of the scene under the cypress! And to think that in all his encounters with this man, he has been unsuccessful; too late—ever too late! The thought is of itself a torture.

Strange the slowness with which Darke draws nigh! Can he still be in dread of the unearthly? No, or he would not be there. It may be that sure of his victim, he but delays the last blow, scheming some new horror before he strike it?

The tramp of the horse tells him to be going at a walk; unsteady too, as if his rider were not certain about the way, but seeking it. Can this be so? Has he not yet seen the head and hound? The moon must be on his back, since it is behind Clancy's own. It may be that Brasfort—a new figure in the oft changing tableau—stays his advance. Possibly the unexplained presence of the animal has given him a surprise, and hence he approaches with caution?

All at once, the hoof-stroke ceases to be heard, and stillness reigns around. *No* sound save that made by the claws of the dog, that continues its task with unabated assiduity—not yet having taken any notice of the footsteps it can scarce fail to hear.

Its master cannot help thinking this strange. Brasfort is not wont to be thus unwatchful. And of all men Richard Darke should be the last to approach him unawares. What may it mean?

While thus interrogating himself, Clancy again hears the "tramp-tramp," the horse no longer in a walk, but with pace quickened to a trot. And still Brasfort keeps on scraping! Only when a shadow darkens over, does he desist; the horseman being now close behind Clancy's head, with his image reflected in front. But instead of rushing at him with savage growl, as he certainly would were it Richard Darke Brasfort but raises his snout, and wags his tail, giving utterance to a note of friendly salutation!

Clancy's astonishment is extreme, changing to joy, when the horseman after making the circuit of his head, comes to a halt before his face. In the broad bright moonlight he beholds, not his direst foe, but his faithful servitor. There upon his own horse, with his own gun in hand, sits one who causes him mechanically to exclaim—

"Jupiter!" adding, "Heaven has heard my prayer!"

"An' myen," says Jupiter, soon as somewhat recovered from his astonishment at what he sees; "Yes, Masser Charle; I'se been prayin' for you ever since they part us, though never 'spected see you 'live 'gain. But Lor' o' mercy, masser! what dis mean? I'se see nothin' but you head! Wherever is you body? What have dem rascally ruffins been an' done to ye?"

"As you see—buried me alive."

"Better that than bury you dead. You sure, masser," he asks, slipping down from the saddle, and placing himself *vis-à-vis* with the face so strangely situated. "You sure you ain't wounded, nor otherways hurt?"

"Not that I know of. I only feel a little bruised and faint-like; but I think I've received no serious injury. I'm now suffering from thirst, more than aught else."

"That won't be for long. Lucky I'se foun' you ole canteen on the saddle, an' filled it 'fore I left the creek. I'se got somethin' besides 'll take the faintness 'way from you; a drop o' corn-juice, I had from that Spanish Indyin they call the half-blood. Not much blood in him now. Here 'tis, Masser Charle."

While speaking, he has produced a gourd, in which something gurgles. Its smell, when the stopper is taken out, tells it to be whiskey.

Inserting the neck between his master's lips, he pours some of the spirit down his throat; and then, turning to the horse near by, he lifts from off the saddle-horn a larger gourd—the canteen, containing water.

In a few seconds, not only is Clancy's thirst satisfied, but he feels his strength restored, and all faintness passed away.

"Up to de chin I declar'!" says Jupiter, now more particularly taking note of his situation, "Sure enough, all but buried 'live. An' Brasfort been a tryin' to dig ye out! Geehorum! Aint that cunnin' o' the ole dog? He have prove himself a faithful critter."

"Like yourself, Jupe. But say! How have you escaped from the robbers? Brought my horse and gun too! Tell me all!"

"Not so fass, Masser Charle. It's something o' a longish story, an' a bit strangeish too. You'll be better out o' that fix afore hearin' it. Though your ears aint stopped, yez not in a position to lissen patient or comfortable. First let me finish what Brasfort's begun, and get out the balance o' your body."

Saying this, the mulatto sets himself to the task proposed.

Upon his knees with knife in hand, he loosens the earth around Clancy's breast and shoulders, cutting it carefully, then clawing it out.

The hound helps him, dashing in whenever it sees a chance, with its paws scattering the clods to rear. The animal seems jealous of Jupiter's interference, half angry at not having all the credit to itself.

Between them the work progresses, and the body of their common master will soon be disinterred. All the while, Clancy and the mulatto continue to talk, mutually communicating their experiences since parting. Those of the former, though fearful, are neither many nor varied, and require but few words. What Jupiter now sees gives him a clue to nearly all.

His own narrative covers a greater variety of events, and needs more time for telling than can now be conveniently spared. Instead of details, therefore, he but recounts the leading incidents in brief epitome—to be more particularly dwelt upon afterwards, as opportunity will allow. He relates, how, after leaving the lone cottonwood, he was taken on across the plain to a creek called Coyote, where the robbers have a camping place. This slightly touched upon, he tells of his own treatment; of his being carried into a tent at first, but little looked after, because thought secure, from their having him tightly tied. Through a slit in the skin cover he saw them kindle a fire and commence cooking. Soon after came the chief, riding Clancy's horse, with

Chisholm and the other three. Seeing the horse, he supposed it all over with his master.

Then the feast, *al fresco*, succeeded by the transformation scene—the red robbers becoming white ones—to all of which he was witness. After that the card-playing by the camp fire, during which the chief came to his tent, and did what he could to draw him. In this part of his narration, the mulatto with modest naïveté, hints of his own adroitness; how he threw his inquisitor off the scent, and became at length disembarrassed of him. He is even more reticent about an incident, soon after succeeding, but referred to it at an early part of his explanation.

On the blade of his knife, before beginning to dig, Clancy observing some blotches of crimson, asks what it is.

"Only a little blood, Masser Charle," is the answer.

"Whose?"

"You'll hear afore I get to the end. Nuf now to say it's the blood of a bad man."

Clancy does not press him further, knowing he will be told all in due time. Still, is he impatient, wondering whether it be the blood of Jim Borlasse, or Richard Darke; for he supposes it either one or the other. He hopes it may be the former, and fears its being the latter. Even yet, in his hour of uncertainty, late helpless, and still with only a half hope of being able to keep his oath, he would not for all the world Dick Darke's blood should be shed by other hand than his own!

He is mentally relieved, long before Jupiter reaches the end of his narration. The blood upon the blade, now clean scoured off, was not that of Richard Darke.

For the mulatto tells him of that tragical scene within the tent, speaking of it without the slightest remorse. The incidents succeeding he leaves for a future occasion; how he stole out the horse, and with Brasfort's help, was enabled to return upon the trail as far as the cottonwood; thence on, the hound hurriedly leading, at length leaving him behind.

But before coming to this, he has completed his task, and laying hold of his master's shoulders, he draws him out of the ground, as a gardener would a gigantic carrot.

Once more on the earth's surface stands Clancy, free of body, unfettered in limb, strong in his sworn resolve, determined as ever to keep it.

Chapter Eighty One
The voice of vengeance

Never did man believe himself nigher death, or experience greater satisfaction at being saved from it, than Charles Clancy. For upon his life so near lost, and as if miraculously preserved, depend issues dear to him as that life itself.

And these, too, may reach a successful termination; some thing whispers him they will.

But though grateful to God for the timely succour just received, and on Him still reliant, he does not ask God for guidance in what he intends now. Rather, shuns he the thought, as though fearing the All-Merciful might not be with him. For he is still determined on vengeance, which alone belongs to the Lord.

Of himself, he is strong enough to take it; and feels so, after being refreshed by another drink of the whiskey. The spirit of the alcohol, acting on his own, reinvigorates, and makes him ready for immediate action. He but stays to think what may be his safest course, as the surest and swiftest. His repeated repulses, while making more cautious, have done nought to daunt, or drive him from his original purpose. Recalling his latest interview with Helen Armstrong, and what he then said, he dares not swerve from it. To go back leaving it undone, were a humiliation no lover would like to confess to his sweetheart.

But he has no thought of going back, and only hesitates, reflecting on the steps necessary to ensure success.

He now knows why Darke retreated in such wild affright. Some speeches passing between the robbers, overheard by Jupiter, and by him reported, enable Clancy to grasp the situation. As he had conjectured, Darke was straying, and by chance came that way. No wonder at the way he went.

It is not an hour since he fled from the spot, and in all likelihood he is still straying. If so, he cannot be a great way off; but, far or near, Brasfort can find him.

It is but a question of whether he can be overtaken before reaching the rendezvous. For the only danger of which Clancy has dread, or allows himself to dwell upon, is from the other robbers. Even of these he feels not much fear. But for the mulatto and his mule, he would never have allowed them to lay hand on him. And now with his splendid horse once more by his side, the saddle awaiting him, he knows he will be safe from any pursuit by mounted men, as a bird upon the wing.

For the safety of his faithful follower he has already conceived measures. Jupiter is to make his way back to the San Saba, and wait for him at their old camp, near the crossing. Failing to come, he is to proceed on to the settlement, and there take his chances of a reception. Though the fugitive slave may be recognised, under Sime Woodley's protection he will be safe, and with Helen Armstrong's patronage, sure of hospitable entertainment.

With all this mentally arranged, though not yet communicated to Jupe, Clancy gives a look to his gun to assure himself it is in good order; another to the caparison of his horse; and, satisfied with both, he at length leaps into the saddle.

The mulatto has been regarding his movements with uneasiness. There is that in them which forewarns him of still another separation.

He is soon made aware of it, by the instructions given him, in accordance with the plan sketched cat. On Clancy telling him, he is to return to the San Saba alone, with the reasons why he should do so, he listens in pained surprise.

"Sure you don't intend leavin' me, Masser Charle?"

"I do—I must."

"But whar you goin' youself?"

"Where God guides—it may be His avenging angel. Yes, Jupe; I'm off again, on that scoundrel's track. This shall be my last trial. If it turn out as hitherto, you may never see me more—you, nor any one else. Failing, I shan't care to face human kind, much less her I love. Ah! I'll more dread meeting my mother—her death unavenged. Bah! There's no fear, one way or the other. So don't you have any uneasiness about the result; but do as I've directed. Make back to the river, and wait there at the crossing. Brasfort goes with me; and when you see us again, I'll have a spare horse to carry you on to our journey's end; that whose shoes made those scratches—just now, I take it, between the legs of Dick Darke."

"Dear masser," rejoins Jupiter, in earnest protest. "Why need ye go worryin' after that man now? You'll have plenty opportunities any day. He aint likely to leave Texas, long's that young lady stays in it. Besides, them cut-throats at the creek, sure come after me. They'll be this way soon's they find me gone, an' set their eyes on that streak o' red colour I left ahind me in the tent. Take my advice, Masser Charle, an' let's both slip out o' thar way, by pushin' straight for the settlement."

"No settlement, till I've settled with him! He can't have got far away yet. Good, Brasfort! you'll do your best to help me find him?"

The hound gives a low growl, and rollicks around the legs of the horse, seeming to say:—

"Set me on the scent; I'll show you."

Something more than instinct appears to inspire the Molossian. Though weeks have elapsed since in the cypress swamp it made savage demonstrations against Darke, when taking up his trail through the San Saba bottom it behaved as if actuated by the old malice, remembering the smell of the man! And now conducted beyond the place trodden by Borlasse and the others, soon as outside the confusion of scents, and catching his fresher one, it sends forth a cry strangely intoned, altogether unlike its ordinary bay while trailing a stag. It is the deep sonorous note of the sleuth-hound on slot of human game; such as oft, in the times of Spanish American colonisation, struck terror to the heart of the hunted aboriginal.

As already said, Brasfort has a strain of the bloodhound in him; enough to make danger for Richard Darke. Under the live-oak the hound would have pulled him from his saddle, torn him to pieces on the spot, but for Jupiter, to whom it was consigned, holding it hard back.

Clancy neither intends, nor desires, it to do so now. All he wants with it, is to bring him face to face with his hated foeman. That done, the rest he will do himself.

Everything decided and settled, he hastily takes leave of Jupiter, and starts off along the trail, Brasfort leading.

Both are soon far away.

On the wide waste the mulatto stands alone, looking after—half reproachfully for being left behind—regretting his master's rashness—painfully apprehensive he may never see him more.

Chapter Eighty Two
A man nearly mad

"Am I still drunk? Am I dreaming?"

So Richard Darke interrogates himself, retreating from the strangest apparition human eyes ever saw. A head without any body, not lying as after careless decapitation, but as though still upon shoulders, the eyes glancing and rolling, the lips moving, speaking—the whole thing alive! The head, too, of one he supposes himself to have assassinated, and for which he is a felon and fugitive. No wonder he doubts the evidence of his senses, and at first deems it fancy—an illusion from dream or drink. But a suspicion also sweeps through his soul, which, more painfully impressing, causes him to add still another interrogatory:

"Am I mad?"

He shakes his head and rubs his eyes, to assure himself he is awake, sober, and sane. He is all three; though he might well wish himself drunk or dreaming—for, so scared is he, there is in reality a danger of his senses forsaking him. He tries to account for the queer thing, but cannot. Who could, circumstanced as he? From that day when he stooped over Clancy, holding Helen Armstrong's photograph before his face, and saw his eyes film over in sightless gaze, the sure forerunner of death, he has ever believed him dead. No rumour has reached him to the contrary—no newspaper paragraph, from which he might draw his deductions, as Borlasse has done. True, he observed some resemblance to Clancy in the man who surprised him under the live-oak; but, recalling that scene under the cypress, how could he have a thought of its being he? He could not, cannot, does not yet.

But what about the head? How is he to account for that? And the cries sent after him—still ringing in his ears—his own name, with the added accusation he himself believes true, the brand, "murderer!"

"Am I indeed mad?" he again asks himself, riding on recklessly, without giving guidance to his horse. His trembling hand can scarce retain hold of the rein; and the animal, uncontrolled, is left to take its course—only, it must not stop or stay. Every time it shows sign of lagging, he kicks mechanically against its ribs, urging it on, on, anywhere away from that dread damnable apparition.

It is some time before he recovers sufficient coolness to reflect—then only with vague comprehensiveness; nothing clear save the fact that he has completely lost himself, and his way. To go on were mere guesswork. True, the moon tells him the west, the direction of Coyote creek. But westward he will not go, dreading to again encounter that ghostly thing; for he thinks it was there he saw it.

Better pull up, and await the surer guidance of the sun, with its light, less mystical.

So deciding, he slips out of the saddle; and letting his horse out on the trail-rope, lays himself down. Regardless of the animal's needs, he leaves all its caparison on, even to the bitt between its teeth. What cares he for its comforts, or for aught else, thinking of that horrible head?

He makes no endeavour to snatch a wink of sleep, of which he has had enough; but lies cogitating on the series of strange incidents and sights which have late occurred to him, but chiefly the last, so painfully perplexing. He can think of nothing to account for a phenomenon so abnormal, so outside all laws of nature.

While vainly endeavouring to solve the dread enigma, a sound strikes upon his ear, abruptly bringing his conjectures to a close. It is a dull thumping, still faint and far off; but distinguishable as the tramp of a horse.

Starting to his feet, he looks in the direction whence it proceeds. As expected, he sees a horse; and something more, a man upon its back, both coming towards him.

Could it, perchance, be Bosley? Impossible! He was their prisoner under the live-oak. They would never let him go. Far more like it is Woodley—the terrible backwoodsman, as ever after him? Whoever it be, his guilty soul tells him the person approaching can be no friend of his, but an enemy, a pursuer. And it may be another phantom!

Earthly fears, with unearthly fancies, alike urging him to flight, he stays not to make sure whether it be ghost or human; but, hastily taking up his trail-rope, springs to the back of his horse, and again goes off in wild terrified retreat.

It scarce needs telling, that the horseman who has disturbed Richard Darke's uncomfortable reflections is Charles Clancy. Less than an hour has elapsed since his starting on the trail, which he has followed fast; the fresh scent enabling Brasfort to take it up in a run. From the way it zigzagged, and circled about, Clancy could tell the tracked steed had been going without guidance, as also guess the reason. The rider, fleeing in affright, has given no heed to direction. All this the pursuer knows to be in his favour; showing that the pursued man has not gone to Coyote creek, but will still be on the steppe, possibly astray, and perhaps not far off.

Though himself making quick time, he is not carelessly pursuing; on the contrary taking every precaution to ensure success. He knows that on the hard turf his horse's tread can be heard to a great distance; and to hinder this he has put the animal to a "pace"—a gait peculiar to Texas and the South-Western States. This, combining speed with silence, has carried him on quickly as in a canter. The hound he has once more muzzled, though not holding it in leash; and the two have gone gliding along silent as spectres.

At each turn of the trail, he directs looks of inquiry ahead.

One is at length rewarded. He is facing the moon, whose disc almost touches the horizon, when alongside it he perceives something dark upon the plain, distinguishable as the figure of a horse. It is stationary with head to the ground, as if grazing, though by the uneven outline of its back it bears something like a saddle. Continuing to scrutinise, he sees it is this; and, moreover, makes out the form of a man, or what resembles one, lying along the earth near by.

These observations take only an instant of time; and, while making them he has halted, and by a word, spoken low, called his hound off the trail. The well-trained animal obeying, turns back, and stands by his side waiting.

The riderless horse, with the dismounted rider, are still a good way off, more than half a mile. At that distance he could not distinguish them, but for the position of the moon, favouring his view. Around her rim the luminous sky makes more conspicuous the dark forms interposed between.

He can have no doubt as to what they are. If he had, it is soon solved. For while yet gazing upon them—not in conjecture, but as to how he may best make approach—he perceives the tableau suddenly change. The horse tosses up its head, while the man starts upon his feet. In an instant they are together, and the rider in his saddle.

And now Clancy is quite sure: for the figure of the horseman, outlined against the background of moonlit sky, clear-edged as a medallion, shows the feathered circlet surmounting his head. To all appearance a red savage, in reality a white one—Richard Darke.

Clancy stays not to think further. If he did he would lose distance. For soon as in the saddle, Darke goes off in full headlong gallop. In like gait follows the avenger, forsaking the cautious pace, and no longer caring for silence.

Still there is no noise, save that of the hammering hooves, now and then a clink, as their iron shoeing strikes a stone. Otherwise silent, pursuer and pursued. But with very different reflections; the former terrified, half-frenzied, seeking to escape from whom he knows not; the latter, cool, courageous, trying to overtake one he knows too well.

Clancy pursues but with one thought, to punish the murderer of his mother. And sure he will succeed now. Already is the space shortened between them, growing less with every leap of his horse. A few strides more and Richard Darke will be within range of his rifle.

Letting drop the reins, he takes firmer grasp on his gun. His horse needs no guidance, but goes on as before, still gaining.

He is now within a hundred lengths of the retreating foe, but still too far off for a sure shot. Besides, the moon is in front, her light dazzling his eyes, the man he intends to take aim at going direct for her disc, as if with the design to ride into it.

While he delays, calculating the distance, suddenly the moon becomes obscured, the chased horseman simultaneously disappearing from his sight!

Chapter Eighty Three
At length the "Death Shot"

Scarce for an instant is Clancy puzzled by the sudden disappearance of him pursued. That is accounted for by the simplest of causes; a large rock rising above the level of the plain, a loose boulder, whose breadth interposing, covers the disc of the moon. A slight change of direction has brought it between; Darke having deflected from his course, and struck towards it.

Never did hunted fox, close pressed by hounds, make more eagerly for cover, or seek it so despairingly as he. He has long ago been aware that the pursuer is gaining upon him. At each anxious glance cast over his shoulder, he sees the distance decreased, while the tramp of the horse behind sounds clearer and closer.

He is in doubt what to do. Every moment he may hear the report of a gun, and have a bullet into his back. He knows not the instant he may be shot out of his saddle.

Shall he turn upon the pursuer, make stand, and meet him face to face? He dares not. The dread of the unearthly is still upon him. It may be the Devil!

The silence, too, awes him. The pursuing horseman has not yet hailed — has not spoken word, or uttered exclamation. Were it not for the heavy tread of the hoof he might well believe him a spectre.

If Darke only knew who it is, he would fear him as much, or more. Knowing not, he continues his flight, doubting, distracted. He has but one clear thought, the instinct common to all chased creatures—to make for some shelter.

A copse, a tree, even were it but a bush, anything to conceal him from the pursuer's sight—from the shot he expects soon to be sent after him.

Ha! what is that upon the plain? A rock! And large enough to screen both him and his horse. The very thing!

Instinctively he perceives his advantage. Behind the rock he can make stand, and without hesitation he heads his horse for it.

It is a slight change from his former direction, and he loses a little ground; but recovers it by increased speed. For encouraged by the hope of getting under shelter, he makes a last spurt, urging his animal to the utmost.

He is soon within the shadow of the rock, still riding towards it.

It is just then that Clancy loses sight of him, as of the moon. But he is now also near enough to distinguish the huge stone; and, while scanning its outlines, he sees the chased horseman turn around it, so rapidly, and at such distance, he withholds his shot, fearing it may fail.

Between pursued and pursuer the chances have changed; and as the latter reins up to consider what he should do, he sees something glisten above the boulder, clearly distinguishable as the barrel of a gun. At the same instant a voice salutes him, saying:—

"I don't know who, or what you are. But I warn you to come no nearer. If you do, I'll send a bullet—Great God!"

With the profane exclamation, the speaker suddenly interrupts himself, his voice having changed from its tone of menace to trembling. For the moonlight is full upon the face of him threatened; he can trace every feature distinctly. It is the same he late saw on the sun ice of the plain!

It can be no dream, nor freak of fancy. Clancy is still alive; or if dead he, Darke, is looking upon his wraith!

To his unfinished speech he receives instant rejoinder:—

"You don't know who I am? Learn then! I'm the man you tried to assassinate in a Mississippian forest—Charles Clancy—who means to kill you, fairer fashion, here on this Texan plain. Dick Darke! if you have a prayer to say, say it soon; for sure as you stand behind that rock, I intend taking your life."

The threat is spoken in a calm, determined tone, as if surely to be kept. All the more terrible to Richard Darke, who cannot yet realise the fact of Clancy's being alive. But that stern summons must have come from mortal lips, and the form before him is no spirit, but living flesh and blood.

Terror-stricken, appalled, shaking as with an ague, the gun almost drops from his grasp. But with a last desperate resolve, and effort mechanical, scarce knowing what he does, he raises the piece to his shoulder, and fires.

Clancy sees the flash, the jet, the white smoke puffing skyward; then hears the crack. He has no fear, knowing himself at a safe distance. For at this has he halted.

He does not attempt to return the fire, nor rashly rush on. Darke carries a double-barrelled gun, and has still a bullet left. Besides, he has the advantage of position, the protecting rampart, the moon behind his back, and in the eyes of his assailant, everything in favour of the assailed.

Though chafing in angry impatience, with the thirst of vengeance unappeased, Clancy restrains himself, measuring the ground with his eyes, and planning how he may dislodge his skulking antagonist. Must he lay siege to him, and stay there till—

A low yelp interrupts his cogitations. Looking down he sees Brasfort by his side. In the long trial of speed between the two horses, the hound had dropped behind. The halt has enabled it to get up, just in time to be of service to its master, who has suddenly conceived a plan for employing it.

Leaping from his saddle, he lays holds of the muzzle strap, quickly unbuckling it. As though divining the reason, the dog dashes on for the rock; soon as its jaws are released, giving out a fierce angry growl.

Darke sees it approaching in the clear moonlight, can distinguish its markings, remembers them. Clancy's stag-hound! Surely Nemesis, with all hell's hosts, are let loose on him!

He recalls how the animal once set upon him.

Its hostility then is nought to that now. For it has reached the rock, turned it, and open-mouthed, springs at him like a panther.

In vain he endeavours to avoid it, and still keep under cover. While shunning its teeth, he has also to think of Clancy's gun.

He cannot guard against both, if either. For the dog has caught hold of his right leg, and fixed its fangs in the flesh. He tries to beat it off, striking with the butt of his gun. To no purpose now. For his horse, excited by the attack, and madly prancing, has parted from the rock, exposing him to the aim of the pursuer, who has, meanwhile, rushed up within rifle range.

Clancy sees his advantage, and raises his gun, quick as for the shooting of a snipe. The crack comes; and, simultaneous with it, Richard Darke is seen to drop out of his saddle, and fall face foremost on the plain—his horse, with a wild neigh, bolting away from him.

The fallen man makes no attempt to rise, nor movement of any kind, save a convulsive tremor through his frame; the last throe of parting life, which precedes the settled stillness of death. For surely is he dead.

Clancy, dismounting, advances towards the spot; hastily, to hinder the dog from tearing him, which the enraged animal seems determined to do. Chiding it off, he bends over the prostrate body, which he perceives has ceased to breathe. A sort of curiosity, some impulse irresistible, prompts him to look for the place where his bullet struck. In the heart, as he can see by the red stream still flowing forth!

"Just where he hit me! After all, not strange—no coincidence; I aimed at him there."

For a time he stands gazing down at the dead man's face. Silently, without taunt or recrimination. On his own there is no sign of savage triumph, no fiendish exultation. Far from his thoughts to insult, or outrage the dead. Justice has had requital, and vengeance been appeased. It is neither his rival in love, nor his mortal enemy, who now lies at his feet; but a breathless body, a lump of senseless clay, all the passions late inspiring it, good and bad, gone to be balanced elsewhere.

As he stands regarding Darke's features, in their death pallor showing livid by the moon's mystic light, a cast of sadness comes over his own, and he says in subdued soliloquy:—

"Painful to think I have taken a man's life—even his! I wish it could have been otherwise. It could not—I was compelled to it. And surely God will forgive me, for ridding the world of such a wretch?"

Then raising himself to an erect attitude, with eyes upturned to heaven—as when in the cemetery over his mother's grave, he made that solemn vow—remembering it, he now adds in like solemnal tone—

"I've kept my oath. Mother; thou art avenged!"

Chapter Eighty Four
The Scout's Report

While these tragic incidents are occurring on Coyote Creek and the plain between, others almost as exciting but of less sanguinary character, take place in the valley of the San Saba.

As the morning sun lights up the ancient Mission-house, its walls still reverberate wailing cries, mingled with notes of preparation for the pursuit. Then follows a forenoon of painful suspense, *no* word yet from the scouters sent out.

Colonel Armstrong, and the principal men of the settlement, have ascended to the *azotea* to obtain a better view; and there remain gazing down the valley in feverish impatience. Just as the sun reaches meridian their wistful glances are rewarded; but by a sight which little relieves their anxiety; on the contrary, increasing it.

A horseman emerging from the timber, which skirts the river's bank, comes on towards the Mission-building. He is alone, and riding at top speed—both circumstances having sinister significance. Has the scouting party been cut off, and he only escaped to tell the tale? Is it Dupré, Hawkins, or who? He is yet too far off to be identified.

As he draws nearer, Colonel Armstrong through a telescope makes him out to be Cris Tucker.

Why should the young hunter be coming back alone?

After a mutual interchange of questions and conjectures, they leave off talking, and silently stand, breathlessly, awaiting his arrival.

Soon as he is within hailing distance, several unable to restrain themselves, call out, inquiring the news.

"Not bad, gentlemen! Rayther good than otherways," shouts back Oris.

His response lifts a load from their hearts, and in calmer mood they await further information. In a short time the scout presents himself before Colonel Armstrong, around whom the others cluster, all alike eager to hear the report. For they are still under anxiety about the character of the despoilers, having as yet no reason to think them other than Indians. Nor does Tucker's account contradict this idea; though one thing he has to tell begets a suspicion to the contrary.

Rapidly and briefly as possible the young hunter gives details of what has happened to Dupré's party, up to the time of his separating from it; first making their minds easy by assuring them it was then safe.

They were delayed a long time in getting upon the trail of the robbers, from these having taken a bye-path leading along the base of the bluff. At length having found the route of their retreat, they followed it over the lower ford, and there saw sign to convince them that the Indians—still supposing them such—had gone on across the bottom, and in all probability up the bluff beyond—thus identifying them with the band which the hunters had seen and tracked down. Indeed no one doubted this, nor could. But, while the scouters were examining the return tracks, they came upon others less intelligible—in short, perplexing. There were the hoof-marks of four horses and a mule—all shod; first seen upon a side trace leading from the main ford road. Striking into and following it for a few hundred yards, they came upon a place where men had encamped and stayed for some time—perhaps slept. The grass bent down showed where their bodies had been astretch. And these men must have been white. Fragments of biscuit, with other débris of eatables, not known to Indians, were evidence of this.

Returning from the abandoned bivouac, with the intention to ride straight back to the Mission, the scouters came upon another side trace leading out on the opposite side of the ford road, and up the river. On this they again saw the tracks of the shod horses and mule; among them the foot-prints of a large dog.

Taking this second trace it conducted them to a glade, with a grand tree, a live-oak, standing in its centre. The sign told of the party having stopped there also. While occupied in examining their traces, and much mystified by them, they picked up an article, which, instead of making matters clearer, tended to mystify them more—a wig! Of all things in the world this in such a place!

Still, not so strange either, seeing it was the counterfeit of an Indian *chevelure*—the hair long and black, taken from the tail of a horse.

For all, it had never belonged to, or covered, a red man's skull—since it was that worn by Bosley, and torn from his head when Woodley and Heywood were stripping him for examination.

The scouters, of course, could not know of this; and, while inspecting the queer waif, wondering what it could mean, two others were taken up:

one a sprig of cypress, the other an orange blossom; both showing as if but lately plucked, and alike out of place there.

Dupré, with some slight botanic knowledge, knew that no orange-tree grew near, nor yet any cypress. But he remembered having observed both in the Mission-garden, into which the girls had been last seen going. Without being able to guess why they should have brought sprig or flower along, he was sure they had themselves been under the live-oak. Where were they now?

In answer, Hawkins had cried: "Gone this way! Here's the tracks of the shod horses leading up-stream, this side. Let's follow them!"

So they had done, after despatching Tucker with the report.

It is so far satisfactory, better than any one expected; and inspires Colonel Armstrong with a feeling akin to hope. Something seems to whisper him his lost children will be recovered.

Long ere the sun has set over the valley of the San Saba his heart is filled, and thrilled, with joy indescribable. For his daughters are by his side, their arms around his neck, tenderly, lovingly entwining it, as on that day when told they must forsake their stately Mississippian home for a hovel in Texas. All have reached the Mission; for the scouting party having overtaken that of Woodley, came in along with it.

No, not all, two are still missing—Clancy and Jupiter. About the latter Woodley has made no one the wiser; though he tells Clancy's strange experience, which, while astounding his auditory, fills them with keen apprehension for the young man's fate.

Keenest is that in the breast of Helen Armstrong. Herself saved, she is now all the more solicitous about the safety of her lover. Her looks bespeak more than anxiety—anguish.

But there is that being done to hinder her from despairing. The pursuers are rapidly getting ready to start out, and with zeal unabated. For, although circumstances have changed by the recovery of the captives, there is sufficient motive for pursuit—the lost treasure to be re-taken—the outlaws chastised—Clancy's life to be saved, or his death avenged.

Woodley's words have fired them afresh, and they are impatient to set forth.

Their impatience reaches its climax, when Colonel Armstrong, with head uncovered, his white hair blown up by the evening breeze, addresses them, saying:—

"Fellow citizens! We have to thank the Almighty that our dear ones have escaped a great danger. But while grateful to God, let us remember there is a man also deserving gratitude. A brave young man, we all believed dead—murdered. He is still alive, let us hope so. Simeon Woodley has told us of the danger he is now in—death if he fall into the hands of these desperate outlaws. Friends, and fellow citizens! I need not appeal to you on behalf of this noble youth. I know you are all of one mind with myself, that come what will, cost what it may, Charles Clancy must be saved."

The enthusiastic shout, sent up in response to the old soldier's speech, tells that the pursuit will be at least energetic and earnest.

Helen Armstrong, standing retired, looks more hopeful now. And with her hope is mingled pride, at the popularity of him to whom she has given heart, and promised hand. Something more to make her happy; she now knows that, in the bestowing of both, she will have the approval of her father.

Chapter Eighty Five
A change of programme

On the far frontier of Texas, still unsettled by civilised man, no chanticleer gives note of the dawn. Instead, the *meleagris* salutes the sunrise with a cry equally high-toned, and quite as home-like. For the gobbling of the wild turkey-cock is scarcely distinguishable from that of his domesticated brother of the farm-yard.

A gang of these great birds has roosted in the pecan grove, close to where the prairie pirates are encamped. At daylight's approach, they fly up to the tops of the trees; the males, as is their wont in the spring months of the year, mutually sounding their sonorous challenge.

It awakes the robbers from the slumber succeeding their drunken debauch; their chief first of any.

Coming forth from his tent, he calls upon the others to get up—ordering several horses to be saddled. He designs despatching a party to the upper plain, in search of Quantrell and Bosley, not yet come to camp.

He wants another word with the mulatto; and steps towards the tent, where he supposes the man to be.

At its entrance he sees blood—inside a dead body!

His cry, less of sorrow than anger, brings his followers around. One after another peering into the tent, they see what is there. There is no question about how the thing occurred. It is clear to all. Their prisoner has killed his guard; as they say, assassinated him. Has the assassin escaped?

They scatter in search of him, by twos and threes, rushing from tent to tent. Some proceed to the corral, there to see that the bars are down, and the horses out.

These are discovered in a strip of meadow near by, one only missing. It is that the chief had seized from their white prisoner, and appropriated. The yellow one has replevined it!

The ghastly spectacle in the tent gives them no horror. They are too hardened for that. But it makes them feel, notwithstanding; first anger, soon succeeded by apprehension. The dullest brute in the band has some perception of danger as its consequence. Hitherto their security has depended on keeping up their incognito by disguises, and the secrecy of their camping place. Here is a prisoner escaped, who knows all; can tell about their travesties; guide a pursuing party to the spot! They must remain no longer there.

Borlasse recognising the necessity for a change of programme, summons his following around him.

"Boys!" he says, "I needn't point out to ye that this ugly business puts us in a bit o' a fix. We've got to clear out o' hyar right quick. I reckon our best way 'll be to make tracks for San Antone, an' thar scatter. Even then, we won't be too safe, if yellow skin turns up to tell his story about us. Lucky a nigger's testymony don't count for much in a Texan court; an' thar's still a chance to make it count for nothin' by our knocking him on the head."

All look surprised, their glances interrogating "How?"

"I see you don't understan' me," pursues Borlasse in explanation. "It's easy enough; but we must mount at once, an' make after him. He won't so readily find his way acrosst the cut-rock plain. An' I tell yez, boys, it's our only chance."

There are dissenting voices. Some urge the danger of going back that way. They may meet the outraged settlers.

"No fear of them yet," argues the chief, "but there will be if the nigger meets them. We needn't go on to the San Saba. If we don't overtake him 'fore reachin' the cottonwood, we'll hev' to let him slide. Then we can hurry back hyar, an' go down the creek to the Colorado."

The course counselled, seeming best, is decided on.

Hastily saddling their horses, and stowing the plunder in a place where it will be safe till their return, they mount, and start off for the upper plain.

Silence again reigns around the deserted camp; no human voice there— no sound, save the calling of the wild turkeys, that cannot awake that ghastly sleeper.

At the same hour, almost the very moment, when Borlasse and his freebooters, ascending from Coyote Creek, set foot on the table plain, a party of mounted men, coming up from the San Saba bottom, strikes it on the opposite edge. It is scarce necessary to say that these are the pursuing settlers. Dupré at their head. Hardly have they struck out into the sterile waste, before getting bewildered, with neither trace nor track to give them a clue to the direction. But they have with them a surer guide than the foot-prints of men, or the hoof-marks of horses—their prisoner Bill Bosley.

To save his life, the wretch told all about his late associates and is now conducting the pursuers to Coyote Creek.

Withal, he is not sure of the way; and halts hesitatingly.

Woodley mistaking his uncertainty for reluctance, puts a pistol to his head, saying:—

"Bill Bosley! altho' I don't make estimate o' yur life as more account than that o' a cat, it may be, I spose, precious to yurself. An' ye kin only save it by takin' us strait to whar ye say Jim Borlasse an' his beauties air. Show sign o' preevarication, or go a yurd's length out o' the right track, an'—wal, I won't shoot ye, as I'm threetenin'. That 'ud be a death too good for sech as you. But I promise ye'll get yer neck streetched on the nearest tree; an' if no tree turn up, I'll tie ye to the tail o' my horse, an' hang ye that way. So, take yur choice. If ye want to chaw any more corn, don't 'tempt playin' possum."

"I hain't no thought of it," protests Bosley, "indeed I hain't, Sime. I'm only puzzled 'bout the trail from here. Tho' I've been accrost this plain several times, I never took much notice, bein' with the others, I only know there's a tree stands by itself. If we can reach that, the road's easier beyont. I think it's out yonnerways."

He points in particular direction.

"Wal, we'll try that way," says Sime, adding: "Ef yer story don't prove strait, there'll come a crik in yur neck, soon's it's diskivered to be crooked. So waste no more words, but strike for the timmer ye speak o'."

The alacrity with which Bosley obeys tells he is sincere.

Proof of his sincerity is soon after obtained in the tree itself being observed. Far off they descry it outlined against the clear sky, solitary as a ship at sea.

"Yonner it air, sure enuf!" says Woodley first sighting it. "I reck'n the skunk's tellin' us the truth, 'bout that stick o' timber being a finger-post. Tharfor, no more dilly-dallying but on to't quick as our critters can take us. Thar's a man's life in danger; one that's dear to me, as I reckon he'd be to all o' ye, ef ye knowed him, same's I do. Ye heerd what the old kurnel sayed, as we war startin' out: *cost what it mout, Charley Clancy air to be saved.* So put the prod to your critters, an' let's on!"

Saying this, the hunter spurs his horse to its best speed; and soon all are going at full gallop in straight course for the cottonwood.

Chapter Eighty Six
Alone with the Dead

Beside the body of his fallen foe stands Charles Clancy, but with no intention there to tarry long. The companionship of the dead is ever painful, whether it be friend or enemy. With the latter, alone, it may appal. Something of this creeps over his spirit while standing there; for he has now no strong passion to sustain him, not even anger.

After a few moments, he turns his back on the corpse, calling Brasfort away from it. The dog yet shows hostility; and, if permitted, would mutilate the lifeless remains. Its fierce canine instinct has no generous impulse, and is only restrained by scolding and threats.

The sun is beginning to show above the horizon, and Clancy perceives Darke's horse tearing about over the plain. He is reminded of his promise made to Jupiter.

The animal does not go clear off, but keeps circling round, as if it desired to come back again; the presence of the other horse attracting, and giving it confidence. Clancy calls to it, gesticulating in a friendly manner, and uttering exclamations of encouragement. By little and little, it draws nearer, till at length its muzzle is in contact with that of his own steed; and, seizing the bridle, he secures it.

Casting a last look at the corpse, he turns to the horses, intending to take departure from the spot. So little time has been spent in the pursuit, and the short conflict succeeding, it occurs to him he may overtake Jupiter, before the latter has reached the San Saba.

Scanning around to get bearings, his eye is attracted to an object, now familiar—the lone cottonwood. It is not much over two miles off. On Darke's trail he must have ridden at least leagues. Its crooked course, however, explains the tree's proximity. The circles and zig-zags have brought both pursued and pursuer nigh back to the starting point.

Since the cottonwood is there, he cannot be so far from the other place, he has such reason to remember; and, again running his eye around, he looks for it.

He sees it not, as there is nothing now to be seen, except some scattered mould undistinguishable at a distance. Instead, the rising sun lights up the figure of a man, afoot, and more than a mile off. Not standing still, but in motion; as he can see, moving towards himself. It is Jupiter!

Thus concluding, he is about to mount and meet him, when stayed by a strange reflection.

"I'll let Jupe have a look at his old master," he mutters to himself. "He too had old scores to settle with him—many a one recorded upon his skin. It may give him satisfaction to know how the thing has ended."

Meanwhile the mulatto—for it is he—comes on; at first slowly, and with evident caution in his approach.

Soon he is seen to quicken his step, changing it to a run; at length arriving at the rock, breathless as one who reaches the end of a race. The sight which meets him there gives him but slight surprise. He has been prepared for it.

In answer to Clancy's inquiry, he briefly explains his presence upon the spot. Disobedient to the instructions given him, instead of proceeding towards the San Saba bottom, he had remained upon the steppe. Not stationary, but following his master as fast as he could, and keeping him in view so long as the distance allowed. Two things were in his favour—the clear moonlight and Darke's trail doubling back upon itself. For all, he had at length lost sight of the tracking horseman, but not till he had caught a glimpse of him tracked, fleeing before. It was the straight tail-on-end chase that took both beyond reach of his vision. Noting the direction, he still went hastening after, soon to hear a sound which told him the chase had come to a termination, and strife commenced. This was the report of a gun, its full, round boom proclaiming it a smooth-bore fowling-piece. Remembering that his old master always carried this—his new one never—it must be the former who fired the shot. And, as for a long while no other answered it, he was in despair, believing the latter killed. Then reached his ear the angry bay of the bloodhound, with mens' voices intermingled; ending all the dear, sharp crack of a rifle; which, from the stillness that succeeded continuing, he knew to be the last shot.

"An' it war the last, as I can see," he says, winding up his account, and turning towards the corpse. "Ah! you've gi'n him what he thought he'd guv you—his *death shot!*"

"Yes, Jupe. He's got it at last; and strange enough in the very place where he hit me. You see where my bullet has struck him?"

The mulatto, stooping down over Darke's body, examines the wound, still dripping blood.

"You're right, Masser Charle; it's in de adzack spot. Well, that is curious. Seems like your gun war guided by de hand of that avengin' angel you spoke o'."

Having thus delivered himself, the fugitive slave becomes silent and thoughtful, for a time, bending over the body of his once cruel master, now no more caring for his cruelty, or in fear of being chastised by him.

With what strange reflections must that spectacle inspire him! The outstretched arms lying helpless along the earth—the claw-like fingers now stiff and nerveless—he may be thinking how they once clutched a cowhide, vigorously laying it on his own back, leaving those terrible scars.

"Come, Jupe!" says Clancy, rousing him from his reverie; "we must mount, and be off."

Soon they are in their saddles, ready to start; but stay yet a little longer. For something has to be considered. It is necessary for them to make sure about their route. They must take precautions against getting strayed, as also another and still greater danger. Jupiter's escape from the robbers' den, with the deed that facilitated it, will by this have been discovered. It is more than probable he will be pursued; indeed almost certain. And the pursuers will come that way; at any moment they may appear.

This is the dark side of the picture presented to Clancy's imagination, as he turns his eyes towards the west. Facing in the opposite direction his fancy summons up one brighter. For there lies the San Saba Mission-house, within whose walls he will find Helen Armstrong. He has now no doubt that she has reached home in safety; knows, too, that her father still lives. For the mulatto has learnt as much from the outlaws. While *en route* to Coyote Creek, and during his sojourn there, he overheard them speak about the massacre of the slaves, as also the immunity extended to their masters, with the reason for it. It is glad tidings to Clancy, His betrothed, restored to her father's arms, will not the less affectionately open her own to receive him. The long night of their sorrowing has passed; the morn of their joy comes; its daylight is already dawning. He will have a welcome, sweet as ever met man.

"What's that out yonner?" exclaims Jupiter, pointing west.

Clancy's rapture is interrupted—his bright dream dissipated—suddenly, as when a cloud drifts over the disc of the sun.

And it is the sun which causes the change, or rather the reflection of its rays from something seen afar off, over the plain. Several points sparkle, appearing and disappearing through a semi-opaque mass, whose dun colour shows it to be dust.

Experienced in prairie-sign he can interpret this; and does easily, but with a heaviness at his heart. The things that sparkle are guns, pistols, knives, belt-buckles, bitts, and stirrups; while that through which they intermittingly shine is the stoor tossed up by the hooves of horses. It is a body of mounted men in march across the steppe.

Continuing to scan the dust-cloud, he perceives inside it a darker nucleus, evidently horses and men, though he is unable to trace the individual forms, or make out their number. No mattes for that; there is enough to identify them without. They are coming from the side of the Colorado—from Coyote Creek. Beyond doubt the desperadoes!

Chapter Eighty Seven
Hostile Cohorts

Perfectly sure that the band is that of Borlasse, which he almost instantly is, Clancy draws his horse behind the rock, directing Jupiter to do likewise. Thus screened, they can command a view of the horsemen, without danger of being themselves seen.

For greater security both dismount; the mulatto holding the horses, while his master sets himself to observe the movements of the approaching troop. Is it approaching?

Yes; but not direct for the rock. Its head is towards the tree, and the robbers are evidently making to reach this. As already said, the topography of the place is peculiar; the lone cottonwood standing on the crest of a *couteau de prairie*, whose sides slope east and west. It resembles the roof of a house, but with gentler declination. Similarly situated on the summit of the ridge, is the boulder, but with nearly a league's length between it and the tree.

Soon as assured that the horsemen are heading for the latter, Clancy breathes freer breath. But without being satisfied he is safe. He knows they will not stay there; and where next? He reflects what might have been his fate were he still in the *prairie stocks*. Borlasse will be sure to pay that place a visit. Not finding the victim of his cruelty, he will seek elsewhere. Will it occur to him to come on to the rock?

Clancy so interrogates, with more coolness, and less fear, than may be imagined. His horse is beside him, and Jupiter has another. The mulatto is no longer encumbered by a mule. Darke's steed is known to be a swift one, and not likely to be outrun by any of the robber troop. If chased, some of them might overtake it, but not all, or not at the same time. There will be less danger from their following in detail, and thus Clancy less fears them. For he knows that his yellow-skinned comrade is strong as courageous; a match for any three ordinary men. And both are now well armed—Darke's double-barrel, as his horse, having reverted to Jupiter. Besides, as good luck has it, there are pistols found in the holsters, to say nothing of that long-bladed, and late blood-stained, knife. In a chase they will have a fair chance to escape; and, if it come to a fight, can make a good one.

While he is thus speculating upon the probabilities of the outlaws coming on to the rock, and what may be the upshot afterwards, Clancy's ear is again saluted by a cry from his companion. But this time in tone very different: for it is jubilant, joyous.

Turning, he sees Jupiter standing with face to the east, and pointing in that direction. To what? Another cloud of dust, that prinkles with sparkling points; another mounted troop moving across the plain! And also making for the tree, which, equi-distant between the two, seems to be the beacon of both.

Quick as he reached the conclusion about the first band being that of Borlasse, does he decide as to that of the second. It is surely the pursuing colonists, and as sure with Sime Woodley at their head.

Both cohorts are advancing at a like rate of speed, neither riding rapidly. They have been so, but now, climbing the acclivity, they have quieted their horses to a walk. The pace though slow, continued, will in time bring them together. A collision seems inevitable. His glance gladdens as he measures the strength of the two parties. The former not only in greater number, but with God on their side; while the latter will be doing battle under the banner of the Devil.

About the issue of such encounter he has no anxiety. He is only apprehensive it may not come off. Something may arise to warn the outlaws, and give them a chance to shun it.

As yet neither party has a thought of the other's proximity or approach. They cannot, with the ridge between. Still is there that, which should make them suspicious of something. Above each band are buzzards—a large flock. They flout the air in sportive flight, their instinct admonishing them that the two parties are hostile, and likely to spill each other's blood.

About the two sets of birds what will both sides be saying? For, high in heaven, both must long since have observed them. From their presence what conjectures will they draw?

So Clancy questions, answering himself:

"Borlasse will suppose the flock afar to be hovering over my head; while Woodley may believe the other one above my dead body!"

Strange as it may appear, just thus, and at the same instant, are the two leaders interpreting the sign! And well for the result Clancy desires; since it causes neither to command halt or make delay. On the contrary impels them forward more impetuously. Perceiving this, he mechanically mutters:

Thank the Lord! They must meet now! Curbing his impatience, as he best can, he continues to watch the mutually approaching parties. At the head of the colonists he now sees Sime Woodley, recognises him by his horse—a brindled "clay-bank," with stripes like a zebra. Would that he could communicate with his old comrade, and give him word, or sign of warning. He dares not do either. To stir an inch from behind the rock, would expose him to the view of the robbers, who might still turn and retreat.

With heart beating audibly, blood, coursing quick through his veins, he watches and waits, timing the crisis. It must come soon. The two flocks of vultures have met in mid-air, and mingle their sweeping gyrations. They croak in mutual congratulation, anticipating a splendid repast.

Clancy counts the moments. They cannot be many. The heads of the horsemen already align with the tufts of grass growing topmost on the ridge. Their brows are above it; their eyes. They have sighted each other!

A halt on both sides; horses hurriedly reined in; no shouts; only a word of caution from the respective leaders of the troops, each calling back to his own. Then an interval of silence, disturbed by the shrill screams of the horses, challenging from troop to troop, seemingly hostile as their riders.

In another instant both have broken halt, and are going in gallop over the plain; not towards each other, but one pursuing, the other pursued. The robbers are in retreat!

Clancy had not waited for this; his cue came before, soon as they caught sight of one another. Then, vaulting into his saddle, and calling Jupiter to follow, he was off.

Riding at top speed, cleaving the air, till it whistles past his ears, with eyes strained forward, he sees the changed attitude of the troops.

He reflects not on it; all his thoughts becoming engrossed, all his energies bent, upon taking part in the pursuit, and still more in the fight he hopes will follow. He presses on in a diagonal line between pursued and pursuers. His splendid steed now shows its good qualities, and gladly he sees he is gaining upon both. With like gladness that they are nearing one another, the short-striding mustangs being no match for the long legged American horses. As yet not a shot has been fired. The distance is still too great for the range of rifles, and backwoodsmen do not idly waste ammunition. The only sounds heard are the trampling of the hooves, and the occasional neigh of a horse. The riders are all silent, in both troops alike—one in the mute eagerness of flight, the other with the stern earnestness of pursuit.

And now puffs of smoke arise over each, with jets of flame projected outward. Shots, at first dropping and single, then in thick rattling fusillade.

Along with them cries of encouragement, mingled with shouts of defiance. Then a wild "hurrah," the charging cheers the colonists close upon the outlaws.

Clancy rides straight for the fray. In front he sees the plain shrouded in dense sulphureous mist, at intervals illumined by yellow flashes. Another spurt, and, passing through the thin outer strata of smoke, he is in the thick of the conflict—among men on horseback grappling other mounted men, endeavouring to drag them out of the saddle—some afoot, fighting in pairs, firing pistols, or with naked knives, hewing away at one another!

He sees that the fight is nigh finished, and the robbers routed. Some are dismounted, on their knees crying "quarter," and piteously appealing for mercy.

Where is Sime Woodley? Has his old comrade been killed?

Half frantic with this fear, he rashes distractedly over the ground, calling out the backwoodsman's name. He is answered by another—by Ned Heywood, who staggers to his side, bleeding, his face blackened with powder.

"You are wounded, Heywood?"

"Yes; or I wouldn't be here."

"Why?"

"Because Sime—"

"Where is he?"

"Went that way in chase o' a big brute of a fellow. I've jest spied them passin' through the smoke. For God's sake, after! Sime may stand in need o' ye."

Clancy stays not to hear more, but again urges his horse to speed, with head in the direction indicated.

Darting on, he is soon out into the clear atmosphere; there to see two horsemen going off over the plain, pursued and pursuer. In the former he recognises Borlasse, while the latter is Woodley. Both are upon strong, swift, horses; but better mounted than either, he soon gains upon them.

The backwoodsman is nearing the brigand. Clancy sees this with satisfaction, though not without anxiety. He knows Jim Borlasse is an antagonist not to be despised. Driven to desperation, he will fight like a grizzly bear. Woodley will need all his strength, courage, and strategy.

Eager to assist his old comrade, he presses onward; but, before he can come up, they have closed, and are at it.

Not in combat, paces apart, with rifles or pistols. Not a shot is being exchanged between them. Instead, they are close together, have clutched one another, and are fighting, hand to hand, with *bowies!*

It commenced on horseback, but at the first grip both came to the ground, dragging each other down. Now the fight continues on foot, each with his bared blade hacking and hewing at the other.

A dread spectacle these two gigantic gladiators engaged in mortal strife! All the more in its silence. Neither utters shout, or speaks word. They are too intent upon killing. The only sound heard is their hoarse breathing as they pant to recover it—each holding the other's arm to hinder the fatal stroke.

Clancy's heart beats apprehensively for the issue; and with rifle cocked, he rides on to send a bullet through Borlasse.

It is not needed. No gun is to give the *coup de grâce* to the chief of the prairie pirates. For, the blade of a bowie-knife has passed between his ribs, laying him lifeless along the earth.

"You, Charley Clancy!" says Sime, in joyful surprise at seeing his friend still safe. "Thank the Lord for it! But who'd a thought o' meeting ye in the middle of the skrimmage! And in time to stan' by me hed that been needful. But whar hev ye come from? Dropt out o' the clouds? An' what o' Dick Darke? I'd most forgot that leetle matter. Have ye seed him?"

"I have."

"Wal; what's happened? Hev ye did anythin' to him?"

"The same as you have done to *him*," answers Clancy, pointing to the body of Borlasse.

"Good for you! I know'd it 'ud end that way. I say'd so to that sweet critter, when I war leevin' her at the Mission."

"You left her there—safe?"

"Wal, I left her in her father's arums, whar I reckon she'll be safe enough. But whar's Jupe?"

"He's here—somewhere behind."

"All right! That accounts for the hul party. Now let's back, and see what's chanced to the rest o' this ruffin crew. So, Jim Borlasse, good bye!"

With this odd leave taking, he turns away, wipes the blood from his bowie, returns it to its sheath, and once more climbing into his saddle, rides off to rejoin the victorious colonists.

On the ground where the engagement took place, a sad spectacle is presented. The smoke has drifted away, disclosing the corpses of the slain—horses as well as men. All the freebooters have fallen, and now lie astretch as they fell to stab or shot; some on their backs, others with face downward, or doubled sideways, but all dead, gashed, and gory—not a wounded man among them! For the colonists, recalling that parallel spectacle in the Mission courtyard, have given loose rein to the *lex talionis*, and exacted a terrible retribution.

Nor have they themselves got off unscathed. The desperadoes being refused quarter, fought it out to the bitter end; killing several of the settlers, and wounding many more; among the latter two known to us—Heywood and Dupré. By good fortune, neither badly, and both to recover from their wounds; the young Creole also recovering his stolen treasure, found secreted at the camp on Coyote creek.

Our tale might here close; for it is scarce necessary to record what came afterwards. The reader will guess, and correctly, that Dupré became the husband of Jessie, and Helen the wife of Clancy; both marriages being celebrated at the same time, and both with full consent and approval of the only living parent—Colonel Armstrong.

And on the same day, though at a different hour, a third couple was made man and wife; Jupe getting spliced to his Jule, from whom he had been so long cruelly kept apart.

It is some years since then, and changes have taken place in the colony. As yet none to be regretted, but the reverse. A Court-House town has sprung up on the site of the ancient Mission, the centre of a district of plantations—the largest of them belonging to Luis Dupré; while one almost as extensive, and equally as flourishing, has Charles Clancy for owner.

On the latter live Jupe and Jule; Jupe overseer, Jule at the head of the domestic department; while on the former reside two other personages presented in this tale, it is hoped with interest attached to them. They are Blue Bill, and his Phoebe; not living alone, but in the midst of a numerous progeny of piccaninnies.

How the coon-hunter comes to be there requires explanation. A word will be sufficient. Ephraim Darke stricken down by the disgrace brought upon him, has gone to his grave; and at the breaking up of his slave establishment, Blue Bill, with all his belongings, was purchased by Dupré, and transported to his present home. This not by any accident, but designedly; as a reward for his truthfulness, with the courage he displayed in declaring it.

Between the two plantations, lying contiguous, Colonel Armstrong comes and goes, scarce knowing which is his proper place of residence. In both he has a bedroom, and a table profusely spread, with the warmest of welcomes.

In the town itself is a market, plentifully supplied with provisions, especially big game—bear-meat, and venison. Not strange, considering that it is catered for by four of the most skilful hunters in Texas; their names, Woodley, Heywood, Hawkins, and Tucker. When off duty these worthies may be seen sauntering through the streets, and relating the experiences of their latest hunting expedition.

But there is one tale, which Sime, the oldest of the quartette, has told over and over—yet never tires telling. Need I say, it is the "Death Shot?"